Praise for THE
SICK
ROSE

'It is hard to find a more impeccably English writer than Erin Kelly, whose debut THE POISON TREE, marked her as a name to watch in British fiction . . . in trademark style [THE SICK ROSE] flits between the 'then' and the 'now', playing with the magic and poison of memories, until the present intervenes with brutal and tragic consequences.' *The Times*

'Kelly writes perceptively and chillingly about the long shadows cast by tragic mistakes . . . she shows considerable promise.' *Daily Telegraph*

'A tense and twisting novel of dark secrets and dangerous desires.' *Grazia*

'Kelly's first novel, THE POISON TREE, earned her comparisons with Ruth Rendell and on the evidence of this second psychologically complex thriller, the accolade is entirely deserved. Like Rendell, Kelly is an expert in suburban macabre, relishing in the kind of domestic scenes we all recognise but giving them a satisfyingly chilly twist.' *Psychologies*

'A compelling suspense novel from crime fiction's freshest voice.' *Red*

THE
SICK
ROSE

ERIN KELLY

HODDER

First published in Great Britain in 2011 by Hodder & Stoughton
An Hachette UK company

First published in paperback in 2012

2

Copyright © Erin Kelly 2011

The right of Erin Kelly to be identified as the Author of the Work has been asserted
by her in accordance with the Copyright, Designs and Patents Act 1988.

A CIP catalogue record for this title is available from the British Library.

B format paperback ISBN 978 1 444 70385 6
A format paperback ISBN 978 1 444 70109 8
Ebook ISBN 978 1 848 94242 4

Typeset in Plantin Light by Hewer Text UK Ltd, Edinburgh
Printed and bound in the UK by Clays Ltd, St Ives plc

Hodder & Stoughton policy is to use papers that are natural, renewable
and recyclable products and made from wood grown in sustainable forests.
The logging and manufacturing processes are expected to conform
to the environmental regulations of the country of origin.

Hodder & Stoughton Ltd
338 Euston Road
London NW1 3BH

www.hodder.co.uk

For my father, who taught me to read

Dead men are heavier than broken hearts.

Raymond Chandler, *The Big Sleep*

PROLOGUE

September 2009

Louisa knew when she woke that she would do it that evening. The feeling had been hanging in the air for days like a gathering storm that only she could forecast. The usual signs were there: music had become unbearable, innocent conversations ticked like unexploded bombs, memories nibbled like fleas in the bedclothes at night.

And then, later that morning, she saw his face. A wisp of cloud, so low she felt she could reach up and pluck it from the sky, took the form of his profile. Fear held her still until the wind dispersed his likeness. From that moment, she was lost: his reflection replaced her own in every puddle and pane of glass. Everyone spoke with his voice. Everything in the garden seemed to shift and grow to spell out the letters of his name: that ladder leaning against the wall formed the letter A, and someone had raked the soil in the empty flowerbeds in a zigzag pattern that described an endless succession of Ms. Only the ruin stayed the same, its three remaining chimneys silhouetted against the changing sky like lightning trees. As morning turned to noon, the sun passed through its glassless windows, marking the hours like some huge, ancient clock. Louisa, knowing what the night would bring, wanted the day to last forever; but it was a blur of administration and conversation, and passed too quickly.

She had been the first one on site and was the last to leave. She made sure the greenhouse door was pulled to and, identifying each unmarked key at a glance, locked up the cabins. She felt her way along the thick cable for the weatherproof switch and, with a tiny pressure, the site was in darkness. There was only a weak moon and she used her torch as she crossed the rubbled surface that would soon be a car park, passed through the thicket and finally, staying parallel to the boundary wall, walked the path only she had trodden. The feeling rose inside her like an itch she had to scratch. This is the last time, she promised herself. The *last* last time. There had been so many.

Once inside, Louisa flicked on the little kettle out of habit, then turned it off before it had a chance to boil; she would not be drinking tea this evening. She busied herself with the ritual of lighting first the oil lamps and then the candles: some of the large ones had burnt almost to stubs and she had to put her hand right down inside the glass jars and vases to light them, scorching her knuckles as the wick took the flame. She double checked all the windows, pulling the thick yellow curtains across so that no one would see. Who would be watching her, anyway?

She sat on the edge of the bed for a minute or two, letting the heater warm the room, and gave herself a chance to back out. But then she was on her knees, reaching under the bed for the bottle. Her fumbling fingers soon closed on the cold glass; it was sticky where the cap met the neck, and wore a collar of fine grey fluff. Louisa winced. How long since she had done it? Spring? Yes, she realised – she had resisted all summer long. No wonder the urge was so strong now. She could forget about him in the months when there was as much work as there was light and physical exhaustion kept her asleep all night. But this was September, the hinge of the year, and the evenings were pulling up short. No matter how early she got up or how hard she worked, there was no escaping the fact that she was forced through her front door a little earlier every evening, each day bringing a few more minutes of that seething silence. The empty hours would stack up as the weeks progressed, and one dark, quiet hour was more than enough. She uncapped the bottle and swigged, the spirit punishing her throat. Now the exorcism could begin.

There wasn't much vodka, but that was fine: she only needed it to give her courage to drink the whiskey. Her legs already unsteady, she climbed onto her bed and reached into the overhead cupboard. The deceptively small door panel concealed a space that went back for two or three feet, and she lost her arm up to the shoulder as she groped around in the carefully arranged stacks of bags and boxes. Eventually her fingers closed on the handle of the right bag. She yanked it with such force that she fell back on the bed, the plastic carrier landing on her lap. A second later, the whiskey bottle rolled out. She tipped the other contents of the bag out like a child upending a Christmas stocking, although there were no surprises in here. She spread her things about her on the quilt, wondering where to begin, aware of a quickening at her throat and wrists and between her breasts. She started with the little green phial of vetiver oil, simply unscrewing the lid and inhaling. It was still a quarter full. Every year the smell got a little fainter and staler but it had been his, he had actually used this, and she could never replace her relic with a new, fresh bottle. She dabbed it on the skin behind her ears, remembering how he had anointed himself with the oil, his thumb pressing it onto his neck and wrists. Essential oils reacted differently with everyone's skin so she would never quite be able to recreate his exact scent, but this would have to do.

The whiskey bottle had not been his, but it was his brand, an obscure, old man's Irish whiskey that no one else their age had even heard of, let alone drank. Hard to find even in London, even then, so getting hold of it now was a labour of leftover love. Pressing the bottle to her lips felt like his kiss and she closed her eyes as though he were really there. She drank as much as she could bear to and shakily placed the bottle next to a candle, where it became an amber lantern.

Bringing her only mirror in from the shower room, Louisa got to work on her face, refreshing the dried-out cosmetics with drops of olive oil from the tiny pantry. The eyeshadow was called Blackpool and the lipstick Black Cherry, and both contained strong pigments intended for supple young complexions. She pulled her hair up to one side, ruthlessly fastening it with a clip so that everything on the right-hand side of her face lifted by half an inch. Now her face looked lopsided. She tousled her hair and swept it over the left side of her face in a long, messy fringe. That was better. She held up the dress: it always looked smaller than she remembered. Had she really gone out in something that short? There was the usual moment of breath-holding tension as she tried it on and the usual relief when it still fitted. If anything, it was looser on her now than it had been then. Blue crushed velvet that used to cling now hung, and if her breasts did not fill it out as once they had, her stomach did not protrude either. She pulled a face; in the dusky glass an approximation of her teenage self pouted back at her. It's not fair, she couldn't help thinking. He will *always* look young. She reached for the bottle, fumbled and nearly knocked it over onto the bedclothes. She was drunk, on the way to being very drunk. She drank some more.

Louisa peered about in the gloom. For a few moments, she had no idea where the television had gone. Then she remembered that it was serving as a pedestal for a bunch of Chinese lanterns she had dried in the summer. She removed the vase of flowers and lifted the draped blanket to reveal the tiny set with its integrated video player. It, too, was smaller than she remembered. The cathode and tape combination had been cutting-edge technology when her parents had bought it for her. There was no aerial and the remote control was long lost. Would it even still work? She felt a flicker of panic as she calculated how many months it had been since it was last turned on. She reunited the plug with the socket and slackened with relief as the screen came to life.

The videotape marked *Glasslake* was, as far as she knew, the only one of its kind in the world. She gripped it tightly, almost daring herself to crush it. It would be so easy to hook her little finger into the body of the cassette and unspool the tape. She knew she ought to destroy it. With every passing season she grew more confident that she would never be discovered – but if she was, if things ever caught up with her, to be found in possession of it would be disastrous. Yet she was powerless to stop herself inserting the cassette and pressing the play button.

She sat through the familiar adverts in their usual sequence: the small-hours commercials for those wavering between brands of coffee and cigars, 0898 numbers for the horny and lonely, the prelude to some long-forgotten Channel 4 show that had been the tape's initial recording. The broadcast footage was soon scratched out by an amateur recording. When the camera closed in on him with its wobbly zoom, she felt the same frisson as the first time she'd seen him. He raised his hand to push his hair out of his eyes; you could just about see the threads where his black jumper was unravelling at the wrist, and the lyrics scrawled on the inside of his arm. Later, when they knew each other, he would tell Louisa that if he was nervous he sometimes forgot the words he had taken hours to write. Next were a couple of other recordings, just as badly lit, sound equally distorted, but they were Louisa's favourites because she had been there. There she was at the first gig in the blue dress; there she was at the second, standing directly in front of the camera so the top of her head was in shot throughout. He had appeared to be singing to the camera although Louisa knew it had all been for, and to, her. It was proof that, whatever had happened between them afterwards, at that time he had wanted her as much as she wanted him. This, she acknowledged, was the real reason she didn't destroy the tape.

Adam looked into the lens during the final screech of feedback. After a couple of fumbled attempts Louisa found the pause button and froze his features. He was looking at her with longing and accusation. Grief so strong it was almost sweet engulfed her. She leaned in towards the television as though for an embrace. She could almost believe that the yearning she felt was powerful enough to pull him out of the frozen picture and back into life, but the only reciprocal warmth was the hot static kiss of the screen.

I

September 2009

They had not yet charged him with anything. That was the main thing. As long as they didn't charge him he could tell himself that he was there as a witness, not an accomplice. Paul looked around the cell. There was no window, just a row of square frosted glass bricks at the top of the wall that let in enough light to show that it was morning again but not enough to warm the cell. Outside it would be warm, hot even, if the days before were anything to go by. He remembered the short staircase he had descended to enter the plain little corridor with its studded doors and calculated that this part of the building was sunk into the ground. Its bare surfaces were all cold to the touch; he could feel the floor, cool and hard through his socks. The brown scratchy blanket hadn't helped; Paul had spent the night alternating between using it as a pillow to stop himself getting neck ache and as a cover to stop himself shivering. The nightmares that had shaken him awake suggested he had managed some sleep, but he felt as though it had been weeks since he closed his eyes. He needed the toilet so badly that he had a cramp in his belly, but there was no paper next to the little steel bowl and he didn't want to call out for any in case Daniel was nearby and heard him. He might even be in the next cell; the silence didn't mean anything.

He was examining his fingertips, wondering how long it would take for the blue ink to fade completely from the whorls, when there was the sound of a bolt being drawn back and the door to his cell was thrown open with a reverberating clang. The acoustics of incarceration were new to him. They were familiar to Daniel, of course, who long before his first arrest had inherited a folk memory of heavy doors and alarmed corridors and who talked about plod and Old Bill and the filth. Paul had always called them the police with the absent-minded respect those who never really believe they will encounter them can afford.

A uniformed officer told him it was time to go back into the interview room. He wondered what they would throw at him today. Yesterday's interview had been an intensive, hour-long inquisition that he had survived, if not won, by putting his training into practice. If they arrest you, Daniel had said, never answer, never explain. If you don't say it, they can't use it. Of course he had been preparing Paul to defend himself against charges of robbery or handling or trespass, but presumably the principle also applied for something like this. The longer he thought about it, the more convinced he was that there was no way for them to prove he had been there.

They passed a bathroom in the corridor: Paul begged and the officer took pity on him, waiting outside the stall. It was like the exams at college, where if you needed to go the teachers would escort you and hover at the urinal, as though you'd written the answers on the porcelain in invisible ink. Just like the school toilets, this bathroom had cubicles that amplified the sounds inside. Paul relaxed his bowels and cringed at the splash. There were more of those glass bricks where the wall met the ceiling; no chance of anyone escaping through a window here. There was no mirror over the sinks, for which he was grateful. The third dispenser he tried actually contained some soap: a little squirt of foam that looked soft and fluffy but when he washed his face with it the skin became tight and sore as though he'd splashed bleach on it. He tried putting some on his little finger and cleaning his teeth, but the taste was so bitter he was forced to spit it into the sink.

It was the same room as before, completely windowless with dark blue walls that made it look like midnight no matter what the time. Only air vent bricks in the door and at knee level reassured Paul they weren't all going to suffocate. The black Formica table had a tatty wooden trim; their chairs were also wooden, with black vinyl seats, but his was orange plastic and attached to the floor with bolts. The reel-to-reel tape recorder took up half the table. The detectives were the same, too: the man called Detective Sergeant Woburn and the woman who had given her title but immediately afterwards asked him to call her Christine, with the result that he instantly forgot her rank and surname. They both looked fresh, and Paul realised that while he had spent the night in the station, they would have gone home to their own beds and showers and toilets. Woburn had shaved – the skin on his cheeks was pink and angry – but there was already a hint of shadow on his jaw. Paul cupped his own chin and wondered when he had last taken a razor to it. Four days ago? Five? And he was still days away from the beginnings of a beard.

He had a hard time believing Christine was a police officer. She wore lipstick and earrings and her hair was cut in a proper style. She couldn't have been more different to the squat, sour little woman who had taken his belt and his phone and his keys and his shoes away from him the previous day. Only the duty solicitor, a man in his fifties called Rob, looked like Paul felt. He was bleary-eyed and greasy-haired and had the appearance of someone who had pulled an all-nighter. Paul remembered that Rob had looked like this when he had turned up to the station yesterday and, judging by his eggy tie and tatty shoes, probably did most of the time.

Woburn stared him out while Christine smiled, then lowered her eyes. He wished he could read their minds. Daniel was big on body language: of necessity, he was better able to read people's minds than anyone Paul had ever met. He always knew what you were thinking. That was one of the reasons it was so difficult to lie to him.

The tape recorder clunked and whirred into action. 'Interview with Paul Seaforth resumed at 09.20 hours, 1st September 2009,' said Woburn. 'We were discussing the events of the evening of 30th August, same year. While you were sleeping, we had a little chat with Scatlock. He's told us the lot.'

Paul was incredulous and insulted. Did Woburn think he was an idiot? Daniel might be many things, but he wasn't a grass. Carl had spoken about the police and the mind games they played: it was part of their training, they used misleading language designed by psychologists that convinced you they were telling the truth when they were bluffing. The meaning of Woburn's words depended on Paul's response, and he breached his wall of silence only to show that it hadn't worked.

'I don't believe you.'

'Fair enough,' shrugged Woburn. He held up a photograph. Before Paul had a chance to look away, he took in a tableau of the scene that had been replaying itself in his mind ever since they had fled it. Woburn tapped the end of his pen on the worst part of the image. Paul screwed his eyes up but the picture didn't go away. He made fists and pressed them into the sockets of his eyes but the picture was only imprinted more permanently. 'Don't be shy,' said Woburn. 'It's not as though it's the first time you've seen it.'

Paul wondered why they weren't using the man's name and hoped it would stay that way. Ken Hillyard. Ken Hillyard. Ken Hillyard. It had been repeating on a loop in his mind and he was afraid that if anyone said it aloud it would break his resolve, like a password. He focused on the table. The varnish had long worn off the wooden trim. He tried to worry at a splinter in it but it had already been rubbed smooth by other guilty fingers. Rob had moved his chair next to the wall and was leaning into it, his left temple pressed against the plaster.

'It's uncomfortable viewing,' said Woburn cheerfully. 'Perhaps you'd like to see this instead.' He produced another photograph, of a little black box with a blank screen. Out of context, it took Paul a few seconds to grasp what he was looking at. When he recognised the sat nav, he felt the individual hairs on his arms raise themselves one by one. A second photograph showed the wiggly country lane that led to the village whose name would soon, for a while at least, become public shorthand for a particular crime.

'Nice piece of kit,' said Woburn. 'This is top-of-the-range stuff. They remember everywhere you ever go. This one even remembers when you went there. Covered in your prints, of course.' A third screenshot from the device showed that they had arrived at the village at 11.20 p.m. Two hours later it had happened. Paul's heart beat fast as he tried to work out what this meant for him. 'Look. Here's how it is. We know you were both there. One of you did it. *I* know which one. *You* know which one. *She* knows which one.' He jerked his head in Christine's direction. She remained inscrutable, the sad eyes, the small static smile. 'Tribes in the Amazon previously undiscovered by white men know who did it. This is a question of when, not if.' Paul shook his head, feeling his brain bounce off the walls of his skull. He needed to think, and fast, but Woburn was still talking. 'Here's what'll happen if you *don't* talk to me. Best case scenario, we charge you with aiding and abetting. Worst case, Scatlock blames you, the whole thing goes to a messy trial, it's your word against his and you go down for something we all know you didn't do.'

Christine leaned in as though to impart a confidence. 'We know it was Daniel. Of course we do. I think you got a bit out of your depth, didn't you, hmm? So I don't blame you for clamming up. But you were there, and this is only the evidence that we found before we've really started digging, so there's bound to be plenty more where that came from. Look, I know you're afraid of him.' Paul felt a stone in his throat and Christine's face began to swim. If he blinked even once he'd had it: her sympathy was not worth Woburn's contempt. 'I know you're afraid of what he might do. But that's exactly my point: the more you tell us about what Daniel did, the stronger our case against him will be and the longer he will go away for.'

'Do you have any *idea* what would happen if I did that?' he blurted. 'You don't know what he's like.' Not until he saw Rob flinch upright in his chair did he realise his virtual admission of guilt.

'On the contrary, I know all too well what Daniel Scatlock's like,' said Woburn. 'I've been nicking his dad since I was in uniform. Junior's got a juvenile file as thick as a doorstep. I've been looking forward to his coming of age for years.'

A future without Daniel in it, was that really what they were offering? He had thought it was the answer to his prayers, but now that it seemed to be a possibility he wasn't so sure. He had wanted to escape, but not like this, with death as the catalyst and liberty as the sacrifice. Despite the plans he had made for life on his own, for the first time it occurred to him that he didn't know how to cope without Daniel, how to *be*.

The only sounds in the room were the soft rhythmic click of the tape recorder and a light nasal whistle every time Rob exhaled. When Paul spoke it felt like jumping off the highest diving board at the pool: you didn't so much decide to do it as find that, after a few seconds of tiptoeing on the edge, the water was rushing up to meet you.

'I'll need protection. Like, a safe house or something.'

'A safe house?' snorted Woburn. 'Have you any idea how much that would cost? That's for serious cases.'

'How much more serious does it *get*?' asked Paul.

'What DS Woburn means is that safe houses are very labour intensive and they tend to be for more vulnerable people, families and those at risk from the public,' explained Christine. 'I'm afraid that the CPS wouldn't see your case as exceptional, or regard you as particularly vulnerable. People have to testify against friends all the time. But we can offer you a degree of witness protection and . . .' A silence followed, during which she searched the air above her head. When she spoke again her tone was breezy. 'I think it's time we all had a cup of tea,' she said.

'*What*?' said Woburn.

'Interview suspended at 09.31 hours,' said Christine and pressed the pause button.

Woburn glared at her but didn't argue. Paul understood suddenly that she was his boss. It was obvious now: Daniel would have sussed it out in seconds. The two detectives rose and left the room together. Their voices, his harsh, hers soft, faded as they walked away. The uniform who'd escorted him from his cell came back to wait at the door.

Rob's spine slackened again: now he had his chin on his chest, in the classic pose of the park bench dosser. 'Well, this puts rather a different complexion on things,' he said. 'Time for a cigarette break, methinks.'

Paul, alone with the uniform now, watched the tape machine, suspended on pause: its two turning circles, one with an orange tag, the other plain white, kept making tiny movements as though straining to get away. Woburn and Christine came back after five minutes or an hour, Paul couldn't tell any more, with tea for all five of them. It came in two plastic cups, doubled up so that you could hold it without burning your hands. Until yesterday, he'd never had tea in a disposable cup. Even at Daniel's the tea had always been in a proper mug. Once you got used to drinking out of plastic, it wasn't that bad. Whoever had made the tea had put just the right amount of sugar in it. He supposed they were waiting for Rob to come back before they could turn the tape recorder on. Christine spoke first.

'We might have found a middle way. Now, you've got blood on your hands, metaphorically speaking, but I think if we, ah, if we *reframe* this case with you as a witness for the prosecution we can get a collar on Daniel without involving you at all.'

'What do you mean?' said Paul. Carl had always told them there was no such thing as a get-out-of-jail-free card.

'I'm going to have a word with an old friend of mine who runs community projects. She's a youth worker, she's helped rehabilitate young offenders and, um . . . vulnerable people for me before.' Despite his history Paul made a small internal objection to the term 'offender' but had no quibble with 'vulnerable'. He felt like a crab without a shell. 'She'll sort you out with some work, somewhere to live – no, not a safe house, but her current project is in Warwickshire, it's far enough away for you to be able to make a new start. It's some kind of gardening project, I think. It'll be hard graft, but it will get you away from Daniel.'

Paul almost replied that he'd happily shovel shit for the rest of his life if it meant he could extricate himself from this mess and put Daniel away. Some part of him seemed to leave his body and swoop around the room, as if giving him a taste of the freedom that could be his. But first he had to make sure he knew what they were saying. He'd had enough of shades of grey, he needed them to spell it out.

'But this is on condition that . . .'

'You tell us exactly what you saw Daniel do.'

'But what about my involvement in it?'

'What involvement? You were a *witness*,' said Woburn.

'But I . . .' Then he understood. Christine sat in quiet composure while Woburn tried to persuade his features into a mask of patience. She placed her palm on the table between them so that her fingertips were inches away from Paul's and he wrestled with the impulse to hold her hand. 'So what do you think, Paul?' she said.

2

April 1989

Louisa's bedroom was at the back of the ground floor of her parents' house, with the garage on one side and the alleyway on the other. Patio doors opened onto a barren little courtyard, giving a subterranean feel.

'I don't know how you can bear to sleep there,' said Miranda, who had the room across the landing from their parents. 'It's so far away from the rest of us.'

'Exactly,' said Louisa.

It was true that in the event of an intruder scaling the mews gate, outwitting the alarm and forcing the steel front door, she would be the first to feel the blade split her skull, but it was a risk she was willing to run if it meant she could play her music loud and have the downstairs shower room to herself. The bottom bedroom had its own early warning system built in: there was always enough time between the sound of the gate dragging open, the car being reversed into the garage and the key turning in the front door to eject her guests. Hooded eyelids and high colouring gave her beauty a feverish, consumptive edge that certain boys, sensitive types on the cusp of manhood, found hard to resist. How many of them had tiptoed, shoeless, down that cobbled side alley? She could also sneak out to parties – the best of which never began until they were all in bed, anyway – and return at daybreak similarly undetected. Louisa's parents were proud of their enlightened permissiveness, a situation she was careful to preserve by flaunting her mildest dissipations and hiding those she knew would genuinely concern them. The trick was to decide for yourself where the line was drawn, then throw in something that completely raised the bar, so that by the time they had conceded the point you were back where you wanted to be in the first place.

She still flinched to recall the threat to her position that had occurred a few months ago, around the time of her eighteenth birthday, when her father had mooted turning the bottom bedroom into a gymnasium and making the guest bedroom over to Louisa. The prospect of being moved into the heart of the house had greatly distressed her, and badly affected her sleep just when she ought to have been concentrating on her A levels. After months of wasted worry, Nick Trevelyan had spent the money on a surround-sound entertainment system from Bang and Olufsen; he and Leah had joined an expensive private gym near Olympia, where they could lift weights under the supervision of personal trainers and swim in the vaulted, saline swimming pool. It was a family membership, meaning their daughters could use the club as often as they wanted. Miranda, who followed their parents in all things, whether that was reading medicine at UCL or the *Guardian* at breakfast, was an instant convert. She called her exercise regime 'training', as though she were limbering up for the Barcelona Olympics. Louisa refused to join them, even though she could see the results were impressive: it was as though someone had laced Miranda into a corset and, every week, was pulling the strings a little bit tighter. It wasn't that Louisa was against exercise per se. There was just something so unorganic and strange about running nowhere fast on a machine.

The three of them would sit at the breakfast table sprinkling bran on carefully weighed portions of muesli; she'd feel their eyes on the back of her head as she fried an egg in butter. They had even started to dress alike, all in pale grey sweats with the gym logo across the back. The clothes blended seamlessly with the colour scheme that ran throughout the house, from the front door to her father's study in the eaves: white walls and carpet with furniture in whispered shades of chalk and pastel. It was like living in an over-exposed photograph, where Louisa, in her blacks and reds and purples, felt like an anomaly, a trick of the dark.

She wanted to paint her bedroom. On Portobello Road, she exchanged a fiver for a nearly full tin of black paint, some gold leaf and two half-rolls of velvet wallpaper in a deep plum colour, a beautiful texture with a pile deep enough to lose your fingertips in. They remained in the drawer under her bed, along with her alembic and her distillery, her meticulously labelled phials and bottles, her books and her sex toys. If she painted the walls and hung the paper while they were all out at work or the gym, how long would it be before they even noticed? No one but the daily (and, of course, her own invited guests) ever breached her threshold.

The right thing would be to do it with Leah's blessing but she had exhausted all her powers of negotiation and persuasion in convincing them that taking the Kensington Market job had been the right thing to do. Her parents, in the wake of her failing to take up her place at university after A levels, were still at the 'pretending to understand' stage. It had been an uncomfortable conversation, one devoid of the usual sport. For once, Louisa was testing a boundary she knew to be inflexible. It had gone more or less as she expected it to, running the gamut from incomprehension to mockery via disapproval in under two minutes.

'Working on a *market stall?*' Leah had said.

'But you said I had to do *something* with my life.'

'Something worthwhile. We had hoped you might study, or at least travel. So far you seem to have spent most of your allowance on getting drunk.'

'I've done enough studying. What I need is life experience. I'm not academic like you and Miranda. I just want . . . oh, I don't know.' She cast around the room for support. Miranda was curled up in the papasan chair with a giant textbook on her lap. The bamboo squeaked as she turned her head to speak. 'Mum, I had a Saturday job when I was eighteen, working in the pharmacy, remember?'

'That was different,' said Leah. 'That was *relevant*.'

Nick said, 'But there isn't a market in Kensington. Or do they have it in one of the squares?'

'It's an indoor market,' said Miranda. 'That big building on the corner opposite Barkers.'

'Can't say I've ever noticed. What do they sell, fruit and veg?'

'No, Dad. It sells, like, alternative clothes and music and jewellery.'

'*Oh*.' He turned his attention back to Louisa. 'And what would you be selling?'

'Oils.'

'Oil? As in olive?' said Nick. 'But I thought you said it wasn't a food market.'

'Oilzzzzzzzzz.' She buzzed the plural.

'But darling, you can't paint,' said her mother.

This rankled with Louisa, who liked to think of herself as a polymath creative who had yet to find her medium. 'Essential oils,' she said with theatrical patience. 'Aromatherapy. Plant essences with healing powers. You know, lavender relaxes you, clary sage is a stimulant—'

'Oh, *healing*,' said Nick. 'Like the crystals and their vibrations.' They were laughing at her now; Louisa felt a bubble of rage. She wished again she had never told them about the crystals. In retrospect, her beliefs did seem rather foolish, but she had only been fourteen then and it was very unfair of them to keep referring to something that had happened four years ago. Not for the first time, she wished she had the kind of family who picked fights rather than ridiculing her; it was the one thing she couldn't bear.

'Oh, lay off her,' said Miranda. 'I think it sounds nice. Much better than an air freshener. And a lot kinder on the ozone layer.'

'But that's the whole point,' said Louisa. 'It's not just a pretty smell. There's real evidence—' She bit her tongue. She shouldn't have used the e-word.

'I must have missed that issue of the *Lancet*,' said Nick. 'Or was it published in another peer-reviewed journal that I don't subscribe to?' Louisa thought, Before this conversation goes much further one of them is going to use the word 'empirical' and I am going to lose my temper. 'Louisa, we've been over and over and over this. Unless there's empirical research to back up these theories, it's all just snake oil.'

'You're so quick to dismiss anything that's even *remotely* alternative—'

'These things are called alternative medicine because they are alternative *to* medicine. If they worked, I promise you I'd be prescribing them. I'm serious, Louisa. I've seen one too many patients hand their life savings over to some quack who promises to make them live forever with smells and bells.'

'Oh, for fuck's sake!' shouted Louisa, and she left the room, wishing there was a door to slam, angry at them for having made her undermine her own argument.

'It's just a phase, like the homeopathy, or the Buddhism,' she heard her mother say.

Nick snorted. 'The fact that this one actually comes with a job attached should ensure it burns itself out within the month. I'm sure the culture shock of having to get up for work every morning will see the novelty wear off soon enough.'

It had been a Pyrrhic victory, her pride the casualty. She descended the stairs as silently as her boots would allow then walked the mile to the market to tell Elvira, as she had always intended to, that she could start tomorrow.

Louisa loved where she lived, the streets off Gloucester Road where looming Edwardian mansion blocks were interspersed with dinky terraces. As a small child, she had always imagined them as streets made of cake with their patisserie colours and swirls; the contrasting shades of brickwork like milk and white chocolate, the intricate scrolls of their stones like piped icing. The cottages and mews houses in the foothills of the mansions were painted in fondant sweetshop colours. Walking through her neighbourhood made her crave sugar.

Kensington Market was a five-floor maze of creeping staircases, twisting corridors and black-walled booths, part dungeon, part disco. Entering it was like going down into hell, in a good way. Elvira's stall was on a mezzanine floor between a tattoo parlour and a shop that sold vintage clothes. At the end of the corridor, near the fire door, was a bright yellow mural showing black men in zoot suits abandoning a card game to dance; looking at it, you could almost hear the jazz.

Elvira had been in Miranda's year at school, when she had been known as Eleanor, but she and Louisa hadn't been friendly back then. When she'd been gone two years and Louisa was in the Upper Sixth, their paths started to cross in pubs and clubs. Even in the gallery of freaks that was the market Elvira stood out, with her waist-length hair extensions, her pierced nose and her painted veil; every day she drew a spider's web across her eyes and nose with the same liquid liner that made her round English eyes into Egyptian almonds. She ran three stalls within the market, and the one that Louisa was going to be looking after was called Volatile Oils. It was set up like a Continental tobacconist, with a few packets of henna and joss sticks on a tiny table before her and the oils displayed in tall, cramped shelves that stretched behind her and on either side, so that people had to ask for what they wanted. Those nearest to hand were the bestsellers, the low-grade oils cut with grapeseed and quick to perish. The real treasure was on the top shelf, the expensive, rare organic oils in their dark blue phials that shone like sapphires. Within a week she could identify every one with her eyes closed: within a fortnight she had blended a concoction of lavender, neroli and patchouli that helped her achieve a sleep so deep she was late for work twice. Most of her customers were tourists. Louisa suspected that their oils would be left to fester in rucksacks or discarded in hostels, although in years to come they'd catch a trace of frankincense or rosemary and remember their London holiday. She felt an almost religious euphoria when she convinced a customer of the necessity of spending more money than they had thought possible on pure rose oil or distilled lemon balm. She loved to sell them a ceramic oil burner and show them how to float the droplets on the surface of candle-warmed water so that it smouldered but didn't fizz.

'This is all a bit beyond the call of duty,' said Elvira, when she found her reading Bartram's *Encyclopedia of Herbal Medicine*. Louisa was almost embarrassed to let Elvira know quite how seriously she took it all.

'It's just something to do when there aren't any customers,' she said.

'I'm not knocking it. You took three hundred quid last Sunday.'

Louisa grew to love the rhythm of her days, the quiet hour at the top of the day before the customers came, her after-work cider with the other stallholders at the Milk Bar or Henry Afrika's. Most of all she treasured her lunchtimes. These hours she spent alone in the rooftop gardens on top of the old Derry and Toms department store. It wasn't until you stood at the top of the city above the pall of pollution and looked down that you noticed how few people ever looked up. There were three separate gardens up here. The surprisingly thin trickle of tourists who found their way up tended to dwell on the show-stoppers: the pink-walled, palm-lined Spanish garden with its Moorish geometricity, or the English Woodland with its ponds and birds. Most people only passed through the walled Tudor garden to reach the balcony that looked out across the Brompton Oratory and the caterpillar trains that crawled through the shallow gorge of the Circle line at High Street Kensington station towards Battersea Power Station in the distance. For Louisa, however, it was a destination in its own right. Of course it couldn't possibly be authentic, sitting as it did on top of an art deco building; but its crinkled walls that captured the scent of the lavender growing in the shallow borders, and the herringbone stones beneath her feet, suggested a different time and place. She defended her territory as ferociously as a cat, slipping down Derry Street without telling anyone where she was going. She lived in constant fear of chancing upon one of the other stallholders, or, God forbid, one of the one-night-stands who wouldn't take no for an answer and hung around the market for days. It was such a shame that they were only attractive for as long as they remained strangers. She always told them this at the beginning. They never got it.

She watched, with an anthropologist's interest, the burgeoning relationship between Matty the tattooist and Roberta, the Italian rockabilly who worked in the market café. Louisa would cover his stall for his almost hourly coffee runs, and in return for facilitating his courtship he offered to pay her in kind. They made her right ear their joint project, Matty fitting as many tiny silver rings as Louisa's flesh would accommodate.

Her parents were irritatingly tolerant of the multiple piercings; the corsets, blue hair and black leather choker strung with an unambiguously anatomical silver pagan fertility symbol also went unremarked. It was only after everything had happened, when her clothes had become drab, her skin was scrubbed clean and her hair reverted to its natural brown, that their younger daughter's appearance gave them cause for concern. But that was on the other side of love, the other side of death, and by then there was nothing they or anyone else could have done for her.

3

Paul took the fast train to Fenchurch Street and from there a short walk to Tower Hill Underground station, passing the Tower of London, which people in work clothes hurried past as though it were just another office block. He took two Tubes across the city, doubting his ability to negotiate the bewildering interchange of Baker Street but arriving at Marylebone two hours after he had left the place he could never again call home. It was eleven o'clock in the morning and the wide, quiet station was almost deserted. He bought a Ploughman's sandwich from Marks & Spencer and ate it on a red bench, looking over his shoulder between mouthfuls. He would have preferred the benches to line the walls but they were hexagon-shaped seats in the middle of the concourse, so that no matter where you sat you had a blind spot. He could not shake the conviction that someone – one of Carl's associates or the man himself – was following him. He fingered the mobile in his pocket, wondering when he would be brave enough to turn it back on. Dozens of times his thumb hovered over the power button and dozens of times he withdrew it. He wanted very much to speak to his mother but could not bring himself to do so until he believed he was safe. Their last conversation had been on a police station telephone; he had told her that he was in trouble in the vaguest terms he could get away with, insisting that she stay where she was. Then she had wanted to know why he didn't come down to her. He could not find a way to explain that would not frighten her, so he had made a feeble promise that everything was going to be fine and then hung up.

He changed carriages twice even though the train was almost empty. He ended up sitting near the toilet because from there he could see along the length of two carriages and there was somewhere to hide. At his knees was a bin overflowing with paper coffee cups, its side streaked with years of spillages. On the wall above his head was a map of the rail network. Unknown towns and famous cities were connected by strips and bolts representing the tracks that climbed to the north and curved subtly to the west. He wondered where Daniel was now and what was happening to him.

Woburn had driven him back to Grays Reach in an unmarked car and waited outside while he let himself into the Scatlocks' house. Carl's car was gone but he could hear the dog barking in the garden and he hesitated on the threshold before running upstairs and picking up the holdall he'd packed days before for a very different sort of adventure. On the way out, he grabbed Carl's tatty old road atlas and slid it inside his jacket. Woburn promised – for what that was worth – that Daniel had been charged and would remain in custody until the trial, which would be months off. Paul wondered guiltily if Daniel had had to make a statement and, if so, who would have read it back to him.

The right-hand window gave onto a bank of balding shrubs but to the left were soft rolling hills in shades of brown and green and grey. He had no idea where he was. Hertfordshire? Bedfordshire? Not Warwickshire, not yet. He took out his phone again but instead of turning it on, he levered the casing apart and removed the SIM card. He crossed the concertina divide between the two carriages and found that there he could open the window a tiny amount. Paul unclenched his fist to release the SIM card and posted it through. He felt his shoulders loosen and drop.

The train slowed so that the countryside outside the window seemed to be ambling along past a stationary carriage. The ticket inspector told him that they'd be getting into Leamington (he didn't call it Leamington Spa, like the maps did) around ten minutes behind schedule. He muttered something about vandalism on the tracks, triggering another reflex reaction of guilt in Paul. He looked up his destination in the atlas. The village of Kelstice wasn't big enough to have its own station: it was halfway between Coventry and Leamington, places he knew the names of but nothing more. It was maybe a quarter of the size of the Grays Reach Estate. It might be far away, but it didn't look big enough to hide in.

At Leamington station, the other passengers dispersed into waiting cars or simply strode off into the unfamiliar town. When they had gone there was only one person left on the forecourt, a boy about his own age, wearing jeans tucked into work boots and a leather jacket Paul wouldn't have minded for himself. They made brief eye contact and the boy broke into a smile.

'Are you Paul Seaforth?' he asked, his voice soft and Scottish. 'I'm Ross. Demetra sent me to come and get you. She's really sorry but one of her girls is ill and she can't get away. I've got your keys and a wee welcome pack.' He fanned out a bunch of leaflets and dangled a single key from a blue plastic fob. 'We're no far.'

The station behind them was grand and vast but opposite the car park was a row of hoardings and the few scattered buildings were faded and peeling. Walking into town they kept pace with the railway line, which overscored them in an iron-studded viaduct. There was a budget supermarket, an off-licence, two sari shops and a couple of down-at-heel estate agents. In a gap between the bridge itself and the back of a shop that had been appropriated by a mental health charity, there was a shoulder-width alleyway. Train tracks towered forty feet above their heads, weeds running down the blackened arches like liquid. A series of gateways gave onto mean backyards.

'This is you,' said Ross, doubtfully.

'I'm not going to be living in Kelstice?'

'Och, none of us can afford to live in Kelstice. They wouldn't have the likes of us, anyway. It's got something like the highest proportion of millionaires per square mile in the county. You'll see when you get there on Monday. Most of us live a bit further out on the Coventry road. I'm not sure why Demetra's put you out here, to be honest.'

'It was all done at short notice,' said Paul.

'Of course. Sorry.' Paul wondered what he knew. 'The good news is that, in Leamington, the posh part of town is north of the railway line. Technically, you're north of it. About six feet north. But still.'

Ross consulted his key fob and stopped at a gate marked 45B. Paul deduced from the duelling clouds of vapour pumping from the two shops below that his flat was above either a launderette or an Indian restaurant. When he turned into his own gate there were a dozen empty vats that had once contained ghee, as big as drums, lined along the path. The front door was a plain red slab and white bars lined the windows of a room that turned out to be a dark, messy little kitchen. A pair of bicycles hung on wall hooks and there was a two-seater sofa strewn with takeaway menus.

'Does someone else live here?' Paul asked. He had never been inside, let alone lived in, a house that wasn't a family home.

'Couple of Polish guys who work on the lorries, apparently,' Ross replied. 'I reckon you'll barely see them. It's as good as having the place to yourself.'

The staircase they crept up had no natural light and the landing on the first floor was in darkness. Only a thin white cord of daylight was visible through the door that, he decided, must lead to the front bedroom. Up a further flight of stairs the only open room, the top front, must then be his. It was a good size, with cheap fitted wardrobes taking up a whole wall, giving more storage space than any one person, even a girl, could ever use. The bed was nestled into the dormer window, the pane of which was gauzy with dirt. It was bigger than the matterss he'd had at Daniel's, smaller than the double he'd had to himself at his mum's. Paul noted in alarm that it was made up with blankets, a slippery beige and brown counterpane with a complex hatching pattern folded stiffly over the top layer. He would have to buy his own duvet.

Ross presented Paul with the leaflets. Topmost was a bus timetable.

'The K12 takes you right up to the site,' he said. 'Yours is the stop just after the village. Blink and you'll miss it.'

'The bus stop?'

'The village. I feel bad leaving you like this,' said Ross. 'I'd stay and have an introductory pint with you but I've got to get back to the site and then after that I'm on a promise with the barmaid at the Kelstice Arms. Monday, after work? We'll have a beer?'

'I'd like that,' said Paul.

He stood on his bed and watched the street. Ross emerged from the alleyway to wait at the bus stop just below his bedroom window, texting constantly. Paul wondered if he should have taken his number, then remembered that he no longer had a working phone. His insides dropped as he realised that he had thrown away Emily's number, and had never bothered to memorise it. Not that it changed things, not that she would want to hear from him again, especially not now.

The rest of the flat didn't take long to survey. There was no communal living room and no television, just the kitchen, one bathroom and three bedrooms. The bathroom backed onto the railway arches. A tattered net curtain was all that stood between his modesty and the commuters.

Paul began tentatively to explore Leamington. Most of the pubs at his end of town had open doors but frosted windows. He turned right at the end of the High Street where there was a park and some pleasant, vaguely official-looking buildings, after which the street changed its name to The Parade and the architecture changed for the better. The Parade consisted of two long, opposing, creamy Regency terraces on a gentle slope, so that the entire street appeared to have been carved through a chalk hill. Shops and restaurants occupied the ground floors: Paul stopped when he came to the plate-glass welcome of a Wetherspoon's. After a couple of pints he was confident enough to go into the Balti house underneath his flat. The chicken curry, which came in a little silver bowl, was the first thing he'd eaten since his sandwich in London and it burned like acid in his throat and ribcage. Back at the flat, there was no sign of his Polish housemates.

He went to bed around ten and woke with a start at midnight to the shouting, vomiting and fighting of closing time. He spent the next few hours in a restless trance. Shortly after five, when he thought things must surely have died down for the night, the trains started again, shaking the house from top to bottom. By about eight, the sound had built up to white noise and through that he slept deeply.

Saturday began with a sense of purpose, but once he'd bought a new SIM card and some proper bedclothes the day lacked focus. Paul grew anxious. His days and nights had been timetabled by Daniel for as long as he could remember and he wore his new autonomy awkwardly. On Sunday, he decided to have a dry run of his route into work. His timetable told him that the K12 bus ran every hour on Sundays and his was right on schedule.

Within minutes they were in the countryside. The roads had

no markings and the scattered houses were all of a uniform pinky-brown brick. Some of them even had actual thatched roofs. The road veered sharply to the right to reveal a little humpbacked bridge made of the same red stone. It would have looked like a picture postcard if it hadn't been flanked by two signs saying *Kill Your Speed: 12 casualties on this road in 2008.* The bus driver took the bridge and the bend so fast that he was almost on two wheels. It wasn't until Paul saw a pub blackboard advertising Sunday lunches at the Kelstice Arms that it occured to him that he must be in the right place. Gripping the handrail and bracing himself, he pressed the buzzer. How were you supposed to know that that was a bus stop? It looked like a garden shed with the front wall missing.

He looked around and found himself in Toytown. The houses were old but immaculate, the gardens plastically perfect; the few cars not parked in driveways were showroom-shiny and perfectly parallel to the kerb. The Kelstice Arms, an old-fashioned pub with ivory-coloured walls, stood on a little hillock in the middle of the village. It, too, had windows that you couldn't see into but there was something welcoming about the tiny diamond panes of glass, each one reflecting sunlight at a different angle. Apart from that, there was nothing. Not a church, not a shop, nothing. There was certainly nobody of whom he could ask directions to the castle. He scrambled up to the top of the hillock looking for a clue, but the gentle rise and fall of the Warwickshire countryside meant that, while it was possible to see fields and treetops waving their way into the distance, it was difficult to gauge more immediate surroundings.

Eventually he found it, up a single-track road. At the end of the road was a sign on a stick, rather like an estate agent's hoarding, announcing that a mysterious body called Veriditas was responsible for the restoration of the Kelstice Lodge Gardens. A further sign announced that the project was due for completion in spring 2012. The signs almost obscured a tiny house, the same pink stone as the rest of the landscape, whose collapsing walls gave Paul the impression of a kicked sandcastle. At its tallest point the bricks reached his elbow. A snarl of plants peered over the top. A Coke can, aged to a pale pink, lay on the floor next to a crushed beer can as shiny as a Christmas bauble and cigarette packets rotted to pulp. Clearly it had once been a gatehouse; perhaps that was why it was so small: a man could not lie down in it and fall asleep on the job.

The road petered into a dirt track, at the end of which were several cabins the size and shape of shipping crates. Cables linked them but no lights shone from within and every door was shut. Through a gap between two cabins, as though through ramparts, he glimpsed the house for the first time.

Kelstice Lodge sat on a small, steep hill. Like its baby, it was a ruin, a wreck. There was no roof and only two surviving windows, their fragile stone frames hanging from disintegrating walls like ragged lace. Three chimneys remained. What structural superiority did they possess that they had weathered the storms or attacks or years that had felled the rest? The bottom of the building was stained dark with damp or moss, so that it appeared to be sucking up water from the ground like something alive.

Paul took the slope at a run to scale it. Once inside the ruin, he craned his neck to look up. Halfway up the remaining walls was a line of thicker stone where he supposed a floor had once been, and an arch of brickwork described the remnants of a huge hearth. A vestige of a spiral staircase came to an abrupt end in mid-air. Whiskery vegetation grew in the cracks between the steps. He walked the ruin's perimeter, surveying the estate below. It was impossible to tell where the Kelstice Lodge land stopped and the surrounding farmland began. Here and there were the beginnings of order; rectangular spaces had been cleared and pathways had been marked, but most of the land he could see consisted of shedding trees and impenetrable thickets. The sky rolled lavender and anthracite above him, big clouds that threatened something more dramatic than rain: he wouldn't have been at all surprised to see a cloud split in two to reveal a giant, glowering eye. Something in Kelstice Lodge awoke long-buried memories of childhood games, make-believe sessions of warriors and kings. Paul clasped his hands together, put his foot on a jutting stone and pretended to pull a sword from deep in the rock. He wielded his weapon, turned to point its tip at an imaginary foe and fancied he could hear the whistle of its blade as it cut through the air. For a minute or two he was lost in foolish fantasy, his imagination free to roam as it had when he was a little boy. He felt like he used to before he met Daniel. When his father was alive.

4

On the morning of his death, Liam Seaforth had sexual intercourse with his wife. Sexual intercourse was the technical term for shagging; Paul's class had done it in a special science lesson only the week before. He had struggled to marry the dry biological descriptions from his textbook with the pictures he'd seen on Jake's dad's laptop, let alone with the giggling and squawking coming from his parents' bedroom. Dad had brushed his teeth beforehand. Afterwards, he sang 'their' song in the shower, the one about doing something to me and hanging on a wire. Mum stayed on her own in the bedroom for ages with the door closed.

Paul had been watching television and chain-eating cereal since half past eight. His heart leapt when he heard his father come down the stairs and then sank again as he saw that Dad was wearing his blue all-in-one. The overalls meant that he was going to be working in his shed.

'Morning, Pablo!' said Dad. He kissed the top of Paul's head and stuck the kettle under the tap. Pablo was Spanish for Paul. Mum always said that the reason they had called him Paul was specifically because you couldn't shorten it, and here was Dad making a mockery of the whole thing by adding an extra syllable. Dad said that he was *really* named after Paul Weller, but that this was their secret.

'Are you working on the shelving project?' asked Paul. Liam, who read nothing for pleasure apart from record sleeve notes, had long struggled to understand his son's appetite for books ('He must get it from you,' he told Natalie, as though it were a heritable disease). Everyone agreed that the current library system, books lining the floor of Paul's bedroom like the aftermath of a domino-toppling experiment, wasn't working. Liam was designing and building a shelving system that would fit into the alcove in Paul's room.

'Sure am, Pablo,' said Dad. 'I've done all the prep. What's the magic formula?'

'Measure twice, cut once,' said Paul. 'Can I help out?'

He was expecting Dad to say, 'Health and Safety wouldn't allow it,' which was his usual response to this request. It was unfair and patronising: last time he'd looked, all Dad's tools had been in holders on the wall in rows so neat and tidy that it looked like a hardware store. Admittedly there were all the power tools, but Paul wasn't asking to be allowed to wield the chainsaw. He just wanted to be in there, maybe hold something down and turn the handle on the vice. Sometimes, thought Paul, his dad acted like he didn't *want* any company in the shed.

'I don't see why not,' said Liam this time. 'You are nearly eleven, after all.'

'*Seriously*?' Paul couldn't believe his luck.

'Hands off to start with, mind you. I've got to take you through the theory before you begin the practical.'

They took their cups of tea outside. Above their heads, two aeroplanes had crossed paths and scored an X in the cloudless blue sky. Paul bristled with anticipation. Until now, the closest he'd got to helping out was turning on the yellow hose which wriggled like a snake when water ran through it.

Dad unlocked the shed. 'I must get rid of those,' he said, toeing the jagged panes of glass that were all that remained of their old greenhouse. They leaned against the shed wall in a stack so thick they looked green. He showed Paul how to unravel the extension lead and thread it through the kitchen window so that they could power their tools from the house. ('Whatever you do, don't unplug the microwave, she'll go nuts.') Dad showed him the red light that meant the supply would automatically cut off in the event of a power surge. ('If that goes out, you tell me right away.') Paul wasn't sure what a power surge was but he liked the idea of it. It made him think of flexing his muscles and lifting weights. He unravelled the skein of orange wire and trailed it across the garden. There was some loose cable where he'd overestimated the distance between the house and shed, so he wound it back into its casing and placed it at the shed door, hardly daring to blink in case the red light went out for a second and he missed it.

'What's the golden rule?' said Dad, before he started.

'Look, but don't touch,' said Paul. He sat cross-legged on the patio table, a platform which was the perfect height for viewing. Dad had a stiff steel tape measure that flew back into its casing if you didn't lock it the second you had the right measurement; he worked it like an expert. When the electric saw was turned on, you couldn't hear yourself think and a sandstorm of dust flew up around Dad, eventually settling to reveal him in the same pose, bent over the workbench, bottom teeth chewing on his top lip. He looked up, winked, mimed a clumsy falling over that made Paul giggle. Then he lost his footing for real.

In the seconds that followed, all senses but sight temporarily abandoned Paul. It was as though someone had turned the volume down on the world. Dad tipped forward, dropping the saw, arms flailing madly for something to hang on to. He missed the workbench but the movement dislodged the topmost pane of glass, which fell slowly away from the wall just as he plunged downwards. The jagged shard met his neck. Blood poured through the cut slowly and easily at first, like an egg sliding out of its cracked shell, then flowing faster and stronger until it was squirting from his neck at one-second intervals. It was as though the blood didn't want to stay in, as though it had been going round and round in Dad's body for years, trapped in his veins, and now it had got its chance it was making a glorious bid for freedom. Paul felt marooned on his table, as if it was an island and the grass was a shark-infested sea; he watched in paralysed horror as Liam's wild swooping movements were replaced by a series of twitches. The neatly coiled flexes at the shed door began to look like spaghetti in tomato sauce. Only when the red river began to flow his way did Paul spring from his cross-legged position, jump down from the table and run back to the house. He saw his reflection in the sliding doors as he crossed the garden: jeans, T-shirt, face. His lips were forming the word 'Mum' but no sound came out. It was as though he was the one who had had his throat cut.

Liam was coffined in his favourite Ben Sherman suit, the one he'd got married in. A Mod flag was draped across the casket. That fucking Paul Weller song was played as the curtains swallowed the casket, and his ashes were scattered in the Thames estuary, in the shadow of the suspension bridge he had helped to build. Paul found his voice again two weeks after the funeral. He was still off school but since both his grandmothers had left he was desperate to go back, just to get away from his mother. She hadn't turned the television off for days – at night, she slept on the sofa in front of it – she couldn't bear the silence, she said, she didn't have to think when the telly was on. It was too hot to touch but Paul kept fingering its scorching surface, terrified that it would explode. His dad would never have let things get like this. He used to turn the telly off at the plug every night.

She was in the bathroom, during the ad break between *GMTV* and *This Morning*, when he heard the scream. It was a high-pitched cry of shock and horror, completely different to the constant quiet crying she'd been doing since the accident. His hamstrings propelled him up the stairs two at a time and he threw open the door without knocking. Mum was sitting on the toilet. In her hands was a ruffle of toilet paper that was bright with blood. Paul began to scream too, in a voice louder and higher than hers, begging his mother not to die. She fumbled with her jeans and the paper and shouted at him to get out, but he couldn't let go of her leg. It ended in a slap, after which he ran into his room. He could not close his eyes tightly enough to squeeze out the colour red.

After a while, she came and sat on the end of his bed. She was wearing different clothes. 'I'm sorry, honey. I shouldn't have cried like that, it's not fair on you. I thought I might be pregnant. But if I was, I'm not now. You do know about these things, don't you?' He did know: he should have known, they'd had to learn about periods and all that before they got to the sex lessons. But the sight of the blood, that shocking scarlet, had erased everything else from his mind apart from the memory of his dad. 'It's just . . . if there had been a baby . . . we both wanted it so much, and it would have been something to remember him by . . .'

Paul envied this neverborn brother or sister. It would never have known Dad, which would be preferable to the pain of remembering and missing him. She pulled him onto her lap; he resisted at first, then climbed on. He was still small and light but placed his tiptoes on the floor to bear his weight nonetheless. He wished he could turn himself into a baby again. 'You've still got me,' he said, and wondered what he would ever be able to do to make that enough.

5

'Now, Paul, this isn't an interview,' said Demetra. They were in the cabin that served as a canteen. These huts might look like shipping crates from the outside but their interiors were well appointed, better than some of the industrial buildings Paul had illicitly shone his torch around. There was an office, a couple of store rooms, this canteen, a cabin with flushing toilets and even a room with lockers, sinks and a shower. He slurped a cup of tea made with water that didn't come from a kettle but from a huge silver container that she called an urn. She was drinking camomile. Paul hated herbal tea. It reminded him of when his mother had gone through a phase of thinking that infusions from the Chinese herbalist were the answer, and the house had stunk of muddy, bitter roots and leaves for weeks.

'It's just a chat for us to get to know each other. I'm not interested in this!' She brandished a sheaf of documents which Paul guessed must be his case notes. With concentration he deciphered the inverted letters and numbers of the top sheet. His mother's name leapt out at him immediately after his own, the letters of it familiar and instantly legible despite being upside down and at an awkward angle; next to it, he made out the phrase 'Emergency contact'. The page listed all the people connected to the case, the police officers and his solicitor flanked by small-print contact details and Daniel included under the word 'Defendant'; there was no number next to Daniel's name but Carl's name and address followed immediately afterwards. This document linked him to all the people he was trying to escape, like a thin, tensile steel thread that could tug him back to Essex at a moment's notice – or lead them to him. Demetra saw him looking and closed it on her lap.

'Don't worry, about this, it's just in case there's an emergency. And it's kept under lock and key,' she said. He relaxed a little. 'And like I said, I don't care about what you look like on paper. No, I want to know *who you really are.*'

Who I really am, thought Paul. That's a loaded question. The dutiless son? The false boyfriend? The faithless friend? The man who let someone die? Demetra picked up on his reticence.

'Well. I suppose that's something we'll find out organically as we get to know each other,' she said brightly. 'I'll tell you a bit about us first, shall I? As you know, this is Kelstice Lodge. Ingram – that's my husband, you'll meet him later – and I bought the estate a couple of years ago with a view to restoring the garden to its Elizabethan glory. So, we set up our charity, Veriditas. Last year, our fabulous plantswoman, Louisa, unearthed a tapestry that shows the grounds exactly as they were in 1563. I suppose you read about it? It was in all the broadsheets, although she let us take the credit, bless her.' The phenomenon of the enthusiast who assumes that all laypersons are at least basically versed in their personal passion was new to Paul and he didn't know how to react. 'Anyway. We all muck in with each other's jobs here but officially Louisa's head gardener, does all the botanical research, Nathaniel's our other gardener, Ingram's the fundraiser, and I'm the, the ... philanthropist, if you like. Essentially, we want the project to be more than just another restoration site, we want to really give something back to the wider community. At the moment, because it's autumn, there are only four young people working with us, including you. You have all, you've all overcome *challenges* and all of you have been referred to me personally. Um, what else? So far we've funded most of the work ourselves but we're in the process of applying for a major grant that will absolutely revolutionise the way we work here. At the moment we're doing it all on calling in favours and volunteers.' Basically, thought Paul, she wants cheap labour to do her dirty work. 'But you mustn't for a minute think that you're just cheap labour doing our dirty work,' said Demetra, disconcertingly. 'The young people who stay the course say that working at Kelstice has had an absolutely transformative effect on their lives. I believe – *we* believe,' she was leaning forward now, elbows on her knees, making Paul shrink back into his chair, 'that working in a garden offers a quite unique and very successful form of rehabilitation. There's real *redemption* to be found simply through hard physical toil and the observation of the seasons.'

Paul wanted to shout at Demetra that he wasn't the kind of person who needed rehabilitating, that removing him from Daniel was the only redemption he had ever needed and that he would be out of here as soon as the trial was over, but he settled for, 'Great.'

'Marvellous!' said Demetra. 'And how do you find your digs?'

Paul panicked. No one had said anything about getting any special kit. 'I haven't got any,' he said. 'Just what I'm wearing, I'm sorry.'

'Your rooms. Your lodgings. Are they OK?'

'Oh,' said Paul, feeling extremely foolish. 'Yes. Thank you. Fine.'

'I'm sorry I couldn't get you in with the others, but it was so last minute. There's always a chance a space in the Coventry house will become available. Not everyone is up to the challenge.' She looked crestfallen, as if she had taken every failure personally. She had a naive, martyrish quality that reminded him of his mother and brought to the fore a strange desire to please her. 'I'm sure you won't let me down, though, Paul. I have a good feeling about you.' She rinsed her cup under the tap and Paul followed suit. 'Do you know much about gardens?'

Paul recalled his own back garden in Grays Reach, ten square feet of planks and panels. Troy, his mother's boyfriend, would have covered the whole estate – the whole of Essex – in decking, given half the chance. He had helped put down a membrane and to lay the boards.

'I've done a bit of landscaping,' he ventured.

'Fabulous!' said Demetra, as though he had disclosed a year's experience at Kew. 'To be honest, we need you to destroy before we teach you to cultivate. At the moment it's only ground clearance. We've got about twenty acres that are thick with brambles, we haven't even scratched the surface. And don't *talk* to me about Japanese knotweed. We're months off even beginning to plant. Stick around until springtime though: that's when things get really exciting.'

'Riiiight,' said Paul, wondering what sort of person could get turned on by the idea of digging out weeds and watching plants grow. It was going to be a long autumn.

6

The fewer and farther between her hangovers were, the longer they lasted. It had been Friday night when she had performed her ritual and the after-effects had written off Saturday entirely; Sunday had not been much better, and now here was Monday morning and she still felt weak. The physical hangover was debilitating but the mental one was unusually enduring, too. The mortification when she remembered that debasing journey from the first sip of vodka to hugging the television, crying, on her knees, was almost intolerable. But it had *worked*, that was the thing. As she made her way to the office she felt light, and not just because she hadn't eaten properly all weekend. She usually felt clean and purged afterwards, but this time there was a sense of finality, a tentative confidence that the demon had been driven out at last. More than that, she felt protected from it, as though the layers of cover she had built up over the years had grown deeper and more impenetrable.

She was on time for work, which by her standards was unusually late. Everyone else was on site by the time she arrived. A light drizzle was falling; the sky was a veil of unbroken grey that didn't suggest respite any time soon. Fine by her: today would be spent on the telephone and at her desk. Ross came out of the cabin they called the boot room as she ascended the two steps to the office.

'Morning, Ross,' she said, realising that he was the last person she had spoken to before the weekend as well as the first one she had seen after it.

'Morning. Oh man, my hair,' he said, turning his face to the fine rain and smoothing his thick fringe down. Louisa was puzzled. She had always supposed Ross's hair was a kind of trichological handicap. He wore his parting at one ear, like a balding man's combover, even though he was young and his hair was thick. That anyone would deliberately wear their hair like that baffled her, and the bafflement dismayed her. It was the same instinct that made her want to reach out to Dilan and pull up his trousers to cover his underwear. She had become one of those middle-aged women who were mystified by youth fashion. It happens to us all, she thought; but at *thirty-nine*?

One look at Ingram, who was already barricaded behind his desk, cheered her. He was two years her senior but he made her feel like a girl of twenty-one. He wore his thick hair in a bluntly fringed, almost mediaeval bob. Matching eyebrows above square glasses made him look like a walking enchanted cottage from a story book. He wasn't helping himself today, wearing a hand-knitted sweater with woollen trees across the breast. Louisa half-expected a talking rabbit or a unicorn to jump out of his armpit and start running around his collar.

'There was an article about you in the paper this weekend,' he said to Louisa. The sedative of release was replaced by the old terror. She felt winded, as though an invisible assailant had delivered a blow to her belly, and bent at the waist.

'What's the matter *now*?' said Ingram.

'Indigestion,' she replied, as her empty stomach was sluiced with acid. Because genuine fear came so rarely now, when it did she was stunned by how quickly it could surface and she suddenly understood that her sense of calm was based on nothing more than a superstition that she thought she had – *ought* to have – outgrown. He gestured with a nod to a sheet of newsprint on her desk. She dragged leaden legs across the room to find that he had clipped and cut an article called

'The Neo-Luddite', about a generation of people who were rejecting technology in favour of traditional, organic methods of living and working. She trembled with relief.

'Ha bloody ha,' she said. 'I know, I'm wasting my life, a gardener who works in the garden instead of staring at a computer screen all day. It's weird, isn't it? Anyone would think I actually enjoyed my job.'

'It's not my job to print out your emails.' Ingram would have this debate daily if she let him.

'Then don't,' she said. 'Let them call me. Let them write to me. Let me go to them.'

An electronic quack from his computer told Louisa that another message had winked its way onto his screen. He winced as he read it.

'We've got another one of Demetra's no-hopers starting today. I suppose you knew about this?' he accused. She remembered now: Demetra had told her towards the end of last week when her discomfort about Adam had been all-consuming, and it had been temporarily forgotten.

'Young People, Ingram.' They had tried a million times to come up with a snappy, PC phrase that better encapsulated the complex reasons the kids ended up at Kelstice. Ex-offenders, vulnerable people, addicts, rehabilitees, youths . . . in the end, it always came back to Young People.

Ingram snorted. 'What's this one done, d'you think?'

'Isn't the whole point that we don't *ask* what they've done?' said Louisa. 'Aren't we supposed to be giving them a clean slate?' She was necessarily big on clean slates, second chances and leopards changing their spots. 'They're not all muggers and rapists. And look at Ross. We've done wonders with him. He's going to university next year.'

'Oh, I know. I've just had to write his referral letter to a polytechnic masquerading as a university. William Shakespeare University, if you don't mind. He's doing a degree in *heritage management.* What does that even *mean*? In my day you started with a Bachelor's in history and *then*, when you had graduated, you were in a position to think about your vocation . . .'

Louisa tuned him out and turned to her desk. She would pay for last week's neglect with a new week of late nights and no lunch breaks. The printed-out emails were piled high, and there were dozens of plants she had yet to track down, let alone order. On her notepad was a doodled list of people she needed to blag favours from, with tick boxes she would fill in when she'd made each phone call. They were all empty. The grant application on which so much hinged was due in two weeks; the forms were still in the envelope. The neglect was unforgivable. She turned the page to find that she had, without knowing it, sketched a rough portrait of Adam. She took her pen and cross-hatched over the image until it disappeared, then tore off the sheet and threw it in the recycling bin.

She spun on her chair to look, as she always did when she needed inspiration, at the tapestry. It wasn't the real thing, of course – you couldn't leave your phone unguarded on this site, let alone priceless, centuries-old textiles – but the print was life-size and of the highest resolution. It depicted an Elizabethan couple, she in her farthingale and he in his doublet and hose, standing before a vast and elaborate garden of herbs and hedges, knots and paths. A stone fountain stood in the centre; orchards and fields rolled in the background. The flat perspectives of Tudor embroiderers gave the background a two-dimensional feel that was perfect for her purposes of research and design. She focused on the intricate border, with its convoluted writhes of leaf and petal. Using these pictures she would recreate the garden as faithfully as she could. She eyeballed a pinky-white bloom that had been plaguing her for weeks. Was it eglantine or just a dog rose? Anyone else would have settled for eglantine and been done with it. The fact that she would not commit to the plant until she was entirely sure, and would refuse to compromise with another variety when she did, was what Ingram *really* paid her for. She could spend hours gazing at a single petal. Work was the only place she could escape. Whether she was hunting down a plant or cultivating it, she was always chasing the moment when her past and her character ceased to matter and she became only a vessel for her skills. She turned back to the page of names and numbers, each potentially a step closer to the garden's completion, and to her relief and delight felt the old passion and capability stir within her. The first call was answered almost before it rang.

'Tim!' she said. 'It's Louisa, Louisa Trevelyan. Now, listen, this is very cheeky of me but I'm going to ask because if I don't, I won't get. I'm working on this amazing community programme at the moment, restoring a Tudor garden in Warwickshire, and I'm looking for some sponsorship.'

'Why don't I like the sound of this?' said Tim. 'Are you on the blag?'

'You might call it blagging, darling, I couldn't possibly comment. But if you could lend us a digger or two, gratis, for about six weeks, you'd get the company logo all over the programme, your insignia on the bumf, all that. What do you say?'

Tim put up a pretence of resistance, Louisa put up a pretence of persuasion, and they agreed to talk again tomorrow when he'd had a chance to crunch the numbers. She put a tick in the box next to his name.

She ate lunch – a packet of offensively processed, just-add-water noodles – at her desk and afterwards went for a walk in the garden. As ever, she felt her spirit soar when she emerged from the counterfeit sunshine of the fluorescent strip into the real thing, even weak and white as it was today. The drizzle had stopped now. It had left the ground moist enough for digging over but dry enough for her boots to grip the earth. Mounting the knoll in four strides, she walked the outer wall of the ruin, surveying Kelstice in 360 degrees. Looking at the estate now, you'd never believe that in two years it would be restored to the splendour rendered by the embroiderer's needle.

Only one neat acre had been begun in earnest; Nathaniel's orchard had been double-dug from border to border and pegs and string marked out the trees' positions with characteristic meticulousness. (Nathaniel was like a Thomas Hardy hero – all rosy cheeks, russet curls and meaningful silences which Louisa had initially interpreted as enigmatic – and she had developed an unnerving crush on him. She had been both disappointed and relieved to learn that he lived happily in Stratford-upon-Avon with an antiques dealer called Ian.) Those parts of the garden not under Nathaniel's jurisdiction were a mess. The greenhouse was still half-empty, the bright green gulf of knotweed invincible. To the right of the Lodge, the wild brush of the old mere was as dense as the day she had first seen it. The sooner she could get that digger the better: in the meantime the kids would have to break their backs tilling and turning by hand what machines could do without effort. Ingram was against the digger, ostensibly on the grounds of expense but secretly, Louisa suspected, because he believed that backbreaking physical toil was vital to deplete the energy of a workforce who would otherwise rise up in violent mutiny. If he had his way the entire project would be completed with scythes and hand trowels. Finally, she squinted at the farthest boundary wall. Now that the leaves were starting to thin there was a telltale flash of whitewashed aluminium but you wouldn't see it unless you were looking and because of its position anyone who did see it would surely take it for a farm vehicle or animal shelter.

Louisa turned her attention back to the ruin. No matter how many times she saw it she could never quite commit the pattern of its stalagmites to memory. She let her hands trail along damp walls, fingers lingering in ancient graffiti faded to indecipherable rune marks, wondering as ever who had stood here before her, what they had seen and how faithfully she would be able to recreate their view. How light her workload would be if walls had mouths as well as ears, if these old stones could guide her through her project.

She did not expect anyone else to be up on the knoll and turned a blind corner without looking, headbutting a chest that was at her eye level. She took a step back and so did he, his automatic 'Sorry' gaining hers. Louisa raised her eyes. The apology died on her lips as she looked into the face of Adam Glasslake.

She gulped air that was like icewater, as though she'd been running on a freezing day. Her first thought was that the strength of her longing had finally called him into being, that she had conjured his spirit. For a ghost it had to be: Adam had not aged a day and automatically, pathetically, she put her hand up to her own cheek, conscious of how different she must look to him, how old. But his breath misted the air like hers did and his chest, when it collided with her forehead, had been warm. This was no face in a cloud, no phantom reflection. Confused, frightened, she flattened herself against the uneven wall, fingers splayed against the stone. Adam looked even more terrified than she was.

'Are you all right?' he asked. 'Have I hurt you? I'm really sorry.'

'No, *I'm* sorry,' she said in a whisper. 'Oh God, I'm so, so sorry.' She almost slid down the slope in her desire to get away, and ran through the unplanted orchard, kicking out markers and churning up furrows. She would have smashed through the glass walls of the greenhouse to get away from him. She would have clawed her way through earth.

7

April 1989

'I can't believe I let you talk me into coming all the way into the West End for this shit,' she said to Elvira. They were in a sticky-floored basement in an alley off a side street at the wrong end of Oxford Street. The venue was a dubious crossbreed between a theme pub and an industrial club: the bars either side of the stage were covered in wooden timbers, but the ceilings were messy with open piping. They were only there because Elvira was friends with Trina, the girl on the door, and she'd offered them free drinks if they paid their way in.

'I know, I'm sorry,' said Elvira. 'We'll just stay for a couple of songs, then we'll piss off.'

They had been waiting half an hour for the band to start playing. There were three of them, two guys and a girl, stacking, wiring and soundchecking instruments. Louisa counted two guitars and at least four synthesisers, although it was hard to tell because they kept rearranging them, linking wires and connecting leads until the whole stage was a cat's cradle of cable. The word 'Glasslake' was tattooed on the skin of the bass drum.

Surveying the meagre audience, she saw promise in a ponytailed man wearing John Lennon glasses and an embroidered waistcoat. Once eye contact had been made, she lowered her lashes, counted to two and looked back. He was still watching her. She smiled, counted to two again, then turned back to Elvira, knowing he would come. Just because it was easy didn't mean it wasn't exciting.

After a screech of feedback, the club was plunged into darkness. Only the green fire exit signs and the lights behind the optics at the bar glowed. In the dark, Louisa became acutely aware of the bodies around her: Elvira to her left, tall and substantial, a skinny girl in front with backcombed hair that tickled her nose and soft, hot figures to her right and behind her that could have been men or women. She could feel someone's breath on the nape of her neck and hear it, too: there was a hush of expectation in the echo. When the lights came on, it was hard to believe it was the same band. The machines and musicians were recessed in obscurity. A spotlight like a moonbeam shone on a microphone stand wound around with dead red roses and barbed wire. Behind this, with a bass guitar at his hips, was the band's fourth member, a boy – a *man* – so violently good-looking that Louisa felt tingly and uncomfortable, as though an unbearably beautiful chord had already been played.

An invisible orchestra struck up, each bar bringing a new layer until the anticipation was intolerable. When at last he sang, his voice was by turns operatic and rocky, wheeling and swooping like a bird of prey. Louisa was rooted. The ponytailed man came over and she actually swatted him away like a fly, her rings catching the lens of his glasses. She didn't acknowledge his *sotto voce* 'Bitch', let alone apologise.

The singer's looks were extraordinary, all Slavic angles and full lips, olive skin with a flush. After a while, she let her eye rove over the satellites to his star. An older guy with salt-and-pepper good looks marred only by a Habsburgian chin had two synths on either side and appeared to be playing them all at once. The guitarist was a skinny boy in eyeliner and a top hat, and the girl was behind the drum kit, a microphone hanging over her head. Best place for her, thought Louisa: with her square frame and coarse hair, she had the kind of looks it was almost impossible to enhance.

'I can't work out if this lot are behind the times or ahead of them,' Elvira shouted, so loudly and so close to her ear that Louisa felt something deep within her neck go pop.

'What do you mean?'

'What's it supposed to be? It's not rock, it's not rave, it's trying to be classical, it's a complete fucking mess.'

Elvira's was not the prevailing verdict: the cheer when they left, all four of them disappearing behind the black sheets to some unfathomable backstage area, was disproportionate to the size of the crowd. Live music gave way to records again, and the dancefloor re-established itself in the centre of the room. Louisa searched for the singer, so intently that the muscles of her eyes ached from trying to focus in the smoky shadows. When she finally located him, a barb of excitement was followed by a slump of disappointment. He was with a girl whose long red hair looked as though it had been poured down her back. Was she a girlfriend or a groupie? Their foreheads were touching as they talked. Their conversation did not look casual, and neither did they look like strangers. The couple actually brushed past her on their way out of the club. Louisa was close enough to count the hairs on his wrist, and to notice that the girl had fair eyelashes at the roots where she could not get the mascara wand to reach. As she watched them disappear through the archway that led to the stairs, she felt an unaccustomed crash of defeat.

Louisa was not above taking men away from their girlfriends, but she was unpractised in it.

'Find out when the next gig is,' she said to Elvira.

'*What*? Once was enough.'

'Please?'

While Elvira talked to Trina and the girl drummer, Louisa played with a flyer, folding it in half as many times as she could, then ripping tiny holes in the red and black paper so that it unfolded into a snowflake. What was that film, the one where the man left little origami animals everywhere he went, like calling cards? Perhaps she would become the girl with the paper snowflakes. It would be something to be remembered for. There was a rush of cool air through the club as the fire doors were opened, and the backing band began to slide heavy cases into a waiting van. It was loaded with a clearly practised swiftness, the three of them passing equipment without communication. The doors slammed and the spell was broken. The stage was just a scuffed block of wood, painted black and covered in bits of gaffer tape.

In the street, Louisa's hearing was distorted. As with finishing a book or stepping out of a cinema into daylight, the real world was always less real than the one she'd left behind.

'They're playing the 100 Club next Thursday,' said Elvira. 'We're on the guest list. Unless I get a better offer.' They turned into Charing Cross Road and were engulfed by a crowd spilling out of the Astoria.

8

There were energies at work that were beyond human control or comprehension. Fate, chi, karma, the stars, destiny – they were all different names for the same thing, that force that brought people to where they were meant to be. What other explanation could there be for the fact that he was standing before her now, in the market? Something had delivered him to her. He was dressed like he was about to go onstage even though it was eleven o'clock on a weekday morning. He wore layer upon layer of dark denim and leather, jeans tucked into boots that came halfway up his shins. She had never known there could be so many shades of black.

'Are you Elvira?' he said. Elvira was working the silver stall downstairs and today she was wearing a dress that looked like three strategically placed eyepatches held together with macramé. No way was Louisa letting Adam anywhere near her.

'I'm sorry, she's not around. Can I help you?'

'She told my guitarist we could leave these here.' He had a fistful of flyers similar to the ones she'd been shredding the other night, the Glasslake logo badly Xeroxed, black on red, and his fingers were grubby where the ink had come off. His speaking voice was flat and middle-class neutral, with no hint of its capability.

'You were good the other night,' she said.

'I'm sorry, I didn't know I'd had the pleasure.' He raised an eyebrow and she felt, what the fucking hell was this, a *blush* creep up from between her breasts and stain her cheeks.

'I meant the gig. I saw you at the Borderline.'

'Really? I wasn't sure, we didn't seem to be getting much back.'

'No, really,' said Louisa. 'Really really.' The usual language of seduction seemed to be beyond her.

'I had the worst stage fright. You wouldn't believe how nervous I get. I have to get pissed just to turn up.' He smiled; two little curved dimples, like sickles, bracketed his mouth. 'I'm going to go now, while there's still some mystery left.'

He picked up a little green phial and rolled it between his fingers.

'That's Vetiver. It reacts differently on everyone's skin, so the skill is in matching the right scent to the right person.'

He unstoppered the bottle and held it to his nose. 'I like it,' he said. 'But does it like me?' He streaked his pulse point with it. Like anyone unused to essential oils, he had used far too much, and it trickled onto his collar. He leaned right into Louisa's booth and offered her his neck like a vampire's willing victim. The dull silver of his earring was warm against her cheek.

'It's perfect on you,' she said. 'Have it.'

'Cheers, I will,' he said. 'I'd better go.'

She waited for the inevitable question. To her amazement and something like horror, the invitation for a drink or out to a club didn't come. He dumped a stack of flyers on her countertop and retreated without asking to see her again. She clicked her teeth; she had been so sure. She arranged the flyers across the front of the counter.

When she left work, he was waiting for her outside. He was wearing his Walkman but not listening to it, the navy foam-padded phones around his neck. Her pleasure at knowing she had been right was spiked with indignation that he was playing games with her.

'I realised that I didn't know your name,' he said. 'I'm Adam Glasslake.'

'Louisa Trevelyan.'

'Louisa Trevelyan . . . That's a very satisfying sound to say. Louisa Trevelyan, Louisa Trevelyan. It's like an incredibly short poem, or a prayer. It's very beautiful. It suits you. Would you like to go for a walk?'

This was more like it. They wandered up Kensington Palace Gardens where the embassies kept a respectful distance from the pathway. Uniformed flunkies were crouching next to Bentleys and Rolls-Royces, checking the underside of the vehicles for car bombs. There were still bomb scares most weeks in that part of London.

'Where did you learn to sing like that?' she said.

'I was a choirboy,' he said. 'My father's a vicar.'

'*Really*?' said Louisa. Leah and Nick, born Jewish and Catholic respectively, took their daughters' atheism for granted. Consequently, Louisa found churches agonisingly sexy.

They cut through Hyde Park and then, when it was dark and the gates shut them out, along Kensington Gore, between the Royal Albert Hall and the Albert Memorial, twin monuments to an infinite love. Cherry blossom was sleeting from the trees: it was embarrassingly romantic. Louisa had the notion that everyone involved in the architecture of Kensington, from Queen Victoria onwards, had contrived the streets to facilitate a first kiss.

But Adam didn't kiss her: he talked. He told her that the band used to be called Void Void, and that his first significant contribution to musical history was renaming it, thus ridding the world of the worst-named band in the history of music. That he was an only child born to ageing parents already twenty years into their marriage. 'They thought I was a miracle baby,' he said. 'Mum still does. That's part of the problem; she still thinks I'm about seven. She'd still be tucking me into bed every night if I let her. I had to leave home just to get away from her.'

'And him?'

'He was glad to see the back of me. He's hated my guts since the day my balls dropped and I left the choir. He still doesn't understand why he didn't produce a clone of himself, another theologian, but I *hate* organised religion. Some of the things he's said in the name of God, it's hateful.'

'Like what?'

'Can we talk about something else?

'Oh, OK . . .' she said, although she was reluctant to abandon this vein and resolved to steer the conversation back in this direction at the first opportunity. 'So, what's on your Walkman?'

His musical influences included the usual suspects like The Smiths and The Cure but also Wagner and Britten and Tallis. She learned that he couldn't drive and that, one day, he wanted to live in Germany. That he thought astrology was a load of bollocks, but then most Scorpios did. That he cut his own hair. That he lived in a shared house in Shepherd's Bush with the rest of the band, and wished he didn't. That he only ever felt really alive when he was onstage. (We'll soon see about *that*, thought Louisa.) That he had been to seven schools between his fifth and sixteenth birthdays. That he had an IQ of 172 but no qualifications because having something to fall back on would be to admit the failure of his musical career before it had begun. That was also why he couldn't take a job. These last were just two of the many reasons why he hadn't seen his parents for over four years.

'Do you miss them?'

'I miss her, I suppose,' he said. 'Or I think I do, and then I talk to her and she's all in my face and I cant wait to get rid of her. Anyway, he's made it quite clear that I'm not welcome until I clean up my act, and the only person she worships more than me is him, so . . .'

Louisa wondered what was dirty about his act and hoped she wouldn't remain in ignorance for long.

'Four years is a long time not to see your mother. I see mine every day, I still live with her.'

'Does that mean I can't take you home?' he said. It was the only change of subject she wanted; she felt like punching the air.

'No, they're cool.' She parted the bangles on her wrist, found the watch face. It was half past eleven. 'Anyway, if we go now, they won't even know you're there.'

They passed no one. After ten, these streets were as deserted as any suburban close. Even though she was the one who knew the way, she got the impression that he was leading her. When she opened the gate to the mews, he actually whistled.

'I suppose I'm used to it,' she said.

The daily had been and there was a clean white sheet on her bed like a blank canvas. The light stayed on. They undressed with neither kissing nor inhibition. She noticed that he wore a silver ring on his left thumb, a four-piece, three-dimensional puzzle. He saw her looking at it.

'I only take it off when I'm in bed with someone,' he said. It fell onto her bedside table with a chime. Seeing his naked thumb was almost more intimate than seeing the rest of him. Suddenly, from nowhere, she was nervous.

'I've seen these before, Elvira sells them. It's a Turkish wedding ring. If you take it off, it falls apart, and there's a secret way of putting it back together again, so the men knew if their wives had been unfaithful while they were away because they wouldn't be wearing their ring any more.' She was prattling; he wasn't laughing at her yet but he would if she continued. 'Stage fright,' she admitted. She wrung her hands, wishing that she had a ring of her own to twist. Adam backed away and sat down on her bed.

'Louisa, I had no idea,' he said. 'God, I'm so sorry, I thought you'd done this before.'

Her laughter broke the ice. 'Oh, once or twice,' she said, and came towards him.

It was like throwing petrol over fire. In the first ten seconds they managed to strip the bed of the sheets, move it two feet across the room and upend a jug of water. The sun was rising by the time he rolled away from her, begging for mercy and sleep. She gave him neither.

'Listen, the other day . . . at the Borderline. You were with a girl.'

He opened his eyes halfway. 'Mmn.'

'Who is she? What's her name?'

'No one.'

'Because I just wanted to let you know . . . I won't be someone's . . .' She searched for words that didn't make her sound prim. 'Mistress' was formal and Victorian, 'bit on the side' too Ealing comedy. 'I'm not the kind of girl to be the *other woman*.' Immediately she wished she could take it back. It was supposed to have been ironic but she just came over as desperate.

'She's history,' said Adam. Did that mean he was ending a relationship or that he had never intended to see the other girl again? Either way, she had won. A shiver of triumph overrode a twinge of misgiving at a man who could dismiss any woman so coolly.

While Adam slept, she inhaled the thick oily skin between his shoulder blades where he smelt most like himself. If you could distil and bottle the essence of a human being, if you could crush skin like petals, then she would do this with Adam Glasslake. The vetiver scent was faint now but his neck still bore the visible traces of the oil he had anointed himself with earlier. It was a faint dark green. Below this, on his clavicle, she had marked him for herself, a vivid red circle, half-kiss, half-bite. She felt intensely female and powerful, like a witch.

9

They couldn't stay in their house. Dad's life insurance policy was invalid because Mum had secretly cancelled the direct debit six weeks before his death, along with the Sky, the Christmas Club, Slimming World and all her magazine subscriptions. She had been saving up for fertility treatment. No one told Paul this: he found out by listening at doors when she was on the telephone and thought that he was asleep. 'There's no way I can cover this mortgage,' she told an unidentified friend. 'On what I earn? Are you having a laugh? If I sell up here and rent somewhere crappy I can live off the equity until Paul finishes school. It's not like I've got a choice, is it?' Paul would have looked up the word 'equity' on the internet, but that had been cancelled, too.

'Are you sure you don't mind leaving?' she asked him as they were packing up his room. His books never had been put on shelves.

'I *promise* you I don't mind.' He would have had to say this whatever his feelings because he knew she didn't have a choice, but it was not a lie. In fact, he couldn't wait to get away. His bedroom window looked out onto the garden and he had nightmares where blood-soaked wires were thrashing at the glass like the tentacles of some terrible alien octopus.

Mum had always looked down on the Grays Reach Estate, even though Dad had grown up there and she hadn't exactly been born in a stately home herself. When they argued, he used to call her a snob and Lady Muck. Grays Reach was literally a sink estate, the grey buildings scattered like dregs in the shallow bowl of an old quarry in the part of the estuary where the tunnels and the suspension bridge loosely stitch Essex to Kent and the river starts to smell of the sea. The town planners who had commissioned the estate in the middle of the last century had had an uncanny prescience of, and sympathy for, the requirements of petty drug dealers in the twenty-first century; it was almost entirely pedestrianised, with no conventional streets but clusters of houses that backed onto little courtyards which were in turn linked by paths and alleyways. An offshoot of the A13 divided Grays Reach from its flanking towns of Grays and Tilbury, and an underpass beneath the railway line that carried the trains between London and Southend led to the High School and the shopping precinct. The precinct housed the estate's only pub, the Warrant Officer, bracketed by two burnt-out shop shells. Paul's new home was in the heart of the estate, the end of a staggered terrace that faced another and backed onto a concrete quad. The day they moved in, Natalie said to herself, 'How the mighty have fallen,' and looked out of the window that faced a brick wall. She was acting as though they were living in a shanty town.

That first summer, Paul quite liked Grays Reach. Being miles from the main road meant that his mother was happy for him to spend all day on his bike. On two wheels he mapped the place for himself. There was plenty of land, wasteland and wild fields, to explore. Unlike most of the estuary estates, which had become absorbed into the surrounding towns, Grays Reach remained surrounded by its own scrubby green belt, like the kid at school who can't shake off rumours of fleas and who no one ever comes close enough to touch. Although the new house was only five miles from the old one it was in a different catchment area, which meant that he wouldn't be going to St Neot's but to the Grays Reach High School. His mother was worried that he wouldn't know anyone there. As far as Paul was concerned, this was good. He was sick of being the boy with the dead dad; sick of the staring; sick of the way people were really nice to him in front of the teachers but had stopped playing with him at break times because of how he'd stop without warning and stare into nowhere, bypassed by the football and ambushed by tears.

On his first day he wore a blazer that cracked at the elbows like dry skin. With his little frame in the big coat he felt like he was wearing a suit of armour. At the gates to Grays Reach High, which incorporated a metal detector and were patrolled by Community Support Officers, he wondered very seriously if he might need one. He had never seen so many people in the same place all at once. For one bewildering second he thought that the staff were wearing school uniform too and then as one of the 'teachers' burst a bubble of gum over his tongue and slung a schoolbag over his shoulder it dawned on him these six-foot creatures, these *men*, were schoolboys like him.

The other Year 7s' main concern was coming to terms with the concept of a timetable and the constant shifting from room to room, but Paul had another fear uppermost in his mind. From week one it was horribly apparent that at Grays Reach there were opportunities for blood to escape everywhere. His junior school had presented nothing more hazardous than round plastic scissors and the odd grazed knee: this building was one big flesh wound waiting to happen. The school knew that the kids carried knives and they were good at spot checks, but confiscating the blades didn't mean he was safe. There were design and technology classes with lathes and craft knives, food technology classes with huge steel blades and science laboratories full of glass jars and test tubes, any one of which might splinter into a dozen lethal shards. The compasses in their brand new geometry sets had points sharp enough to break the skin and if you snapped one of those protractors or set squares in half they would have a jagged edge like a sheet of glass.

Paul knew that he was only of average ability – he worked hard for his B-grades – but at Grays Reach he was considered the class intellectual. Despite this handicap, he was assimilated into a loose posse of boys in his form. None of them shared his passion for reading fantasy novels, but you couldn't have everything. He had people to walk home with and people to eat lunch with and until he found a kindred spirit (in books, you always found your kindred spirit eventually, after a long and arduous journey), they would do. He'd once gone to a lunchtime chess club meeting hoping to find some like-minded people – he couldn't play, but he liked the idea of the game with its antiquity and mystery – but it had been just him and Mr Bradley, his history teacher, who didn't bother to hide his disappointment when nobody else turned up but had taught Paul the basic moves nevertheless. After three weeks Mr Bradley's dejection was more than he could bear, and although he was getting into the game, he felt that it would be kinder to release the teacher from his commitment.

He survived most of his first year intact and then, at the beginning of the summer term, they studied genetics in biology. All of them were sticking out their tongues, trying to see if they could roll them into a pipe or not. Miss Grewal, who always wore a white coat like a doctor, couldn't roll her tongue. Paul could do it: the boy next to him was a double roller, making a sort of wavy pattern like the letter W that no one else on their table could do. Miss Grewal had explained that tongue rollers inherited this ability from their parents: if neither of your parents could do it, you would never be able to, no matter how hard you tried, and if they both could, it would come easily to you. If one parent was a tongue roller and the other one wasn't, you had a fifty-fifty chance of inheriting it. Their homework was to find out how many people in their families could roll their tongues and plot it on a family tree diagram and see if there was a pattern.

'That's discrimination, miss,' said a boy called Curtis Goddard, who was big on human rights. 'Not all of us know our dads.'

Paul thought that he would never know whether his father could roll his tongue, and although he tried to picture Dad's face and recall whether he'd ever seen him pull this expression he couldn't. In fact, his mind's image of Dad's face had taken on a hazy quality. The only way he could see him vividly was with his neck slashed and the blood pouring out. The tears seemed to come from nowhere and before he knew what was happening he was running from the classroom, blind with them.

Miss Grewal found him in the corridor where he gulped an explanation. Teachers weren't supposed to touch you but she gave him a light hug. When she ushered him back into the classroom, a few boys at the back gave a wolf whistle, were immediately given detention and then looked at Paul as though it had been his fault.

'That was a bit *gay*, Seaforth,' said Curtis. All his friends were a little more distant with him that lunchtime but he probably would have recovered from that if it hadn't been for the Abigail Burden incident a few days later. Their French teacher handed out a set of brand new textbooks whose pages had edges like razors. Abigail got a paper cut on her finger, deep and wide, the flesh parting like a little mouth. The scarlet stream was disproportionate to the size of the wound. Paul felt iron bands constrict around his chest. Afterwards he had not really been able to remember much about it apart from lying on the floor with a rushing noise in his ears. The other kids told him he'd been screaming for his daddy. From then on, he was on his own.

Grays Reach was dangerous without a force field of friends to protect you. The corridors were fine, you could just attach yourself to any random group of boys by walking close enough, but the walk to and from school was an assault course of lurking bullies. No matter how early he left in the morning or how late he left in the afternoon, they would always find him. If they didn't get him in the underpass they'd find him on one of the footpaths. On a good day, it would be name-calling, threats, no-holds-barred descriptions of all the sex they were having with his mother, who apparently loved young cock, especially up the arse. On a bad day, it would get physical. There was nothing left for them to steal; he made his own sandwiches so he didn't have to carry lunch money, but that didn't stop them ripping his backpack from his shoulders and emptying the contents down the drain. After the bag, they'd start on him. He was surprised to learn that he did not mind blood so much when it was his own; when his own skin was broken, he felt a strange detachment that was the opposite of panic. He started getting up in the middle of the night to wash the stains out of his school clothes. While he was waiting for the tumble dryer to finish its cycle, he read, disappearing further and further into the fantasy worlds where friendship mattered more than anything else and codes of honour were unbreakable.

He longed for a friend, he prayed for one. Then, when he was thirteen, Daniel came.

10

Of course it wasn't really him; she should have known that at once instead of skittering off into fantasy and superstition. The next time she saw him, in the canteen, she was ready for it, she had calmed down enough to see that it was only (only!) his doppelgänger, an uncanny likeness. The differences grew clear, like a picture being pulled into focus or seen through an eye adapting to different levels of light or dark. He was taller than Adam and broader, his cheekbones were softer and his eyes were green, not blue. But the hair was the same, strand for strand, curl for curl, and the mouth was Adam's exactly, although the smile it formed was shy and uncertain, not the swaggering lopsided smirk that Adam had worn. Her starved eyes gorged themselves on the sight of him. Sometimes it was too much to look at him, and yet she could not turn away.

Louisa let her research slide again as she took to stalking him around the site, pushing an empty wheelbarrow to the places Paul was likely to be. She saw the lines of his body through his T-shirt and jeans, the perfect inverted triangle of his torso, the lean thighs, the belly as flat as his back. She found him alone, conducting a fingertip search of a newly cleared and freshly dug garden, picking out the sycamore seeds that littered the estate. It was painstaking, boring work, a job doubtless delegated by Ross, the classic initiation task. Once or twice she saw him pick up a sycamore seed just to let it spin to the ground like a helicopter. He looked very young.

He was eighteen, that much she had gleaned from listening in on conversations in the canteen. She had once believed in reincarnation and the dates were right: she had last seen Adam twenty years ago, just the right amount of time for the vagrant soul to find new flesh. That this chronology offered a more banal possibility did not occur to her until a week or two later. She was in the greenhouse, scrubbing the potting shelves with an organic fungicide, when the idea of Adam fathering a child with another woman came to her. The pain of betrayal, imagined, delayed, was as acute as it had been back then. Knowing Paul's exact date of birth would set her straight. But how could she find out? Demetra wouldn't let her see his file even if she could find a plausible reason for asking. She guarded her charges' privacy fiercely.

Louisa was tormented by Paul's proximity and what it might mean. There was no ritual to cast out this living ghost, no drink that would sink this spirit. If Paul was Adam's son, what was he doing here? And if he wasn't, what was he doing here? Who else from her past was about to trespass on her present? Would the Other Man, the witness or the man who had declared death, be next? Would his bandmates come and find her? Had they all been conspiring, waiting until she thought she was safe? The possibilities wheeled around her mind, the earthly menace and the unearthly omen. She was not sure which was the more terrifying.

She was surrounded by people all day every day but as soon as the last of them had left the site loneliness enveloped her like freezing fog. In the evening she would sit in the office, staring into space, wishing desperately for someone she could hold and confide in. The only person she could really say she was close to now was Miranda, and even her she only saw three or four times a year. There had been a time, six or seven years after it had happened, on Miranda's son's first birthday, when she had come close to telling her. After a raucous children's party, their parents had taken a taxi back to Kensington and Dev, exhausted by catering the whole thing, had gone straight to bed. The sisters had stayed in the huge kitchen, ostensibly to clear up the mess, but they had ended up finishing one bottle of wine and then opening another. Miranda kept making clumsy attempts to wipe down surfaces and load the dishwasher, glass in hand the whole time.

'Do you ever sit still?' Louisa had asked. 'Your life looks like such hard work.'

'Ah, it's worth it though,' said Miranda. 'You'll find out one day, when you meet the right man.' Louisa reached for the bottle as her sister went on, 'Have you *really* never met anyone you wanted to settle down with?' The question was asked in a kind of drunken innocent concern but Louisa felt her answer, detailed and incriminating, roar up out of nowhere. She actually got as far as drawing the breath that would fuel the words but the baby beat her to it, crying out for his mother from his cot. Miranda had leapt up to comfort the child, smashing a wine glass on her way out of the kitchen, shattering Louisa's resolve to share. By the time Miranda came downstairs, the kitchen was clean and Louisa was making coffee, shaken by how close she had come to exposing herself.

It was four years after the near-miss in Miranda's kitchen that she had met Laurence, the only man among Adam's would-be successors whose face as well as body she could remember. Over the years she had lost count of the lovers she had taken, mostly one-night stands and a handful of fledging relationships whose wings she had clipped early on. Laurence had been different, the only other person she might ever have told. He had run a wine merchant's in the small Hampshire town where she had briefly freelanced as garden designer for a big private house. He took her to a restaurant and then back to his flat; he elicited nothing like the passion she had had for Adam, for which she was grateful, but he was kind and tender and she felt a corresponding softening of something inside her. After just two or three times with him she began to think of him as her Dev, a steady, decent man with whom she could become a steady, decent woman. Her mistake had been to get complacent (drunk, again) and invite him back to the tiny unfurnished bedsit that was then her home. After Laurence had fallen asleep Louisa realised her mistake and had lain awake, staring at the starkness of the room, the jangling clothes rail and the conspicuous cardboard storage box that stored her memories. In the small hours she had hidden everything in the only fitted storage the studio had to offer, the kitchenette cupboard with its cutlery for one. She had tried hard to stay awake but the sleep she eventually surrendered to was so deep that Laurence, on waking, had gone looking for tea and cups. She awoke to find him sitting on the end of the bed, leafing through her scrapbook, and had screamed at him to stop looking through her things and to get the hell out of her flat, pushing him up the stairs. He had come round the next day to offer a bewildered apology through the letterbox, but she had stayed on the bed, scrapbook in her arms, locked in grief. She was mourning not only the loss of Adam but the death of the version of herself that was able to put down roots, find love, make a family, live a good life.

Louisa never went back to work at the big house. The weeks that followed had been some of the darkest she could remember; with no employment, she had only herself to live with and there had been some nights when even that company had been unbearable and she had considered – fleetingly and with terror, but considered it nevertheless – the ultimate release.

The job at Kelstice, advertised in a trade journal, had saved her from herself. The salary offered was incommensurate with the experience they were asking for, and this, she supposed, was why she was the only applicant. In the wreck of the site and the amateurish crew she recognised a place she could finally lose herself. For the first few months of the job she lodged with an elderly woman on the Leamington road and it was here that the others believed she still resided, although she had arranged to have her meagre post redirected to a post office box when she had bought the caravan. While she was settling into her four-wheeled home she was afraid the others would notice that her car was often parked in the same spot for days on end, that she was always the first one on site and the last to leave, but she had overestimated the curiosity of others. Demetra, despite the calibre of the young people they worked with, was the kind of person who just assumed everyone was telling the truth, all the time. Why would anyone lie about something like that? The young people, who all lived in the opposite direction of Coventry, showed even less curiosity about her private life. They only *really* saw each other, and she wondered if she had been like that when she was young. To deepen her cover (and because she no longer dared to drink in public) she became the site's designated driver, always offering Ingram and Demetra and even Nathaniel lifts home when they needed them, dropping them at their doors and driving home the long way round, looping the country lanes until she ended up back at Kelstice, its unofficial porter, its secret sentinel. Every night she locked the door of the office and stood in the moonshadow of the Lodge. If the night was mild she took her time on the walk home, knowing that no one would be waiting for her.

11

Paul found that there was a different language at Kelstice, a centuries-old vocabulary. Much of the terminology that they used was to do with horses: the paths that cut through the New Wood were called gallops, and the wild rutted avenue that framed the house they called a ride, not a driveway. At the back of the site there was a stagnant mass of water known as the Mere. Smelly gas rose off it like something out of a horror film, and if you were unlucky enough to get downwind of it you had to breathe through your mouth. The intention was to clean and restore it to an ornamental lake, a job with which he wanted no involvement. The Mere was bordered on one side by Nathaniel's nascent orchard and on the other, close to the perimeter wall, was territory colonised by real trees – as opposed to brambles, ivy and weeds – called New Wood, although it looked as ancient as the Lodge itself.

Very little seemed to be expected of him, and he suspected that he could have spent most of his days wandering around the site, but he didn't want to get into trouble and have them throw him off the project, so whenever he found himself at leisure – or it was raining – he took himself back to the cabins to receive instruction.

One afternoon rain *and* idleness drove him to climb the stairs to the office. Louisa and Ingram were in heated conversation about some benches that Ingram had ordered, clearly to Louisa's great displeasure. They had their backs to the door; that, and the thunder of raindrops on the roof meant that they did not hear him come in. After standing in the doorway for what seemed like entire minutes, cold rain finding its way down the back of his jacket, he decided to seat himself at the spare desk until they had finished arguing.

The desk was strewn with books, none new, some with desiccated spines that snapped in two when you opened them and threatened to disintegrate in his fingers. One account of a castle garden had previously been a library book; the stamp in the back revealed that it had been borrowed just once, in 1972. Tucked into its pages was a facsimile of a map of Kelstice in the 1850s, showing neat little parcels of land and a scattering of long-gone outbuildings. Louisa's voice suddenly became clear and sharp.

'Ingram, if you want a suburban back garden I can make you one, but you hired me to recreate a historically accurate Tudor garden and you can't go around undermining my designs like this.'

'The visitors have to sit somewhere,' said Ingram.

'Yes, but on these? They're going to make it look like a fucking Essex patio!' Paul felt a little surge of indignation on behalf of his home county. 'We'll be a laughing stock.'

'But I've ordered them now,' protested Ingram, passing her a catalogue flagged with sticky notes.

'*How* much?' Louisa cried when she got to the relevant page. 'That's the last time I let you lecture me about budgets. I don't spend my life in that greenhouse coaxing things to life from seed to save money so that you can blow it all on patio furniture!' Ingram flounced to his desk and hid behind his computer, his hair a pale aureole.

'I'm not having them in my garden,' Louisa shouted in his direction, then turned back to the room. When she saw Paul sitting at the spare desk she gasped as though he had ambushed her, putting her hand on her chest and taking a step backwards.

'Sorry,' he said, not because he had done anything wrong but because he was still mindful of the way he'd frightened her on their first meeting. 'I haven't got anything to do,' he continued, by way of explanation for his presence. She sank into her chair, flushed and silent.

'You might try and get that desk into some kind of order,' called Ingram. 'It's a disgrace. Some of those books are out of print, rarities, not that you'd know the way *she* handles them.'

A hostile atmosphere settled over the office, with Ingram making little indignant parping noises from behind his screen and Louisa alternately glaring at Ingram and looking at Paul as he shifted the books around the desk, wishing that he had stuck to doing nothing in the rain. He tried to break the tension with a question.

'Why do they call it New Wood?' he said.

'Well, it was new once,' said Louisa, whose complexion had gone back to normal. 'It was planted just after the war.'

'That's mad, that it can get so wild after, like . . .' he mentally calculated '. . . nearly seventy years?'

'The *Civil* War,' said Louisa. She lowered her Mona Lisa eyelids and smiled to herself, and in that moment there was a schoolgirl haughtiness about her that evoked someone else, someone it took him a while to identify as Emily.

In the first week of October a furious gale blew and winter came suddenly, like turning the page of a calendar. Paul went home from Kelstice on Friday night in a long-sleeved T-shirt but on Monday morning he needed a fleece under his jacket, the navy blue one with the Veriditas logo embroidered on the breast that was the nearest thing they had to a uniform. The trees had shrugged off their remaining clothes, meaning that the journey to work went from golden to silver in a weekend.

The only plant tenacious enough to hold its leaves was the one which literally covered the site, the rampant weed that Louisa and Nathaniel called fleeceflower, the rest of them called Japanese knotweed and everyone regarded as a cross between a triffid and radioactive waste. It towered above Paul's head and to his eye it was rather beautiful in a wild, jungly sort of way, with little chandeliers of white flowers that hung against flat, vivid leaves. But apparently it was a weed, so virulent that it was classed as toxic refuse. You couldn't compost it; every bit of the plants, from leaf to root, had to be burned in giant braziers that they kept in the centre of the Lodge, so that sometimes it looked as if the ruin's crumbling chimneys were once again the conduits for smoke. Cutting it down and removing the roots was like wrestling a bear. He stopped seeing the permanent ache in all of his muscles as punishment and started to view it as reward. The novel sensation of pride and satisfaction after a day's hard physical graft made him feel connected to his father and had the added benefit of knocking him out at night. On the days when he had to work in the office, sitting in a swivel chair, answering the phone and trying to decipher Ingram and Demetra's haphazard filing system, his brain went into overdrive to compensate for the lack of physical activity. Those were always the nights when he found it hard to sleep, tortured by thoughts of Daniel. He would hang out of his bedroom window and look down at the late-night stragglers on the High Street, reflecting guiltily that Daniel would give anything to have even such a meagre view as this.

Their progress was steady but slow. When the trees were nude you could see more: the density of the brambles that clawed at your ankles like man-traps; the distance yet to be cleared. The day he found the cable he was working on his own, tidying up the space around the cabins. All the electricity on site came from a single source; the cabins were connected to it by thick green cables. There were six cabins but seven cables, one of which abruptly disappeared underground. Intrigued, Paul followed its path. He nearly lost it a couple of times – whoever had buried it had done a good job. It threaded along the edge of the car-park site, which was still a choppy sea of clay and hardcore, and then followed the perimeter wall where it surfaced to trail alongside the bricks dividing Kelstice from the farmland that locked around it like puzzle pieces. Paul had no idea whether the walls were as old as the Lodge itself, but they had weathered better, almost entirely intact. In the few tumbledown breaches, the neighbouring landowner had erected a snarl of barbed wire that reached to the waist. Paul peered through one gap and was alarmed to find himself almost nose-to-nose with a masticating cow, her hide the same deep terracotta as the local stone. The longer the wall went on, the more he wondered if he wasn't somehow going round in a huge circle, about to find himself back where he had started.

He knew when the cable vanished under the gate that this was not the case. Even without the cable as a marker, he would have remembered something like this strange portal, with its crumbling brick frame and its rotting green wood. Even the iron bolts and hinges looked frail. He nudged gently at the door. It almost gave, but he was worried about barbed wire or worse on the other side and decided not to push it. He gave the wall itself a good kick. It seemed sturdy and, using worn-away bricks for hand and footholds, he climbed. He found himself looking at the dull silver roof of a motorised caravan. The brow of the vehicle jutted like a frown. Its paintwork was greying and lime-coloured moss grew around the door and aluminium window frames like a velvet trim. It had obviously been driven here, but not recently; there were no tracks, one tyre was flat and grass grew in between the fat spokes of the wheels. The porthole windows were blind with books, pages to panes. Outside, there was a square patch of tilled land with little sticks in it and shoots sprouting up here and there, a miniature version of the big garden they were building on the other side of the wall. Gas canisters lined up like soldiers and sheaves of lavender, neatly arranged in muddy trugs, sent up a sickly-sweet smell.

Paul dropped to his feet on the other side of the wall, making sure to bend his knees to absorb his bodyweight like Daniel had taught him, but his fall was intercepted by nature's barb; his jeans were pierced and the flesh on his arms was ripped by what felt like hot needles. He found himself lying on the ground in a tangle of stems and branches, fat white flowers all around him, and saw that he had pulled the plant clean away from the wall it was trained on and had severed it, almost at the root. His skin, when he rolled up his sleeve, looked like it had been studded with rubies. He leaned the rambling rose back against the wall. To his inexpert eye, it looked all right. Suddenly he was desperate to leave. He did not even know whether this was still Kelstice land, but he felt acutely ashamed of his intrusion, like a voyeur. This thief of electricity clearly did not want to be found and he had more cause than most to respect that. He made an easy exit through the gate, which he now saw was operated by a couple of simple latches, then retraced his steps to the car park. The journey seemed much shorter this time, as return trips usually do.

There was nothing more to tidy up. He was still afraid to take the initiative when it came to vegetation, convinced that he would clear a patch of 'weeds' only to find he had destroyed a precious cultivation. All of the cabins were empty. He walked around the site looking for someone to tell him what to do but found no one. He used the break to call his mother. Her phone gave out the flatline beep of the unobtainable number, which puzzled him. When Troy's phone made the same sound, Paul was instantly on high alert. Years ago, Daniel had said that in the event of Paul ever crossing him, it was Natalie he would target. Afraid of what he might learn, he called the landline for the first time. The sound of her voice made him feel drugged with relief.

'Hello, baby!' said Natalie. 'When are you going to come down and see me?'

'Soon, when I'm properly settled.'

'I can't bear to think of you going through all that on your own, living in the middle of nowhere. I should never have left you behind with those people, I blame myself . . .'

'Don't be silly,' said Paul. 'I'm fine here, I'm making friends. What's wrong with your mobile?'

'It got nicked out of the van when I went back to Grays Reach.'

'Mum! You went back there! What the bloody hell for?'

'I had to, to the dentist to get my filling mended. I can't get an NHS dentist down here yet, although they'd have to if I was pregnant and I'd get all my treatment for free.'

'Are you mad? Carl could have seen you, or anything!'

'It's OK, Troy was with me.' Paul suppressed a snort. 'The little fuckers took my handbag, my purse, a hundred quid's worth of fertility drugs and . . .' Her voice faltered. 'They took that picture of you and me and your dad the day you were born. It was the only copy.'

Paul knew the photograph she meant, an overexposed snapshot of the new family in the hospital ward that she kept in a little leather frame. He hadn't known she still carried it around; the knowledge made him feel warm, like a cuddle, until he heard that his mother was crying. Troy took the receiver.

'Sorry, Paul,' he said. 'She's been really cut up about that photo. She's missing you a lot and . . . she reckons that losing it was like losing your dad all over again.' He said it without resentment or jealousy. 'I'm going to go and look after her now, we'll call you soon.' Paul gave Troy his new number; it was repeated back to him twice, no questions asked.

'Well, I'd better get back to your mum. Take care,' he said. The more Paul thought about Troy, the more he came to view him as a kind of saint. No way would *he* be able to tolerate being a substitute for the real love of someone's life.

12

April 1989

Twenty-three nights, nineteen of them together. For the first time it wasn't enough to lie there, be beautiful and receive pleasure. Adam demanded reciprocal worship.

'I recognised you as soon as I saw you,' he said, his hands pinning hers to the bed. 'We're two of a kind, you and me. Do you know how rare that is? Sometimes it frightens me.'

'Me too,' she whispered into his mouth.

'I like it,' he said, gripping her wrists so tightly that she cried out. 'Scary's good. It reminds me I'm alive.'

The most ridiculous things about him turned her on. The sound of his ring as he set it down on the glass of her bedside table. The way his pelvis seemed made to tessellate with hers. Sometimes she looked down at her breast expecting to see a pulsating cartoon loveheart that she would have to catch and stuff back into her ribcage.

Adam liked the fact that no one in his world knew about her and no one in her world knew about him.

'When I'm with you no one else exists,' he said.

'It's a shame that feeling can't last forever,' said Louisa.

'Can't it?'

'Real life has to intrude at some stage. You'll meet my parents, I'll meet the band.'

'I won't meet your parents,' he said with a vehemence that surprised her. 'I don't do family.'

'Well, at least I'll get to know the band, I hope.'

'I just hate to burst the bubble. This bit. Like we're the only man and woman on the planet. Hey, do you know what that means? If I'm Adam, that must make you Eve.'

'*God*, that's cheesy. You can do better than that.'

'Why? I like it. That's going to be my new name for you: Eve.'

'I bet you say that to all the girls.'

'You *are* all the girls.'

Three afternoons and two nights a week he rehearsed. On those nights he did not come to her. If he could, he called, late, to say goodnight. He didn't have a telephone at his bedsit, not even a payphone. He had a pager instead. Her parents carried pagers, only they called them bleepers. When they were on call they took them everywhere, even to bed, and when the bleep came, they dropped everything. Of course no one was depending on Adam Glasslake to step in and save a life, which was fortunate as Louisa soon learned that the gap between leaving a message and hearing back from him could be hours. Most of the telephone booths on his street in Shepherd's Bush had been vandalised, he said, sometimes he had to walk for miles to find a working one, and moreover there was a band rule that rehearsal time was uninterruptable. She was reluctant to leave her room until she had heard from him, pulling the extension next to her bed just so that she could ignore it for a few seconds when finally it rang. The longed-for conversations were fraught, on her part if not on his; even when he said beautiful things to her, she imagined she heard the chirrup of female laughter in the background. She felt imprisoned, like some fairy-tale princess in her tower, or a mistress in her married lover's pied-à-terre.

The other people in his life – his band members in particular – became mythical creatures to her. They gained glamour and power the longer they remained strangers. Getting him to talk about them was like trying to prise open a bad shellfish. She gleaned only that he didn't seem to have much time for the boys, Ben and Ciaran, but he did confess that he was close to Angie.

'You're lucky she's ugly,' he said.

While she waited, she still had his company in the form of twelve songs spread across two cassettes. She set up Nick's decommissioned tape deck in her room so that the music was on a continuous loop. At some instinctive level she knew that he must not know how often she did this; it was the behaviour of a groupie, not a girlfriend.

Miranda came home one day to find Louisa cross-legged on her bed, having a staring contest with the silent telephone. 'Someone playing you at your own game?'

It was a throwaway, affectionate remark that articulated for the first time the relationship's appeal and its danger. 'No,' she said. She would have loved to confide in her sister but what would Miranda know about passion? She'd been with Devendra since their O levels and as far as Louisa could see, the couple had plunged headlong into mild affection and things had cooled rapidly from there. The closest she'd ever seen them come to sexual abandon was when Dev had squeezed her sister's toes through her socks and Miranda had spilled her coffee on her lap in surprise.

She knew the number of his pager by heart, the digits a rhyme in her mind. She wished she could put some kind of bug on the device, or on Adam himself, that would show on a map of London where he was at any given time. She would never have thought that about any man but Adam and if a previous lover had said such a thing about her she would have been repulsed. Lately, she didn't recognise herself. The sooner she broke into his life and let reality colour the blanks in her imagination the better.

13

Daniel Scatlock was a year older than the rest of them, a mystery which was never publicly solved, and he wore his school uniform like a Savile Row suit. He towered over Mrs Fox who introduced him saying that he was new to the area, which was usually a euphemism for 'excluded from every other school in the county'. Where you went after you were expelled from Grays Reach High was anyone's guess. She appointed Paul as Daniel's guide for the day because their names were adjacent on the register. Paul's dismay was keen. He only hoped that Daniel would recognise his minnowish status and show him the contemptuous disregard he deserved. Invisibility was the pinnacle of his social ambition.

During English, Daniel didn't even make an effort to look at their shared copy of *The Diary of Anne Frank* and when the teacher was talking he didn't open his notebook but just doodled. In French, he wrote his name on the front of his exercise book, forming the letters as deliberately and laboriously as a primary school child, but after that seemed to lose interest. In History, they were given a spot test. The class cried their protests; Daniel, who had more reason to complain than most – he could hardly be expected to complete a test based on a syllabus he had never studied – remained silent, merely adjusting his posture and flinging his legs out in front of him. They were so long he could hook his feet onto the chair of the boy in front of him, a nasty piece of work called Hash, who had bright red hair and a lunar complexion and went nuts if you called him by his real name, Hamish. Hash turned to glare at Daniel, immediately identified a higher authority and squared his shoulders to the front again. Daniel made no attempt to answer a single question. As they were read out, Paul soon got lost in the test, quietly confident of all the answers except for the first one, about why the Nuremberg trials were held there instead of in Berlin.

'Nuremberg was the only prison in Germany that wasn't bombed out in the war,' said Daniel under his breath. 'Berlin was all rubble. I'm right, go on, put it down.' Paul shrugged, wrote the answer and watched for Daniel to do the same. But he didn't, just scowled at the blank page before him. Paul remembered the effort it had taken Daniel to inscribe his French book and understood suddenly that he couldn't read or write properly. Before he knew what he was doing, he'd leaned across and started to jot the correct answers on his neighbour's page. The look Daniel gave him made Paul wish that he had never been born. Daniel didn't turn up to Maths, the last lesson of the day, and during it Paul resigned himself to the fact that the list of people who might give him a kicking on the way home had just got one name longer.

He could not avoid the underpass that connected school and home without jumping across live train tracks. (Sometimes he had been tempted to do that.) The urine-scented tunnel was a further example of the Grays Reach architects' unwavering commitment to fear and brutality. The most hazardous obstacle was a concrete island thick with municipal shrubbery. It usually screened at least one person intent on causing him pain. Tonight it was Simeon and Lewis, two of his regular bullies. Not for the first time, he wondered how come rival thugs never turned up on the same patch. Did they have a rota? Did they meet at the mouth of the underpass after school, saying if you hurt him tonight we'll just go for a bit of verbal abuse tomorrow? They didn't even bother to goad him any more, just got straight down to the violence. Paul knew that the more tense he was, the more it would hurt, but he couldn't make his muscles relax. Simeon smacked the side of his head, a ring catching Paul at the point where his jaw met his ear. The pain was deafening. He tried to walk on but felt his upper body jerk backwards as Lewis stuck out his foot and brought Paul onto the pissy concrete in a pratfall. They both bent down. Tears already on their way, Paul prepared his ribs for the boots.

The third figure came up behind them like a gust of wind, it was so fast and so silent. There was an elegance to Daniel's movements as his hands encircled both their necks and forced their heads together, once at the forehead and the second time bringing Lewis's nose down hard on Simeon's mouth. Paul recognised the sound of a split lip, quieter when it wasn't his, and closed his eyes.

'Fuck off, the pair of you. Pick on him again and I'll kill you, do'you get me?' It was a man's voice, not a boy's, and Simeon and Lewis ran away like children. Daniel crouched down to where Paul lay. His voice droned in and out of intelligibility due to the throbbing in Paul's ear. 'Man, what *is* this?' said Daniel; his anger seemed, if not disproportionate to the attack, certainly inconsistent with the faintness of his connection to Paul. 'Buzz buzz buzz pair of *wankers*. Buzz buzz buzz you're a chicken.'

Then something in Paul's ear went pop and he heard with perfect clarity: 'I said, do you want to go and get chicken?'

There were two fried chicken outlets on the precinct, one halal and one regular. Paul had walked past them a million times but never once been in: they were not the kind of place you went into on your own if you were undersized and unaccompanied. He remained wary: the initial window for violence had closed but perhaps Daniel intended to take him somewhere public before humiliating him. If this was the idea, Daniel evidently didn't plan to do it on an empty stomach. Without looking at the menu, he ordered chips, two colas and two boxes of wings. They ate the food in the window. Curtis Goddard walked past and did a double take. Paul tried to look nonchalant but hoped that word would get out.

'What you did in class,' said Daniel. 'I appreciate it. It was good of you, man.' The way he said it made it sound like a threat. 'But I don't want it getting out.'

Paul mimed zipping his lips. 'Can I ask you something, though?' he said. 'I don't get it. If you can't read, how come you know so much about the Second World War?'

'History Channel,' said Daniel. 'My dad's obsessed. He has it on all day. And if it's not that, it's the Discovery Channel or . . . what do you call the one that's always got *Top Gear* on it?'

'My mum has the telly on all the time, but she never watches anything that interesting,' said Paul. They licked the chicken off their fingers. The grease and salt had given Paul a raging thirst that the cola didn't seem to be slaking.

'I've got a sort of proposal for you,' said Daniel. 'I'm gonna fuck off school as soon as I'm sixteen and the social are off my dad's back, but until then, you cover for me, yeah? And I'll look after you.'

The agreement was apparently effective immediately. They left the chicken shop together and from the moment they fell into step Paul felt the benevolence of his protection. Daniel was Aragorn to his Frodo, although he would rather have died than admit that to anyone.

He lived in a house identical to Paul's, although his was in the middle of the terrace. An England flag hung limply in the kitchen window and a pallet of flattened cardboard boxes was rotting next to the wheelie bin.

'I'm just over there,' said Paul, pointing across the courtyard to the back of his own house.

'Look at that,' said Daniel. 'You go past me on the way in every day.'

What must it be like not to be able to read? Paul found it easier to imagine being blind or deaf or without limbs. It wasn't just that you couldn't lose yourself in a book, although that was bad enough. How did you know you were on the right street, how did you even know which channels you were watching on television, or who was calling you on the phone? And how could you be exposed to letters and words all day every day and not absorb anything but the letters of your own name? Paul dug out a takeaway menu from the halal Indian and tried to decipher the Arabic lettering. The longer he looked for patterns, the more they all looked like dots or squiggles and he could only see three, maybe four, separate recurring shapes or themes. Maybe this was what English looked like to Arabic people, or to people like Daniel. Why hadn't anyone ever taught him to read properly? Maybe his parents weren't very literate either, but how had he got to the age of fourteen without anyone picking up on it? Without anyone *helping*? How was someone like Daniel supposed to get by? No wonder he was angry.

14

In the days and weeks that followed, the usually empty seat next to Paul was filled. It quickly became apparent that Daniel's way of coping was a head-down silence that, if anything, marked him out as a diligent student. The teachers at Grays Reach were riot police in mufti. If homework was handed in it was a miracle: they didn't notice a similarity between the graphology and content of Daniel's work and that of his constant neighbour. Paul wondered if they even read it. There were two hours between school finishing and the end of his mother's shift at the bookie's and every day they were spent with Daniel. The pockets of dereliction that had crawled with threats when Paul had been alone now became their playground. They bunny-hopped their bikes along the chalkpits and construction sites, performed wheelies on the river wall in defiance of the toothy black rocks that jutted from the beach at low tide. They'd ride out to the big mall at Lakeside and wheel around the multi-storey car parks and coast down the spiralling exit ramp against the direction of the traffic. Daniel did it with his eyes closed, and Paul pretended that he was shutting his, too. The challenge was to see how many levels they could descend without the security guards intervening; often they got all the way to the bottom to find two or more security guards there, arms folded across their hi-vis jackets. Then they would duck under the barriers and pedal away, risking their lives on the access roads, legs pumping until their muscles were on fire. They'd keep going until they reached the accessible verges of the riverbank, where it would finally be safe to laugh, and they would freewheel along the coastal path, the salty riparian wind up their noses, in their mouths and wringing tears from their eyes.

If the weather was bad, they'd hang out at Daniel's after school. The Scatlocks' living room was dominated by a giant widescreen television connected to a winking stack of equipment that included a set top box, a wifi rerouter, a DVD player, an ancient VHS machine, a massive amplifier and at least three different games consoles. Two gaming chairs, the kind that looked like ripped-out car seats, faced the screen and they had a glass-fronted fridge rammed with cans of Coke and beer like the ones in the corner shop. Paul knew instantly that this was a house without a mother; it was the converse of his own home, where the lack of masculinity was evident in every ruche and flounce in the abundant soft furnishings. Even the dog, Diesel, a huge but unassuming Alsatian, was blokeish.

You could always tell when Daniel's dad was coming home because the whole living room went dark and cold. Carl Scatlock managed to park his car – a black Land Cruiser – in the space outside the front window. How did it *get* there? The residents' cars were all, in theory, kept away in parking bays and lock-up garages on the periphery of the estate. Daniel's house, a staggered terrace like Paul's, was accessible only by a zagged footpath, gaps too narrow to accommodate a car without mowing down most of the fences and possibly taking down some walls, too. It must have been a slow, painstaking manoeuvre, but if anyone was capable of that it was Carl. He had been a driver in the Army and still drove everywhere as if pursued by the enemy, with reckless speed that he insisted was 100% controlled and necessary 'to keep my skills fresh'. It was true that Carl still looked like the kind of person who often needed to leave places in a very great hurry. As well as doing something nebulous in construction that meant he was often away for days on end, he also took the odd job in security. You could see why he got the work; unlike most built-up blokes, his bulk didn't taper off at the lower half of his body. His calves and thighs were as awesome as his arms and chest and his neck was almost as thick as his head.

'You here *again*?' he said one afternoon, even though it had been weeks since they had last met. 'You homeless or summink? Don't worry mate, I'm only taking the piss. You're as thick as thieves, you two. I had a mate like that when I was your age. Frank Jackson. D'you remember him, Daniel?'

'Of course I do,' said Daniel, with the eye-rolling resignation of one who has heard a story many times.

'He was killed in Bosnia, must be, what, twelve years ago now,' said Carl. 'I still miss him. Losing him was much worse than when this one's mum left us.' Daniel's chin hit his chest and stayed there. 'We signed up together, me and Frank. We was blood brothers. When we was about your age we cut our thumbs and made our blood run into each other. It was all the rage.' Carl Scatlock took a knife out of his pocket. It flashed like a light and he pressed it to the soft fleshy pad of his thumb. Paul felt dizzy. 'You can't do that any more, of course, we didn't know about AIDS and all that . . . What's up with him?'

The idea of deliberately cutting your thumb made Paul feel like his lungs were filling up with blood. He was slowly bending down into a foetal position, self-control slipping away like liquid through fingers.

Daniel dropped to his level, his concern evident. 'Paul! Paul! What's happening? What's wrong?'

'I can't breathe,' said Paul.

'Whoa there,' said Carl Scatlock.

'Don't let him cut himself,' wheezed Paul.

'You're all right, mate,' said Daniel. 'No one's going to cut anyone.'

'The idea of it . . . the thought of it. The thought of the – I can't stand even the word. Please, make him stop.'

'What is it, like a phobia?' said Daniel. Paul nodded. 'I saw a thing on them. He's all right, Dad.'

'Jesus, Daniel,' said Carl in a disgusted sort of way. 'For a moment there I thought something was really wrong with him.' He walked off to the kitchen, cleaning his nails with his knife.

'He can't talk,' said Daniel, when Carl was out of earshot. 'You should see him when a shark comes on the telly.'

Paul managed a thin smile. 'Don't spread it about, will you?'

'You kept my secret. I know yours now. That makes us even.'

Paul found out about the name thing one day after football. They were in the boys' changing room with its prison-issue lockers and its stench of adolescence.

'Nice pass, Danny boy,' said Max Grant, who was a footballing legend and a decent bloke by Grays Reach standards. Once Max had warned Simeon off him in the underpass. In fact, before Daniel, Max was the nearest thing Paul would have had to an ally.

'What did you call me? My name's Daniel. Not Danny boy. Not Danny. Not Dan. *Daniel.*'

Max raised his palms conciliatorily. 'All right, mate.'

'I'm not your mate,' said Daniel. 'Say Daniel.'

Max actually obeyed. 'Daniel.'

Daniel slapped Max lightly on the cheek, which was more humiliating than a punch. The funny thing with Daniel was that while the threat of violence was always there he rarely – bar his double assault on Simeon and Lewis in the first week – raised his hand. He didn't carry a knife, but even the boys who did gave him a wide berth. After initial attempts at recruiting him proved futile, and it became obvious that he had no interest in taking or selling drugs, even the gangs ignored him. But his quiet authority was palpable. There was a thrill, a kind of fear, about going in his slipstream.

Thanks to Paul, he gave in just enough work to be able to slide under the radar. Paul sometimes wished that Daniel would make more trouble for himself, knew that then he might be rescued by 'the system' – you saw it happen, every now and again, these kids got hauled out for extra tutoring, but it was always the mouthy ones and Paul secretly wondered if the extra attention was for the pupil's benefit or just to make crowd control a little easier.

Paul worried about how Daniel would ever pass any exams. So far it was all coursework, which he could help with, but he couldn't sit papers on his friend's behalf (at any rate, not at the same time as sitting his own). One of his dad's favourite sayings had been 'Give a man a fish, you feed him for a day. Teach him to fish, you feed him for a lifetime.' It gave Paul an idea, a brilliant idea. He would teach Daniel to read. He thought he'd be a good teacher because it didn't always come easily to him, either. Some teachers, like Mr Taylor, you could tell they'd been to good schools and that at those schools they'd always been top of the class. If you didn't get the poem the second it was read out to you, he had this way of taking off his glasses and looking at you like you were a slug. Paul wouldn't be like that: he'd encourage his students to take their time and tell them it was OK if you didn't memorise it all straight away, OK to go away and think about the poem. In fact it was better to do it that way. Otherwise, it was like eating your food without chewing it.

He gave the books to Daniel on the evening of his fifteenth birthday. They were in Daniel's front room playing *Grand Theft Auto III*. Paul hated the kinds of games Daniel liked. He preferred the ones that were more like versions of the books he read (much less than he used to: Daniel didn't like him reading, not for pleasure anyway), the ones with a bit of history or fantasy and where the women were just as beautiful but they hid it under long flowing gowns rather than bending down over cars in cropped tops. He could see enough of that just looking out of the window or going to the precinct. Daniel got up to fetch a can from the fridge and Paul saw his chance.

'I got you something,' he said. He'd thought about wrapping the present up but then decided that might seem a bit gay, so he taped the carrier bag down instead and just handed it over. Daniel's face darkened as he opened it.

'Are you taking the piss?' said Daniel.

'No, hear me out. I want to teach you to read. I've been looking it up, I can help you. I want to be a teacher.'

'You little *prick*,' spat Daniel. Paul had not been prepared for this. He'd expected embarrassment, diffidence, but not this rage. Too late it occurred to him that he wasn't allowed to mention it, that apart from that first encounter in the chicken shop they'd never explicitly spoken about Daniel's illiteracy, they'd just got on with it. Daniel had him by the scruff of the neck. Paul had grown unused to violence and his self-defence muscles had lost their memory; he couldn't remember whether to cover his face or to curl up.

'I thought you got it! I thought you were my *friend*.'

'I'm sorry! Daniel, I'm sorry! We won't talk about it again.'

'Fuck off out of my house,' said Daniel, 'before I do something I regret.'

The knock on the door came a couple of hours later. Paul checked his reflection in the hallway mirror. The graze on his neck was livid but the puffiness around his eyes that betrayed his quick, hot tears outside Daniel's house had almost gone down. Daniel sank into the sofa and sat on a copy of *Gormenghast* that was open face-down, cracking its chunky spine in half. Paul wished he'd been watching telly or listening to music or playing the Wii or doing anything other than reading.

'I shouldn't have hit you. It's just ... it takes me back to being a kid again. I didn't like learning to read then and I won't like it now. And our system works, doesn't it? I like things the way they are, you know?'

The weight of Daniel's need tempered the lightness of Paul's relief.

'But what about the exams?'

'Oh my God, you're obsessed. I don't need exams. I'll work for my dad. He hasn't got an exam, it never did him any harm.' He paused to crack a knuckle. 'Did you mean that about wanting to be a teacher?'

His tone made it clear that there was only one possible answer. 'It was just an idea.'

The funny thing was that his failure to help Daniel only strengthened Paul's resolve to teach. Daniel might be a lost cause but that was because they hadn't got to him early enough. Paul would become a teacher and help all the other Daniels out there, catch them before they became young men. Of course he understood that this dream was incompatible with Daniel's idea of their relationship, but that did not worry him too much. Once Daniel had left school – earlier than him, as he must – their friendship would naturally change. In the meantime, Daniel was right: the current arrangement suited them both. They had fun together, didn't they? And it wasn't as though they were going to be tied together like this forever.

15

With some crude detective work she had managed to find out his date of birth. She had had to ask Ross, probably at the expense of her own dignity; that boy saw sexual intrigue even where there was none. But she had got the information she wanted, and the result she had hoped for. The dates did not tally. Paul was only a couple of months into his nineteenth year. Even someone as promiscuous as Adam could not have managed posthumous impregnation. The relief when she found out was intoxicating, like wine. She had in fact drunk wine that evening to celebrate but one glass had led to another and she had finished the night dressed up and painted and weeping apologies at an old videotape. She was trying to discipline herself to dismiss superstitious and supernatural thoughts – there were no ghosts, no reincarnations, and the only destiny was the one you carved out for yourself – yet she clung to her ritual with both hands. Three mornings in the past week she had woken up in her costume with a throbbing head. Each time it had been a relief to wipe her face clean, leave her secret self behind and lose her worries in her work.

The switch of focus required by the grant application had saved her sanity. If necessity was the mother of invention then panic was its pushy father. Playing chicken with the deadline, she had handwritten one thousand words of the most persuasive prose she was capable of. The best lines had been crafted in the office when everyone else had gone home; she liked to work with the cabin door open, so that the wild land and the ruin could keep an eye on her. Ingram had proof-read the document, declared her a genius and come with her to the post office where he had kissed the back of the envelope for luck. Exactly a week later they received a one-page reply from the Heritage Gardens Trust, inviting them to their London office to make a formal pitch. Ingram was ecstatic, convinced that the invitation was a precursor to acceptance. The jungle drums of the heritage management community had told him that only twenty per cent of applicants were granted an audience, and that the pitch itself was little more than a formality.

'Listen to this,' he said, brandishing the letter and bouncing in his ergonomic chair. 'They want us to bring an expanded business plan. *Expanded.* We might yet be able to create my vision. What kind of figures do you think we're talking?'

'I don't dare to hope.'

They had worked out that nothing short of two million would allow them to turn the garden from a community project into a thriving tourist attraction, with an exhibition, a café, and her personal baby, a nursery growing and selling heritage plants. They would be able to erect a walkway within the ruins so that visitors could view the garden from above, as the original residents of the Lodge would have done, as the original garden designers would have intended. She kept cool in front of Ingram but inside she was cheering.

'It says here that they've been looking to sponsor a project in this region for some time now and that they're intrigued by the work we do with young people. D'you want to see for yourself?'

To humour him, she scanned the letter that he had read aloud three times now. There was a postscript in small print below the signature. *As our Pimlico premises are currently being*

*renovated, we would be grateful if you would attend at our interim
offices, 72 Warwick Gardens, London W8.*

The words reared up off the page and slammed into her.

'I can't go,' said Louisa.

'Yes you can.' Ingram flicked through the diary. 'We've
nothing booked on the twenty-fifth.'

'I can't . . . you'll have to go without me.'

'What are you talking about?'

How could she tell Ingram the truth? For her, the streets
of London were paved not with gold but with pictures from
the past. They flickered before her now like images from a
terrifying film, and the climactic scene, the one where the
violins screeched their warning and the audience hid behind
their fingers, took place on Warwick Gardens. She saw the
faces now of all the other players, Adam of course, and the
other men and the woman, too. She shook her head hard, as
though she could fling the memories from her mind.

'I can't tell you why, Ingram. I just can't go.'

It was not like her to oppose him without giving a good
reason and Ingram was losing patience. 'If you can't even give
me a reason . . . You do know what this grant means to us. If
I were a theatrical man I'd go so far as to say that the last five
years have been leading up to this moment. You're coming,
and that's that.'

She tried to be rational, telling herself that she was no more
likely to be discovered there than anywhere else, that it had
been more than twenty years, that the residents would have
moved on . . . It was no good. She could not go back. She
would give herself away, she knew she would, her smokescreen
of control diffusing at the sight of the street where it had
happened. She would be exposed, as sure as if the bloodstain
was still on the ground.

'Why don't we get them up here for a site visit?' she ventured.
'We could do a better job of convincing them that way.'

'Listen, dear,' said Ingram. 'When the HGT says jump, you say, "How high?" You don't say, "I'll jump on my terms." '

'I think it's a *good* idea,' she said, but she could not change his mind without telling him the truth. At three o'clock she faked a headache and left for the caravan, knowing that she would have to go the long way round, up to the gatehouse, out of the perimeter wall followed by a careful trespass through the farm.

Paul was in her way, like he always seemed to be. This time he was clearing litter from around the gatehouse, gloves on and a bag at his hip. It was as though the same invisible hand that had delivered him to Kelstice was deliberately plucking him away from other parts of the site and setting him down in her path. Could the summons to Warwick Gardens really be a coincidence, so hot on the heels of his arrival? She chided herself for letting superstition sweep her away again. He set down his bag and blew a curl out of his eyes, the way Adam used to do.

'Knackered,' he said.

'That's a good sign. Are you getting on all right?'

'Yeah, it's good,' he said. 'I'm getting quite into it now.' The smile he gave her looked like the kind reserved for friends of his mother's and his friends' mothers, which made the little charges of electricity it set off in her pelvis feel even more inappropriate.

'Well. I'd better go.'

'See you later.'

How could such a banal exchange make her feel desire so strong that she could not believe that he did not feel an answering tug of it?

Back at home, she locked the door. She found an unopened bottle of wine among the clinking empties, uncorked it, poured a glass and chased oblivion.

16

May 1989

Elvira had discovered acid house and switched tribes overnight. Her new uniform consisted of white cycling shorts and a white hooded T-shirt, and around her neck hung a CND symbol the size of a small plate. Hooped earrings almost as large brushed her shoulders and she had pulled the tongues out of her trainers so that they lapped against her shins. She had stopped going to gigs and clubs in London and started going to raves in Essex. Essex! Elvira used to complain if she had to venture further east than Tottenham Court Road. The friendship had been based on shared passions; it was hard not to take Elvira's rejection of their old lifestyle personally. She had even reverted to her old nickname, Ellie; Louisa refused to use it. She looked with dismay at the day-glo badges that littered her countertop like radioactive pebbles on black sand. Two dozen fluorescent smiley faces laughed back at her. She was trying to be open-minded but she couldn't see what they had to do with essential oils.

'Don't you think this rather compromises the integrity of what we're doing here?'

'It's a market stall, not an altar,' Elvira said. 'They'll sell, that's all I give a shit about. What's up with you, anyway? Trouble in paradise?'

She couldn't resist the opportunity to talk about Adam. 'Not trouble, not as such; it's just all so intense. It's *consuming* me. I feel like he's taking me over.'

'Yeah, that's what Trina was like,' Elvira said carelessly.

'Trina?' Louisa tried to keep her voice light.

'She had a thing with him over Christmas. I thought you knew? Didn't I tell you that night at the Borderline?'

Louisa shook her head.

'I can't believe I didn't tell you this. God, she was a nightmare when she was going out with him. It was like she'd had a personality transplant, she turned into this little mouse running all over London after him. One day she was all happy because he'd rung her, and the next day he hadn't called or he was being all distant and she'd be going on about how miserable she was and just when I'd talked some sense into her and she'd ended it, he'd come back with his tail between his legs and we'd be back to square one.' Elvira was telling the story with relish, like she was relating the plot of a soap opera. 'Well, *obviously* he was shagging around.' She saw Louisa's face and assumed a patronising air that suggested she was two decades rather than two years older than Louisa. 'What? I'd want to know if it was me. Anyway, I hope you're using protection. You don't know where he's been, you know, with AIDS and everything.'

They had been relying on the pill. Still, automatically, she leapt to his defence. 'He's changed,' she said. Hadn't he told her that? Hadn't they both agreed that what they had was new to both of them?

Elvira finished pinning the badges on to the soft cloth backdrop. 'Let me tell you something about men. They're congenitally incapable of change. All of them. Well, you can't say I didn't warn you. Just don't come crying to me when it all goes wrong.' She pulled a white and silver bandana out of her waistband and held it tight against Louisa's hairline. 'Do you know what, you'd look great like this. Aren't you sick of mooching around looking like a goth? It's 1989, for fuck's sake. And summer's coming, you look like you're going to melt. Go on, let me give you a makeover.'

Adam loved the way she dressed, loved the fusty femininity of what he called her widow's weeds.

'He might not like it,' she said without thinking. Elvira's eyebrows seemed to float above her head.

'Since when did *you* let a man dictate what you wore?'

'What's wrong with wanting to look nice for him?'

Elvira stood back with her arms folded, looked Louisa up and down.

'What's happened to the old Louisa who got any bloke she wanted and didn't take any bullshit? Don't let him do this to you.'

'Do what, make me happy?'

'If this is you happy, I'd hate to see you sad.'

The pavements were crowded and sticky, but Louisa and Adam were six storeys above street level and up there noon was crisp and pale. They both had a free day – Ciaran had cancelled rehearsals in order to go and show his support to the striking dockers down at the Port of London – and they were drinking champagne in the art deco sweep of the Roof Gardens bar. Adam had said it was a shame to come there so often and not to get drunk. The other diners were men in suits and ladies who lunched; Louisa and Adam fed off their disapproving looks. She knew how they must look, she with her black lace and blue hair, him dressed like the rock star he already was, keeping his sunglasses on even indoors. He spent like a rock star, too, ordering by the glass and paying their bill with cash. They ordered no food.

Afterwards they wandered through the gardens. She picked the purple heads from the lavender and showed him how crushing the flowers between her fingers released their pungent oil; he did the same.

'There's a theory about why smells are so evocative. They say that because we don't need scent for survival any more, like our ancestors did, it's become a kind of luxury sense, associated with emotions rather than life or death stuff. That's why nothing brings back a memory as sharply as smell.'

If she had said anything like this at home, she would have been asked to name this authoritative 'they' and laughed out of the room, but Adam was always up for discussions like this; he took her ideas and ran with them.

'What, more than music?' he said, playfully, then grew serious. 'I think music affects us in ways we can't even begin to understand yet. D.H. Lawrence called it "the insidious mastery of song". D'you know that poem? It's about a man who listens to a woman playing the piano and he's transported back in time until he's a little boy again, listening to his mother play. It's beautiful, it makes me cry. I wanted us to set it to music, but Ciaran wasn't up for it. I hate having to depend on him to write.'

Louisa made a note to find the poem, read it, memorise it.

'Does your mum play the piano, then?'

'I believe she did, before I was born,' he said. 'But I only ever knew her to play a church organ.'

Flamingos looked on, unimpressed. From the balcony Louisa's London shimmered in the early summer heat. The sky was huge.

'This is what the human eye was meant to see,' she said. 'A proper horizon, not that bloody courtyard outside my bedroom window.'

'Well, I'd better get rich and famous so that I can buy us a nice big penthouse to live in,' he said. 'We'll have a house in the countryside too; I'll have a recording studio there and you can have a herb garden and grow all the lavender you want.' It was the first intimation he had given of a future beyond their next meeting. Her heart turned cartwheels. Elvira could say what she liked; this was real.

Two Japanese teens, effortfully styled in crepe-soled shoes and red rubber catsuits, were mucking about with Polaroid cameras, pretending to push each other over the edge. The railings were too high for anyone to topple over and were in any case crowned with spikes. After an exchange of mime, Adam took their photograph, the girls giggling at him. Louisa and Adam posed for their own snapshot; he had gone on to photoshoot autopilot, pouting at the camera. She was looking up at him in adoration. She waved the Polaroid dry between her fingertips.

Adam took her face in his hands and kissed her. It was a perfect moment so she sabotaged it by asking the question that had been swelling her throat.

'I didn't know you used to have a thing with Trina.' He pulled away from her so quickly that it felt like a slap.

'Why should you?'

'I just think it's weird that you didn't tell me, that's all.'

'I didn't tell you because I never think about her. Your past doesn't matter to me, and don't look at me like that, I know you've been around the block. That's the whole *point* of us, isn't it? That's why we work, because we're equals. What matters is that we're together now.'

'Yes, but—'

'Louisa, I hope you're not going to get all clingy and possessive on me. It kills love, all that stuff. It *chokes* it.'

His mood had jackknifed. His eyes remained on the skyline. She took a step towards him; he shrugged her off. She felt like impaling herself on the railings.

'Right, I'm off,' he said. 'You stay here and finish your drink.'

'But I thought we—'

'I've got to meet someone.'

'*Where?*'

Did she imagine the micro-pause before he spoke? 'Not that it's any of your business, but I'm going to rehearse.'

She retreated into the Tudor garden and waited until

she was sure that he really wasn't coming back to her. His departure had been so abrupt that it took her a while to spot his inconsistency. They couldn't have a rehearsal if Ciaran wasn't there, could they? With no evidence other than the memory of a spill of red hair, she knew at once that he was with *her*. No wonder he kept Louisa at arm's length. He was everything to her, and she was sharing him with someone else. The walls of the garden seemed to draw in and tilt. Something cold unfurled in her stomach. She was not yet ready to name this tentative green shoot as jealousy, but the tendril curled out and it grew and it grew until it was strangling her from the inside.

17

March 2007

'I don't know why you have to have your hair like that,' said his mother, pushing his fringe out of his face. 'It's like a mop, I can't see your lovely face. You look like something out of the seventies. In my day all the boys had proper, sharp haircuts. Your father had his hair cut Up West every six weeks, without fail.' Paul reached for the thin wire band he'd bought to keep his hair out of his eyes. Mum flicked her eyebrows. 'And I'm not sure about the girl's hairband.'

'But blow-drying with a girl's hairbrush and a girl's hairdryer is OK?' This was deliberate: Troy began every day in front of the mirror working on his own hair, a rock-solid wave that broke abruptly in a thick wedge three inches above the nape of his neck. Troy and his mother had started going out eighteen months ago, when Paul was fourteen, and he had been living with them for half that time. He had his own business cleaning ovens (domestic and industrial, no job too large or too small) and wore baggy shirts tucked into tight jeans which emphasised his skinny limbs and soft belly. It was hard to imagine a less Trojan figure.

'Stop it, you,' said his mum, with a smile. She sat at the head of the kitchen table, where the surface had been swabbed so many times that the walnut veneer had gone white. All the accoutrements of her fertility treatment were laid before her: a row of rubber-sealed ampoules, needles in their sterile plastic, the needle gun and two cotton balls ready-steeped in antiseptic solution. She rolled up the leg of her tracksuit bottoms, grabbing the flesh to locate the muscle on the front of her thigh. Paul turned away: he knew that he would not see the needle go in and that no blood would flow but sometimes there would be a pinhead of scarlet and that was enough. He would never, ever get used to the idea of his mother puncturing her flesh. He heard her suck her teeth as she gave herself a shot of hope.

'What you up to this weekend, anyway?' she said. 'You seeing Daniel?'

'We haven't made plans,' said Paul. In over two years of knowing Daniel the two had never made plans to see each other, and still they met up almost every day. He had made good on his promise to leave school on his sixteenth birthday, or so near to it that the teachers were happy to turn a blind eye. The friendship had naturally changed but not in the way Paul had imagined; he had supposed that Daniel would be absorbed into the adult world, Carl's world, the world of work and drinking and women, and would have better things to do than hang around with a schoolboy. Now seventeen, Daniel could pass for much older, old enough to get served in any of the bars in Southend with an over 21s policy. He caught the odd day's work – Carl always knew someone who knew someone who wanted muscle – but his social life didn't extend beyond the occasional pint with his dad in the Warrant Officer. Paul was uncomfortably aware that this was not normal, that while the rest of the boys in his year were out getting high and catching chlamydia, he and Daniel were still in their bubble of computer games and bike rides.

His evenings might still have belonged to Daniel but his days were his own and, in a reversal of his peers' patterns, he lived for them. Spending every lunchtime revising in the library would normally have singled him out for violence but he was one of the oldest kids in the school now and one of the tallest, too. Most of his tormentors were long gone and in any case the legacy of Daniel's protection loitered in the collective memory. He still walked beside him, an invisible presence. He was predicted decent GCSEs – he'd got mostly Bs and a single, shining A★ for his English Language mock – and had a place waiting for him at the sixth form college in Tilbury town. He dared to dream of university and teacher training after that. He didn't care how much debt he had to accrue; education was his ticket out of Grays Reach. He supposed that the friendship with Daniel would naturally cool then. The time when he would be desperate to escape him, would do anything to get away from him, was still a couple of years off.

Daniel came round at the same time as Troy arrived home.

'Someone's parked a bloody great jeep in my space,' grumbled Troy. Parking at Grays Reach was unallocated but if Troy couldn't leave his van in the same bay, the one that was visible from the bedroom window, he became agitated and would leave the house at hourly intervals in case the usurping motorist had moved his vehicle. 'It's not much to ask, at the end of a working day, is it, for a man to park his van where he wants?'

Behind him, Daniel pushed his tongue under his lower lip and crossed his eyes. Paul swallowed a laugh, kissed his mother goodbye.

'But you haven't had your tea!' said his mum. 'Have you eaten, Dan?'

Paul's mum was the only person who got away with shortening Daniel's name. When she did, he got a weird look on his face, soothed and stressed at the same time, as though the comfort he took was too painful to bear.

'We'll get chicken or something, don't worry,' said Paul.

The jeep in question was Carl's Land Cruiser, occupying not only Troy's space but the one next to it, too. Paul looked around for Carl, wondering why anyone would drive when the two houses were almost within hollering distance. He was astonished when Daniel brandished the keyring and climbed into the driver's seat.

'What the fuck?' Daniel's seventeenth birthday had only been a week ago. What was he doing with a car already?

'Get in, then,' said Daniel.

Paul almost never went anywhere in a car; his mother didn't drive so all outings were made in Troy's indiscreetly bright orange work van, Paul forced to ride in the windowless rear of the vehicle which stank of cooking fat and chemicals. Sitting in the passenger seat of a car, on the other hand, reminded him of trips with his dad. The click of the seatbelt and view over the dashboard rescued a dormant memory of a fishing trip to Canvey Island; they had pitched a two-man tent and stayed the night and in the morning, when the dawn had filtered through the green canvas and woken them, his dad had told him he was a real man now. He couldn't have been more than about five.

'How did you pass your driving test?'

Daniel gave him a look that was part contempt, part amusement.

'I haven't got a licence, you dickhead,' he said. Paul should have known better and his relief at Daniel's mild reaction outweighed his shame. Daniel's lack of qualification was evident within seconds of the key turning and the first raucous rev; he reversed out of the parking area with only the briefest of glances over his shoulder. There was a dull clanking from the boot, as though it were loaded with clapperless bells.

'Did your dad teach you to drive?' he said, recalling with discomfort Carl's arrogant, lawless speed.

'When I was fifteen. You didn't know that about me, did you? I can drive *anything*. Manual, automatic, left-hand drive, whatever. I could drive an HGV if I had to.' He reached down into the footwell and pulled out a giant AA road atlas with a handwritten page of directions sticking out of the top. 'Read that, will you?'

Carl Scatlock only just had the edge over his son when it came to the two literary components of the three Rs, and it took Paul a few seconds to deduce that Pizzy must be Pitsea. Paul opened the map on the relevant page and began to direct Daniel onto the A13, from where they would follow signs to the A127.

'Where are we going? I mean, I know where we're going, but why?'

'My dad's working on a big refurb job up London,' he said. 'He's ripped about three ton of piping out of some old Victorian house. The woman who owns it told him to make sure it was recycled. She hasn't got a clue you can sell it, silly bitch.'

'Right,' said Paul. 'You want to take this next slip road.'

There was no way Daniel would have been able to do this without him. Paul had never considered how much reading drivers had to do. How were you supposed to know where you were going if you couldn't read road signs? There were no landmarks here; each scrubby verge, each slip road and roundabout looked exactly like its predecessor.

The scrapyard was half a mile from Pitsea market. Carl had turned cartographer for the last few hundred yards, sketching the side streets they needed to cross. They took a left at a disused petrol station, pumps ripped out, buddleia replacing them on the forecourt, and found themselves in an expansive, menacingly silent industrial estate.

'There's no sign,' said Daniel. 'It hasn't got a name. You've got to look for a green fence with a wheel hanging over the door. You don't even tell him who sent you. If he doesn't know, he can't tell.'

They supposed that the leaning carapace of corrugated iron to their left was the fence in question and when Paul spotted the tyre suspended from a girder Daniel let go of the steering wheel and hit the dashboard in delight. The open gateway was wide enough to accommodate the vehicle, and Daniel drew it in in a clumsy manoeuvre. They found themselves facing a giant hangar. Old white bathtubs filled with taps flanked the entrance like two stone lions. Daniel sounded the horn and a man in navy overalls with a camouflage of black grease on his face emerged.

'Gavin?'

Daniel leapt from the driver's seat, leaving the engine running, and shook Gavin's hand as though they were friends and equals. He did not give his name. Paul felt as though he were seeing Daniel for the first time all over again. He had forgotten how impressive, how confident he could be.

'Let's have a look at it, then,' said Gavin, and threw open the back doors.

When they had finished unloading the pipes, Gavin filled a white kettle that was fishscaled with greasy fingerprints and made them tea so sweet that Paul's teeth hurt. The negotiations were conducted out of his earshot. Before they left, Gavin peeled some layers from a roll of notes in his pocket and handed them to Daniel, who pocketed them without counting.

'I can't get rid of it quickly enough at the moment,' said Gavin. 'It's ever since the Chinks got the Olympics, they've gone building mad out in Beijing. It's caused a world shortage of scrap, I'm not taking the piss.' He tapped the side of his nose with a grime-encrusted fingertip. 'No questions asked.'

It was the most fun he'd had with Daniel in years.

There was some coursework to be finished at home and he was glad of it; what with the excitement and the rush from Gavin's sugary tea, it would be hours before sleep came. Daniel insisted on dropping Paul as close to his front door as he could. Troy's van was back in its rightful place. Paul wondered if he had identified the cuckoo in his nest. If he had, he'd hear no end of it tomorrow.

Daniel handed over £90. It was more money than Paul had ever held before.

'What's this for?'

'You've earned it. I couldn't have done it without you, could I? There's gonna be loads more jobs where this came from, my dad's too busy to do it himself. And we'll have to do pick-ups as well as drop-offs, all over Essex. Sometimes up London, even. I'll need your eyes.'

Paul thought of all the things he could do with £90. A job a week like this and he could set up a college fund. It was certainly better than playing computer games, and he liked how Daniel was in this context: cool, in control but not controlling of him, someone he could admire again.

18

He would never have got involved with the stealing if it had been suggested that first time. The line into unlawfulness was crossed so gradually that, looking back, he could not isolate the moment. Carl would occasionally hand them goods that no sane person would ever dump – a drum of copper wire, uncoated, that glittered and rolled like a Catherine wheel as he threw it into the back of the car, sheets of lead so brand new they were millpond-smooth – but by then the trips to Gavin's yard had become a habit, like getting up for school in the morning. By the time the grey area had unambiguously blackened, Paul's ideas of what was and was not normal had been distorted.

It was inevitable that Daniel and Paul would, at some stage, look to source their own materials. Even when it was all over he could never be entirely sure whether the first theft was impulsive or the climax of a master plan that he had been too naive to suspect. If he had been plotting, Daniel certainly put up a convincing show of spontaneity.

He had his own car now, although it was necessarily registered in Carl's name. It was nothing special, just an old Volvo estate. Blooms of rust flourished all over its body but if you folded down the back seats, pulled the front ones forward and didn't mind the odd bit of piping prodding you in the back of the head, there was as much interior space as in a small van.

The first time it happened they were deep into Essex, driving around for fun. You had to get a good half-hour inland before you hit proper countryside, the kind that was honeycombed with green and yellow fields and unbroken by the heavy industry that characterised the estuarine stretch of the county. There were no pedestrians and few cars, which Daniel interpreted as a chance to take the Volvo up to a hundred miles an hour. The car shook in protest at eighty but Paul knew better than to ask him to slow down: if you did that, he just laughed and floored it. Paul's finger traced the B-roads on the map, trying to keep up with him, and it was either ask Daniel or get hopelessly lost.

'Slow down, mate. Those signs might as well not be there. I can't keep my place on the map.'

They passed a complicated, five-armed junction with bewildering asymmetrical Give Way lines and a vast array of signs pointing to towns, villages and roads that were only vaguely familiar. They had no idea who had the right of way, and were lucky that there were no other vehicles in sight or earshot.

'In fifty years, no one will use road signs any more,' said Paul, a mile or so down the road. 'It'll all be done by sat nav.'

'Genius idea,' said Daniel. He hit the brake and reversed back so quickly that it took Paul's stomach a second or two to catch up with the rest of his body. They came to a lurching stop not back at the junction but at a parking spot dominated by another road sign, this one pointing the way to a nearby antiques market, white lettering on a chocolate brown background. Daniel got out of the car and examined the sign, tapping its surface and peering round the back. Meanwhile Paul sat in the passenger seat and tried to remember having voiced any idea, genius or otherwise, in the recent past.

'First sound of a car, you call me and we leg it, OK?' Daniel appeared at the passenger window with a smile on his face and a bolt-cutter in his hand.

'Be careful you don't cut yourself.'

'Oh, for fuck's sake,' said Daniel. 'Eyes and ears, all right?' He flipped his eyes upwards and Paul understood that he was supposed to climb on top of the car. He ascended the bonnet in one stride and the roof in another. There was a hollow thud as his weight made a faint impression on the metalwork. From this makeshift crow's nest he looked out over miles of flat countryside. If he turned his back on Daniel, he could even see the QE2 bridge, hazy in the distance.

'Can you see all right?' said Daniel.

'For miles and miles,' said Paul. 'But what am I looking for?'

Daniel was too focused on his task to reply. He made dismantling the sign look as easy as opening a can. When he had finished, the grey signposts stood empty. It reminded Paul of the time they'd been to the fair and his dad had hit every single target at the coconut shy and they had left a row of empty poles behind them. Daniel threw the sheet of metal into the back of the car. It landed with a thunderclap and Paul was dragged out of his memory.

'Pure steel, this,' he said. 'You heard Gavin. He can't get rid of it quick enough.'

'Daniel, I'm not sure,' said Paul.

'It's the ultimate in recycling,' said Daniel in the voice he used when the case was closed. 'Use it again and again and again. I like to do my bit for the environment.'

They got back in the car, Paul not quite able to believe what had just happened. Five minutes further down the road, a couple of miles deeper into the country, Daniel made a rapid, centrifugal U-turn on a country lane barely big enough for two cars to pass. Paul saw what he was looking at; the black and white chevrons that indicated a steep bend. He had forgotten that Daniel didn't know his Highway Code.

'No,' said Paul, astonished at his own bravery.

'*No?*'

'Look, if we're going to do this we need to do it ... responsibly.' Daniel rolled his eyes. 'No, listen, I'm serious, Daniel. These arrows tell people about the bend. You take this away, someone's going to drive straight into that bank and die. I don't mind helping you out but I don't want anyone's death on my conscience.'

Daniel listened to Paul's lecture, but with bad grace. When they got back to Grays Reach, he waited until Paul had got out of the car then swung the passenger door closed so swiftly and violently that his fingers were almost crushed. Paul instinctively recoiled and crossed his arms in front of his body, as though bracing himself for a blow. As he cowered, he felt that the facade of friendship had been torn away to reveal the true balance of power in their relationship. It was like ripping off a sticking plaster and being confronted with the wound beneath.

'Don't shit yourself!' Daniel was laughing at him. 'Did you really think I was gonna hit you?'

'No,' lied Paul.

'I wouldn't hurt you, anyway, not even if you fucked me over,' said Daniel. Paul felt himself relax and allowed himself a little smile. But Daniel had stopped laughing. 'No, I wouldn't hurt you. I'd hurt your mum.'

19

Paul made his second discovery a few days after he had found the caravan. He was working alone, hacking down brambles to the left of the ride, then clearing the soil that was matted with the roots of murdered plants. It was hard to concentrate; he kept breaking off to stare at the Lodge. It looked different every day, depending on the angle of your approach, the time and the weather conditions. From today's vantage point, with the low sun silhouetting the structure, it looked like the jutting lower jaw of a half-buried beast. He was digging deep when he hit something hard beneath the loam. Using the tip of his shovel as a chisel and then a lever, he exposed a bed of compacted gravel six inches deep. He called Ross over and the two of them rolled back the earth like peeling a carpet away from floorboards. It made a faint road leading from the gatehouse to the Lodge, parallel with the dirt track they currently used as a guide. When Ingram and Louisa saw it they literally danced with excitement. You'd think he had uncovered a Roman mosaic rather than a gravel driveway.

A fortnight later a new ride had been established, one that swept to the left of the gatehouse rather than the right of it. It changed the whole feel of the estate, gave it a framework. The gardens might still be an abstract mess and the Mere a stinking quagmire, but here was a pathway from which people had approached the Lodge in centuries gone by. Paul had helped Louisa to plant oak saplings on either side. They looked puny now but Louisa said that the beauty of gardening was that it made you think about time and life in a completely different way. 'Oak trees take three hundred years to grow, three hundred years to live, three hundred years to die,' she said. 'Humbling, isn't it?' She had a way of explaining things that made you see the point.

Paul was slowly falling in love with his life at the Lodge. Sometimes he forgot the circumstances that had brought him there for hours at a time. He forgot about Daniel and the impending trial, he forgot about Ken Hillyard and what they had done to him because he was lost in his work, so perfectly suspended between history and the future that he was able to live genuinely in the present. He wouldn't have dreamt of telling the others, who either really didn't care, like Dilan, or who secretly cared, like Jodie and Ross, but were too busy being ironic or cool to admit to it.

Dilan reminded Paul of Daniel. He had that same street confidence with an undertow of violence. 'I hate the countryside, man. Shit clothes and no reception,' he said, looking from his wellingtons to his phone, which he shook like a maraca in an attempt to attract a signal. 'You know, my girl doesn't believe I can't get bars out here. She thinks I'm hiding from her.'

'That's because you usually are,' said Jodie.

'So would you if she was your girlfriend.'

'If you don't like her, why are you going out with her?' said Paul.

'You've got to have a woman, innit? Anyway, no one else can get my hair the way I like it.' Patterns as elaborate as any Tudor parterre had been shaved into his short black hair. Stiff black bristles were filling the gaps between the furrows. 'You seeing anyone?'

He thought of Emily, and then of Gemma. 'Not at the moment.'

'I'm up to here in pussy,' said Dilan, saluting five inches above his head. 'Want me to send some your way?'

'No need,' said Ross. 'Louisa fancies him.' Paul cringed. Ross had got it into his head that Louisa had some kind of crush on him. It was a ridiculous idea; all they'd done was plant a few trees together, and besides—

'She's *well* old!' interjected Jodie.

'Och, she's mum old rather than nan old, perfectly respectable,' said Ross. 'I know *I* would.' He checked the time. 'I don't know about you guys but I make it beer o'clock.'

In fact it was not yet five, but still they filed into the boot room to wash up and change, Dilan replacing the offending wellingtons with box-fresh white trainers. The rest of them slipped into clothes that were barely distinguishable from their uniforms.

'There's a pint behind that bar with my name on it,' said Ross. 'It's payday today. I'm gonna get *twatted*. You never know, Yummy Mummy might be there.'

'Piss off,' said Paul. Ross winked.

Paul could not understand where the people who drank in the Kelstice Arms came from. The village was like a ghost town: you only saw people on foot if they were walking to or from their cars. Perhaps they came in their cars from surrounding villages or even from Leamington or Coventry and stuck to soft drinks, or perhaps they just drove home drunk. The pub was as unlike the Warrant Officer as the Lodge was unlike the precinct. It was crooked with age but decorated in those colours that posh people liked to see in pubs, muted greeny blues that came out of the tin genteelly faded. The pictures on the walls hung on hooks so that anyone could nick them. His favourite was a watercolour, some artist's impression of Kelstice Lodge at the height of its glory. Paul looked at the six towering chimneys, the haughty house, the elaborate order of the gardens and the symmetry of the trees flanking the ride.

It was unsettling, unfair somehow, like seeing a picture of someone now old when they were young and beautiful. He wondered how the collection of misfits currently rammed into the snug would ever restore it to anything like that.

A debate was raging among his colleagues, the subject being that if you *had* to be locked in one room of the house which room would be best? Ross was chairing the dispute with his usual good humour. Paul was in awe of Ross; whatever he said, people always took it the way he had meant them to. Paul wondered what he had been thinking when he had decided to sell drugs, and what his own life would have been like with him for a friend instead of Daniel.

He was four pints down and on the cusp of drunkenness by the time the people he still thought of as the adults – Demetra, Ingram, Nathaniel and Louisa – turned up. Ross got them all pushing the tables together so that nobody was left out. The tables were the old-fashioned sewing-machine kind with smooth wooden tops and wrought-iron legs with *Singer* woven into the pattern, and they didn't sit comfortably on the uneven flagstones of the pub floor. Paul dropped to his knees and got to work with folded beermats, identifying the wobbly legs and righting them. He found himself at eye level with Louisa's knees in their jeans and from nowhere he was all but overwhelmed by the compulsion to cling to her legs and bury his face in her lap. He could have killed Ross; ever since he had started making his insinuations, Paul had started having weird Pavlovian erections whenever he got close to her. He stayed crouching, pretending to fiddle with the table legs, until cramp in his knees distracted his body's attention away from his penis. When he looked up, Louisa was staring right through him, nursing a glass of cloudy juice. If she had noticed the nudging and the name calling, she showed no sign of it. He hoped that his face was as inscrutable as hers.

Paul stood a round, served by Kylie this time, who virtually threw the drinks in his face.

'What's the matter with her?' he asked, when he had distributed the contents of his tray and started on his fifth pint.

'Ross was caught *in flagrante*,' said Jodie.

'In who?' said Dilan. You had to hand it to him; he wasn't afraid of looking ignorant. In that respect at least he differed from Daniel.

Ingram sighed. '*In flagrante delicto*, Dilan. It's Latin.' His voice was heavy with the weight of the explanation. Paul hated the way Ingram thought a poor education was a character flaw and not an accident of circumstance, as though anyone from anywhere could waltz into Eton if only they bucked their ideas up. That kind of thinking was the reason people like Daniel were able to fall through the cracks in the system. 'In the blazing offence. Blazing being a metaphor for vigorous, highly visible action.'

'Say that in English, man?' said Dilan.

'Caught with your pants down,' said Jodie. 'Kylie saw Ross trying to get off with one of the conservation volunteers.'

Dilan's eyes widened and he slapped the palm of his left hand with the back of his right one. 'Oh my days!' he said.

'Kylie *thinks* she caught me trying to get off with one of the conservation volunteers,' corrected Ross. 'When in fact she saw me making innocent conversation with a fellow student.'

'Innocent conversation with your hand on her arse,' said Jodie.

'It's very easy for these things to be misunderstood,' slurred Paul. 'It's not always as straightforward as it seems.'

'Get you, man of the world,' said Dilan.

'I'm serious. I was caught at it. It wasn't nice.' He had their attention now. They weren't to know his entire sex life could be condensed into a few minutes.

'Who found you? Your mum?' said Jodie.

'No, it was his mum he was in bed with,' said Dilan, to much laughter.

'My girlfriend,' said Paul. The word still felt funny in his mouth. 'Ex, now, obviously.'

'That's *harsh*, man,' said Dilan, with great respect.

Across the table, Paul saw a change come over Louisa's face; the tussle for control of the lips that usually precedes tears. He understood in a flash that it had happened to her.

At the bar, Kylie rang the bell for last orders. There was a corresponding vibration somewhere near his hip. He frisked himself for his mobile and pulled out a screen displaying unfamiliar digits. The thought fluttered within him that Emily had somehow found his number and was reaching out to him in spite of what had happened. He climbed over his friends, pressing the answer button as he went so that the call would not be diverted to voicemail. At the doorway, he elbowed his way past a shivering smoker who was trying to light the wrong end of her cigarette. Even as he raised the phone to his ear he could tell that it was a male voice, although reception scrambled the sound. Trepidation replaced his foolish hope.

'Sorry, who is this?' he said, walking into the car park.

'It's me,' said a voice that was like a fist to the face.

'Carl . . .' He wheeled around and peered into the darkness behind him, as though expecting the voice to embody itself. How the hell had he got this number?

'Where the bloody hell have you got to? You've left my boy in a right state.'

'I'm sorry,' croaked Paul.

'I don't know what you think you're playing at. Listen, no one wants this to get nasty, but you've got to change your statement otherwise Daniel's gonna go down for this. Listen. You come back to Grays Reach tomorrow, I'll drive you down the station and you can tell them you made a mistake first time, all right?'

'I'm not coming back to Essex,' said Paul.

'Don't make me come and beat it out of you.' He was bluffing. He must be bluffing. But if he had the phone number, maybe he had the address too . . .

'I only told the truth.'

'Fucking hell, Paul. I've spent all day visiting my boy. He's in bits. He's sharing a cell with some nonce. I know he fucked up, but he doesn't deserve *this*. You don't deserve him as a friend . . .'

No, thought Paul, I don't. He cut Carl off. He stood alone in the car park, charged and hot with fear and shock. A gust sent leaves scurrying across the road. The phone rang again, same number. He switched it off but still it seemed to buzz and hum with missed calls and threatening messages. He could handle the threats, he reflected; it was hearing about Daniel he couldn't bear. He took comfort only in the fact that Carl had not seemed to know where he was; if he had known, he wouldn't have called, he'd have turned up. Procrastination was not his style.

What if Carl had not found his number, but it had been given to him? Carl's contact details were on his case notes, printed just above his mother's. It would be easy for someone with access to his folder to work out the relationship and play a spiteful cat-and-mouse game with him. But who, and why? He returned to the emptying pub to retrieve his coat. Ross was at the bar talking to Kylie, who had a wet rag in one hand. She was supposed to be wiping the tables but some kind of reconciliation was evidently on the cards: Ross was tracing her palm with his fingertip, making out that he could read her fortune, and she was letting him. Dilan was rolling a spliff under the table and Jodie was texting furiously. All of them had his number, as did Ingram, Demetra, Louisa and anyone else with access to the Lodge records. What was I thinking? he wondered. Kelstice was such a microcosm that it was easy to forget that half the staff were there because they were in trouble at home, or were undergoing some kind of rehabilitation. He looked at Dilan (driving and taking away), Jodie (aggravated burglary) and even Ross (possession with intent to supply). He had been naive, he now saw, not to assume the worst about everyone. He should have learned that by now. He would have to change his number for the second time in two months. He did not understand how they had found Carl Scatlock's number or why they would want to do this to him.

Paul went into the Gents, opened up his phone and removed the SIM, bent it out of shape and tried to tear it. It was harder to destroy a metal-and-plastic rectangle the size of a fingernail than it was to dig out a clump of knotweed. The exertion brought him out in a beery sweat. Once he had managed to twist it into two pieces he tried to flush the halves down the lavatory but they kept bobbing to the surface, chasing each other around the bowl like tiny golden fish.

When he came back into the pub, the tables were on the chairs and Kylie was just about to draw the bolts across the front door. That meant that everyone had got the last bus back to Coventry, which meant that the Leamington bus would be leaving in . . . shit shit shit.

He stood in the little shelter, trying to strike the balance between making himself visible to the driver and making himself vulnerable to the late-night cars that took these lanes at speed. The yellow wash of light that heralded the bus's arrival did not come. He read the bus-stop timetable twice to confirm the departure times he knew by heart and tried to turn on his phone for the clock but his fingers were cold and clumsy and he couldn't get the battery back in. Without a SIM card he had no way of calling for a taxi, even if he had had the money. A car approached. He locked eyes with its headlamps, turned to full beam, and was blinded for half a minute. When the white blobs and splashes cleared, the car had pulled up parallel to his stop and Louisa was lowering the window. In the dark she looked about the same age as him.

'Have you missed your bus?' she asked.

'Doesn't matter, I can walk,' shrugged Paul.

'Walk? To *Leamington*? How many have you had? Get in, I'll give you a lift. I've just driven Ingram and Demetra home, it's no bother.'

The interior smelt strongly of something herbal and churchy underlaid by a heavy, eggy smell that made him feel seasick. The silence in the car filled up as though it would burst the windows. He didn't know what to do with his hands so fiddled with his fleece, worrying at the hem and then pulling at a loose thread in the embroidery on the breast, unravelling the letters until they just said 'as'.

'I'm sorry if I hit a nerve earlier,' he said. 'When I was talking about what happened with my girlfriend. I think it was a bit insensitive. I didn't mean to upset you.'

Her laughter was sad. 'You don't need to apologise to me for what you did to your girlfriend.'

'I'm not, I don't think. More like, I'm sorry someone did it to you.' He hadn't meant to share his theory with her: it had just slipped out. They were approaching Leamington now, and she stopped at a red light.

'No flies on you, are there?' she said, in a tone that put an end to the conversation. 'Whereabouts d'you live?'

He directed her to his flat. When she dropped him off, he didn't know how to say goodbye. Should he kiss her on the cheek? What if Ross was right and she saw that as a sign? How embarrassing would that be? He settled for a mumbled thank-you and then tried to make a fast getaway, but his seatbelt caught and he had to twist his whole body around to release the tangled strap. In the back seat, sitting upright and belted

in like three well-behaved children, was a trio of orange gas
canisters. He knew at once that he had found the occupant
of the secret caravan but he kept it to himself; he had already
blurted one of her secrets this evening.

The alleyway was moated by a steaming puddle of vomit,
which Paul cleared in a flying leap he would never have
been able to repeat sober. He had just missed his elusive
housemates: the kitchen windows were weeping with fresh
condensation and a comforting cabbage smell lingered. He
lifted the lid of the pan on the hob: there was an unidentifiable
but appetising stew inside. He ate the lot, standing up, with
the wooden spoon and then in a rush of guilt emptied his
pockets, arranging four pound coins in the bottom of the
dirty pan. In his room, he didn't get undressed, just kicked
off his shoes and trousers. He kept his socks on and even his
fleece. The smell of the gas clung to his clothes and skin like
a veil. Before sleep mugged him, he held two thoughts in his
mind. The first was that Louisa's lift had distracted him from
the Carl problem. The second was that it was a pity she was
so old. That night he had his first wet dream in years, waking
with a start at four in the morning to find that he had made a
bog of the cold, empty bed.

20

'How's it going with that girl?' said Daniel with unconvincing nonchalance.

'Emily? Yeah, she's all right.' Paul wished he had never mentioned Emily, but it was hard when she was his default thought. She was in the year below him, Year 12 and taking AS levels while he was in Year 13 and hurtling towards A Levels. She had a round infantile face and soft wispy hair and her breath was pure and milky, like a child's, but from the neck down she was all woman; when she let him touch her, his hands swerved like an out-of-control car. She could have got away with tight clothes like the girls from the estate but she wore dresses that floated around her; like Paul, they only got to skim, never to cling.

Emily read for pleasure the kind of books that Paul had only read for school. She had lent him her copy of *Great Expectations*, a second-hand paperback with a wrinkled orange spine. After a couple of chapters he'd got really into the story, but was learning that enjoying a book and being able to talk impressively about it were two different things. He read the Dickens in tandem with a York Notes guide to help him through the bits he didn't get. So far, she was impressed with his take on the book; he lived in mortal fear that she would one day catch him in the act of reading the study guide.

It had taken three months for Paul to speak to her and another three to progress from that to their – his – first kiss. That first time, she'd been allowed to drive her mum's car to college and she had driven him out to the quarry. She had been wearing a flowery dress, a denim jacket and a pair of baseball boots. Her hair had been washed that day and was more flyaway and babyish than ever. She kept putting up her hand to smooth it down and at one point Paul reached out and tucked a strand behind her ear. She had blushed furiously, a bright coral that had stained her cheeks and the skin above her breasts, but she hadn't taken his hand away and he had known that she wanted him to kiss her. But kissing was still all they did. He hadn't even seen her bra beyond the strap. The pattern had not changed or progressed in the term they had been whatever it was they were – weekly conversations which would progress to hand-holding or a bit of tickling, whichever seemed more likely to culminate in a fully clothed snog. He was sore and swollen with wanting her. He wished he could just bypass this stage and somehow magic the pair of them to a clean bedroom, clothes already off, permission already given, preferably with Emily already having done whatever girls had to do to warm themselves up for the event. He would be as gentle with her as he could. He was in a rush to be able to take his time.

Emily was the reason Paul had not yet applied to university, although he had not told anyone this, not even – especially not – Emily herself.

He told his mother that he wanted to work for a year or so first, to put aside a bit of money so that he wouldn't spend the rest of his life in debt. She was delighted; her pride at the thought of a graduate son had always been tempered with worries about money. If Paul worked locally and lived at home, in two years he would have saved enough to cover rent, fees and living. He felt bad about lying to her about his intentions; the minute Emily was off next year, he would follow her.

He told his tutors at the sixth form college that, seeing as he intended to spend the rest of his life in the education system, he wanted to experience real life for a while. They were less enthusiastic, and not just because of the insult implicit in his excuse. Why not apply this year, they said, secure a place, and then defer? They pretended it was for his own good but he knew that the more students they sent off to higher education, the better ratings the college would score. He stood his ground. A year from now, he was confident he and Emily would be sleeping together, a proper couple. What if he was accepted onto a teaching course in, say, Bristol or Exeter and then a year later when she started looking at courses, she found that the university for her was in Edinburgh or Glasgow? She was cleverer than he was, he didn't expect to go to the same university, but he knew that all of the big university towns also hosted less elite universities, former polytechnics. Perhaps they could even live together.

So far he had managed to keep her apart from Daniel but that could not last forever. Emily would never understand the nature of their friendship and he knew she would disapprove of where they went to at night; he disapproved himself. And Daniel would never understand what he felt for Emily. Girls flocked to Daniel 'like flies to shit', as Carl put it. It was his looks, of course, but the raw material was well packaged. While Paul saved almost every penny of his share of their takings, Daniel spent the lot on designer clothes. Unless they were working, he never wore sports gear or trainers but worked a sort of high-fashion formal look that the girls couldn't get enough of. For someone who had terminated his relationship with education at fifteen, Daniel was pretty well known at the sixth form college, especially among the girls. Once, when he'd met Paul at the gates, a girl had invited him to some party she was having and ignored Paul. Not that anything long term ever came of this popularity. Soon after leaving school, Daniel had had a thing with a girl called Nicola which had spanned a good two months. Paul had hoped that he would get her pregnant, marry her and emigrate to Australia. But Nicola had dumped him for being moody and shut-off. Paul deduced that the closer they got, the harder it became for Daniel to hide his illiteracy. Knowing Daniel better than anyone, Paul guessed that he had masked his panic and shame with truculence and stonewalling. Daniel had spent the night after she broke it off in custody, after uprooting a post and using it to smash in the window of Ladbroke's in the precinct. It was the first time Daniel had been arrested, and Paul had been as frightened by the lick of the law as if he were the one spending the night in the cells. That fear, though, was nothing compared to seeing Daniel cry when he came home again. He had never seen his father in tears but he imagined that it would feel like this, panic and a strange sense of betrayal at such weakness from a strong man.

In the immediate aftermath of Nicola, Daniel had seen some programme about the history of male friendship and discovered that in ancient Greece platonic friendship between men, not sexual unions between men and women, was the elevated relationship, the one all the great art was about. He had pressed the record button halfway through and made Paul watch it. Watching the bad actors playing Achilles and Patroclus, Paul understood what Daniel was trying to tell him: that their friendship was the bedrock of his life and there was no room for women. It made Paul feel claustrophobic and prematurely but passionately angry, as though Daniel had already come between him and Emily.

'Troy not in?' said Paul, dumping his bag on the kitchen floor.

'He's at the Warrant Officer,' said his mother. 'He thought he'd give you and me a bit of time together.' The house stank of the Chinese herbs she took in conjunction with her acupuncture. The bag of curling leaves and dried-out roots was acrid and choking when it was dry; they had to be boiled for half an hour before she could drink them and when the pan was on the hob, the smell was repulsive. His mother used honey to make the tea go down; she spooned almost half a jar into the cup, gulped it, shuddered, then peered into the mug, clearly dismayed to find there was still so much left.

'Sit down, baby, I want to talk to you,' she said, when she had recovered. Paul was immediately on guard. Did she know what they'd been up to, and if so, how much did she know? Did she only know about the legit stuff or was she on to the stealing, too? He tried to compose his features into an expression of puzzled innocence.

'Me and Troy have been talking about things,' she said. 'You know that my last IVF cycle didn't work, because Troy was still working?' Paul nodded. Natalie had made poor Troy give up his business, concerned that the chemicals in the oven-cleaners were somehow disabling his sperm. He had heard them rowing about it in the night; his mum had threatened to leave if he didn't change his career and eventually Troy had agreed. Paul would not have understood before, but since he had met Emily he was beginning to see why men did completely stupid things because women asked them to. 'Well, that was the last of the money. I only had one go on the NHS and we can't afford any more private ones with Troy being out of work.' Was she going to ask him for *money*? He was suddenly conscious of the roll of notes in his jeans, as conspicuous and mortifying to him as any erection. 'The rules are different in different parts of the country. In some counties you can get three goes up to the age of forty. It's a postcode lottery.'

'So?'

'You know Troy grew up on the south coast? Well, I've made some phone calls and it turns out that if we move in with his mum there, we'll be eligible for two more cycles on the NHS. To cut a long story short, we're moving.'

Paul remained still while his mind turned cartwheels. He wasn't even sure where Sussex was, to be honest, although he guessed it would make commuting to Tilbury Fort Sixth Form College quite a challenge, and if she thought she was taking him away from Emily before he had sex with her she had another think coming. He folded his arms.

'And when's all this supposed to happen?'

'This is the thing. Me and Troy are going next month.'

Not 'we' but 'me and Troy'.

'And where am I supposed to go?' said Paul.

'I saw Carl Scatlock yesterday. Him and Daniel would love to have you for a few months.' Now Paul's silence was stunned. Being friends and working with Daniel was one thing, but living with him? There was no *way* he could keep Emily away from him if they were living together. He put his head in his hands.

'I thought you'd be pleased,' she said. 'You virtually live there anyway.'

'Why can't you wait until the end of term? I'll be finished in a couple of months.'

'I haven't got a couple of months, love,' said his mum, as though she were a terminal cancer patient. 'I'm forty-one on my next birthday. It's the cut-off age. We won't be in Troy's mum's house for long, the council will rehouse us as soon as I'm pregnant and there'll be room for you there. Paul, please. You know how important all this is to me.'

Of course he knew, but he would never begin to understand it. For an only child, he was getting pretty sick of all these brothers and sisters coming between him and his mother. If the ones that were never born were this intrusive, what would the real thing be like? She put her hand over his. She was still wearing her wedding ring. Something in Paul dissolved. 'You know that you only have to say the word if it's not OK.' But how could he deprive her of the thing she wanted so much? He knew before he had let go of her hand that he would do what she wanted.

'Did you tell Carl *where* you were going?' asked Paul. Since Daniel's loose threat to his mother, he was determined to protect her.

'I don't believe I did,' she said. 'I think I just said we were going to the south coast.'

'I wouldn't if I were you,' said Paul. 'Keep it to yourself.'

'Why?' said Mum.

'You know what people round here are like,' said Paul. 'What if someone reports you? Like they do with benefit fraud? Maybe they'll take it away from you.'

'Carl Scatlock is the last person who'd report anyone for benefit fraud.'

'Not just Carl,' argued Paul. 'People in general. If no one knows, no one can tell.'

She brightened. 'Are you saying you'll stay, then? I'll miss you, but it'll all be worth it when you get your little brother or sister.'

She seemed so convinced that it would work this time. He couldn't bear to think what might happen if it didn't.

21

The floor plan of the Scatlocks' house was the same as Paul's, two big bedrooms and a box room with the bathroom on the ground floor. He had never been upstairs in their house before, but assumed that they would have made up the tiny third bedroom – the one that his mother had set aside for a nursery – for him. He was dismayed to find the room full of broken appliances, dismantled bicycles and one neat stack of identical microwave ovens still in their boxes. You couldn't even shut the door, let alone get a bed in there. He was expected to sleep in Daniel's room. The mattress they had provided was brand new – it still had the plastic on the day he moved in – but it was a double, too big for the floor space available, and it tipped to one side so that three or four times a night he would find that he had rolled off into the unlovely space underneath Daniel's bed. The only comfort to be gained was that sometimes in the night Diesel would creep into bed with him. Paul loved the solid warm body of the dog beside him.

They were together more than ever. Carl was juggling construction work with nightclub security and was often away for days on end. When he was away, Paul wondered why Daniel didn't sleep in his dad's bed but Daniel said that he couldn't be arsed to change the sheets. If Daniel pulled, he took the girl downstairs on the sofa while Paul was sent to their room like a ten-year-old. They never discussed what the arrangement would be if Paul ever got to bring Emily home; he had stopped mentioning her, and Daniel seemed to presume that it would never happen.

He saw her two evenings a week, pretending that he was having driving lessons. (He was actually learning to drive, but these were early-morning sessions, his instructor picking him up at first light while Daniel was still asleep and teaching him until it was time for college.)

'You don't need to pass your test to drive, it's a waste of money,' said Daniel. 'I can teach you for nothing. You're addicted to exams. It's not normal.'

His cover was blown one day after college when he'd forgotten to tell Daniel he was 'having a lesson'. Emily had left her car in the street outside and was fishing in her bag for her keys when a nearby car sounded the horn so loudly that every student turned to stare. Daniel was leaning out of the window of Carl's Land Cruiser. Paul stood between his best friend and Emily, feeling like the rope in a tug-of-war.

'I'll see you later,' said Paul to Daniel, wondering if Emily had any idea of the courage this took him, and how she would repay him if she did. 'I'm going to get a lift with Emily.'

Emily smiled and began to wave at Daniel but he revved his engine and drove off so quickly and haphazardly that one boy actually had to do a stuntman's dive out of his path.

'Who was that?' said Emily. She looked intrigued without being impressed.

'My friend, Daniel. He's a bit intense.' He caught a glimpse of blue bra cup between the buttons of her dress, felt the inevitable journey towards disappointment begin. She said she was nervous, she said it was a big deal, but sometimes he wondered if she was playing a game with him. All he could do was give her the benefit of the doubt. 'Let's not go straight home, let's go for a walk or something.'

They went to the quarry that had been turned into a nature reserve. From up there you could see the motorway and the chalk pits and if you stood on tiptoe you could see the suspension bridge as well.

'My dad helped to build that,' he said to her. He hadn't said it to gain sympathy or for effect but she kissed him lightly on the cheeks, as though brushing away tears, and then on the lips with promising intensity. Paul wondered briefly about the ethics of exploiting his father's death to seduce Emily and swiftly concluded that it was what his father would have wanted. Soon they were down in the grass. Beneath him she felt light and weak. For a terrifying second he saw how easy it would be, that he didn't *need* her permission. He parted her legs with his knee and put his hand in the hot space between them. Months of frustration were ready to burst out of him and he told himself that he was just trying to see how far she would let him go, that he would stop the minute she said—

'Paul, *no!*' There was nothing contrived about the panic in her voice. He sprang away from her, flushed and ashamed.

'When I'm ready, it'll be you,' she said. 'I'm not saying no, I'm just saying not yet.'

He made her pull up a block away from Daniel's. Her goodbye kisses were always the most passionate. He was harder than the handbrake and desperate for two minutes alone with his right hand but Carl was in the bathroom and anyway Daniel was waiting for him, playing *Assassin's Creed* in the darkening living room. On the screen, a Crusader in a chain mail tunic emblazoned with a St George's cross leapt between two buildings in a notional Holy Land. Daniel would have been there anyway but Paul could tell he'd been actively, anxiously waiting for him rather than just sitting there.

'So that was Emily,' he said, thumbs working frantically, not taking his eye off his game. 'She looks like a right snob. And a prick tease.'

'Leave her alone,' said Paul, feeling his hands turn into futile fists.

'Has she let you shag her yet?' The Moor chasing Daniel's Crusader fell to his death from a tower. Daniel gave a little smirk of triumph.

'We're waiting until she's ready,' said Paul, and immediately wished he'd lied.

Daniel's laughter widened the chasm between their experiences. 'Good luck with that.'

He had let his guard down only fractionally but another Moor had caught up with the Crusader and knifed him in the back. Daniel shouted, '*Fuck!*' and threw the control at the wall, where it smashed into pieces. He punched the empty chair, hard, four or five times, until it fell on its side. The dog ran into the room and began to growl.

'It's OK, boy,' said Paul, his hand on Diesel's collar. 'It's only us.'

Daniel calmly picked up the other handset and attached it to the box. Paul turned away from the screen so he would not have to see the Crusader bleed to a virtual death, the cross disappearing as the white of his tunic turned scarlet.

22

May 1989

Louisa wore the empire line gown in duck-egg blue that Adam said made her look like a Jane Austen heroine, although Elizabeth Bennet or Emma Woodhouse would never have accessorised with a pair of army boots and a tasselled leather jacket with a strawberry blond Jesus spray-painted on the back. Outside it was the kind of hot sticky weather that presages a thunderstorm: inside the venue it was tropically muggy. The Underworld in Camden Town was bigger than the Borderline but it was still a basement. Long before the support act took to the stage beads of condensation had started to form on the ceiling and, by the time Glasslake were scheduled to come on, fat drops of God knew what were splashing at random intervals onto the dance floor.

Louisa resented having to check her jacket into the cloakroom, feeling that she should have been able to leave it in, what, the dressing-room area? Backstage? The van? The rituals and spaces of the warm-up remained alien to her. She had desperately wanted to come and see them sound check but Adam had forbidden it and she had been afraid to press him. He had given her a taste of what would happen if she pushed him too far in the days after the scene in the Roof Gardens; for three days, he had not returned any of her pager messages. She had been pitched and thrown between worry that he had come to harm and anger that he was toying with her. On the fourth day she gave him up for dead, or lost, it was all the same to her, and stopped trying to contact him. He had telephoned her later that afternoon and her relief was so great she found herself stumbling over her words, so urgent was her need to apologise to him.

Ben was the first onstage; he wore a woman's leopard-print fur coat and eyeliner, and would likely be carted off with heat exhaustion before the end of the show. Angie and Ciaran were in the regulation black. Adam wore only a pair of black leather trousers and a low pendant of an Egyptian ankh. Someone nearby sneered, 'Christ, another one who wants to be Jim Morrison when he grows up,' and she was astonished at the surge of violence, an animating force, that rose up within her. But they were silenced when he began to sing. His voice was too big for this space: he was too beautiful for this little band. Ambition rose off his body like steam.

When Angie played the drums, the muscles on her bare arms flexed like a weightlifter's. Ciaran's mastery was evident even to someone like Louisa who knew nothing of the technicalities of live music. He controlled a flight deck of synthesisers as calmly as though he were operating a microwave. In the gaps between the songs she indulged in a little self-torture, searching the audience for a skein of auburn hair with no idea what she would do if she saw one.

Afterwards, Adam disappeared again while the rest of the band cleared the equipment, slaves to their emperor. When he materialised he was still in his stage clothes, a jacket thrown over his shoulders. She felt a sharp contraction of pride and possession.

'Let's get out of here,' he said, before she could praise him.

'What, now?'

'There are two ways to come down after a gig. One is to drink and smoke until you haven't got any voice left, and the other is to go to bed with a beautiful woman.'

'Can't I meet the others tonight?'

'I can't even bear to *look* at them after we've come offstage. It's a completely irrational feeling but totally overpowering: you know, like when you've just had sex and you have that overwhelming urge to just get the fuck away.' Her face must have been stricken, because he said, 'Not with you, obviously.' He linked his fingers through hers. His hand felt different, smaller and softer.

'Where's your ring?' she said.

He looked down at his thumb. 'Oh, that. I'm always losing it,' he said.

'But you said . . .'

She didn't get to finish her sentence. They were swept almost to one side by Ciaran, carrying a synth over his shoulder like a ladder in a Buster Keaton sketch. His lapel was studded with badges like a pearly king's coat, each bearing a cramped, angry little slogan. *Kick Out the Tories* and *Sinn Fein* shared space with *Red Wedge*, *Socialist Workers Party*, *Workers for Freedom* and *No Trade with South Africa*. Up close, she could see that he was older than she had first thought; even older than thirty, perhaps. The look he gave her was one of hunger swirled with disgust and Louisa recognised it instantly. She'd been on the receiving end of looks like that a million times and always from men like Ciaran, not unattractive but probably inexperienced, usually intelligent and bitter that this alone could not get them the women they wanted. From her new position of understanding, Louisa felt superior and could not resist pressing against Adam to highlight what he was missing and clarify who he was losing out to.

'I'm Louisa,' she said. 'It's so lovely to meet you properly at last,' but her words bounced off his retreating back. Angie followed close behind, carrying the bass drum that was half her size. She looked at Adam.

'On a scale of one to ten, you're a ten and he's an eleven. Or are you an eleven and he's a ten?'

'Eh?' said Adam.

'I'm trying to work out who's the biggest arsehole, him for being such a moody bastard or you for being such a lazy cunt. Are you just going to watch me lug all this shit up the stairs?'

'Yes,' said Adam fondly.

'Wanker,' she replied, with the same affection. 'Van's waiting, when you're ready.' She looked at Louisa and smiled expectantly.

'This is Louisa,' said Adam with a sigh, as though the information had been dragged out of him by an interrogation squad. 'I'm going to walk her home now.'

'Good luck, it's pissing down outside,' she said brightly. 'Where d'you live?'

'Sort of Gloucester Road, South Ken,' said Louisa.

'But that's on our way home! Why don't I drop you off?'

She felt Adam stiffen beside her. 'I like walking in the rain,' he muttered.

'Suit yourselves,' Angie said.

The noise from the rain was as loud as traffic. It fell at an angle and drove the filth and litter into the gutter. Drenched clubbers sheltered in chip shop doorways and under the ineffective bus shelter. The only bus that passed them was headed for the mysterious elevated hinterland of High Barnet in the north. The hem of Louisa's dress was already heavy with water. Walking back to Kensington would be romantic for about five minutes and then it would be miserable. She gathered the strength to challenge him.

'I'd quite like that lift, you know. It's a long way to walk even in the dry. And I *have* been on my feet all day.'

He said yes in a way that made her feel it was her fault it was raining.

Now that she was in the van she could see that it was actually a customised minibus, with most of the back seats ripped out.

Metal stumps poked from beneath the pile of equipment and redundant seatbelts dangled lifelessly from the walls like streamers after the party was over. Angie was driving while Ben was in the front seat with his feet up on the dash. Louisa could see his face in the rear-view mirror. He was attractive in a small, French sort of way. In a band without Adam, he would have been the looker. He was counting out the money they'd made from the gig, excited because they'd actually managed to turn a profit, even if it was only ten quid each, which he handed out to the other members in coins and notes. Ciaran took his with mumbled thanks; she still hadn't managed to meet his eye. Adam handed his to Louisa for safekeeping. She was touched by the old-married-couple nature of this trusting gesture and made a big show of putting the money into her own purse so that the others wouldn't miss it. She felt an unexpected diffidence and was happy to listen while they spoke.

They had to shout to make their voices heard over the drumming of the rain on the roof. Ben had got them an unpaid gig at the polytechnic in Luton and opinion was divided over whether they should accept. Angie and Ben argued that all exposure and experience was good, Adam was insulted that they should be asked to play for free and Ciaran was saying, in a voice that sounded almost tearful, that he'd been doing this for ten years and he had never heard of anyone being spotted by an A&R man in Luton. *Ten years*, thought Louisa. How old *was* he? Ciaran was like a warning from history. By thirty you should be coming out the other side of your career, not still hoping that it would one day take off. She wondered why he had not yet achieved success and how he could bear to be surrounded by such blistering youth.

'I think we should all get hideously pissed,' said Ben.

'Everywhere's shut,' said Angie. 'Unless you want to pay to get into a club, and I need that tenner.'

Louisa's parents were in Devon with Miranda and Dev. Louisa weighed up bonding with the rest of the band versus bed with Adam and decided to play a long game.

'You can all come back to mine.'

'But your folks!' said Adam, as though it was a trap.

'At the cottage, and so's my sister,' said Louisa.

They all pulled into the mews. The van had to be the cheapest vehicle that had ever graced the cobbles.

'Nice gaff!' said Ben.

Ciaran looked up at the mews and then at Adam.

'I'm sorry, all of a sudden I'm not thirsty.' He slipped through the gate as it closed, swinging his long black trench coat around him like a toreador and splashed his way into the night.

'Well, at least that answers my question about who's the biggest arsehole,' said Angie. 'Tonight, anyway.'

Once in, Louisa set about raiding her parents' wine cellar, which was recessed in the floor of the utility room, starting with a Liebfraumilch, a gift from one of her father's grateful patients, that she knew her parents would never touch. She noticed that, when it was free, Adam didn't insist on whiskey but drank the white wine he professed to despise. When she came back up, all three of them were crouched by her father's Bang and Olufsen.

'Nice kit,' said Ben. 'This must have cost a grand, easy. What have you got?'

'Nothing much, I'm afraid,' said Louisa, who still listened to everything on cassette. She opened the glass-fronted tower that housed her father's CD collection. 'Only classical.'

'*Only* classical?' said Adam. 'My dear girl, I have so much to teach you.' He pulled out a recording of Britten's *War Requiem* and turned it up so loudly they all jumped in surprise. Angie spilled her glass down her front.

'Damn, that was the last of it,' she said.

'Plenty more where that came from,' said Louisa.

'I'll get it,' said Adam. 'I'm going to the loo anyway.'

Ben leaned in so close that for a disorienting moment Louisa thought he was about to kiss her. 'I'm sorry about Ciaran. That right there is your typical love-hate relationship. Ciaran resents Adam because he's the front man and he gets all the glory and the credit, not to mention he's fighting off the girls with a stick, the bastard.' Ben didn't seem to see Louisa's face crumple at this. 'And Adam resents Ciaran because I think that deep down he knows Ciaran's the real songwriting talent in the band.'

'If Ciaran hates Adam so much why doesn't he go and form a band on his own?' said Louisa.

'Because Adam is beautiful, and he can sing,' said Angie simply. 'And that's where the magic is. Also, Ciaran's thirty-four. Adam's young. *We're* young. We could all start again. Ciaran thinks this is his last shot at success.'

'He's right,' said Ben.

'The thing is, they've both got that unteachable quality, that talent. Me and Ben, we're plodders – we are, Ben – we work hard, but they don't even have to try. And with that comes the artistic temperament, which brings us back to the fact they're a pair of arseholes.'

'He's started talking about Hamburg again,' said Ben. Angie rolled her eyes. 'Whenever there's a schism in the band – well, whenever Adam doesn't get his own way, which is much the same thing – he throws a tantrum and threatens to go and live in Hamburg.'

'It's Berlin now, haven't you heard? Ciaran's convinced him the Wall's going to come down. Adam thinks he's going to soundtrack the revolution.'

'As *if*!'

'*Mein Gott!*'

They were crying with laughter, as though Adam leaving

the country was no big deal, as though it wasn't the worst thing that could happen. Maybe to them it wasn't. 'Don't worry, I'm sure you'll cure his wanderlust,' he said in a way that made Louisa feel the joke was on her.

Adam came back with a box of wine. After another glass, Angie fell asleep on the sofa. She had taken her wet shoes and socks off to reveal toenails like pieces of gravel. Louisa felt a stab of pity and frustration. You'd think she could at least try to do something with her hair: a henna rinse would give it a bit of depth.

'Sleeping Beauty herself,' said Ben nastily; when Adam joined in the laughter Louisa was ashamed of her relief.

'Let me get her a cover,' said Louisa. 'You two can crash here if you like.'

She went upstairs to the airing cupboard for the spare blankets. The sooner she could get Ben to drop off, the quicker she could take Adam downstairs.

The CD came to an end as she descended the stairs. Her bare feet made no sound on the carpet and she stopped halfway down, the better to hear them talk. Adam and Ben had been raising their voices all night and through habit or intoxication did not think to lower them now.

'She's nice,' said Ben. She wondered what gesture Adam's silence contained: she imagined an arrogant shrug that confirmed he was due nothing less. 'Does she know about . . .?'

She could almost hear him shake his head.

'No,' said Ben. 'They never do, do they?'

23

Paul passed his driving test first time with only three minor faults at 2.53 p.m. on 29th May 2009. He knew as he watched the examiner complete the paperwork that it would be one of those dates that you never forget, like a birthday or a deathday. He was right about that, but not in the way he thought.

That evening Michaela Johnson, who was in his English class, threw her eighteenth birthday party. Emily knew about the party but she wanted them to go to the cinema instead. She didn't like Michaela Johnson; she thought that she was promiscuous, emphasising each syllable. ('A right slag, that one,' said Daniel, with less eloquence, but more justification; Michaela had been one of his more vocal sofa conquests.) But Paul didn't get invited to many parties, still less have a genuine reason for celebrating, and Emily's primness, usually part of her charm, had annoyed him. The week leading up to it had been tense, with tearful phone calls from his mum (not pregnant again), juggling Daniel and Emily, sitting his last A level and having extra driving lessons; he wanted to let off steam properly, the way people his age were supposed to do. An evening of serious cinema followed by the usual protracted sexual rejection was more than he could take. He tried to persuade Emily to come – even good girls were famously loose at parties – but she stood her ground.

Michaela had a baby brother, and someone had filled the child's plastic bath with fruit juice and spirits to make a punch. People were pouring cans and bottles in. Paul dipped a paper cup into the mixture. It tasted like Troy's hairspray. Within seconds he felt calmer and happier. Almost everyone from college was there along with a few stragglers from Grays Reach High, including, Simeon and Lewis – who had graduated from bullying twelve-year-olds to selling them drugs – and Hash, who drunkenly greeted Daniel like a long-lost brother. Paul hid his laughter as Daniel tried to disentangle himself from the embrace; by the time Hash had really hit his stride as a bully Paul had been safe under Daniel's wing, and so he had never been on the receiving end of his petulant brand of violence. He wanted it to stay that way.

There were too many people; the press of bodies was actually not unpleasant – squeezing past her in a rammed corridor he got closer to Michaela Johnson's bare stomach than he had ever managed to Emily's. Teenagers spilled out of the house to litter the grassy banks outside. The houses on either side of Michaela's were vacant: the front door of one had been battered down before 8 p.m., and the empty rooms contained the overflow. Twice the police were called, but both times they just sent Community Support Officers on pushbikes who told them to turn the music down only for it to resume, louder and faster than ever, once the boys in the wrong shade of blue were out of earshot.

'They clock off at half ten,' said Daniel, 'and after that, they won't send plod out for a teenage party. Not unless something really kicks off.'

Normally Daniel didn't like Paul to drink in case he needed him for some unspecified high-precision emergency, but tonight he was encouraging him, producing cans of Special Brew from somewhere and telling him that he was proud of him for passing his driving test. In the living room, the two of them commandeered a sofa. Girls in tiny clothes were gyrating in front of them, but it was still too early for any but the drunkest boys to dance. Though all of the girls naturally looked over at Daniel, once or twice Paul couldn't help wondering if some of their glances had been directed at him. He looked as good as he was ever going to get, in clothes that Daniel had chosen for him: a grey T-shirt with a low V-neck and charcoal linen trousers.

'Gemma likes you,' said Daniel, gesturing to a girl in the eye of the dancefloor.

'Gemma *Collins*?' said Paul in disbelief and amusement.

Popular wisdom held that Gemma was the most beautiful girl in Grays Reach, in all Essex. Paul didn't understand why she would go for him, and if he was honest he didn't see why he should go for her. She had an undeniably lovely face and was always beautifully dressed and made up, but there was something arch and brittle about her looks. She looked like a model – but the skinny, fashion kind, not the soft, welcoming glamour models that he preferred.

'You're well in.'

'Nah. What about Emily?'

Daniel clicked his teeth. 'Look, do you want to be a virgin all your life or not? More experience you have, the better time you'll be able to show this Emily. This is *Gemma Collins*.'

'I'm not sure.'

'It's no skin off my nose whether you do or not. I've had sex, you haven't.'

'Jesus, Daniel, d'you want to say that any louder?' Paul, emboldened by punch and beer, pushed himself up off the sofa and huffed his way towards the bathroom. Gemma Collins was on the stairs. She had done something to her hair; it was twice its usual size and hung in fat curls.

'Your hair looks nice,' he said.

'Thanks,' she said, as though compliments were immeasurably boring. But five minutes later he was following her up the stairs. The only bedroom not yet occupied by at least one couple was the box room. Evidently it belonged to a little sister; the half-size bed was covered in Disney toys and a poster of Ariel from *The Little Mermaid* was peeling away from the wall. Gemma closed the door behind her; a tiny pink dressing gown swayed on its hook. Someone had covered the back of the door with stickers and then tried to peel them off again, giving the paintwork a lichened effect. She sat down on the bed and patted a space beside her. Paul joined her, feeling awestruck rather than desirous. Gemma's kiss was perfunctory, almost professional; after ten seconds or so, she broke off in a way that made Paul feel she'd been counting down. Then she undid the top button of her jeans, pulling at his own buckle with her other hand. He barely had time to register what she looked like naked, only that she had even more bones and fewer curves than her clothes suggested.

All that time with Emily when he had fantasised about having a naked, willing female body in his arms, it hadn't occurred to him that when it happened he would not know what to do with her. Fortunately, Gemma took the lead. She rolled the condom – her condom – onto him without even looking and, with a decisive hand, guided him in. Her head was level with his armpit and his own face was buried in a pink pillow. Once the euphoria and novelty of devirginisation had worn off, he started to get a bit of a rhythm going. It was almost meditative; he felt as though he were hovering above the bed, looking down on himself, already embarrassed on his own behalf and hurt and angry on Emily's. Apart from the obvious sensations, he was quite uncomfortable; Gemma was stiff and unresponsive, although for all he knew that was the norm. The thought came to Paul that he might as well have thrown off the mattress of the bed and fucked the slats that supported it for all the softness and welcome Gemma's body gave. Despite this, things seemed to be drawing to a conclusion with more than their usual rapidity. Suddenly Gemma, who was bucking underneath him in a motorised sort of way, froze with her hips in mid-air. It was like being stuck at the top of a ferris wheel that had stopped without warning.

'Do you want to finish off up the bum?' she said.

'Do I . . . *what*? No!'

'Whatever.' Gemma shrugged, sending a zip of white lightning up his spine that signalled the point of no return. She didn't react as he cried out. In the echoing seconds after he came, she wriggled out from under him, making him wince. He fell onto his side, wondering what to do with the condom. Gemma folded up a tissue and put it in her knickers before pulling on her jeans; she handed another tissue to him and he wiped himself and wrapped the condom in it, hiding his shrivelling penis from the Little Mermaid. The inappropriateness of the location finally hit home.

'We're not going out,' she said.

'I'm sorry?' said Paul.

'Just because we slept together, it doesn't mean we're going out.'

'Oh. Right.' Paul groped for the right phrase. 'I, ah, I hope we can still be friends.'

'Yeah,' said Gemma. As she pulled her T-shirt down over her head there was a quick ripping sound and she let out a gasp of pain; a chunk of her hair had come loose, a toffee-coloured tendril that Paul thought must have been ripped out at the root until he saw the nylon stitching at the top of the lock that revealed it to be fake, an extension. She frowned at the inconvenience and clipped it loosely back into her hair. Now that she was clothed again, her body made sense; tight jeans hung off her linear frame and she regained that expensive look that her reputation was based on. As the event shrank into history Paul allowed himself to think, I just had sex with Gemma Collins. He could already feel it assuming the stuff of myth rather than reality. Thinking along those lines made him feel less wretched.

'Will you tell Daniel we did it?' she said. 'Make sure you tell him I was good.'

Was she saying she wanted him to provide her with a *reference*? Paul tried not to consider that possibility. His thoughts were only of Emily, how different it would be when he finally got her to have sex with him, how they would find a safe place, take their time, fall asleep together afterwards. Gemma checked her bag as though Paul might have rifled through it and stolen her purse during the act. She squeezed a tube of gloss over her lips and, with Paul still naked from the waist down, stood and opened the door.

'Give us a chance!' he shouted, but it was too late. The landing was rammed with people, all of whom turned to laugh and whoop and slow-clap his humiliation. Only one of the faces was familiar. Emily's expression ranged from recognition to disbelief to grief in a heartbeat.

Pulling on what clothes he could, carrying his shoes and socks and giving his pants up for lost, Paul flew down the stairs, his peripheral vision briefly registering Daniel and Gemma in conversation. Outside, Hash had set fire to an abandoned mattress and the acrid smoke temporarily blinded Paul. By the time he caught up with Emily she was unlocking her car. Her beautiful, babyish features were hard with rage.

'I thought you *liked* me,' she said. 'I thought you liked me enough to wait.'

'I do like you! I love you!' He had rehearsed this declaration many times; never had it come out quite like this.

'But you've had sex with her?' said Emily.

'You said you weren't coming!'

'And that makes it all right, does it?' said Emily. She was crying now; a little black blob of make-up that had been lodged in her tear duct worked its way free and ran in a sooty drift down the side of her nose.

'God, Emily, no, I'd hate you to think that . . . Oh, I don't know what to say, I'm pissed. It's just, you know, it was *Gemma Collins* . . . Daniel said . . .'

'I might have known fucking Daniel would be at the bottom of this,' said Emily. It was the first time Paul had heard her swear. 'I don't know why I let him talk me into coming here.'

'*Daniel* invited you?'

'Yes, he was there after college today. He said it would mean a lot to you if I—' Emily's voice broke.

'It does mean a lot, it's lovely to see you. Please, Emily, nothing's more important to me than you are.'

'You've got a funny way of showing it.'

'But I love you!' How many times did he have to say it before it cancelled what he had done?

'Forget it. It's over.'

'But what about college?'

Her crying increased in volume now. He held out his arms to comfort her knowing that he had revoked his own licence to do so. She kicked his shins with a force he knew would leave a bruise. The only way to stop her getting into the driver's seat would have been to grab her by the arm. Instead, he lay on the bonnet of her car. Emily revved the engine twice and then slowly began to drive.

'Emily, please,' he shouted through the glass. She braked softly and he slid off, landing on the tarmac with the bouncing grace of the truly drunk. Emily leant out of the car window to look him over, assess and then dismiss him with a coolness he would not have believed her capable of. When he staggered to his feet she reversed out of the car park and tore into the night. Paul felt like crying. His perfect day had descended into farce then tragedy in less than an hour. He was drunk – though sober enough to see that the main fault was his – but no one else's actions seemed to make sense either. Why had Gemma Collins waited until he had a girlfriend to decide she fancied him? Why had Emily turned up at a party thrown by a girl she couldn't stand? Why had Daniel even *gone* to college today? He had known that Paul wouldn't be in today, he'd known it was test day—

A terrible notion sent a sobering rush of adrenaline through Paul's veins. He dragged his bruised limbs back into the party, charging his way through sagging intoxicated bodies. He looked in every room, searched the garden and the bare rooms in the violated house next door, but there was no sign of Daniel or Gemma. His mind was spinning and his guts were churning. He staggered back to the Scatlocks' house. It was empty.

At about three in the morning, Paul awoke to hear Daniel with some girl on the sofa. He wondered who it was. It couldn't have been Gemma, though; he heard movement and moaning and later soft laughter bubbling up the stairs. He lay awake for hours, devising ways he could get back at Daniel for this. There was no equivalent, no reciprocal sabotage; the only relationship Daniel seemed to prize above all others was their own friendship. But in wrecking things with Emily, Daniel himself had destroyed that. How could they come back from something like this?

The next morning he tried to read but he couldn't concentrate, his mind buzzing with the confrontation he knew he had to have when Daniel came downstairs. When footsteps were overhead he automatically went to hide his book between the sofa cushions. Lifting them up revealed a wisp of honey hair, sewn together at the top.

The knowledge that Daniel had been able to coax from Gemma the responsiveness that had eluded him stripped Paul of his remaining confidence. When Daniel came downstairs, he simply told him the bones of it. He waited for Daniel to deny or explain or apologise. It's not too late, he thought, you can still say the right thing and we can be friends again, although he didn't know what that right thing might be.

'Frigid,' said Daniel conclusively, when he had finished his story. 'You're better off without her.' He looked happier than Paul had seen him for months.

24

Louisa was in the Portakabin office, watched over only by the couple depicted in the replica tapestry that hung behind her. The Heritage Gardens Trust letter was in a document holder before her and she had the feeling that the embroidered figures were reading it over her shoulder. She clicked a new cartridge into her fountain pen and took out another fresh sheet of Kelstice Lodge headed paper, trying not to think about the nine in the waste basket. She dated it, addressed it, and while she was thinking about the perfect opening line, she found that she had doodled little knot gardens all over the corner of the page. She crumpled it up and made a start on the eleventh draft. When she lost count of the number of drafts, she reconsidered not the request but the medium of its asking. Perhaps this was the kind of thing that had to be done on the telephone after all. If her plan did not come off she would jeopardise not only her career but the entire garden project. If her suggestion was taken the wrong way – and Ingram seemed convinced that the arbiters of the grant expected applicants to abide by a whimsical, fluctuating etiquette that was easily and fatally breached – it was important that she be able to perform damage limitation on the spot. Offending the Heritage Gardens Trust would mean losing the grant, which would mean struggling on for years with volunteer labour and borrowed equipment. They would be able to build the garden, yes, but not to afford the infrastructure that would attract visitors.

But she had no choice. She absolutely could not set foot in Warwick Gardens, even if they took her there blindfold (an option she had actually considered for a fleeting, crazy moment in the middle of the night, lying on her back and trying to find a plausible excuse). It was the place where she had lost control in the past, and she knew it would trigger a similar impulse in her now. She inhaled and exhaled deeply before dialling the number at the bottom of the Heritage Gardens Trust letter. Even knowing that the person who picked up the phone would likely be sitting in a house in Warwick Gardens made her uneasy.

'Joanna Bower,' said a voice as sharp as secateurs. Every upper-class lady gardener Louisa had ever met – and there had been plenty – had shared the same strident, no-nonsense tone. It made it hard to decipher the sentiment behind their words, although disapproval tended to be the default setting.

'Joanna, my name's Louisa Trevelyan, I'm calling from Kelstice Lodge in Warwickshire. I believe you're in charge of—'

'Tudor garden!' said Joanna Bower. 'Yes, exciting stuff, I've got your application in front of me now. You're coming down to see us after Christmas, aren't you?'

'Well. That's the thing. I, we, thought it might be rather nice if the Trust came up to see us here instead, to give you an idea of the way we work, to see the place three-dimensionally and—'

'Hold it *right* there!' boomed Joanna Bower. Louisa tried to decode the ensuing silence and concluded that she had caused offence.

'I'm so sorry if—'

'It's a brilliant idea,' she said. 'We'll make a day of it.'

'Oh! Great.'

'We'll bring the cameras.'

'Excuse me?'

'We've got a film-maker following us around at the moment, wants to do some little trailers for the website, says he might even make it into a documentary. What fun to film your pitch, get an idea of the funding application process.'

Louisa felt all the saliva disappear from inside her mouth.

'I'll have to check with Ingram,' she said. 'He has the last word on this kind of thing.'

'Nonsense!' said Joanna Bower, in a tone that left no room for misunderstanding about who was in the powerful position here. 'He'll love it. Everyone wants to be on the box, don't they? Fabulous publicity for your garden, even if we don't end up working together.'

Louisa hung up with a grave heart and a head that felt too heavy for her neck. A new worst-case scenario was looming, and it was all her fault. She had thought that nothing could be worse than returning to Warwick Gardens, but at least there the only threat would come from within. If she was filmed, though, if she was broadcast ... *Someone* was bound to see her face on television. The Other Man had seen her face but not known her name. The rest of them knew her name but not where to find her.

She dug her nails into the flesh of her forearm, a tiny punishment for her own stupidity. Most of the time she thought that the intervening years had toughened her up, made her paranoid, wary, wise. Then there were the times like now, when she felt as incautious as a teenager, as though no lesson had been learned.

25

Paul had not celebrated Hallowe'en since he was a little boy. At primary school, he had enjoyed bobbing for apples and picking coins out from flour cakes with his teeth. He had had a black bodystocking from Woolworths, decorated with bones, that he had worn for three years running. After his father's death, however, even pretend gore was enough to endow the feast with genuine fear. At their house in Grays Reach, Paul and his mother had usually stayed indoors with the curtains closed and the TV off to avoid feral children demanding money with menaces. Daniel and Carl Scatlock might have watched a horror film on an obscure satellite channel but that was as close as they came to celebrating it.

But in Leamington it was harder to avoid. The joke shop opposite his bus stop had swapped its usual window display of clown suits and feather boas for a macabre tableau of green-faced witches and dancing skeletons. In the middle was a shop mannequin in a wig and a long white nightie; like the eponymous girl in the film *Carrie* she was soaked in blood. It never went dark brown like normal blood but stayed scarlet day after day. Paul knew it was only food colouring or fabric dye but still it turned his stomach and made him shake and after a few days he had to walk three hundred yards along the High Street to the next stop because twice he had had his eyes closed tight against the image and had missed his bus.

The young people at Kelstice Lodge were off to a Hallowe'en party in Coventry, some student house a few doors down from their own. Paul had not yet thought of a convincing reason not to go. He was desperate enough to consider telling them the truth, that celebrating the dead was no fun when your own past had a body count. Admitting to his blood phobia might have got them off his back about the party, but telling them might have led to talking about his father. Then the floodgates would open, they would all want to know more and more, and he was afraid that once his secrets began to spill they would be difficult to stem. He reminded himself again that one of these people had almost definitely passed his number to Carl Scatlock. Although he couldn't work out how or why they had done it, he was still sure. Until he had solved that mystery he wasn't going to confide in any of them, not about his father and certainly not about Ken Hillyard. If forced, he would have put his money on Dilan. Dilan had no motive – as far as Paul could tell, they had always got on well – but he was the only person at Kelstice whose background had been seriously criminal and for a while Paul wondered if he knew the Scatlocks through some nationwide network of violent petty criminals. He also wondered if it could be the police themselves; they had already proved that they could be manipulative by tricking him into his court appearance, and that Woburn was a heartless bastard who had hated Paul on sight. He wouldn't have been surprised to learn that Woburn was torturing him for a laugh. The problem was, even if he worked out who was responsible, he would never understand why. These days only his mother, the police, Ross and Demetra had the number. Carl had not called again, although Paul always made himself qualify that thought with the word 'yet'.

He was home early on Thursday afternoon and bought a curry from the hatch on the High Street, waiting with his back to the joke shop. When it was ready he carried his takeaway around the back of the alleyway so that it ended up back where it started, the lights of the Balti house kitchen casting a dim glow on his own front door. He didn't want to stink out his bedroom so he ate it straight from the foil under the strip-lighting of the kitchen, clearing a space for himself on the sofa among the spread of local newspapers that were weeks old and nothing but adverts anyway. As usual, he had the place to himself. The red bike was gone from its hook on the wall, although the silver one still hung there. Tyre marks made it look like it had actually been ridden up the walls. Paul wished he had thought to bring his own bike. If he could navigate the ring roads and A-roads of estuary Essex then the winding lanes of Kelstice would prove no problem. He thought about the last time he had ridden a bicycle – it had not been his own – and forced himself to derail that train of thought. One of the Poles had evidently been in at some point that day because someone had slid a letter underneath his door. The crisp white corner pointed at him. It made him nervous. It was not usual for him to get post here. Officially, he was living in Goring; his mother had paid to have the whole family's post redirected there. It was only the police who knew his address. Of course there was also Demetra and Ross, possibly Ingram, and now Louisa knew where he lived, but why would any of them write to him when they saw him every day? He looked at the franked envelope: fat, milky, thick quality paper. The logo on the front said CJS, a familiar set of initials but one he couldn't quite place. He held it in his hands for a few minutes, willing it to be good news; but it had to be something official, and official could only mean bad.

The letter was from the Criminal Justice System and called him Mr Seaforth, which made him think of his dad. It confirmed – as though he had already known, as though he had been waiting for verification – that he would be called as a witness for the prosecution at Daniel's trial, and informed him that although a date had not yet been set it was likely to be in the new year. The letter said that he would be hearing from them nearer the time so that he could set aside a fortnight to come to court. The second sheet of paper was a glossy leaflet entitled 'What to do if you are a witness'. Paul read the letter twice. It was obviously a mistake, and one that needed to be corrected as soon as possible. Instinctively he shut the bedroom door and turned the key as though someone was coming after him. He felt as frightened as he would if Daniel or Carl had delivered it by hand.

He knew who he had to talk to. He vaguely remembered using the business card as a bookmark. He had been sure he wouldn't need it again. His bookshelf was quite full now; it could be in any of them. He took the first couple of paperbacks and held them by the covers, spine up, to see if anything was pressed between the pages. Nothing. He became increasingly frantic with each empty book, shaking them violently as though they themselves were in trouble. After a while he stopped working systematically and began to pick them up at random, unable to tell which he'd already searched and which he hadn't. He threw a charity shop Terry Pratchett across the room in frustration and panic and something fell out. It lay on the rug, a tiny white rectangle with the Essex Police logo in the top right-hand corner.

'Hello?' The voice was female, but not the one he'd been hoping for.

'Can I please speak to Christine?'

'Detective Chief Inspector Shaw is on annual leave,' said the woman. He thought it was the squat little woman with short hair who'd processed him on arrival at the station. 'Who's calling?'

'My name's Paul Seaforth, it's to do with Daniel Scatlock's trial.'

'Who? Oh, hang on, I know. I'm going to put you through to one of her team.'

He just knew it would be Woburn.

'Mr Seaforth.' The detective sergeant's voice was freighted with sarcasm. 'How's life in the cabbage patch? Got to ride on the big lawnmower yet?'

'It's the wrong time of year for that,' said Paul automatically. Woburn laughed. 'Listen, I think you've made a mistake. I got a letter this morning saying I need to go to court when Daniel has his trial. But I've already given my statement.'

'Yes, and very useful it was too.'

'So I thought that meant I didn't have to go to court?'

'Where did you get that idea?'

'You *told* me. You said—'

'I said that we wouldn't charge you in relation to the offence, and we haven't. This is a murder trial. You're our star witness. It's your word against his. It's your performance in the witness box that's going to put him away.'

Paul could not believe how naive he had been. He would see Daniel again, and in the worst possible circumstances. He pressed the phone into his neck. It was a moment or two before he could speak. In the interval Woburn started chewing something noisy, gum or toffee, and Paul could hear the click of his fingers on a keyboard.

'I think you've tricked me into this.'

'Oh, man up,' said Woburn.

'When's Christine back?' said Paul.

'A week Monday, but she won't tell you any different to me,' said Woburn. He stopped typing and eating. 'Listen, let me dig out the number for Witness Support. They'll tell you what to expect, how to deal with the briefs and silks. You'll be fine.'

There was the click of a receiver and the line went dead. Paul dashed across the landing to the bathroom and threw up £4.95 of lamb balti.

26

The next day, Hallowe'en itself, seemed to dawn earlier than usual. Paul woke up with a start at 5 a.m., just as the night music of pigeons and lone motors gave way to the lumbering rumble of lorries on the High Street. Five was the psychological cut-off point: if the clock had said 4.59 he would have tried to go back to sleep but at five it was time to begin to carve out a day. He consoled himself with the knowledge that exhaustion would take the edge off the next night's insomnia and used the time to rearrange his scattered books onto their shelves, taking the opportunity to reclassify them into author groups. They were all in place long before 7 a.m. He had memorised the letter, of course. Its content, and yesterday's conversation with Woburn, replayed themselves over and over in his mind until the words condensed into a scream in his throat. He couldn't stay in his room.

He got a much earlier bus than usual; it was full of commuters rather than students, and morgue-silent. A few of them had university staff ID cards on ribbons around their necks. He wondered what these people did with themselves in the two or three hours before the students came onto campus. He forced himself not to think about the parallel life where he was one of them, Emily coming to visit him at university, Daniel left behind in Grays Reach wondering where he had gone.

Louisa was the only one there. She, who had the shortest commute, was always the first to arrive. She was coming out of the toilet block in her usual jeans and jacket but with a white towel wrapped around her head. This solved the mystery of where she bathed at least. It could not have been comfortable washing her hair in that shower; the water may have been hot but it came out in a compact jet, like a hose, and the cabin was unheated.

'You're early,' she said, with a stare that dared him to comment on her incongruous turban.

'Couldn't sleep,' he said.

'I know the feeling.' She gave him a sad, slow smile.

Ingram assigned Paul to Louisa for the first hour of the morning. In the office, he printed out emails and posted requests on websites for gardening geeks who swapped seeds and bulbs like kids swapped football cards. At first he had thought that her astonishment – 'But it's so *quick*! You make it look so *easy*!' – was mockery. He had never met such a technologically illiterate person before. For all her obvious intelligence, she needed as much help as Daniel.

Just before lunch, he took delivery of a tray of saplings, little shoots in compost that looked like weeds on the brink of death but had cost, according to the docket he signed, £200. He scrunched up the docket, stuffed it in his fleece and took the plants straight to Louisa, now kneeling over mysterious implements in the greenhouse. When she saw what he had brought her she clapped her hands in excitement. As he walked away, he could hear her chatting to them in baby talk. She was absolutely barking mad. He meant to tell Ross and the others what he'd seen over lunch in the pub, but when it came down to it he found that betraying her little moment wasn't worth the points he would score.

Lunch lasted for two hours and they had only been back at the Lodge for half an hour when Demetra came to collect Ingram to take their twins trick-or-treating. This left Louisa the most senior person on site; at four o'clock she handed the keys to Ross and asked if he wouldn't mind locking up for her today. A carnival atmosphere prevailed. Someone had retrieved a few feeble little pumpkins from the greenhouse and Jodie was carving crude eyes and mouths into their flesh with a knife Paul didn't like the look of. Dilan produced a crate of Guinness from a cupboard in the canteen and passed them around.

'Why Guinness?' asked Paul, who would have preferred lager or cider.

'It's traditional, innit?'

'That's St Patrick's day, you fool,' said Ross, cracking open his can. They took the crate up to the Lodge. Paul racked his brains for a reason to go back to Leamington, even contemplating running away while they weren't looking, but his thoughts kept turning to his long-term problems and brainwaves were thin on the ground. At five, he found himself waiting at the bus stop with the rest of them, drinking in the shelter, Ross flicking Jodie with the tip of his scarf until she screamed and ran out into the road. A car kerb-crawled its disapproval then sped up again when Dilan grabbed his crotch and made an unmistakable gesture in the driver's direction. Paul found their good cheer unbearably oppressive. If he had anything more to drink, his guard would slip and he would surrender to his growing compulsion to recite the CJS letter word for word. And if he stopped drinking he would stay edgy and oversensitive throughout the party, on high alert for fake blood, real blood, dead men who haunted him and the living ones out to get him. Whatever he did, he was damned. Five minutes before the bus was due, he clapped his hand to his jeans pocket and said:

'Shit! I've left my phone behind. I'll catch you up, OK?'

'You'll miss the bus,' said Ross.

'I won't, I'll leg it,' said Paul, breaking into a run that slowed as soon as he was out of sight. He froze at the top of the newly planted ride, waiting for the sneeze of brake and door that would tell him their bus had gone and he was alone. A breeze sent the saplings swaying in their high collars. In the shifting twilight the ride seemed twice its usual length. The Lodge presided over all, its spikes and spires blacker than ever, scudding clouds behind it giving the illusion that the ruin was thundering down the avenue towards him. He was suddenly, childishly aware that it was Hallowe'en. He had drunk enough to make him paranoid but not enough to make him forget. The obvious solution was to keep on drinking, and he knew that Dilan had left a few cans under a tarp in a corner of the Lodge. He looked at his phone; there was still an hour before the next bus to Leamington left. He texted Ross a promise that he would catch them all up later and climbed the knoll. Four cans of Guinness remained. The crack of the ring-pull echoed like a gunshot.

Sometimes alcohol worked for him, sometimes it didn't. Today was one of the bad times. Instead of obliterating his worries it intensified them. He pictured the inside of a courthouse and could draw only on television dramas, all old men in grey wigs. It would be the first time he had ever really stood up to Daniel. A crown court was a pretty public place for their first confrontation. He got to the bottom of the fourth and final can and still relaxation did not come. He grew reckless. There seemed little point in self-control when his fate was so clearly in the hands of barristers and policemen. He took a noisy piss over the side of the Lodge, then climbed onto a crumbling ledge. The dark was broken only by a few sequinned clusters denoting villages, and that orange glow rising from behind the low hill in the distance must be Leamington. He twisted his body and saw another light, a silver glow rising over the crooked horizon of a brick wall, which meant that Louisa was at home. He rose on his tiptoes to gain a better view. Something underneath his feet shifted and gave way. Paul teetered over the steep edge of the knoll and only a valiant windmilling of his arms made him fall back into the shell of the Lodge. He landed on his coccyx and burst into short-lived tears. He was shocked rather than badly injured, but the pain brought everything into focus, his loneliness and his fear. Suddenly he wanted physical comfort; he needed to be held by someone or soothed by a soft voice, but his mother was miles away, Emily would never touch him again and even Christine, whose soft voice had promised protection, had betrayed him. He just wanted someone gentle to tell him everything was going to be all right. It didn't have to be true – it couldn't be true, he had long passed the point of anything being all right ever again – but he still needed to hear it.

The wind blew the smell of stale water into his nostrils as he fought his way through the wickerwork of naked brushwood. He kept one hand on the boundary wall. Turning a degree or two in the wrong direction might mean that he stumbled into one of the murky puddles that surrounded the Mere, or disappeared into the trees and spent the night here. Louisa might be able to walk this path blindfolded but he had only ever trodden it in the day and his way seemed strewn with traps and trips. Branches rattled like bones around him; twice he almost lost his nerve but he was driven by a primal need for the comfort of touch. The light grew subtly brighter as he made his clumsy progress along the gentle curve of the wall. He fumbled with the latch until the gate opened, light shining through the arch as though from a room.

'Who's there?' came a tremulous voice from within. Too late, he realised that his bumbling passage must have been a racket of snapped twigs and swearwords. She must be terrified. He stopped dead.

'Louisa, it's only me, it's only Paul.' Shadows shifted inside and then there was the sound of a bolt being drawn. Louisa opened the door; hot air blasted from inside like an oven. It took the breath from his lungs and the words from his lips. She looked different, both younger and older than usual, with her hair teased over one eye and her face painted with dark colours. She was wrapped in a navy blanket brocaded with moons and stars. Only her feet and neck were visible but both were bare. She held out her arms and wrapped him in the soft folds of cloth. Beneath it she was naked, as soft and hot as he was hard and cold, but she didn't flinch from his touch. He could not say who initiated the kiss but it was as inevitable as it was natural. She tasted like whiskey. He kicked the door closed behind him and surrendered to the warmth of her wordless welcome. Anyone would think she had been waiting for him for years.

27

Daniel's suit was by Paul Smith and brand new, purchased on a rare father-and-son outing to the West End. He modelled it for Paul, sardonically walking an imaginary catwalk in the tiny living room, striking ridiculous poses, pointing into the middle distance like a catalogue model and pouting at a pretend camera. Paul, who was finding it hard to even look at Daniel after what happened with Emily, laughed despite himself. He might be sending himself up but he looked the business and he knew it. The logic behind the purchase was unclear, however. It had cost £650; for that, Daniel could have bought himself an entire wardrobe of clothes that he was actually likely to wear.

'Is someone getting married?' he had asked Carl. It was easier to talk to him than Daniel at the moment. He hoped it wasn't a funeral. They all reminded him of his father's.

'No,' said Carl.

'Christening?' said Paul, knowing how unlikely this was.

'Nope,' said Carl, enjoying the game.

'So what's the occasion?' said Paul. 'Why the suit?'

'It's for court, you bell-end,' said Carl affectionately. Daniel scowled, the spell of his suit broken. Paul took time out from being angry with Daniel to be angry on his behalf. At that point Daniel had been cautioned by the police, but nothing more. It was bad enough for society at large to write you off as a member of the underclass, but when your own father assumed you would need a defendant's outfit you didn't stand a chance. He knew that Carl would never have seen it that way, that he saw the suit as a rite of passage and the pre-emptory purchase of it as a way of investing in his son's future the way other parents bought driving lessons.

Paul only saw Daniel in the suit once after that. He had arrived at college without the memory stick containing his history coursework, a lengthy assignment due in by noon that day. He had been working and reworking the essay until the small hours and upon waking (late), been so tired that he had forgotten to bring the bloody thing with him. It was only ten o'clock when he got back to the Scatlocks'. With the likelihood that Daniel and Carl were both still asleep, he let himself in quietly. Diesel, snoring at the foot of the stairs, opened one eye, registered Paul and gave his hand a half-hearted lick before falling back into his doze. Paul took his shoes off and tiptoed up the stairs, hoping that he could retrieve the stick without waking Daniel.

Daniel was already up. Through the crack in the bedroom door, Paul saw him, hair done, suit on, in front of the full-length mirror. For a bewildering moment Paul wondered what the appointment was that could get Daniel into a suit this early in the morning. Then he noticed what Daniel held across his palm. It was a history textbook, a fat account of the Civil War, a dense, dry text that even Paul, who loved the period, was struggling to read. It was open at the halfway mark. Daniel was flipping through the tissue-thin pages, occasionally looking at his own reflection. These glances were furtive, fleeting, as though he would catch himself reading if only he were quick enough. Paul was mortified. Better to catch him on the toilet or masturbating than to intrude on his wretched little fantasy. Daniel shifted position, sat down on the edge of the bed which was Paul's customary studying place. Again, he leafed through the pages that could not have meant anything to him. At one point, he looked in the mirror and nodded to himself, as though considering and agreeing with the point he had just read. That was the part that went straight to Paul's heart, bypassing their recent history and taking him back to the early days of their friendship.

He wished he could turn off the umbilical tug of guilt, wear lightly the knowledge that when he abandoned Daniel for bigger, better things, this was the life he would leave him to. He held his breath all the way back down the stairs. In the hallway he slammed the front door loudly and began to make an ostentatious fuss of Diesel before heading to the kitchen where he made toast with percussive exaggeration. By the time he went up to the bedroom to retrieve his memory stick Daniel was down to his boxers, standing by the unmade bed as though he had just got up. Only his hair, slick with gel, gave him away. The Civil War textbook was second from the top of the pile, exactly where Paul had left it.

28

May 1989

Louisa pulled the grey hood of Miranda's sweatshirt over her head and checked her reflection in a shiny black car. She didn't recognise herself, in any sense, but Adam had left her with no choice. It was the only way she could think of to get to know him properly. Not knowing where he went when he left her bed was torture. The obvious thing was to ask him, but even asking for an invitation to his house was enough to tip him headlong into one of his sulks. Every day she swallowed so many questions that the words were pushing against the side of her throat like little hands. She tormented herself with worst-case scenarios and when he arrived, surreptitiously checked his clothes for long red hairs. This was the kind of stress that gave people cancer; she could almost feel her body changing at a cellular level. She was living off Bach Rescue Remedy rather than food but the little phial wasn't strong enough to work its magic any more. Knowing was the only cure. She had more or less resigned herself to another woman. Now it was all about the details.

She bolted through the mews gate just as it was closing. He was a hundred yards ahead of her. Instead of doing the expected right turn for the Cromwell Road and the bus that would take him home to Shepherd's Bush, he took a left. She had been following him for thirty seconds and already she had caught him out in a lie. He came to a halt at a stop where all the buses were travelling in the direction of Hammersmith. She leant on a wall and watched him wait. He took his Walkman from his backpack, plugged himself in and closed his eyes. Louisa was too far to catch the metallic overspill from his headphones but she read his lips and saw that he was listening to his own music. She dared not risk lowering her hood even though she was starting to feel as though she was wearing a bearskin on her head. A Sloaney-looking girl walking her poodle stopped in her tracks to admire him. Louisa had a brief and vivid image of pushing her under the wheels of the approaching bus.

It was the easiest thing in the world to jump on the Routemaster behind him. He took the stairs two at a time: she clung to the pole until the bus was on the move before following him up. She peered over the handrail, slowly, like an animal emerging into unfamiliar territory. He was in the front seat, thank God, so she went to the back. When the conductor asked her where she was going she realised she didn't know, so she whispered, 'To the end,' and he charged her 70p. Adam had a Travelcard, the kind that was kept in a wallet with a photo ID card. She had never seen it before. She wondered what else he kept in his pockets and if it was time to start going through them. That would depend on what today yielded. An appetite-sapping adrenaline coursed through her as they rode along Hammersmith Road, passing Olympia at a pace that she could have outwalked in heels. There was some kind of wedding show on; young couples and daughters with their mothers spilled onto the pavement clutching branded carriers. Adam had his feet up on the ledge below the front window, the soles of his boots pressed against the glass, and he kept checking his watch.

She went over the facts and the fantasies. He had a history of promiscuity. He was mysterious and made himself unavailable. And she had caught him out in a lie. The conclusion that he was meeting someone else was inescapable but the possible details and specifics were as numerous as the women in London. Was he going to meet the redhead? To the house of some married woman while her husband was out? A schoolgirl on her lunch break?

The windows opened only fractionally and the top deck of the bus was hot and airless. Swooning beneath her hood but afraid to take it off, she wondered when she had become the kind of woman who had to skulk around on buses following her lover. It was Adam's fault, he had driven her to this with his secrecy and his lies. A conversation with an old boyfriend echoed in her mind; what had he said? 'If I'm possessive it's only because I love you so much.' She been unspeakably turned off and had dumped him, of course, but now she forgave him because she understood. She knew now that jealousy wasn't a choice but a curse, that no one would ever choose to feel this.

He got to his feet as the bus swung under the Hammersmith flyover. She curled into a ball as he rounded the top of the spiral staircase, close enough to touch, but he didn't give her a second glance. Louisa misjudged the step down and had to grab onto a passer-by to stop herself falling into the gutter. It took half a minute to convince the middle-aged woman that she wasn't trying to mug her, during which time the city had swallowed him. Hammersmith was not as familiar to her as it used to be; the big roundabout was a building site, an office block half-built on top of the Tube station. A pneumatic drill struck up and confused her senses. The pavements were swarming with pedestrians – shoppers, office workers, and pensioners – milling in all directions. He could be anywhere. She almost screamed his name.

Eventually she saw him on a traffic island opposite the Odeon, hostage to the red man. Despite its name, the Hammersmith Odeon wasn't a cinema any more but a huge theatre that staged gigs for bands at the other end of the career ladder than Glasslake. Did being so near to such a prestigious venue inspire Adam, daunt him or make him bitter? She would give anything for an hour's access-all-areas pass to the inside of his mind. The row of front doors were all closed. Adam walked past these, into a little side yard between the Odeon and the back entrance of a shabby pub with a peeling mural of a toucan on the wall. By the time she had made it over the three pedestrian crossings that divided her from him, he had disappeared behind a barricade of silver beer kegs. Heavy with sweat, hood still up, Louisa walked the length of the yard twice. The only place he could have gone was through a side door of the Odeon marked *Staff Only*. A keypad kept her out.

What did it mean? Had the band made some breakthrough he hadn't told her about? Had she misjudged him? She barely had time to consider her new questions before the side door opened and he came out. She crouched behind the beer kegs. Adam was wearing a pale blue tabard, the kind tea-ladies wear, and in either hand he had a black bin liner full of rubbish that he lobbed into the dumpsters lining the wall. Louisa tried to deal with what she was seeing. A minute or so later he emerged again, this time carrying a mop and bucket. What she saw broke her heart and fixed it at the same time. No wonder he was secretive and ashamed; he was sweeping the stage he should have been treading. It would not be lack of trust but an excess of pride that made him hide it from her. She held her breath; for him to spot her now would be disastrous. Something about the sight of him in dirty overalls made her love him more than ever. She would wait for the right time to tell him she knew about his secret job. Perhaps she never would. It was such an innocent secret.

She waited until she was back on the Hammersmith Road to take her hood off. The spring breeze on her face was the sweetest relief she had ever known. The only pity was that he had not felt he could tell her himself, but that would come, that level of trust and intimacy would come if only she could resist the temptation to force it.

She could tell that Dev was at the mews before she opened the front door; the smell of spices and garlic and onions curled down from the extractor fan. Dev's cooking was the best thing about him. Yesterday she wouldn't have been able to stomach his food but today she had second helpings of the vegetarian curry, then thirds. He was having a good-natured argument with Nick about how a little bit of ghee didn't hurt anyone in moderation. Nick was intransigent in his defence of sunflower oil and the benefits of polyunsaturated fat. Whatever this was cooked with got Louisa's vote: she ladled the third helping onto her plate.

'It's nice to see you eating properly,' said Nick. 'You know, if you want to lose weight the best thing is balanced diet and exercise. Starvation diets only lead the body to lose water and muscle, not burn fat. You've still got that gym membership whenever you want it.'

'I've got a better idea. Why don't you just give me the money and I can go clubbing? Dancing's exercise.'

'Nice try, but I don't think swaying gently to The Sisters of Mercy after six pints of cider counts,' said Leah. 'You're in a good mood today. What's his name?'

'Ha bloody ha,' said Louisa. She shot Miranda a warning glance but her sister did not seem in the mood for point-scoring: rather, she was looking at her with an almost parental concern. The problem with Miranda was that she would never understand any relationship that wasn't exactly like her own.

Because she was no longer waiting for his call, it came. This time, her breezy tone was not an affectation.

'Is everything all right?' said Adam, 'You seem a bit distant.'

If by distant he meant that she wasn't begging to see more of him, he was right. It worked in a way that fake calm never did, because he invited her to come and watch him rehearse in the Shepherd's Bush studio the following day. Heavy with the opiates of satisfied curiosity and spiced carbohydrates, she stretched out on her bed. She was asleep within minutes.

29

Paul awoke with a jolt, remembered, disbelieved, then looked two inches to his left for confirmation of the truth. Louisa was still now but a couple of hours ago she had been everywhere at once. The thing he couldn't get over was the *movement*. Was that how it was supposed to be? It was the opposite of his rigid experience with Gemma. Not that that meant it had been good. The opposite of bad sex, he now knew, was just a different kind of bad sex. Of course it had been intensely pleasurable, at least for ten seconds, but he knew he hadn't performed well or even understood what was happening for much of it. He had come here because he had wanted to tell someone about Daniel; he had sought an ear and got a whole body.

His mouth was dry; he peered around the room for some water. It was lit only in patches by several old-fashioned, health-and-safety-contravening oil lamps that stood about on tables and ledges. He was pretty sure they had already been burning when she let him in. He could smell their faint petroleum odour and that sickening eggy gas smell, too. These were overlaid with the strange herbal scent that seemed to follow Louisa wherever she went. He saw no bottles or jugs of water, just books on every surface. There was a ledge stacked with them directly by his head. They weren't normal books like the ones he enjoyed; the shapes, sizes and covers were all wrong and they had titles like *Grow Your Own Drugs* and *A History of Women in the Garden.*

Throwing off at least two duvets and a slippery counterpane, he got out of bed. Immediately his skin goosefleshed. He made his way over to the pull-down table and felt its surface for a glass or bottle. There was a framed formal photograph of her with a girl who must be her sister, both of them wearing saris, and a dozen curling snapshots of two dark-eyed, curly-haired children were Blu-tacked to the peeling veneer walls. Still there was no water. Dozens of bottles lined the shelves but they were strange undrinkable potions, from large plastic containers to smaller ones with oily labels. Here was where the strange smell was at its sweetest.

At last, in the murky depths of the back of the caravan, he found a tinny little sink with a tap. He put his mouth underneath the tap to drink and misjudged: the water clattered noisily into the basin. Paul turned the tap off quickly, and looked over at Louisa. She didn't seem to have stirred. He tripped over a fat wormy pipe which supplied the gas fire that dominated this half of the van. Its surface was slightly warm but it gave out no heat.

Cold and exhaustion suddenly got the better of him and he slipped back under the covers. Louisa's body was a combination of spongy flesh and unyielding muscle and her skin was the softest thing he had ever touched. He wondered if she would want to do it again in the morning. The thought thrilled and terrified him. Despite his thirst, he felt a faint pressing in his bladder and knew he'd have to piss before he could fuck again. On the horns of this eternal dilemma, he went back to sleep.

Louisa heard the water attack the sink and felt Paul get back into bed but she played dead until his breathing became slow and even. What had she been *thinking*? She reflected on the men she had been with since leaving London: until now she had chosen her partners well, her unerring instinct for physically *simpatico* lovers only growing sharper with age. The men had had little in common but their sex, she had known brown skin and white skin, middle-aged flesh and young, although never this young. None had suspected that, when it all happened, she would close her eyes and pretend it was Adam on top of her, underneath her, behind her, inside her. Like the ritual, she knew that it was an absurd, almost dangerous compulsion, but she couldn't resist feeling close to him again. And anyway, it was the only way she could come.

The proxy lust she felt for Paul had been building for so long that it had not occurred to her that being with him would be less than perfect. She had been expecting the impossible, she saw that now; the resurrection of the dead. The first kiss had been promising but he had floundered as things progressed. When she had had Adam's likeness in her arms, she could open her eyes to the image but not close her other senses. Afterwards there had been a brittle silence in the room and the facts presented themselves to her like a list of criminal charges: he was young, he was vulnerable, he was inexperienced, perhaps to the point of virginity, she was old enough to be his mother, and though not his employer she had a duty of care to him that did not extend this far under any interpretation of the phrase. He was also the first man – the first *person* – she had allowed into her caravan, the first man in her home since Laurence and only the second since Adam, and in doing so she had put herself in a position of weakness. She should have hidden, never opened the door to him, but she had heard his voice and thought – what? That it was a sign? That it was fate? Inwardly she chastised herself for allowing her grief and a stupid romantic notion (and the drink) to get the better of her. It could not happen again.

All she could do at this stage was think of damage limitation strategies, but none were forthcoming.

Paul rolled over onto his back and, despite herself, something in Louisa stirred. He *was* beautiful, and ridiculously young – how long had it been since she had lain with a boy like this, smooth flesh with the skin over his abdomen as tight as a tambourine? The more she looked at him, the less like Adam he seemed. Crop the black hair that fell in his eyes even when he was asleep and she might never have noticed a resemblance in the first place.

Without his back story it was impossible to know the truth about him. How long had he known where she lived? Had he been to the van before? If so, this either made him touchingly sincere or horribly calculating. She forced herself to remember that no one at Kelstice had a clean past, although not everyone had their transgressions carefully documented in Demetra's files. How many days or weeks had he been keeping her secret? (Her secondary secret, of course, for no one knew about the primary one apart from the Other Man and he had his own reasons for keeping quiet.)

The next time she woke up the hands on her alarm clock glowed a pale green 6 a.m. It would not get light for another hour or so but she knew she would not go back to sleep; on a weekday, she would be up by now. She wrapped herself in her moon-and-stars coverlet, tiptoed to the washroom, pulled the door behind her with the softest of clicks. She had got used to the volume of the chemical toilet flush. Now, she heard it through her guest's ears. There was no way he could have slept through that.

He hadn't. He was sitting up as she came in, his hair having doubled in size in the night.

'Can I go to the toilet, please?' he said, like a five-year-old in class.

'Of course you can.'

He cupped his hands over his groin and sidled into the washroom without meeting her eye. She heard him splashing about with soap and water and wondered if he was using her toothbrush. When he came back, he took a mincing little run at the bed before hiding himself under the covers. This time he did look at her, as though he was waiting for her to tell him what to do. It was obvious that she was going to have to steer this situation and she had absolutely no idea how to begin. To buy herself thinking time, she fell back on the time-honoured English strategy for alleviating social excruciation.

'Um. Would you like a cup of tea?' she said.

'Yes please.'

She busied herself about the small ceremony, glad of the engulfing steam and the roar of the boiling water.

'How do you take it?'

'Milk and two sugars, please.'

'Oh. I haven't got any sugar, how awkward.'

She thought that his burst of laughter surprised him as much as her. 'What's funny?'

'Well. You've woken up with one of your staff. Lack of sugar isn't the awkward bit.'

She joined in his laughter and then looked at the bed. 'Do you mind if I . . .?'

'It's your bed,' he said, but threw back the covers proprietorially. She got in but didn't take her blanket off and they drank their tea in self-consciously chaste companionship.

'I'm sorry,' they both said at the same time. She was taken back to their first meeting at the top of the knoll; then, as now, it had been all mutual apologies and brittle tension.

'What for?' he asked.

'Jumping on you like that,' she said. 'I didn't really give you much choice in the matter.'

'I'm not,' he said, blushing. 'I *am* sorry that I crept up on you, though.'

'So how long have you known about my home?' How could she make him see that it was a secret without making herself desperately defenceless? Paul did not seem to know how heavily the balance of power was weighted in his favour. An older man would have intuited it in a second. A certain kind of man would have exploited it.

'A few weeks, maybe a month. Although I didn't know you were the one living here until you gave me a lift the other night. I saw the cans in the car. Doesn't the smell give you a headache?'

'No. Does it you?'

'Dunno. Could be the booze. Doesn't it get claustrophobic?'

'It probably would if I worked in an office or a shop,' said Louisa. 'Or if I lived in a city. But after a day out in the elements I just want to feel . . . enclosed.' She supposed that the truth was as good a policy as any. 'I'm not doing anything illegal.'

'You're paying Ingram for the electricity, are you?' he said, but he was smiling.

'I like to think of it as in lieu of overtime pay,' she answered, then grew serious again. 'I barely use it. This isn't even Kelstice land. I lease it from the farmer for a peppercorn rent. I paid him up for three years. I don't see him from one month to the next. Listen, Paul. I've never brought anyone connected to the Lodge here, and I'd appreciate it—'

'But the others must have asked where you live?'

'Not everyone's as curious as you. Look, I'd really—'

'Yeah, all right, you don't want me to tell anyone. It's OK, I get it.' He looked her in the eye, unguarded. She was surprised to find she trusted him. It was so long since she had trusted anyone that it took her a few seconds to identify the feeling.

'I'm not being funny,' he said, after a while, 'but are you on some kind of community service as well?' She would have laughed if it hadn't been so dangerously parallel to the truth. She bought time with a question of her own.

'Why do you ask?' None of the young people had ever asked her that question before either. In that self-absorbed way teenagers have, it never occurred to any of them that she could have her own grisly history.

'It's just that I'm on, like, minimum wage and even *I* can afford a room in a house.'

She did laugh then. 'I'm not here because I have to be,' she said. 'It's my choice. No one goes into heritage management for the fabulous wealth but I do OK. I'll tell you another secret – one more can't hurt – I'm saving up, I have been for years. I'd like a garden of my own, not just to restore and then move on, but to live in forever. A little cottage garden or something like that. Something I can design myself, be really creative, not just recreate something from history. One day somewhere will come on the market and I'll be able to afford it outright.' She didn't mention the more prosaic reason her savings were gathering dust in a low-return, instant-access account – insurance, escape, blackmail. 'Everyone should have a grand plan. What do you want to be when you—' She had been going to say 'grow up' ... '—after this?' she tailed off, but the unsaid words hung in the air as though she'd written them on a blackboard.

'I wouldn't call it a grand plan,' he said. 'But I know what I want to do. I want to be a teacher.'

'Are you going to university?'

'I was going to,' he said. 'And I will, after . . .' He shrugged. 'Everything's kind of on hold at the moment.' He was evidently referring to the events that had brought him to Kelstice in the first place. She could no more guess his past than he could divine hers. What could this diffident, innocent young man have done? Who were they sheltering him from? He yawned and burrowed under the covers; a freezing foot brushed against her thigh. At her yelp, he retracted it.

'Oh God, sorry.' His mortification at this trespass was touching. 'I'll go.'

'Stay.' The word was out before she had time to consider it, and she was surprised to find it was the right one. What harm could it do to cling a little longer to the fantasy of Adam? The boy in her bed was clumsy and shy but he was warm and willing and there was comfort, if nothing else, to be derived from his body. 'Stay,' she repeated.

His hand was as cold as his foot, but she didn't flinch when his fingers brushed the dip of her waist. He asked the question with a tentative look and she answered it by rolling her body over his. She kept her eyes open.

30

One dull, drizzly Friday afternoon, Carl arrived home with such force and speed that for a moment Paul wondered whether he had broken his own front door down. One side of his face was an empurpled bulge, much like Paul's had been whenever it had made swift connection with a hard surface. The eye that he could still open was wide and white in panic.

'Where's Daniel?' he said, a post-exertion wheeze to his voice.

'He's taken Diesel out for a crap,' said Paul, noticing that Carl was bare-chested underneath his jacket.

'Listen, get rid of this for me, quick.' He handed Paul a supermarket carrier bag containing what looked like clothing but felt heavier, as though weighted with a single stone.

'What is it?' said Paul, pulling open the bag for a closer look. Carl snatched it back, folded it over itself, thrust it into Paul's armpit.

'Just do it, OK? Now!'

Paul took the bag and ran out of the front door. Briefly he wondered about trying to find Daniel but the roared instructions had left no room for curiosity detours. He kept going until he reached the riverbank. The urgency of Carl's command propelled him through the subway that had been the scene of his childhood beatings. A train thundered overhead. With swollen lungs he reached the footpath on the side of the river. There did not appear to be anyone else around, no kids, not a single buggy-pusher or dog-walker. He turned a full circle to cover his back. To his left the arachnid hoists of the dock hid the horizon; the yuppie flats on the Kent side of the river and the bridge were silhouettes in the mist. His only witness was a single tug on the water. It was high tide, and the rocky black beach was submerged. He drew back his arm and bowled the bundle into the water, hoping it would travel far enough for the current to drag it to sea. Its contents came loose as it flew. The bag blew away on the breeze, and the bloodstained T-shirt caught a breeze and floated gently for a few seconds but the knife fell straight and swift, blade down, into the Thames, piercing the brown foam. His legs felt wobbly, as though he'd run a marathon rather than a mile.

He was afraid of Carl and afraid to be involved with him. It was the first time he had seen, let alone disposed of, evidence of Carl's life outside the house. At home they only ever got to see the affectionate, loyal side of him but he remembered that the man had been a soldier before he was a father. Paul wondered how many people he had killed, not just during his time in the forces. It was a long while before he felt confident enough to return to the house. When he did, Carl was showing a couple of uniformed policemen out of the front door with a sardonic flourish, a cocky smile and the words, 'Told you you wouldn't find nothing, didn't I?'

Daniel was eating pizza in front of the Discovery Channel, picking little scraps of something off the top and feeding them to the dog.

'They've put fucking anchovies on it, man,' he said, as though nothing out of the ordinary had happened. Carl opened three tins of beer and shared them out. Before Paul had a chance to drink, he was pulled into an embrace that resembled a headlock Carl might use to throw punters down the stairs at a nightclub.

'You're a good boy, you are, Paul. Loyalty, that's what it's about . . . I've got two sons now. You just think of me as a second father.' Paul would have physically reeled from the insult if he hadn't been so aware of the frailty of his neck compared to Carl's arm. How dare this thug compare himself to his own gentle, funny, dreamy father? 'There's a home for you with us for as long as you want it, isn't there, Daniel?'

Daniel nodded. The dead weight that always seemed to be pressing down on Paul's chest these days suddenly doubled, as though Carl had just sat his substantial form down beside his son. It was getting harder and harder to breathe.

31

Shepherd's Bush was two postcodes away and another country. Louisa looked out of the bus window at the market where the nearest stall sold three pairs of vast knickers for 50p. Strange smells and sounds boomed from the shops. Life here seemed to be lived on the street, and she was conscious of her white skin and her alternative clothes and above all of the *A–Z* that she clutched in her hand, marking her out as a visitor. She turned off the Uxbridge Road and into a maze of side streets lined with Victorian houses, at first imposing townhouses but seeming to lose a storey at each corner until she got to Cedar Avenue. The road was treeless despite its name and comprised two mean low terraces, most of which were pebbledashed, stone-clad or rendered. Number ten had a pockmarked surface, aluminium doors and windows that seemed loose in their rotting wooden frames. She experienced the same tender compassion she had felt when she found out about his cleaning job: no wonder he had wanted to keep her away. She vowed not to let her disgust show, no matter how awful it turned out to be inside. But for now she wasn't going into the main house; she let herself down the side alleyway, picking her way through overgrown tyre tracks and squeezing past smelly metal dustbins as she followed the music that she could hear coming from the . . .

Well, it was a garage. They could call it the studio all they liked, but the ugly little prefab with its glassless windows was a garage. Inside the . . . would she *ever* be able to bring herself to call it the studio? . . . the concrete floor still bore the oil-stains of a car, and a faint smell of petrol lingered.

They were mid-song and there was no welcome hello, just a nodded acknowledgement of her presence from Adam and a mouthed invitation from Angie to make herself at home. The place was simultaneously damp and dusty and there was nowhere for her to sit but an old-fashioned, high-backed armchair with the seat cushion missing. It was dark, too: the only light came from an industrial-looking spotlight without a stand that had *Hammersmith Odeon* stencilled onto it with thin white paint. They kept trying to balance it on its side to light the stage, but it just rolled back in its round shell. In the end they left it lying on its back so that it threw up light like a volcano, meaning that only the ceiling – corrugated iron, thin wooden rafters – was illuminated, and the band played in darkness.

Adam had been gallingly right: she hadn't been missing much. Louisa had imagined that it would be like a private show just for her but they hadn't played a single song she knew. Instead they were working through new tunes in a stop-start fashion, each interval punctuated by technical disputes that meant nothing to Louisa. Adam and Ciaran were having an intense disagreement about mixes and monitors: Adam thought that Ciaran was trying to lose his voice and Ciaran insisted, with diminishing patience, that that was the point of this track, that the vocals were buried in feedback. Ben smirked, using the downtime to paint his nails black. Angie interjected where she could, playing devil's advocate, but it was clear that the argument was one-sided. Adam's will was stronger than the rest of them combined, which was as it should be, Louisa thought; without him, what were they? A songwriter and a couple of session musicians. Ciaran seemed physically to diminish as Adam lambasted him. His slight frame was lost in his greatcoat with its breastplate of badges. He's softer than he looks behind that sloganeering, thought Louisa, and she wondered if his defensive manner was overcompensating for shyness. He still hadn't made eye contact with her.

'All right!' Ciaran threw up his arms. 'Have it your way. Again.'

She wondered if the antipathy and tension between singer and composer was necessary for their creative process, and whether the music would have been as good if they'd actually liked each other.

At the foot of the armchair was a pond of paper scraps, flyers and tickets, fanzines and photographs. There were tickets from gigs dating back over a year, and a photograph of the band on a fire escape. The other three were dressed in black while Adam wore a white vest and white jeans which ought to have made him look embarrassingly mainstream but which he managed to subvert. Louisa could not believe that such precious records of the band's early months were lying around so casually; this collection was crying out to be ordered and saved in a scrapbook. If they wouldn't get round to it, she would: it would be a way of showing them she was on their side, and perhaps it would encourage them to let her in. One of the girls at the market sold beautiful Indian notebooks where the paper was handmade and the covers were black velvet brocade. She had often browsed the stall, liking the feel of the rough, pulpy paper underneath her fingers, but never known what she might fill the books with. Now she had finally found contents worthy of their pages. It would be something for Adam to show his children: *their* children, she let herself think. She smoothed the pieces of paper out, squared them off and slipped them into her Bartram's where they would be pressed flat. She also found a stack of videotapes of live performances; she remembered Ben saying that they needed someone with a reel-to-reel recorder to make them into one continuous showreel. She could do that too, they had a tape-to-tape VHS player in their sitting room. There was just about room for the tapes in her duffel bag.

Adam's pager started to bleep, slowly at first and then with increasing rapidity and insistence.

'Oh, Adam, how many times have we asked you to turn that thing off during rehearsal?' pleaded Ciaran. Adam ignored him and pretended to tune his bass. His mouth creased at the corners; he was enjoying Ciaran's rising annoyance. Eventually Ben picked it up. He looked at the message, then at Adam, and said, '*Her*?'

The constricting feeling in Louisa's belly was back, as though it had never been away. It was unsettling how near the surface the old suspicions were. She studied Adam for signs of guilt and saw only that his features went blank.

Ciaran's reserves of patience were finally exhausted. 'Can you please tell the members of your harem to leave you alone during rehearsal?' he snapped, as though Louisa wasn't there, or perhaps because she was.

Adam walked, with a slowness that must have been deliberate, to the window ledge where his pager rested. He moved nearer to the spotlight, the better to read the message, and when he did, he blinked and swallowed.

'What is it today?' said Ciaran. 'Got someone pregnant again? Given someone the clap?'

'Fuck off,' said Adam. From his jacket pocket he retrieved a bright green Phonecard and flexed it once or twice as though deciding whether to use it.

'What's wrong, Adam?' said Louisa from her place in the shadows.

He answered without looking up at her. 'I'll be back in a bit.' Louisa stood up, but he said, 'I'll be quicker on my own.'

Angie and Ben sent a couple of nervously sympathetic glances in her direction but did not speak to her, which was a good thing: her voice would have broken if she'd had to reply. Louisa tucked her knees under her chin and listened to the others twiddle about with a riff as though nothing was wrong. It seemed like hours before Adam came back. When he did, he looked like his own ghost, his complexion the colour of granite. He was more inscrutable than ever but it wasn't the contrived deadpan of before. It was enough for even Ben to break through the irony barrier.

'Jesus, Adam, what's happened?'

'Nothing,' he said into the microphone, then withdrew from it as though surprised. 'Nothing important, anyway,' he repeated in an unamplified voice. 'My dad died this morning.'

Louisa stood up. All three band members held out their arms to him, exchanged matching horrified looks and then dropped them.

'Adam, we don't have to carry on if . . .' began Ciaran, his voice saturated with pity and something else – guilt for the way he had spoken to him earlier, no doubt. Adam looked at him so fiercely that for a moment Louisa was genuinely worried he was going to hit him, and Ciaran took a step back.

'I told you, nothing to worry about,' said Adam. 'I just want to sing. Come on. Where were we? We haven't got all day.' And he started to sing in a voice that never wavered once. If you closed your eyes you would never suspect anything had happened; he was note perfect. It was only if you looked at his face and saw that terrible blank expression that you would know something was wrong.

They did not go to his room afterwards; he wanted to go back to the mews. It gratified her that he needed her at such a heightened time. 'When's the funeral?' she said. 'Do you want me to come with you?'

'It doesn't matter, I'm not going.'

'Oh, *Adam*.'

'Why are you making such a fuss? I haven't seen him for four years, I wasn't ever going to see him again, so what's changed since this morning?'

Louisa had a sudden vision of herself, Miranda and Leah at her father's funeral, all dressed in black and crying behind veils. Tears brewed at the thought and she hoped it wasn't a premonition. Elvira knew a woman like that, who foresaw deaths. Maybe she was becoming psychic.

'But won't you want to be there for your mum? She'll *need* you. You can have her back in your life again, with him out of the way.'

'She made her choice between me and him years ago,' said Adam. 'She can go to hell as far as I'm concerned. Or heaven. Don't look like that, she'll be fine. I'm sure he's saving her a seat.'

32

He made his phone calls in the secret locations from which he used to phone Emily, the wheelie bin port or the empty lock-up with the door hanging off. It was a long time since she had accepted a call from him and he was aware that he was chasing her out of habit now. Even if he could engineer a reconciliation, the relationship would never be as pure and perfect as it had been before he had gone with Gemma. Daniel had seen to that. The only benefit was that without Emily he was free to go wherever he liked. His new secret phone calls were to the Clearing people, the service that matched leftover university places with those who hadn't got the grades to go to their first choice of college, or people like him who were trying to get a place at the last minute. They told him that there was little they could do without his results but sent him some preliminary paperwork which he passed off as a bank statement when Daniel asked why he was suddenly getting so much post.

There were only weeks until the start of the university term. In the meantime, he longed to get away, but where could he go? He was the only child of only children. His only surviving grandparent, his Nanna Seaforth, had followed her second husband to Australia where, according to Natalie, she drank all day and sunbathed until her skin looked like Spam, bright pink and mottled. Contact with her had petered out a couple of years ago. He had only his mother, but she was in no fit state to host him; the last time he had called, Troy had picked up the phone and filled in the gaps between her chirpy assurances that everything was going well. The latest drugs she was taking were making her 'mad, hairy and fat', said Troy, 'all crying and slamming doors'.

Paul knew that the sanctuary he craved would not be found with his mother. Troy was still out of work, as Natalie would not let him do anything that involved chemicals and confined spaces, and his skills were almost impossible to apply within those restrictions. Paul took comfort at least from the fact that Troy must love his mother very, very much to go through all this for her. Briefly he toyed with the idea of going inter-railing or taking himself to Ibiza for the summer, but pitching up in a strange place solo and having to seek out company was not his style. He told himself there was no point making a dent in his savings when university would give him all the new experiences he needed. He had nearly £3,000 stashed in the building society now, surely enough to live off for a year, and in the time he had left he could put away another five or six hundred.

He tried not to think about what Daniel would do without him. At a level of almost inaccessible depth, he still felt guilty about abandoning him. With the end in sight, his boiling anger had begun gently to recede. It was always there, but Paul turned it down to a manageable simmer. Daniel had, after all, been his protector for five years and a threat for a matter of weeks. They continued to work at night, defiling industrial estates and street furniture along the estuary and into the Essex countryside. On the rare occasions Daniel noticed Paul's silence he put it down to the loss of Emily with platitudes like 'She just wasn't the right one for you, mate.' Paul concentrated on work and money, taking extra care now that his dream of becoming a teacher was a step closer.

* * *

'We're expanding into lead,' said Daniel, which made Paul think of frozen water in a pipe.

'Oh?'

'The problem with lead is that you need a team to make it worth your while. We're selling ourselves short taking only what we can carry. With two men on the roof and one on the ground we can double the amount we take, easy.' There was a knock on the door. 'That'll be him now.'

Through the peephole Paul saw a thin face and a torch of hair. '*Him*?' he whispered, in incredulity. 'I haven't seen him since . . .' The memory of the party still smarted.

'I'd forgotten he even existed, to be honest. He was in the Warrant Officer the other lunchtime with my dad. He's working the door at Boulevard with him.'

Boulevard was the biggest nightclub on Southend seafront; Carl had recently started the notorious Saturday night shift. Its bouncers were legendarily corrupt and violent. No careers officer could have made a better match.

'I think he's calmed down a bit since school. And my dad seems to think he's all right, so . . . let's call it a trial. If he doesn't fuck it up, we'll bring him in.'

Hash strode into the house on long, wiry legs. He hadn't filled out much since school but he seemed to have condensed, packing more muscle onto a slim frame than most men twice his bulk carried. Diesel growled and Paul gave him an appreciative pat.

'It's a proper bloke's house, this,' he said, eyeing the drinks fridge. 'Your dad not in?'

'He's working,' said Daniel. 'And so are we. Come on, let's go.'

They stopped off at the scrapyard to offload the previous night's spoils, a wrought-iron gate they'd found propped against a wall. It was eleven o'clock at night but Gavin was still there, mug in hand, greeting them as casually as if it were the middle of the afternoon. Paul wondered if he ever went home. It was quite easy to imagine him sleeping in one of the old bathtubs, warmed by the furnace.

'Nice,' said Gavin. 'I can sell this on as architectural salvage. I've got a woman from Brentwood wants some Victorian chimney pots, if you ever see any lying around.'

Hash introduced himself to Gavin by name, something Daniel still hadn't done despite the frequency of their visits. He asked Gavin what else he was in the market for in a loud, obvious sort of way. He'd missed the point about Gavin, that you never did anything directly, that it was all about the subtleties.

'These boys'll tell you what you need to know,' said Gavin. When Hash's back was turned he mouthed to Daniel, 'Where'd you get him from?'

'That place was brilliant,' said Hash, when they were back on the road. 'How d'you know about it?'

'My dad put me onto it,' said Daniel.

'Your dad's well cool,' said Hash. 'If I had one I'd want him to be just like yours.'

Hash's fatherless family were infamous even by Grays Reach standards. As well as Hash, his formidable mother had half a dozen daughters, all of whom had inherited her red hair, the genes of their various fathers evidently in timid recession.

'Is he seeing anyone? Because my mum—'

'Hash, I'm trying to concentrate on driving.'

'Oh, OK.'

White lines flickered in Paul's peripheral vision as Daniel recounted his rules of theft to Hash. He regurgitated Paul's own imperatives about road signs and added some that adhered to his own strange and arbitrary moral code; Catholic churches, for example, were fair game because the Pope was a Nazi and all the bishops were paedos but Church of England ones were off limits. Hash listened with rapt respect.

'Is that for real, that stuff about Catholics?' he said. A mad wish rose within Paul that Hash could take over his job as Daniel's reader. He still had time to train a replacement before his flight to university.

'Swear to God,' said Daniel. 'I read all about it.' Paul felt hope implode. Of course Daniel had picked up the information the same way he learned everything else, from a television documentary. For Hash to become part of their inner circle of petty theft he would have to know the truth about Daniel's illiteracy. Daniel himself would never volunteer that information and for Paul to do so was out of the question.

'Why don't you just get a sat nav?' said Hash. 'Save all this map reading.'

'It's Paul's job,' said Daniel. 'He likes doing it.'

They went through a narrow Victorian arch that cut through the high embankment of a train tunnel. There would only have been room for one car at a time, the signs with the red arrows telling them that they had priority over oncoming traffic. On the other side of the bridge they came to a stop. Paul peered into the darkness; there was nothing but a steep bank. Daniel's eyes were raised to the heavens, their whites glistening as his pupils retreated almost up and under his lids, and he was smiling. Paul's own eyes climbed up to where an overhead wire scored the navy sky. There was a greenish glow on a pole that looked like a traffic light, but what would a traffic light be doing on a—

'Oh, no,' said Paul. 'Oh, mate, no.'

A few weeks back, Gavin had mentioned that railway signal boxes were a great source of copper wiring if you were brave enough to go and get it. Paul had googled it and learned that a boy their own age had suffered seventy per cent electric burns after trying something similar in the north. He had refused to have anything to do with it.

'Oh *yes*,' said Daniel.

Without warning, Hash took the slope at a run, letting out a long whoop like a football cheer.

'Shut up, Hash,' said the other two in unison. It wasn't until faced with Hash's amateurishness that Paul realised how professional he had become. He followed them over the fence. The track itself was a shimmering, humming strip of steel. It was two o'clock in the morning now. Paul knew that the last train for Shoeburyness had left Fenchurch Street a good two hours ago, and the last train from the coast to London earlier than that, but it was still unnerving. There was a yellow sign warning *Danger of Death* and picturing a man with a lightning bolt running through his body. You didn't have to be literate to know what that meant but he read it aloud anyway for Hash's benefit as well as Daniel's; the redhead was hopping from foot to foot like an excited child. Come to think of it, it wouldn't be any great loss if Hash was zapped out of existence. Paul had a pleasant vision of Hash experiencing a violent but (crucially) bloodless death, his lanky body thrown into the air by a rogue arc of electric current.

'Danger of death my arse,' said Daniel. 'That's the tracks. We're only nicking a bit of signalling wire. It's not like we're stealing the brakes or anything. Just a few commuters a little bit late for their office jobs. They'll probably be *grateful*. They'll probably go home and go down the pub.'

'Come on, Paul,' said Hash. 'Play with the big boys.'

Paul felt the familiar surrender of his own will to Daniel's and hoped that Hash didn't think it was because of anything he'd said. He held the torch while Daniel jemmied open the signal box door. Even Hash must have been able to see that Daniel didn't know what he was doing; he pulled at the box's multicoloured intestines with no clear intent. Paul felt a very faint vibration beneath his legs. Seconds later a black engine yanked past a string of windowless carriages, like a ghost train ferrying the dead, so close and so fast that it made their hair fly and their ears ring. All three of them lost their nerve and their footing at the same time and went rolling down the hill of the embankment, arms and legs colliding, giving Paul as sure a hiding as if he had been beaten with an iron bar.

'I can't believe we're leaving empty-handed,' whinged Hash, when they were back on the road.

'One of the most important things about this business is knowing when to call it a night,' Daniel told him, his voice heavy with condescension. 'My father taught me that.'

'Your dad's well cool,' said Hash again. His tumble hadn't knocked any of the nervous energy out of him. He was making everyone tense. On the outskirts of Grays Reach, they pulled up on the kerb outside a service station with an all-night garage and sent Hash in to get some crisps and sweets for when they got back.

'Is he coming back to ours, then?' said Paul.

'Is he fuck,' said Daniel. 'I'm waiting till he's in the shop and then I'm gonna leave him here.'

But Hash didn't make it into the shop. He paused by the driver door of an empty, dark grey Peugeot, showroom-shiny, and tried the handle. Paul watched in sickened fascination as he opened it up and grabbed something from inside, then turned and ran back to the boys' Volvo, shouting 'Go, go, go!' like something from a TV show. The street revolved around them as Daniel executed a powerful three-point turn; he screeched away from the petrol station at speed that made Paul feel he'd left his internal organs behind.

'Got you a sat nav, mate,' said Hash.

'I know, but there?' said Daniel. Paul could tell he was only just managing to keep a lid on his anger. 'That's my local garage! You don't shit on your own doorstep!'

'It's yours,' said Hash, but the swagger was gone from his voice. He handed the little black box with its wire tail to Paul. 'We can use it next time we go out.'

'Next time? I tell you what. Don't call us, Hash, we'll call you.'

Finally Hash was silent. When they got back to Grays Reach, he dragged his feet across the courtyard and disappeared into a tunnel between two houses. Paul wondered if he knew the extent to which he'd blown it, for both of them.

Up in bed, Paul tried to read but the words on the page seemed crooked and close, like Chinese characters. He was still awake when Daniel came up. Diesel jumped off Paul's duvet and onto Daniel's.

'He's a fucking liability. That thing with the sat nav, what was that all about? He's like a little kid.'

'I dunno,' said Paul. 'Couldn't you, like, train him up or something? What if I can't come out one night?'

'Why, where are you going?' Paul sensed Daniel sit up in bed.

'Nowhere, nowhere. But what if you want to drive out, not for work, just to see a girl or something. You don't want me everywhere you go.'

'Don't I?' said Daniel. Is it because he wants me with him, or because when I'm with him, he knows where I am? thought Paul.

'You can always use that sat nav,' suggested Paul.

'I can't programme it, can I, you prick?' said Daniel in triumph as well as anger.

'I didn't think. I'm sorry, Daniel.'

'It's OK,' said Daniel, laying a hand on Paul's arm like a pardoning priest. He did not remove it and Paul listened to the slowing breath and felt the deadening of the weight until he was sure that Daniel was asleep. Only then did he pick up the hand by the wrist and place it on Daniel's bare chest. He fancied that he could still feel it: every time he was about to drop off to sleep, he was jolted awake by a phantom touch, but every time he looked over to check, all of Daniel's limbs were where they should be.

Paul resigned himself to another sleepless night. The only reason the situation was tolerable, the only reason he had not had some kind of nervous breakdown, was that an end was in sight. Soon he would be at university, off to start a new life for himself. He had nightmares that night about being imprisoned in a cage made of lead and gilded with copper and aluminium.

33

November 2009

He learned to tolerate the idiosyncrasies of life in her caravan. Aware that he was essentially her guest, he tried to carry his weight, taking over the heavier jobs. Maintenance of the three panels on the side of the caravan, the ones that opened to reveal the electricity socket, the gas supply and the tank for the chemical toilet, became his responsibility. The gas was easily changed, especially now she had switched to an odourless kind, the chemical toilet was only gross the first time, but the electricity was a perennial problem, forever coming unstuck at the mains. Reconnecting it meant a fifteen-minute traipse back to the cabins, and he always forgot to pull down the trip switch that cut the electricity off; if you reconnected without pulling the trip, the power surge blew the fuses in the light and the kettle, and you had to go back to the cabins and reconnect it again. He made a big fuss about it, but he didn't really mind. It felt reassuringly masculine. These were the kinds of jobs that his father hadn't let his mother do.

Louisa never stopped growing things. It was as though she had to have her fingers in the earth to function. As well as working in the garden all day, they worked at weekends in the tiny vegetable plot alongside her caravan, pulling up carrots and swedes and leeks that she threw into a slow cooker and made into soups and stews.

'It's funny, I never thought about growing stuff before,' he said. 'You just get used to seeing everything come out of a packet.'

'I don't suppose I gave it much thought when I was your age either. I was a real city girl. I'd have concreted over every blade of grass in the country if I could have.'

'But you hate concrete! You said that people who pave over their front gardens should go to prison.'

She laughed. 'Ah, but that's me *now*. I told you, I wasn't like that when I was younger. Well. There was one garden I loved . . . but even that was planted in concrete.'

He wondered what had happened to change the way she thought. Spending time with Louisa was changing the way he looked at everything; it was as though he saw the earth from the ground up, rather than the sky down, for the first time. He wondered who had done the same for her, what the experience had been that had turned the teenage Louisa into the woman he knew, and he wondered if it was to do with the way there sometimes seemed to be a screen of glass between them.

He finally admitted to destroying her rambling rose one day when he found her tracing its dying tendrils with a look of sorrow on her face. Now that the wild flowers around its base had died he could see the full extent of the damage he had caused. The plant had been almost completely severed just above the root. Its naked stems, which should have remained green all year round, were so dark brown they were almost black. She snapped off a brittle shoot; it was hollow and dry. Thorns fell off it like needles from an old Christmas tree.

'It's had it,' she said.

'I'm sorry, that was me,' he said. 'I broke it when I climbed the wall, the first time I came here. Don't worry, I'll plant a new one for you.'

'That's sweet, but it won't work,' she said. 'The soil will be rose-sick.'

'What's that?'

'When a new rose is planted on the same spot as an old one, you get a sick rose; it doesn't bloom and it'll probably die. No one really knows why, but it's not worth replanting. I've seen it happen lots of times.'

'It makes sense, in a way,' he said. 'You can't expect something that beautiful to bloom twice.'

'Yes, I suppose so,' she said. A change came over her face, as though something obvious had finally dawned on her. 'I never thought of it like that.'

Paul didn't buy her a new rambling rose, but he did buy her a rosewood chess set whose board was carved with an intricate floral pattern that he thought she would like. It was nothing special, only a charity shop find – he had checked his bank balance at the building society and been horrified at the crater his new lifestyle had blown in his savings – but he had never bought a present for a woman who wasn't his mother before, not even Emily, and he was nervous about giving it to her. The moment he eventually picked was a darkening weekend afternoon. They were in bed together, the faltering electric bulb and the blinking oil lamps bathing them in a flickering cinefilm light.

'I got you a present,' he said, drawing the package out of his bag. 'To say sorry about your rose.'

She unwrapped it and ran her fingers over its carved surface like someone reading Braille.

'It's beautiful, I love it,' she said. 'But I don't know how to play.'

He was shocked. 'What was the point of your posh school if they didn't teach you to play chess? You'll be telling me you didn't walk around with books on your head next.' She wrinkled her nose at him. 'I'm only teasing, it'll be nice for me to teach you something for a change. Not that I've played against anything other than a computer for years.'

Wrapped in blankets and throws, they sat cross-legged opposite each other and balanced the chessboard on their knees. He instructed her carefully, enjoying the process of handing down information and the flush that crept over her lips while she was concentrating. For the first few games he tried to lose and won, but as she got the hang of it, the challenge became genuine.

'Checkmate,' she said suddenly, childishly pleased with herself. 'I'm right, aren't I?'

Paul studied the black pieces ringfencing his white king.

'Bloody hell, you are as well,' he said. She leaned across, her bare arm gleaming, and deposed his monarch with a flick of her fingertip.

'Do you forgive me? 'Yes,' he said.

'Trusting fool,' she smiled. He traced a line from her wrist to her neck, let his hand cup her chin.

'I'd forgive you anything,' he said, without really knowing where the words had come from. She didn't move her lips, but her smile dimmed somehow.

'You don't know what you're saying,' she said. He felt the mood shift. The look in her eyes mystified, excited and frightened him. He had clearly hit a nerve, although he didn't know how or why; but he did know, with sudden but absolute certainty, that she was wrong. He meant it, he meant it twice, the words were doubly freighted with meaning.

By pre-empting forgiveness on his own part he was paving the way for the terrible confession he had yet to make to her, and he also wanted to show her what she meant to him.

'I mean it,' he said, his other hand reaching out to thumb the petal-soft skin on the inside of her elbow. Louisa flushed, took both of his hands and held them in her lap.

'Sweet boy,' she said, pushing his hair away from his brow and putting her thumb on his lower lip. Tell her now, whispered a voice inside his head, look at her, she'll understand, but he lost his nerve and resorted to humour.

'Who are you calling a boy?' he said, pulling her free hand underneath the chessboard and into his lap. She smiled and took his cue; he wondered if he would ever take for granted the other things she could do to him and the things he was allowed to do to her. The chessboard and all the pieces were thrown off the bed. Kings and queens, knights and bishops, rooks and pawns all rolled across the floor, a scattered court.

34

December 2009

The diggers arrived, navy blue machines that perched on the edge of the car-park plot like giant insects. Ingram gathered everyone together and made a big announcement about the power of Louisa's cajoling, and how it boded well for the grant application. Paul felt a surge of something warm and sweet when Ingram said her name and identified it as pride. He winked at her across the sea of hardcore and mud that divided them and, after a brief glance around to check that no one was looking in her direction, she made a suggestive gesture, her tongue probing the inside of her cheek, then resumed her previous expression of cherubic innocence. Paul let out a shocked, delighted laugh that he had to cover up with a cough.

There was a surreal interlude while everyone stood before the diggers in admiration, like a bunch of Edwardians oohing and aahing over a motorcar. 'Isn't it thrilling?' said Demetra, who was wrapped in fuzzy, sludge-coloured wool.

It was the first time he had seen her for weeks; he had been waiting for an opportunity to talk to her since Carl's phone call had come, but it had to sound casual in order not to raise the alarm, so he couldn't have made an appointment.

'Demetra, does anyone apart from you have access to my file?' he asked.

The skin between her eyebrows folded into a column of concern. 'Of course not. Why would you think that?'

'I was just wondering if anyone could find out about me, why I'm here ... contact details for people at home. Where I'm living now, that kind of thing.'

'The whole point of you being here is that your past stays in your past,' she said. 'I don't even keep the notes here, they're all filed at home. Literally no one but me has seen them.'

'Not even Ingram?' he said, although he didn't seriously suspect Ingram of anything.

'Absolutely not. What's this all about, Paul? Do you think there's been some kind of breach of security?'

'No, not really. I was just wondering. You know, with the trial coming up and everything.'

'I haven't forgotten about that, you know. Christine's going to put you in touch with the Witness Service people, they'll take the edge off it all for you. But that's not till next year. I'd put it to the back of your mind for now, if you could. Oh, look, Nathaniel's starting!'

Only Nathaniel was allowed to operate the diggers, on the grounds of age and responsibility, although he was more accustomed to using seed dibbers and fingertips than powerful machinery. Dilan, who had extensive experience of mastering the dashboards and controls of strange vehicles in seconds, would have been the better choice (he had begged Ingram to let him behind the wheel, but to no avail). There was good-natured catcalling as Nathaniel swung the machine's jaw around so quickly that for a second it looked as though the whole vehicle would topple into the mud.

Within an hour it was plain that this new machine could achieve in a day what usually took them months to accomplish. Nathaniel laid waste to an acre of sycamore stumps, clearing the land all the way to New Wood, and turned his attention to the remaining knotweed that grew eight feet high behind the gatehouse. Once the vegetation was razed, it became apparent that sections of the site had been used as a dumping ground

by local fly-tippers for months or even years. The wildings
had been hiding everything from old mattresses to domestic
bin bags.

'What is *wrong* with people?' said Ingram. 'There's a
perfectly good civic amenity centre on the Kelstice road.
Surely it's more trouble to throw all this over our wall?'
He instructed Paul and Ross to take it to the tip, although
he didn't help them to load the festering contents into the
back of the truck. Then there was a scrape and a crunch as
the jaws of Nathaniel's machine closed over metal. He left
the cabin and jumped down to the jumble of tubing. Paul
was close behind him and instantly recognised it as lead. It
wasn't that old, it had no patina, so it must have been recently
dumped. Now it was Paul's turn to wonder what was wrong
with people. He saw not litter or vandalism but a couple of
hundred quid jutting from the brambles. Daniel would have
made the 'Kerching!' sound of a cash register. A bold, stupid
idea came to him and he was glad that Ross would be with
him to stop him acting on it.

'I wonder who dumped this?' he said.

'What is this, *Time Team*?' snapped Ingram. 'It's just a pile
of old metal, dear, where my nice gravel car park ought to be.
Shift it, someone, will you?' And then, as though he hadn't
been the one who had called them away from their jobs in
the first place: 'It's a one-man job. I don't want all of you
disappearing for the day. There's a lot to do.'

Paul wanted someone else to volunteer, to save him, but
no one was going to fight him for the task of single-handedly
disposing of scrap metal. His morning with Louisa had left
him feeling invincible and reckless, and some crazy force
within him spoke on his behalf. 'I'll do it,' he heard himself
say. On the way out he said to Ross, 'Listen, the right-hand
wipers have gone on the truck. I don't think it's legal to drive
with them like this, and if it starts raining I'm fucked. I'm

going to pop into the garage on the way back. If I'm late, that's why. Square it with Ingram, will you?'

He felt a forgotten life force bubble up inside him as he sailed past the tip, took the A45 to Daventry and joined the motorway to London. At this stage he was still telling himself that he didn't necessarily have to go to Gavin, that there must be thousands of scrap dealers in England and that he would just keep driving until he passed one, but the motorways were lined with service stations and he knew as he left the M1 for the M25 that he had been fooling himself. He had never approached Essex from this angle before but he needed no map. Paul was calculating again, in hours not pounds now: with clear traffic and minimum hanging around at Gavin's – not usually a problem, you didn't go there for the hospitality – he would be back at Kelstice in four hours. He had not eaten since breakfast but he was running on adrenaline. The fluttering excitement he felt came not only from doing a deal or playing hooky, but from the sense that he was coming home. Was it possible to call somewhere home when you knew you would never live there again?

He had no idea what the stash in the back of the van was worth, but the drag of the extra cargo, making itself felt with every depression of the accelerator, confirmed that the sum was worth the risk. He saw several signs for a luxury hotel with its own spa and organic restaurant, and wondered if the haul would yield enough cash to take Louisa somewhere like that for the night. How lovely it would be to eat and drink in a restaurant where no one knew them and where the bedroom they came back to had its own en suite; where they could drink wine in the bath, or watch a film in bed.

In the privacy of the van he started talking to himself, telling the story of what had happened with Daniel and Ken Hillyard out loud. He had started doing this lately to relieve the pressure of bottling it up. It reminded him of all those times with Emily when the words 'I love you' had filled his mouth like too many sweets and the effort of not spitting them out had been painful. That experience had taught him that if you didn't say the words, at least to yourself, they might explode out of you at the wrong time. He was desperate to tell Louisa about the court case and the way the police had misled him and his own unforgivable part in things, but the timing was never right. If he told her before having sex, she might not let him do it. Afterwards would be better, but it seemed that that perfect shining moment of absolute relaxation and trust that always followed sex immediately preceded sleep, and when he woke up the perfect moment was gone and it was time to wait for the next one.

On the forecourt of Gavin's yard he sat at the wheel, suddenly nervous. When was the last time he had been here? Oh Jesus God. It had been the day before it had happened; they had promised Gavin a haul of copper that had never materialised. Gavin was casual about promises, but would he remember their no-show in the light of their subsequent disappearance? Paul shifted the van into reverse, but before he could move it there was a thudding noise behind him. Someone was banging on the side of the van.

'Oi, oi!' said Gavin, appearing at the passenger window, sweaty in black overalls and eating a sausage sandwich. He brought his fist down again, a double punch on the bonnet this time. 'Long time no see!'

Paul had no choice but to ease the vehicle into the front yard now, while Gavin walked alongside him like a man leading a horse. He gave himself a short silent pep talk; all he had to do now was get in, do the deal and get out. He leapt out of the door with a swagger he hoped would fool both of them. He landed in an inch of runny mud but inside the hangar it was so hot that he could almost see the clay drying and caking on his boots. The furnace was as noisy as a train and it glowed red like hell.

'Let's have a look at you, then,' said Gavin. If he knew what had happened to Daniel, he made no mention of it. Paul opened the back of the van and started to pull out the scraps of lead. He had underestimated the task; without Ross to help him it was hard, hot work. The lead was sliding in his hand. He took off his fleece and slung it over the back of a chair. His hands were sweaty and he tasted the salt on his upper lip. The inside of his mouth was, by contrast, uncomfortably dry.

Gavin held a few pieces in his hand, a human scale, assessing the value of the whole lot based on the heft of these few pieces.

'Call it £400?' he asked. Daniel would have haggled, and successfully, but Paul tried only to hide his glee.

'Nice one,' he said.

Gavin had the notes in a tin on a shelf. He peeled them off in twenties. It didn't make a dent in the size of the roll, which must have been thousands of pounds thick.

'Can you get any more where that came from?' said Gavin.

'I'll keep my eyes open.' It was easier than saying no.

'Good lad. Cup of tea, see you on your way?' At the mere mention of tea Paul's desiccated mouth filled with saliva, and his thirst trumped his desire to leave. Gavin spooned three sugars into a mug that had a picture of a woman in a bikini on it. The hot liquid was supposed to make her bikini disappear but this one was so old that the woman was permanently naked in see-through patches, trapped between decency and nudity forever. The tea was delicious and refreshing despite a fine film of machine oil marbling its surface.

'I seen your mate last week,' said Gavin.

Paul almost choked. They had promised him Daniel would not be bailed before the trial. Promised. If he had been bailed, surely Christine or even Woburn would have called him or written. He had not been in his flat for two nights. *Shit.* Perhaps even now there was a letter under his door. He cursed himself for coming back to Essex.

'Are you sure it was him?' said Paul.

'Swear to God,' said Gavin, although not confrontationally. 'He still comes once a week or so. You might catch him if you hang about for long enough.'

'You're all right, mate, I've got to head.'

Paul drove with the windows wound down but he remained feverish with worry. He would not go back to the Lodge at all but drive straight to 45B and check for post. There was a jam getting off the M25 to the M1 and he used the dead time to call Christine. She sounded pleased to hear from him, like he was a favourite nephew, and told him that yes, Daniel was still in custody. Hadn't she promised him?

Immediately Paul's temperature returned to normal, although he did not feel the cold until he was on the M1, creeping through the roadworks. It wasn't until he reached over to the passenger seat for his fleece that he visualised it still hanging over the back of Gavin's workshop chair, green trim against navy, warming itself as the furnace blazed away. He swerved as he recalled the identifying Veriditas logo; the car in front sounded its horn and put its hazard lights on, while a lorry behind him flashed its headlamps in anger. When he had pulled the vehicle back into the middle lane, he clapped his hand over his heart where the lettering had been. Only then did he remember that he had unpicked the stitches. His relief was physical; even if Gavin was still in touch with Carl, which seemed unlikely given his recent bonhomie, there was nothing there to lead anyone back to Kelstice. He drove home with extra care, stopping only to buy a burger and chips. It wasn't until he came to dig the coins out of his pocket that he realised how much he was shaking. On the way out of the service station, he used some of Gavin's cash to buy Louisa a bottle of sparkling wine and a bunch of flowers, as though by spending it on her he could make his dirty money clean.

35

According to legend, vampires cannot cross a threshold without an invitation from the master of the house. Louisa knew how they felt. She had been poised to knock on Adam's door for five minutes. Five days had passed without him returning her call, a record even by Adam's standards. When, in desperation, she had called the Hammersmith Odeon they said that he had not been in to work all week, and that if she saw him first she could tell him not to bother coming back.

There was a rapping noise and a sharp pain and Louisa saw that her knuckles had struck the glass without her ordering them to do it. Ben opened the door, wearing a chiffon dressing gown with a marabou trim and a pair of novelty boxer shorts, black printed with red lipstick kisses. He blinked through a fug of marijuana smoke.

'Louisa,' he said eventually.

'Is Adam in?'

He pulled his dressing-gown belt tight. 'Just me,' he said. 'Come in, though.'

It wasn't until she was in the hallway that it hit her how much she had built Adam's house up in her mind: despite its unpromising exterior, she had imagined that inside it would be a cross between a church crypt and an opera house, with mirrors and drapes and candelabras on every surface. Instead she stepped into a world of sludge-coloured anaglypta wallpaper and matted brown shagpile. On the left was a door to the front room, which was being used as a bedroom – Angie's, she surmised, from the huge bra lying on the floor. Ben hurriedly pulled it shut. There was a right-handed open-plan staircase with a single brown banister. The back room, where he had been watching *Neighbours*, contained no furniture apart from a peach velour three-piece suite. The walls here were pictureless and the shelves in the recess of the chimney breast only thinly scattered with books and cassettes. The place seemed entirely irreconcilable with its inhabitants and the music they made. Ben turned his attention back to the screen where Harold Bishop was holding court in the coffee shop, coffee pot in hand, jowls wobbling. Madge was rolling her eyes at him.

'Joint?' Ben offered. Louisa shook her head. She was quite paranoid enough.

'Make yourself at home. Sofa's here, kitchen's out the back. They'll be back soon,' he said.

'They?'

'Him and Angie. They've gone to the funeral.'

Louisa flicked on a smile. 'Of course! Yes, I'd forgotten. He did tell me.'

'Oh, right. I thought they only decided at the last minute. Make yourself at home.'

Just as the credits were rolling, and that awful song was playing, the key went in the door and Adam and Angie came in. Ben smiled and cracked his knuckles as though turning his attention from one soap opera to another. The look Adam gave Louisa chilled her blood. If I *were* a vampire, she thought, that look would revoke my permission to be here, some force would suck me back out of the house, because it is very clear that I am not welcome.

'Can we talk?' she said. Angie tipped her head at Ben, who pouted but did then follow her behind a frosted door that presumably hid a kitchen. Adam had barricaded himself into his body with folded arms and legs. 'We don't have to talk. Let's go to bed. I can make it better.' He wrapped himself tighter in his own embrace.

'To be honest, Louisa, I just want to be on my own.'

The sting of rejection diminished her sympathy.

'Why do you shut me out of everything that matters?'

'For exactly this reason. Because you're too intense, OK? Because you'd want to analyse my relationship with my dad all the way up there and then to meet my mum.'

'And why not? I'm supposed to be your *partner*. I should have been there for you!'

'It's quite amazing that my father dies and this is all about *you*.'

Where had that come from? Up until now, he hadn't given a shit about his father. Now he was using his grief as a weapon against Louisa.

'That's not fair,' she said. 'I just want to look after you.'

'Jesus Christ, Louisa, you're as bad as my mother, trying to control me, checking up on me,' said Adam. 'I *told* you what would happen if you got all possessive.'

Louisa sank into the sofa. 'What are you saying?' she said. Fear drained the fight from her but in a dark corner of her mind a tiny flare of something unexpected glimmered – relief? Release? The little flame sputtered and died. Freedom from Adam was the last thing she wanted, it was the end of the world.

'You work it out,' said Adam. He turned on his heel, cutting a swathe through the piled carpet. The front door slammed. Seconds later, Angie's head appeared around the edge of the kitchen door.

'I couldn't help but hear that,' she said. 'I'm sorry if I trod on your toes. He only decided to go this morning, and I think he just wanted to be with someone a bit neutral, do you know what I mean?'

Poor Angie, in her role as asexual mediator, was neutral in every sense of the word.

'What was she like, his mother?'

Angie shrugged. 'I didn't speak to her. We didn't go into the church; he made us hide behind a tree in the graveyard like something out of a bad film. We just hung around for the burial bit and then we went home again. I don't think anyone noticed us. There were millions of mourners, all Jesus people. More dog collars than Crufts. I tell you what, though, she was really *old*. She must have been about seventy when she had him.'

'Where do you think he's gone?' Louisa said. 'Who else would he go to?'

Ciaran, who had evidently been upstairs the whole time, walked into the kitchen, snipped a corner of a carton of orange juice with rusty scissors and drank straight from it.

'Ah, Louisa, the obtuse tip of the love triangle,' he said.

'*What*?' said Louisa.

'He's being a prick,' said Angie, flushing. 'It's just a lyric we've been playing with. Shut up, Ciaran, she's upset.'

His smile revealed a gloss of juice on his teeth. She hoped it rotted them.

'What do you mean?' Louisa asked. 'Love triangle? Who *is* she?' Ciaran and his orange juice left the kitchen and Angie looked at her feet.

'I told you, it's just a lyric. Don't let him get to you.'

'I can't bear people laughing at me, I won't have it!' She grabbed hold of Angie's hands. 'Listen, Angie, tell me what's going on. Be level with me. As a *woman*.' Louisa saw and ignored the irony of invoking a sisterhood she had willingly betrayed when she first went to bed with Adam. 'Is he seeing someone else? Is it that red-haired girl? Is that where he's gone now? It is, isn't it? Where does she live?'

'Who? Rebecca?' Finally jealousy had been given a name. 'Christ, no, I haven't seen her for ages. Look, I know he doesn't have the best track record, but at the moment I don't know of any other girl but you.'

'Can I wait here for him?'

Now Angie looked at her with nothing but pity.

'Any other day, I'd say yes, but today, I think he just needs some space. I'll make him call you. I promise.' Louisa had very little trust left, but she handed the crumbs of it over to Angie. She had no choice.

All her clothes had been folded away and the bedlinen was fresh. Louisa buried her face in the pillows, tried to lose herself in Adam but there were no stray hairs in her bed, none of his scent on her pillow. When she had stopped crying and only the sharp sudden aftershocks of tears were ragging her chest, she pulled the extension cord out of the wall. She wanted more than anything for him to call her but if he wasn't going to, she could not bear to know.

The next morning she saw things with a clarity that made her cringe. He was grieving for his father, even if he couldn't name or admit to the process, and she had desecrated that grief with her petty jealousies. She paged him the words 'Forgive me' and plugged the phone back in. He returned the call so quickly he must have sprinted to the telephone box.

'Am I still your Eve?' she asked, desperate now to own the nickname she had hated at first.

'Of course you are.' He sighed. 'I think we need to spend some time just the two of us. No more hanging out with the band. We were happier before you started tagging along, weren't we?'

He was right, and she acknowledged it. In a way, it was nice to surrender. It was certainly easier.

'So what's the moral of the story?' he asked her.

'I don't know.'

'That things work better when we do them my way. Listen, I'm busy with the band tonight but I'll see you the next day, and the one after that, and the one after that. It'll be just like it was in the beginning. I'll meet you at the Roof Gardens tomorrow lunchtime.'

'I can't wait.'

She vowed to herself that she would make the most of this second chance, that her role from now on would be to make his life easier, not to heap more stress upon him. Something had to give if their relationship was going to work, and it couldn't be Adam's music, which would clearly suffer if she was a distraction for the rest of the band. It would require a twist in her nature but surely all relationships had an element of compromise.

The next morning, she had company at breakfast. Leah was sprinkling brown sugar on a grapefruit, a serrated spoon by her bowl.

'Hello, stranger!' she said brightly. 'Would you like the other half?' She held up a yellow hemisphere.

Louisa pulled a face. 'Thank you, but I prefer to eat actual food,' she said, and peered into the fridge.

'We haven't spoken properly for ages,' said Leah. 'Let's go out for dinner tomorrow night, just the four of us. Somewhere local, nothing fancy.'

'I'd really love that,' said Louisa, and meant it. 'But I'm busy tomorrow night.'

'Bring him along,' said Leah, in the voice she used when she was trying especially hard to be casual. Louisa shook her head, for once wishing she could say yes. After years of hiding boys from her mother, now she was having to hide her mother from a boy. Incredibly, her fantasies had now evolved to the point where she dreamed that one day Adam would be assimilated into the family, comfortable in their company, not a moody outsider but just another face at the dinner table, like Dev.

'Well, you know you could always have boys to stay over if you wanted. Your father and I are very liberal about things like that.'

'Thanks,' said Louisa. 'I'll let you know if it comes to it.'

Her plans to get an early night backfired. It was June 21st, the summer solstice. The sun shone until nine, her body clock was firmly set at midnight or one and she wasn't at all tired. Scanning her shelves for a novel or something else light, her eye lingered on the black velvet scrapbook she'd bought from the market and the papers wedged into the Bartram's next to it.

She had already made a copy of the video on her father's reel-to-reel VCR, but had forgotten all about the book. That part of the project had been neglected but if she did it now she could present both to him in the Roof Gardens tomorrow. She opened the book, tracing the silver thread that was chain-stitched so tightly that it looked like wire and held tiny amber-coloured beads in the formation of stars, cheap metal and plastic so skilfully embroidered as to look ancient and precious. She blew dust off its pages and surrounded herself with scissors to trim, a stick of glue and a fountain pen that Adam had left behind in her room on one of his visits. He believed that important words deserved pen and ink. He hated anything disposable.

The first page was thicker than the rest and cried out for an inscription. Holding it, she hovered over the page, unsure what to write: she had not yet decided whether this was a public or a private document. In the end, she left space on the first page and turned to the second, where she wrote *Glasslake* in her best hand. The nib had been worn down by Adam, who was left-handed, and the slant was in the wrong direction. The pen skidded so that the writing was unrecognisable as hers, but then the paper soaked up the ink like a sponge and the edges blurred, giving it an antiquey look that suited the book.

She crossed her legs and spread all the scraps before her. On top of the pile was the Polaroid that the Japanese girls had taken of them on the Roof Gardens. She wasn't sure whether or not to include it; strictly speaking, it was nothing to do with the band. After deliberating, she decided not to and was proud of herself: she was learning not to overdo it, not to be too intense and make everything all about her. She leaned the photograph against the wall, where it kept her company.

Her first task was to arrange the remaining papers in date order, although much of this was guesswork, as none of the photographs was dated and most of the tickets and flyers gave the day and month but not the year. She was vaguely aware that the middle of her back was starting to ache and that pins and needles were developing in her left leg, but she shifted only slightly, too absorbed in her task to move.

The project was most enjoyable when she came to the gigs that had been played and the photographs that had been taken since she had met the band; so many memories accrued in such a short time. She was able to contribute a couple of her own keepsakes: a beermat, a lavender stem that she'd purloined from the Roof Gardens and pressed, the set list, scrawled on the back of an envelope, from the Luton Poly show, and then of course the black and red flyer that had played its own part in bringing them together. Finally she unfolded the last document, an A4 poster with a badly reproduced photograph of the band that had advertised a gig out in Vauxhall; she had particularly fond memories of this one. They had all travelled together in the van, and all five of them had gone to a party afterwards. Angie had driven home over Waterloo Bridge as the sun came up. Ciaran had jumped out at Embankment to buy a first edition of the *Guardian* and they had parked on a double yellow, all differences forgotten as they stared in united horror at the picture of the lone Chinese student squaring up to the tank.

It had only been a fortnight or so ago, but already the poster felt ragged and velvety with age. She turned it over to gum its back.

The pen used had been cheap, but it was an elegant hand.

To my darling Adam,
   I am so proud to share tonight with you.
      All love forever,
         Your Eve.

It wasn't her writing.

36

The gardening programmes on the radio were already warning of the Big Freeze of 2009. Icy Siberian winds had decided to go south for the winter and were turning the whole continent white. They were in for a record-breaking cold snap. Every day the forecast got more apocalyptic: Louisa listened with rising anxiety, terrified for the heritage seeds she had coaxed into shoots. The only comfort she took was the novelty of being worried about something other than the impending visit from the Heritage Gardens Trust and their cameras; if she still cared about her work, her current self was not yet lost to her past crime. She blew her budget and turned up the heat in the glasshouse a degree, deciding to leave it on all night. She even thought about cancelling her Christmas leave. Ingram and Demetra had promised that they would come in while she was in London; they were looking forward to showing their twins around the site. This worried her too, not because she was concerned about them finding her home – she would detach the cable and wind it up before she left – but because Ingram, for all his flair for research and design, had the opposite of green fingers; like frost or fire, they blackened everything they touched. He was bound to leave a door open or turn the heating off or something; she resolved to take Demetra and the twins to one side and instil in them the importance of protection.

The university bus that so many of the Lodge workers relied on stopped running on the 16th of December and would not recommence its timetable until the second week of January. Christmas holidays at Kelstice Lodge were therefore academically long. One by one the staff had fallen away. Nathaniel and Ian were staying with friends in a Portuguese villa, in one of the flashes of glamour that illuminated their ostensibly mundane existence. Ross was going back to Scotland ('The McProdigal returns,' said Ingram darkly), and Jodie, no longer welcome in her own parents' home, was going to stay with Dilan, who was still welcome, or at least tolerated, in his.

Without discussion, Paul stayed on. Ingram had found him cross-legged on the floor of the office one afternoon, making little newsprint jackets to keep Louisa's hyssop saplings warm while she was away. Ingram's reaction was the closest he had ever come to an outright declaration that he hated Demetra's rehabilitative notions about garden restoration and confirmed Louisa's suspicion that he was simply enduring the young people because of the cheap labour. He had actually taken her by the arm and marched her outside into the shadow of the Lodge.

'What do you think you're doing?' he barked.

'What d'you mean?' she said. 'It's another pair of hands. The more prep we do now, the less work you'll have to do in the holidays.'

'I'll be glad when this bloody grant comes through and we can afford to hire proper workers. I know Demetra's vetted them and everything but I worry about you alone on the site with them. I mean, this Paul. You don't know him from Adam, do you?'

For a chilling second she wondered how he knew, but when she saw his puzzled blinking eyes she laughed as she had not laughed since she was a girl, although these were not the carefree giggles of youth. This was a raging, hysterical laughter that threatened to turn into something else: tears, a panic attack, an aneurysm.

'What is *wrong* with you lately?' said Ingram.

It was funny because she *did* know him from Adam, or she was beginning to. She no longer had to pause before speaking his name in case the wrong one came out. After over a month in his company, he was Paul, a beautiful boy who, in a certain light or an uncertain mood, looked like Adam. After the initial awkwardness, his company had turned out to be surprisingly easy. She was careful to guide the tiller of their conversations through the shallow waters of work and their mutual acquaintances, in case either of them went under in the swirling seas of their hearts. They never discussed their pasts, or if they did, it was only in playful terms that made light of the years between them.

She was unused to having anyone in her space and initially worried that she would hate the intrusion, that she would have to entertain him and that this would drain her. As it was, Paul made few demands on her attention, happy to curl up and read in silence. He got through a novel every few days, always worlds of wizards and warlocks, and they seemed to occupy him completely in a way that created space between them, even when they were spending twenty-four hours a day together. Miranda, when in a restaurant or travelling, was only ever completely at ease when her children had a book or a toy on the go to distract them; Louisa understood how she felt now. He drew out another instinct in her too; the unaccustomed joy of looking after someone. She had replaced her old butane gas canisters with the odourless propane because butane gave him headaches. She started to eat meat again because, while he professed to like the one-pot vegetarian stews and curries she cooked, he said they were starters, not mains, and a man couldn't live off them. He looked bashful when he referred to himself as a man.

She felt as though she had entered a period of hibernation, of suspended reality. The sexual stamina of teenage boys was legendary but she had forgotten how much young people could *sleep*, and with relief she had surrendered to his own circadian rhythms, marathons of sleep followed by marathons of sex. Her desire to somehow recapture Adam had meant that she did not give up on Paul after that first, disastrous experience. It took a dozen times or more, drawing on non-verbal communication skills she didn't know she had – a carefully placed hand here, a well-timed sigh there – before he had interpreted them in a way that made the teacher proud of her pupil. She was happy to ride it out until the sex wore off, as people said happened if you kept sleeping with the same person for long enough. Even at thirty-nine, she had no experience of this. Her three months with Adam remained the longest relationship of her life.

She was aware that when things cooled off between her body and his, when the chemical hit of attraction inevitably succumbed to the law of diminishing returns, she would be left with a situation that was bizarre, even grotesque. Every now and then he would do something, like eat sweets for lunch or turn the *Today* programme over to a music station, that made her wonder what the hell she thought she was doing, but he also had an endearingly unguarded romantic side that she would never have found in a man her own age. Everything was new to him.

'We'd never have got away with this in the olden days,' he said suddenly one day when they were walking through the middle of the Lodge. 'Can you imagine what it was like here? Everything would have happened right here in this spot. In the olden days, the *real* olden days, I'm not talking about the 1980s,' – he ducked to avoid her swipe – 'they'd have done everything in the same room. The whole household would have lived together. Had all their meetings, eaten all their meals, traded, argued, had sex, given birth, died. At this time of year there would have been a great fire and people would have slept under furs and skins if they were rich and hay and sacking if they were poor.' He paused, his eyes half-closed. He had a way of looking like he was *remembering* something rather than simply imagining it. Then he smiled. 'Can you think of a worse passion-killer than having Ingram snoring and farting in his bearskin a few feet away?'

When he made her laugh, she forgot about his age.

It was as though two relationships were glinting in and out of view, like two different images contained within the same hologram. It was easier to see it for its surface attractions of sex, playfulness, comfort. But there were flashes and winks of something deeper, a concern for his happiness, a need to know he was going to be there tomorrow, that bore no resemblance to the panicked possessiveness she had felt with Adam. The images changed places daily, sometimes hourly. Louisa genuinely did not know whether the image would ever still, and if it did, which of the pictures it would be.

She did not plan to tell him. It happened so quickly, as incidents of life-changing stupidity always do. They were in the greenhouse, working under artificial light, even though it was only three o'clock. It was 21st December, which last year she had thought of as the shortest day of the year, but this year, with Paul in her bed, she had reframed as the longest night. Louisa had inevitably flirted with paganism in her teens and could never forget that this was the winter solstice, one of the most sacred days of the pagan calendar. Although she was trying to put away the childish things of esoterica and arcana, the 21st of December never lost its significance, not least because of its terrible opposite.

Paul had been behaving strangely all day, saying her name as though he was about to tell her something and then mumbling, 'Oh, nothing,' as soon as he had her attention. He had not spoken for hours, unnaturally absorbed in the unpleasant task of scrubbing the empty benches and shelves with an organic disinfectant. Louisa was dressing the smaller plants in their newspaper jackets and wrapping the fruit trees in large horticultural blankets. She whispered soft season's greetings to her plants as she went, and internally debated whether to leave Radio 4 on over the Christmas period. A thought suddenly struck her. Had he been building up to ask her if they could spend the holidays together? Was that the question he'd been trying to ask her all day?

'You are going back for the holidays, aren't you?' There was a world of difference, a universe of difference, between enjoying his company and his body here and taking him to stay with Miranda and her family in London.

'Yeah, I'm gonna see my mum. I booked my ticket online last week, I'm travelling tomorrow.' She sagged with relief. 'I get the train from Leamington to Marylebone, then the Tube to Victoria, then another train to Sussex.'

'I'll come down with you. I'm going to stay with my sister in London.'

'That'll be nice,' he said to the wooden slats. He had been scrubbing the same area for about ten minutes; if he kept going, the wax would come off and the wood would rot.

'Paul, is everything all right?'

He shrugged.

'Is it to do with us? Because, you know, I'm very happy with what we've got.' She paused. 'The way things are.'

Violent shaking of the head.

'OK, if you're sure . . .'

She tucked the hyssop saplings into their winter coats. 'I thought you came from Essex?' she said, and immediately wondered if this was something he had ever told her, or if it was part of the information she had scraped together from Ross and Demetra. How awful, at this stage, for him to find out the reason for her initial interest in him. She shuddered at the thought of him discovering her hidden reliquary, the tapes and the photographs of his likeness. How incriminating for her, and how hurtful and awkward and—

'I can't go back there!' he burst out. 'Not *ever*.' His reaction was violent, like steam suddenly blowing the lid six inches off a pan. 'It's more than my life's worth. Have I ever said the name Daniel to you before?' Louisa pretended to consider this, knowing that Paul had never mentioned a single name from his past any more than she had. 'Daniel is – he was my – I suppose you could say he was more like a brother than a friend. That was certainly the way he saw it, anyway. We looked after each other; he stopped the bullies from kicking my head in and I helped him read and write. No, that's not true, I did it for him. He couldn't read at all, apart from his own name and a handful of words. God, it feels so weird telling you that. He never wanted anyone to know. He would have killed me for saying it, I never would have dared.'

'What do you mean, "was", "would have"? Is Daniel dead?'

Paul exhaled, sending a plume of steam into the air. 'I used to wish he was, but no. He's in prison. Basically, I put him there. For the last couple of years, we used to, ah, you're not going to like this, we made money by nicking scrap metal and selling it on. Not violent robbery, we never did anything like that until . . . one day, in August, we were on a job and something really bad happened. If I'd thought for a second that . . . we didn't mean, we didn't *plan* . . .' He cracked his knuckles and looked over his shoulder before continuing. His voice had dropped half an octave and grown so quiet that she had to lean close to make out his words. 'Someone – we – a man died, Louisa, because of us. I'm the only one that saw it happen – well, apart from him, obviously. That's why I'm here. The police put me here until the trial, so that I'm out of the way of his dad. It's my statement that's going to get Daniel sent down for murder. I'm their star witness.' He spread his fingers, held out his hands in star shapes, grimaced. 'He'd kill me to stop me testifying, he'd do anything.' Louisa put down the terracotta pot she was holding and sank down onto a bench. It felt as though something inside her had burst open. 'The trial's in three months. You can't imagine what it's like to have a date looming in your future like that, a day you know is going to be terrible but there's nothing you can do about it.'

Try me, she thought. There were only three months to go until the meeting with Joanna Bower, the Trustees and their film-maker, a date which, to her, was as terrifying as any courtroom cross-examination.

'I was his only friend and I betrayed him, d'you get me? Daniel would never ever have done this to me, he's not a grass. He still hasn't sold me out.' He was whispering now, perhaps to cover the crack in his voice. 'Guilt is the worst feeling in the world. And do you know what the worst part is? If I had to do it again, I would.'

His terrible secret made her feel less alone. But she was so caught up in the magnitude of what he was saying that she was in danger of losing the detail. Was he saying that Daniel hadn't killed the man, or that he had? She must choose her words carefully. Paul was in full but fragile flow. If she misjudged her reaction he would retreat into silence again. He was standing before her in his muddy T-shirt looking absolutely horrified, as though he had been the recipient of shocking news and not its bearer. He looked about twelve years old.

'It doesn't matter,' she said. 'Come here to me.' For a moment she thought he was going to try to sit on her lap, but instead he burrowed into her arm.

'How come you're not angry with me?' he said, into the fold of her fleece. 'How come you're being so nice?'

'Because I understand.'

Pity and gratitude did battle on his face.

'It's nice that you're trying,' he said. 'But you *can't*. The only way you could understand guilt is if you'd been through it yourself and I'm not being funny, but someone like you, you're . . . all clever, and *good*, I mean that's why I like being with you, but please don't think you can understand.'

At the time, it felt like his speech had been designed to drag the confession out of her. She rolled the words around her mouth, murmuring them to herself for the last time before speaking them aloud. They would either bind her to Paul or sever the link forever. She felt a strange calm steady her voice.

'Paul, listen to me. I do understand, I do. When I was eighteen, I killed my lover. His name was Adam.'

37

June 1989

She hailed a cab on Gloucester Road. The lumbering, arrhythmic pace of the taxi was at odds with the pounding velocity of her thoughts. Her first instinct had been right all along, the paper in her hand evidence of suspicions she had convinced herself were unfounded. There had only been one other woman with them on the night of the Vauxhall show, the woman who was always there, the one he confided in, someone who might not be beautiful but who had nevertheless accessed the private part of Adam that Louisa had never been able to touch. She didn't know who she was angrier with: herself, for having ignored all the signs and warnings about Adam; him, for the lies he had told her and for making her fall in love with him in the first place; or Angie, who had listened to her talk about the problems she had caused, crafting a reputation for peace and mediation when all the time she had been fucking him behind her back. Not just Angie. They had *all* been in on it, all four of them, they must have. Every snigger, every snide aside they had ever made was now recast in the light of his betrayal. They would have laughed themselves stupid when she wasn't there. Nothing hurt Louisa more than the thought of being a laughing stock. Why had they chosen *her* to play their cruel game with?

Shepherd's Bush Green was settling down for the night; dossers were colonising shop doorways and the dark triangle of the park. Only a couple of kebab shops and off-licences remained open. As they joined Uxbridge Road, the meter told her that the fare already exceeded the cash in her pocket: she had to get out half a mile away from the house. She ran. Her feet were light but her hands were hot, hard fists. She felt capable of battering the door down with her bare knuckles; she felt capable of blowing it down.

Electronic music tumbled from an upstairs window but the only light in the house came from the downstairs room, the one where Angie slept, a pinkish glow through a chink in the curtains. Louisa crept across the knee-high weeds of the front garden to squint through the curtains, knowing that she might see them together and liquid with fear at the thought of it. Angie lay alone on top of the duvet, a paperback propped up on her pillow. She was wearing glasses and a pale blue dressing gown. She looked unforgivably plain. Louisa went to the front door and knocked with surprising restraint, as though saving her energy for the violence that must come later. A blue blob swam into focus as Angie opened the door fractionally. Her face was a mask of surprise and then she composed herself and almost shouted:

'Louisa! It's late, I was just going to bed,' and then, in a normal tone, 'This is a surprise.'

She got another surprise when Louisa grabbed her by the shoulders and threw her into the sitting room. Angie lost her balance and fell on her backside, dressing gown riding up and open to reveal an oversized grey T-shirt (Adam's?) and thick bare legs peppered with stubble.

'Who with?' snarled Louisa.

Angie pulled the dressing gown across herself and drew her legs in. 'Louisa, what the fuck?' she said.

'Who were you going to bed with? My boyfriend?'

'No.' Angie got to her feet.

'Don't deny it!' said Louisa. She unfolded the poster. The image had smudged but the biro on the back had not. When

Angie saw the writing her whole face changed, not into the expected expression of exposure and remorse but something closer to pity.

'Listen, it's not what you think . . .' Louisa raised her hand, noticing as she brought it down that her silver rose ring had twisted so that the flower was on the inside. It caught Angie smack on the cheekbone and she staggered back. She was clearly shaken but her voice was the same even tone she used to arbitrate band disputes. 'Stop it, Louisa. Calm down.'

'Don't tell me to calm down, you patronising . . . you lying *bitch*. Acting so friendly to my face and the whole time . . . What is it, can't get your own boyfriend so you have to steal someone else's?'

Angie remained silent. The nature of the wound changed with every second. There was a blushed handprint on her cheek, a ring of white skin around the red gash. 'You sad, fat little cow,' said Louisa. 'You know he laughs at you behind your back? He thinks you're ugly, he told me.'

'Do you know what?' said Angie, throwing up her hands. 'This has got *nothing* to do with me. Tell him yourself. I've had it with the lot of you. First-floor landing, it's the only door.'

The stairs felt like sponge. She hesitated fractionally at the door, which was closed, then kicked it, obeying the same act-now, think-later instinct that had brought her here in the first place.

Afterwards, when she thought about it, she found that she saw two separate images in quick succession, and that she held them in her head quite separately. The second image that she registered was the bedroom itself. A single Anglepoise lamp showed her beige walls, uneven Venetian blinds, piles of notebooks and a wardrobe full of black clothes with its doors missing. But she would not recall that until days later.

What held her attention at the very first look was the foreground. Adam knelt on the bed, a stride away from her.

He was shirtless, a string of jet beads she had never seen
before reaching almost to his navel, his jeans rucked down
around his thighs. His eyes were closed but his face wore an
expression she was used to; she watched his features crumple
in surrender. She did not need to count the seconds – one, two,
three, four – until his eyelids flickered apart as they always did.
This time, they went on to widen in terror, the spaces between
his features growing too large as panic rearranged them. Look
at me, she thought, the least you can do is keep your eyes on
mine – but he allowed them to flick downwards. Kneeling on
the floor as though in prayer, his hands on Adam's thighs and
entirely unaware of her presence, was Ciaran.

38

She zigzagged through the indistinguishable backstreets trying to find the Uxbridge Road. It was the other side of midnight and there were few cars. The only people she passed were a couple of men in jeans and Queens Park Rangers T-shirts. They exhaled lager and belligerence but she met their aggressive stares with a challenge of her own. She had enough rage inside her to take on a coachload of football fans.

She recognised his footsteps. His tread was measured and even but his breath was ragged, as though he'd been running. He put one hand on her shoulder like an arresting officer. She shrugged it off.

'Louisa, stop,' he said. 'I can explain.' She turned to face him. 'Oh, Louisa, please don't cry.' He looked stricken but not sorry, as though someone else had done this to her. He thumbed away a tear before she could stop him.

'How can you . . .' she began, but she was crying too hard to get the words out. 'How can you explain, what can you . . .' She gained control of her breath. 'I suppose you're going to tell me it's not what it looked like?'

'It's not.'

'Because it *looks* like I just saw you getting sucked off by another bloke.'

'Look, it was just a one-off.'

'I don't believe you.' She would never believe anything anyone said ever again.

'It was just a laugh. Look on the bright side, we could always have the best of both worlds, make it a threesome.' Those sickle-shaped dimples that heralded a smile were there, then his lips parted and he was laughing at her. She went to slap his face but he was quicker than Angie and he caught her at the wrist. His grip was light but instinct told her not to struggle. 'Oh, come on, Louisa, it was a *joke*.'

'Do I look like I'm laughing? Was Ciaran laughing when he wrote this?' With her free hand she pulled out the love note. A mad little surge of hope was dancing inside her ribcage, although she didn't know what it was that she was hoping for. That it *was* Ciaran's writing? That it *wasn't*?

He let her arm drop. 'Ah.' He wasn't going to deny it.

'But you don't even like each other, you're always fighting.' There was a shrivelling feeling in the pit of her abdomen. She recalled every one of Ciaran's jealous, hungry glances in her direction. Refracted through the prism of her new knowledge, the pictures were completely different. She had recognised thwarted desire, but not its object.

'It's complicated.'

'I'll fucking say so. I mean, what *is* this? You calling him Eve? That's supposed to be my name. Is it just easier to call everyone Eve? How many of us are there? It's fucked up, you're *sick*.'

'There's just the two of you.'

'Oh, I'm honoured.'

'Look, it doesn't mean anything. He's got this *thing* about me.'

'I was there, I *saw* you. He wasn't forcing himself on you.'

'I'm not *queer* if that's what you think.' He spat out the word like poison. In any other circumstance she would have been sickened by this homophobia, would have launched into a disgusted, righteous tirade. Now, she was appalled to realise, she was reassured by it.

'I find you with your – your – your . . . and you say you're
not . . . Oh God, Adam, we weren't using protection. I might
have AIDS.'

'You haven't, I promise, I never let him . . . Look, Ciaran
was just a . . . situation that I got myself into. I wish I could get
myself out of it without breaking up the band. It's not easy for
me, keeping you apart, trying to make sure neither of you got
hurt. It's been killing me.'

'Are you asking me to feel *sorry* for you?'

'I'm just trying to make you see things from my point of
view,' he said. 'I'm not used to saying no to people, it's hard.
It's *you* I love. I could have carried on shagging this girl I was
seeing before you and I didn't.'

'Are you telling me I'm lucky it was *only* Ciaran?' she said.

'Yes! No. I'm saying that in all the ways that count, I'm
faithful to you.'

He actually seemed to believe it. Louisa couldn't bear to
hear any more. She began to walk, all the way up Uxbridge
Road, past the rattling skeletons of stalls at Shepherd's Bush
market. She ought to be exhausted but she wasn't tired, she
could have walked until she reached the sea. He trod on her
shadow all the way.

'What do you think you're doing?' she said.

'Walking you home.' He kept pace with her as she crossed
the Shepherd's Bush roundabout at street level. It was a warm,
breezy night; wind whipped up little whirlpools of litter in the
gutters. He followed her to the top of Holland Park Road.
She turned left to cut through Warwick Gardens, where big
pillared houses gave way to pretty Georgian terraces. Here the
air was perceptibly cleaner. Instead of carrier bags and crisp
packets, leaves and petals chased each other on currents of air.
She knew that she would never be able to tread this pavement
again; there were so many streets now that were infused with
memories of Adam. In the future, London would be a grid of

forbidden streets, she would have to avoid the landmarks he had made. Because it had to end; no high was worth this low. There was nothing he could say that could undo what he had done.

'I've told him it's over,' he said in a voice that was little more than a whisper. 'Him, the band, everything.'

Except for that. She halted as though he had pulled on her reins. He could not have chosen words better to halt her . . . and he knew it, she realised. They were only words. It was only a game. She picked up her pace again.

'Did you hear what I said?' He kept his voice low and tried to hold her hand. 'Don't walk away from me, Louisa!'

At the other end of the street, a door slammed and there was the sound of car keys being dropped on the pavement; the road was so quiet the clink of metal on stone resonated like the proverbial dropped pin. He tilted her chin. She wanted, despite everything, to give in to his kiss. That was the thing about life with Adam. It was sensational. Was she really ready to let it all go? But something inside her would not allow it.

'I just don't believe you any more.' Her voice was almost lost under the sound of a key turning in an ignition. The fingertips that had been stroking her skin suddenly dug into the hollows of her cheeks, pressing the insides of her cheeks together, forcing her tongue between her lips. There was nothing beautiful about her now; the car driver stopped being a potential audience and became a potential rescuer. Adam's arm curled round her in an iron clinch.

'You ungrateful little bitch,' he said.

He had held her mock-captive before in bed but this was different. The disparity between his physical might and hers hit home for the first time. A fortifying surge of panic allowed her to shove her way out of his embrace, bringing her hands up between his arms and forcing them sharply outwards. She felt all the lost power of the last few months come surging through her palms. The push of her hands against his chest was the best feeling she had ever known.

Adam staggered backwards and lost his footing on the edge of the kerb.

Something strange happened to time. The car was moving fast, too fast, but the seconds started to stretch out. Louisa saw the car coming towards them, saw the slow-motion trajectory Adam's fall was going to take and knew that he would not regain his balance without her help. He saw it too and reached for her. She stretched her hands out far enough for him to brush her fingertips but not to grip; his knuckles bent to form a desperate hook, trying to lock on to her. He lurched backwards again, into the path of the car. Louisa darted forward and in that slowed-down second she saw his face relax into its customary arrogance, as though he had known all along that she would save him.

The hands that had been outstretched flicked upwards at the wrist, and she pushed.

He made contact with the bonnet of the car. At the moment of impact, Louisa felt a strange detachment take hold, as though she were watching fictional events unfold on a screen. He looked like a big black spider tumbling over the braking vehicle. She noticed that the car was a convertible and thought, that's good, that shouldn't hurt too much; he'll survive that, she thought, as he tumbled across the soft roof; and then, as his head hit the asphalt with a crack, she thought, oh, no, he might not.

His left cheek was pressed against the ground and his face was entirely obscured by his hair. The shape of his body was all wrong: his legs looked like they were on backwards. His right thumb stuck up as though hitching a ride. He was entirely without motion. The driver brought the car to a sudden, screeching halt fifteen yards away, then reversed until he was a car's length from Adam's body. The man who half-climbed out of the driver's seat was youngish, with a loosened tie and pink eyes. He was close enough for Louisa to smell the booze on his breath and he had a manic, coked-up look around the eyes. She was already starting to think of him as the Other Man, her anonymous partner in crime.

'Fuckfuckfuckfuckfuck,' said the Other Man. He saw Louisa then. His expression was one of horror, panic and self-preservation, or was he only mirroring her own? For the few seconds their eyes connected there seemed to exist a moment of complete, pure complicity between them. He was gone as quickly and as noisily as he had arrived, and she was alone with Adam for the last time. She would have gone to him, but across the street, a light went on in a window. Someone opened it and a man's voice made a wordless expression of shock. Louisa reflexively jumped back into the shadows, hiding herself between two parked cars as another car rounded the corner. The new vehicle was a shabby navy Ford Sierra and it drew to a halt in front of Adam's crumpled body. The driver, a skinny, handsome black man around Adam's age, got out and started jabbering in an unidentifiable foreign tongue. The *A–Z* on the dashboard and a windscreen sticker gave his profession away.

'I'll be right down,' shouted the man from the window and then, over his shoulder, 'Marina, call 999. *Call 999!*'

The minicab driver was rocking on his heels and looking up and down the street. The man from the window reappeared in his doorway, ran down the steps and bent to crouch over Adam. Louisa was rooted to her gloomy hideaway.

'It wasn't me,' the minicab driver said to the man.

'I know it wasn't, you fool. Out of the way, let me have a look.'

'Are you a doctor?'

'No, I'm ... I've done a first aid course,' said the man. 'Can you move, please, you're blocking the light. Where's that bloody ambulance?' He alternated between blowing into Adam's mouth and pumping his chest. The man's breathing was noisy and deliberate, as though making a pantomime of respiration would force Adam to do the same. He picked up Adam's wrist. He shook his head. His fingers travelled to Adam's beautiful neck and pressed down in three or four different places.

Little yellow boxes of light appeared in windows up and down the street. Doors opened. The woman called Marina came down her front steps in a red velvet dressing gown, carrying a towel and a bottle of mineral water. 'They'll be here in two minutes,' she said.

'I don't think he's got two minutes,' said the man. 'Oh, shit, Marina, I can't find a pulse. He's dead.' He carried on performing the procedure nevertheless.

Louisa thought distractedly that she ought to be the one to give him his last kiss. A small crowd gathered around Adam, the man she would forever think of as the man who declared death, the taxi driver and Marina. Concerned voices and the hum of the Sierra's engine masked Louisa's footsteps, and nobody was looking in her direction. She crept backwards into the recess of the night, which she threw over her like a cloak. She did not run. She walked with a calm, even gait along Cromwell Road. An ambulance and a police car streaked past her, lights on, sirens off. The two vehicles chased each other like a pair of boy racers. Their pursuit was futile; the drunk driver was long gone, she had gone and so, in every sense that mattered, had Adam. They could drive as fast as they liked; they were already too late.

39

December 2009

Paul hung back while Louisa queued at the ticket window. She kept giving him nervous glances and he hoped the smiles he bounced back were reassuring. This was the first time he had been with her in any context other than Kelstice. She had more formal clothes on than her usual uniform of fleece and jeans; a dress that wrapped her up like a present, and over that an expensive, tailored coat of dark blue wool teamed with black suede boots with heels like knitting needles that clicked when she walked; he had been impressed when he saw her dressed up and had insisted on carrying her, with much laughter, from the caravan to her car so that she wouldn't muddy her boots. In the strip-lit reality of Leamington station the clothes made her look older, *other*. She wore make-up too; it settled in faint creases around her eyes he hadn't noticed before. She had told him that sharing her secret made her feel eighteen again but she looked twice that today. The difference in their ages charged towards him and punched him in the stomach.

A fat white hexagon of snow blew in from the platform and settled on her shoulder, a guiding star on a navy night.

'It's evens for a white Christmas,' said the man in the ticket office.

When they passed through the barrier he had to show the guard his Young Person's Railcard. The photograph had been taken when he was sixteen, when he was just starting to grow his hair out. He looked like a mushroom. Louisa looked at it, said, 'Oh, sweet Lord,' and had one of those wild giggling fits she only got when something wasn't actually funny.

'I should never have told you,' she said as the train clattered through a greeting-card landscape of naked trees and spooling white mist. 'I've ruined it.'

'It's fine,' said Paul. It was true, up to a point. He had lived with the Scatlocks long enough to know the difference between a good person who did a bad thing and a person who was bad to the bone. Her confession in the greenhouse had come as a shock, but only for a minute or two. His reaction had been one of disbelief, chased by indignation on her behalf and anger at the dead man. This was the fourth terrible thing in his life, after his father, and Emily, and Ken Hillyard, and each time there was such a revelation the impact was a little less devastating. At this rate, he'd have a heart of stone by his twenty-first birthday.

She reached for his hand. He took it but put his scarf over it so that other people wouldn't see the gesture. He was acutely aware of what they must look like. If someone mistook her for his mother, which newly seemed possible, he was afraid it would ruin her for him forever.

There was a brass band playing at Marylebone station, a huge, real Christmas tree and holly and ivy and lights. A young woman with tinsel in her hair was throwing up into one of the clear plastic bags that served as litter bins. Bodies thronged the concourse, making Paul nervous. It was as though Marylebone was the portal linking his recent life at Kelstice with his past life of Daniel and Carl and policemen and trials. It made everything at Kelstice seem dreamlike. Who had he been kidding? *This* was the real world.

'I wish you had a mobile,' he said as the band barrelled into 'God Rest Ye Merry, Gentlemen'. Suddenly her not having a phone was another unappealing symptom of the generation gap.

'We'll still talk,' she said. 'I'll call you. It might be a bit weird if you ring me at Miranda's.'

He nodded. Keeping their relationship secret from everyone at Kelstice was a habit so deeply ingrained that evidently they were both to keep it from their families too. 'If I don't pick up, it'll be because I can't, not because I don't want to.'

Paul's ticket to Goring had a built-in Travelcard that allowed him to cross London. He turned towards the entrance to the Underground.

'Honey, I don't do the Tube,' she said, in a voice he'd never heard before; arch, cynical, impatient. 'There's only one way to survive in London, and that's by spending money.' She headed for the taxi rank. He didn't recognise this urbane woman with her confident edge. It seemed to him that a hardness went with her clothes and her make-up. Her confession had not seemed to tally with what he knew of her character but it was easy to believe that this new Louisa – or was it the old one? – was capable of anything.

The queue of snow-dusted black cabs was long but moving swiftly.

'I was thinking,' said Paul, although he hadn't been, the words tumbled out unexpected and unrehearsed.

'*Oh?*' It sounded like a warning.

'Why don't I find out what happened next?'

'Next after what?'

'What do you think? After he . . . after you left him there?' She winced but didn't say anything. 'You said yourself you never looked into it. What if I found out what happened to the Other Man?'

'Oh, *yes*,' she hissed. 'Hi, I killed my boyfriend but I want you to find out if someone else went down for it. I can just see that making a private detective's day.'

Paul tutted. Couldn't she see he was trying to help her? 'Not like that. On the internet.'

'You can really do that?'

'I've got nothing else to do, have I?'

'What if I don't like what you find out?'

'At the moment you don't know, and it's killing you.'

'There are worse things than not knowing,' she said. 'Me *knowing* was how all the trouble started.'

A red-faced taxi driver broke into their conversation. 'Do you want a cab or what?'

Paul kissed her goodbye through the window and was surprised to find tears pricking his eyes. It was not so much a parting as a severance, and the effort of it took him by surprise. Of course she was snappy, London made her nervous and hadn't she opened her heart to him, hadn't she put her life and liberty in his hands? As the taxi pulled away, he heard her voice instructing the driver that under no circumstances was he to travel through Kensington but to cross Westminster Bridge and go down through Wandsworth. He hoped that she would be all right without him.

Down in the Tube carriage, he felt lost and hollow. The train came into the weak winter daylight for a minute or two as the tunnel receded at High Street Kensington and there was a corresponding lucidity in his thoughts. Their ages were only numbers. After everything she had told him and despite his creeping doubts, it had never once occurred to him to be afraid of her. He wondered whether this was faith or stupidity, which were, when you thought about it, two of the cornerstones of love.

40

How the hell were they going to have twins in a house this size? If he was them, with two children on the way, effectively homeless and with neither of them working, he would be terrified. His mother and Troy, however, were walking around with dumbly beatific smiles on their faces, touching each other whenever they passed, which was a spatial inevitability as well as a demonstration of affection. There wasn't room to move in this house. If you wanted to go up the stairs and someone was coming down you had to double back on yourself and go into the living room to let them pass.

Before last autumn, Paul had only slept under three roofs in his whole life, not counting holidays – their first house, the house in Grays Reach and then Daniel's – and now here he was sleeping somewhere new every month, the standard of accommodation and comfort going slowly downhill every time, from 45B to Louisa's caravan and now this. He was sleeping on the sofa – if you could call it sleeping, and indeed if you could call it a sofa. It wasn't a soft couch like the one in their old house or even a leather one like the Scatlocks' but a padded bench with lace doilies draped over the thin wooden arms. It was a foot too short for him to be able to stretch out properly, so he would wake most mornings at around four with cramp in his legs. He missed Louisa's big pull-down bed and her two duvets and the way she threw out heat like a furnace.

Troy's mother, who made him call her Mrs Ball, got up at six every morning and put the television on at a volume that made the water in her fish tank jump. She was a pinched, morbid little woman who wore dull gold sleepers that pulled her earlobes so low you could see daylight through the holes. She aroused in Paul something like the opposite of desire: if Louisa was someone whose body he couldn't get enough of, he couldn't get far enough away from Mrs Ball. She flicked between two television channels that showed seances and ghost hunts and fortune tellers. She was always on at Natalie to come with her to the spiritualist church; every time she returned she had tales of someone 'coming through' from the dead, usually Troy's father or one of her many deceased friends. Although Paul no more believed in psychic powers than he did Father Christmas, there was something unnerving about the way she looked at him, as though she knew what he was thinking. Daniel had had the same knack; if they looked at you for long enough you'd find yourself blurting out your secrets.

He forced himself out of the house every day even though the coastal air was a knife to his skin. The first day he tried to go for a walk along the shore the freezing salty wind blasted his face so that he had red marks on his cheeks and eyelids like sunburn; it hurt to blink. Even the beach was boring, nothing but identical pebbles and replicated groynes as far as the eye could see. If you walked for half an hour you arrived in Worthing but that was little better: half the shops in the town centre were empty and the rest sold comfortable shoes and nan-shaped clothes. Old women seemed to outnumber old men by about twenty to one and everything about this edge of England was geared towards their needs. Paul had never seen so many ramps. You could go for miles without encountering a single stair. He took to sitting in pubs on his own in the afternoons, savouring cheap pints in the kinds of chain pubs that did two lasagnes for £6 and were frequented by, yes, old women. He even tried to persuade Troy to join him for an evening drink.

'What, and leave your mum on her own, in her condition?' said Troy, as if she were a week overdue rather than nine weeks pregnant.

When the snow came the house was more claustrophobic than ever. It happened a couple of days after New Year's Eve (what a miserable experience *that* had been; watching Graham Norton on television and then missing Louisa's midnight phone call because he had been filling up a hot water bottle). The severe weather warnings were by now such a regular feature of the forecast that they had lost their power to caution, but it was still a surprise to go to sleep one evening and wake up to find the windowsills inches deep in thick snow.

Mum had brought his old laptop with her when she had left Grays Reach. It wasn't as fast as the brand new one Carl owned but it was easy to piggyback onto a neighbour's unsecured wifi connection. He checked the travel updates hourly, watching the animated map of England that turned pale blue in patches where the snow was falling. Trains were being cancelled across the country and in the event that all his connections were running, the roads in rural Warwickshire were evidently impassable with whole villages cut off because the council hadn't provided enough gritters. He and Louisa had agreed to return to the Lodge on the 4th of January, as soon as the trains were running, but she called him that day to postpone their reunion.

'I'm going to stay in Wimbledon for a couple more days, darling,' she said in one of their whispered phone calls, made from Miranda's landline late at night. 'I'm being thoroughly spoilt. I'd forgotten how lovely a hot bath on a cold day can be.'

'I miss you,' said Paul.

'Me too. I *ache* for you. I can't wait to be with you again.'
The sound of her voice worked the same magic as the tips of
her fingers. He wished he could say something elegant and
erotic to her but he was not as good with words as she was and
anyway, she always took the lead in things like that. Instead,
he closed the living-room door, put a dining chair under the
handle and trawled the internet for actresses who looked a bit
like her doing things he wouldn't dare to ask her to do, and if
he did he wasn't sure he'd have liked her to say yes.

41

The streets got more treacherous as the snow was packed down into icy slides. The elderly women of West Sussex all stayed indoors. Paul considered writing to the government suggesting that the Psychic Channel be used as an instrument of non-violent torture against terrorist suspects. Mrs Ball was watching, enraptured, as a camp middle-aged man with fluorescent yellow hair ran his fingers over a gravestone with his eyes closed, evidently in deep communion with the spirit of the deceased. He thought about his own father's memorial, a pale pink plaque in a wall of more of the same. He forced himself not to think about the memorial to Ken Hillyard but it was relatively safe to wonder where Adam Glasslake might be buried.

He had said he wouldn't go snooping in Louisa's past, but perhaps it would do her good to see the grave. He thought back to the bereavement counselling the school had made him have after his father died. The counsellor had been really into headstones, benches, plaques and trees. She had said that without a physical representation of your loved one you could never really complete the grieving process – that some people could never even begin it. What if Paul could find Adam Glasslake's gravestone? He would go with her to see it, he wouldn't mind. It was obvious to him that if they hadn't caught her so far then they wouldn't now. What she needed was to come to terms with the loss of him and move on.

He flipped his laptop open. If Adam had been killed today his death would have been recorded a million ways, from straightforward court reports to tabloid investigations to Facebook pages in his memory. He wasn't sure exactly when Louisa had been eighteen but was pretty certain that the internet was still in its infancy then, judging by her reluctance to adopt it. Probably they had all still been on dial-up connections and only using the internet for sending emails. Mrs Ball looked up and Paul shielded the screen from her, even though his search had so far yielded nothing apart from several different listings for a clothing importer from Arizona. He put the name in inverted commas and tried again. He had scrolled through three pages of guff about the sale and distribution of ladies' fashions, increasingly convinced that he was wasting his time, when he came across a music website containing the words 'Lyrics Adam Glasslake'. Once into the site he had to search all over again. It belonged to a band called Springhead and was badly designed, with black letters superimposed over dark photographs. The pictures were arty and blurred, showing two vague pale faces that could have been either sex and any age. The music was in the same vein: ambient, abstract, electronic. It wasn't Paul's kind of thing and he could not imagine it had ever been Louisa's either. Paul clicked every button with no luck until he came to one marked *Archive*. The caption read: *Back in the day! Our first band, Glasslake. Lyrics Adam Glasslake, music Ciaran Richards*.

That took him through to another photograph, this time taken onstage. It was of appalling quality, evidently a scan of a photocopy. That shape there must be Adam; it was impossible to make out any of his features; the dark hair and eyes could have been any colour in the original. The track playing was called 'Chapter and Verse'. On this page the music was completely different, rocky and complex, the low quality of the recording failing to disguise the purity of the voice. The sound was more evocative than any image could have been. For the first time the magnitude of what he was doing hit Paul: he was listening to a ghost voice. He felt a new flare of anger at the man who had let Louisa down so badly and something else, too, a need to find out all he could about Adam's life as well as his death. His curiosity went from idle to industrious in four bars of music. He had to know everything.

'For the last time, will you turn that music off,' said Mrs Ball, even though he had never before played any music through his laptop and it was the first time of asking. Paul unplugged the computer and took it upstairs, making himself as comfortable as was possible on the bed that his mother and Troy shared.

There was a message board on the Contacts page. Paul posted a message saying that he was looking to trace anyone who had known Adam Glasslake. Before he even had time to wonder what he was expecting to hear, a response was typed out.

I'm intrigued, his correspondent wrote. *Give me a call.* He attached a mobile number. Paul knew if he hesitated even for a moment he'd never actually do it. Withholding his own number – after Carl Scatlock's call, he took no chances – he dialled.

'Ben speaking,' said the voice.

'Oh, hello. It's Paul here, from . . . the internet,' said Paul, immediately regretting giving his own name and having no idea what he was going to say next. He should have waited a few minutes, made some notes, devised a strategy. His flustered eye snagged on Troy's bowl-haired, skinny-tied school photograph. 'I was at school with Adam, and I was just trying to find out what happened after he left.'

'Which one? He was expelled from most of them,' said Ben but before Paul could think of an answer there was a muffled disturbance in the background and Ben said, 'Put that down,

Grace. Grace! *Grace*!' A small child started to cry. The phone was let go and at a remove Paul heard the voice shout, 'Angie, can you see to her?' There was more action and a woman's voice chimed in soothing admonishment in the background.

'Sorry. You have my undivided attention now. There's a name I haven't heard for, what, twenty years? I'd almost given him up for dead.' Ben laughed; so he didn't know. 'We all had a big bust-up and never saw him again. What do you want him for?'

Paul fought the urge to blurt the truth. You couldn't just go around phoning people out of the blue and telling them their old friends were dead in any circumstances but especially not when your girlfriend was the undetected murderer. Inspiration struck just in time.

'I'm organising a reunion, I—'

'Hang on, how come you asked for Adam Glasslake?'

'I'm sorry?'

'Adam Glasslake wasn't his real name, was it? That was only his stage name, he adopted it when he came to London. He got it off some gravestone at his dad's church. At school he would have been known by his real name, Alan Murray.'

'I, ah . . .' stammered Paul.

'What do you really want?' said Ben, suddenly suspicious.

'Thank you so much for your help, that's brilliant, I'll let you know if I find him,' said Paul, and hung up, his heart hammering.

Entering Alan Murray returned millions of hits. He refined his search, combining the name with the words 'dead', 'funeral', 'obituary', 'killed' and finally, after his fingers hovered nervously over the keys for whole minutes, 'murdered'. If he was staggered how many Alan Murrays could be alive, it was yet more astonishing how many Alan Murrays had died. For half a day he trawled obituaries of men called Alan Murray, the middle-aged, the young, a couple of children, good men, bad men, indifferent men, strokes, heart attacks and at last two murders – but one in 2001 and another in 2006, neither compatible with Louisa's timeline and in any case both outside London.

He found a couple of sites that offered tantalising glimpses of reports that could only be accessed in full by subscribers. A further search turned up a site where you could, using a credit card, buy yourself some time to look through the archives of every newspaper in English. From his wallet he drew out the credit card pressed upon him by the building society and so far unused, and bought himself two hours' access. Three decades of British newsprint were soon available at the click of a mouse. Paul was thrilled, never having known such a thing existed. He had expected to find facsimile pictures of actual printed pages but the format was just the bare facts delivered in generic plain font, like a no-frills email. This made concentration all the harder and he was soon sweating with the effort of it, completely lost in the process. He felt like a detective or a private eye, like he had been given a passport into a secret world of intelligence. Excitement turned to stress as the clock in the corner of the screen ticked down and still he found no record of Alan Murray's death. He allowed himself to wonder briefly if Louisa was telling the truth at all, if she hadn't made the whole thing up for a joke or as some kind of test of his loyalty.

His eyes were dry and so was his mouth. As quickly as he could, he went downstairs to make himself a cup of tea. He looked around the tiny kitchen and reflected that at least it was a haemophobic's paradise; the only blade in there was an ancient breadknife that was butter-blunt. While the kettle boiled, he tried to recall exactly his conversation with Louisa. Hadn't she told him the street where it had happened? It had rung a bell, had something to do with Kelstice ... Leamington, Conventry, Warwickshire ... Warwick Gardens, that was it. Back upstairs he entered the address and Alan Murray and was rewarded with a positive hit. Suddenly Paul was breathless, as though he was physically chasing the man himself through the streets.

The report that came up was dated 19th October 1989. So, Louisa had been eighteen in 1989 which meant that now she was ... *Christ* ... He filed his reaction away to be dwelt upon later. That revelation shrank into the background in the light of the report that followed. It was only a few lines long but it changed everything.

Mystery Coma Man Rev's Son
The previously unidentified man who spent three months in a coma in St Mary's Hospital following a hit-and-run on Warwick Gardens in June has been named as Alan Murray, 21, of Haywards Heath, East Sussex. Mr Murray, who regained consciousness last month with no memory of his accident, is the only son of controversial Anglican clergyman Reverend Radclyffe Murray, who died in the spring.

Mr Murray is still recovering from a serious head injury and will complete his convalescence at home with his mother, Mrs Theresa Murray.

Louisa, who had spent the last twenty years living as a murderer, had not killed Adam. Everything she thought she knew about herself was wrong. His heart swelled at the thought of being able to give her such amazing news. If he had felt like a secret agent before, now he felt like a god, able to resurrect the dead and pardon the guilty. He would tell her in person when they were together again; he could not wait to see the look on her face. He would have to choose his words carefully. He had never had such huge news to break. If Louisa had been religious, he would have been announcing the difference between her soul being saved or damned, which was as big as news got.

With twenty minutes of his search still left, Paul tried to find out where he might be now. Alan Murray might be a common name but, as far as Paul could detect, the world had only ever played host to one Reverend Radclyffe Murray, which was just as well as he did not sound like a very nice man; he had evidently spent the last years of his life campaigning hard for gay clergy to be banned from the Church. He had died of heart disease in May 1989, just weeks before Adam had been hit by the car. He had a fleeting image of Louisa comforting him after his father's death; it was far more disturbing than the idea of them in bed together. Radclyffe's controversial opinions hadn't stopped over six hundred parishioners attending the memorial service, which was held by the Bishop in Chichester Cathedral. Obituaries mentioned him being survived by a widow, Theresa Murray, who was sixty-four, and their only son Alan, twenty-one. Paul sipped at his tea, found it had gone cold and spat it back into the mug. He turned his attention to Mrs Theresa Murray, combining her name with her son's. The archive presented the search results chronologically. The rest of 1989 and the early nineties yielded nothing but there was a 1994 report from the Brighton *Evening Argus*.

Vicar Widow Seeks Son
The widow of Reverend Radclyffe Murray, the controversial clergyman who died in 1989, has been admitted to the Roseberry Nursing Home in Eastbourne after a series of small strokes. Theresa Murray, 69, is said to have been heartbroken after the recent disappearance of her only son, Alan, now 26, who was left brain-damaged after a hit-and-run accident soon after the Reverend's death. Anyone with information about Alan is urged to contact the Missing Persons Bureau.

At the foot of the piece, in square brackets, was the word 'image', presumably pertaining to a photograph of Adam.

What had he looked like, this man Louisa had loved enough to kill? Paul tried to picture him, as though if he thought hard enough the vague fuzzy image he had seen on Ben's website would suddenly pull into sharp focus. He tried to resign himself to not knowing. Louisa had already told him that she hadn't kept any photographs after the event, that it would have been too hard.

His connection was about to time out: he emailed the relevant documents to himself. Finally he had time to order the concatenation of conflicting realities. Twenty minutes ago, Adam had been dead, then resurrected; the most recent available intelligence suggested that he was now alive but missing. One truth shone brighter than the rest: the fact that Louisa was not a killer.

Idly he googled the Roseberry Nursing Home, Eastbourne, and called to the screen the home page of a site only slightly more professional-looking than Ben's, with a crappy stencil-effect rose pattern bordering the frugal pages. He supposed that Adam's mother must be long dead by now so it was with low expectations that he made the call. On a whim, he gave his name as Dan Smith; uttering the forbidden diminutive gave him an uneasy thrill, like a swearword in church. The manager who answered told him that Mrs Theresa Murray was their longest-term resident, and although very feeble was still alive. Visitors were welcome.

Goring was in West Sussex and Eastbourne in East Sussex. The paired counties were huge but the line between the towns was a direct one, snaking along the brim of the English Channel. Paul looked out of the window at the darkening sky. If the snow held off, he could be there this time tomorrow.

42

On the morning after, the Friday, the phone by her bed rang and rang but she didn't answer it. In the end Miranda knocked on the door and came in without knocking.

'It's Elvira,' she said. 'She wants to know why you're not at work.'

'Tell her I'm not coming in,' said Louisa, from underneath the duvet. 'Tell her I've got the flu.'

'Tell her yourself. I'm not doing your dirty work for you.' Louisa turned her face to Miranda and must have looked pretty horrific because her sister recoiled and said, 'Just this once, then. That's quite some hangover you've got.'

Elvira came round on the Monday, sat on the edge of the bed, said, 'That's not flu,' and told her that Adam wasn't worth it, with uncharacteristic and unbearable tenderness. Louisa didn't speak. Elvira came round again two days after that and said that if Louisa wanted to keep her job she had better be at the stall by midday or she was going to give it to a friend of Roberta's who was over from Italy.

Louisa couldn't stop looking at her palms. She expected them to be blistered, the skin seared where she had touched him. She felt raw. There was nothing on the radio; she flicked between the news bulletins on Capital and GLR but no one mentioned it. She was afraid to watch the television, even if she was on her own. She developed an Orwellian conviction that it was spying on her. Her parents did not take the *Fulham Chronicle* or even the *Standard* (it was unthinkable that she could venture the two hundred yards to the newsagent) and there was nothing in the *Guardian*. Murder they would report, guns or knives or fists, but not necessarily a hit-and-run death. Dozens of pedestrians were killed by drivers every year in London; the only cars the press were interested in were the ones being blown up by the IRA.

Journalists might not care, but the police would. If they caught the driver they would catch *her*, she was sure of it, and she waited for the knock on the door. The Other Man was her only witness; he could not mention her without incriminating himself, but if they did catch up with him it was only natural that he would put the police on to the girl with the blue hair and the long black dress. A problem shared is a problem halved, after all.

Miranda was amazing: sympathetic to the heartbreak it was impossible to conceal, ignorant of the horror it was necessary to hide, and discretion itself when it came to protecting her from their parents. When Louisa hacked into her hair, cutting out the blue streaks and losing five inches of length, it was Miranda who sat with her in the utility room, patiently giving her a damage-limitation haircut that would last until she felt well enough to go to a stylist. Later that day, Louisa took all her clothes, including the ones she had been wearing on the night, to the housing charity shop at Notting Hill Gate. She was astonished by the bustle and traffic on Kensington Church Street. So many cars, each one a killing machine. So many people, each one of them a killing machine too, although none of them would believe it of themselves if you told them.

The knock on the door came after two weeks. It was not the expected uniformed duo, but it *was* a good-cop-bad-cop, black-clad couple. Miranda ushered Angie and Ben into Louisa's room with a puzzled, concerned expression on her face that said, Do you want me to stay? Louisa shook her head and closed the door, hanging onto the knob as though the harder she pulled it, the greater the soundproofing.

Everyone was upstairs, so she did not offer them a drink although she would have liked one for herself. They sat on the bed. Underneath it were their videotapes, their flyers and the book she had made them. She was terrified that they would somehow sense the proximity of their own captured images, that they would delve under the bed and in looking at her stash of memorabilia somehow divine what she had done. There was a scab on Angie's cheekbone but it didn't look like the kind that would leave a scar. Louisa was flooded with a surge of remorse for lashing out at her and wondered why she did not yet feel something similar for her more terrible transgression. Shockingly, shamingly, it was Angie who apologised.

'I'm sorry for the way I dealt with that, the way I sent you up there. It was really nasty of me.'

'I'm mortified by what I said to you,' said Louisa, meaning it. 'I was just upset. I thought it was you.'

'You had every right to be,' said Angie. Her dignity was admirable and deepened Louisa's regret. 'I don't think either of us exactly covered ourselves in glory, did we?'

'I suppose not.'

'Your hair looks nice.'

'Thanks.'

She fiddled with the drawstring of her trousers while she waited for them to do away with the small talk and tell her that Adam was dead, that his mother had been informed, that someone had turned up in the small hours with his wallet.

'He's not here, then?' said Angie.

'What? Why would he . . . ?'

Ben and Angie's eyes clicked together for a second.

'When he didn't come back, we just assumed he'd gone to you. That's what he told us when he went after you. He said he was glad the Ciaran thing was out in the open, and he was going to go and be with you. It was like, you could see Ciaran's heart breaking in front of you.'

He had been telling her the truth; he had chosen her, and what had her response been? 'I just don't believe you any more,' followed by that final, fatal connection between her body and his. That his ultimate choice had been her seemed to cancel all his previous crimes and withdraw from her the motive, the already flimsy justification, for her own. Louisa drew on all her reserves of discipline to disguise the impact of the revelation, tried to focus on the fizzing sound in her ears, like the noise after the music at the end of a record or cassette, but Angie was still talking.

'. . . so he goes to Adam, I don't believe it, you'll never go to her, but Adam just walked off. I was convinced he'd be here, but when Ciaran went to look for him, I said to Ben we'd better go and check.'

Not trusting herself to talk, Louisa raised her eyebrows. It felt like lifting a weight.

'Ciaran's gone to Hamburg,' said Ben. 'He's convinced that that's where he is. And if he isn't here, I think he's probably right.'

'You really haven't seen him since that night?' said Angie. 'I'm sorry we're just blurting it all out like this, it must be awful for you.'

Louisa shook her head. Another spike of guilt prodded, but failed to penetrate, the rubbery cocoon of disbelief in which she seemed to have shrouded herself; it was a strange, puzzling reaction inconsistent with what she had done. She felt guilty because she was lying to Angie, not because of what she had done to Adam.

'That's it, then,' said Ben. 'We'll either see him on *Top of the Pops* or he'll end up some bitter old man drinking in a bar on the Reeperbahn telling people he could have been a contender. My money's on failure. Music's changing. No one wants a histrionic pretty boy in leather trousers any more. They want jeans and T-shirts, sweat and beats. I'm glad to be rid of him, to be honest. He would only have held us back, musically.'

'So what are you going to do?'

'Carry on as a two-piece, I suppose. Ciaran's left all his kit, he said we could have it. After he'd set fire to all Adam's stuff, that is. Almost burned the studio down.'

'Jesus, what a mess,' said Angie. She linked her fingers and stretched her arms out before her. 'You know how they say about someone, "He always has to have the last word"? Adam is the opposite of that. He always lets you have the last word. It's much more powerful, because then he knows you'll be waiting for him to answer.'

'God, you're right,' said Louisa. 'I suppose you knew him better than anyone.' She felt a rush of blood to her cheeks as she realised that she had used the past tense, but Angie didn't pick up on it, just gave an embarrassed shrug.

'I can't tell you how many times she wanted to tell you about Ciaran,' said Ben, nodding at his bandmate. 'She was all for clearing the air but she couldn't bear to do it to either of you.'

'Really?' said Louisa.

'Yeah,' said Angie. 'You were nice. He was *better* with you.'

'So *why*, then?' she said. 'Why did he do it?'

'Adam just can't resist the idea of someone being in love with him, man, woman, whoever. It's a drug to him, like being onstage. He's a spoilt brat, and gets away with it because of how he looks and how he sounds. Ciaran was mad about him, he worshipped him. I know you wouldn't think that to see them together but that was just Ciaran being defensive. I mean, look what he put up with. Not just you, but loads of girls over the last couple of years. He knew what Adam's like, and he let it carry on because the alternative was to lose him.'

'I loved him too, you know,' said Louisa.

'I like the way you're already talking in the past tense,' said Ben. 'Shows that you can move on.'

What was left of Glasslake stood up to leave.

'Keep in touch,' said Ben.

'I don't think that's a good idea, do you?' she replied. 'Good luck and everything, but let's agree that we should break the chain here. I'm serious. Don't come here again.'

'Charming!' said Angie.

'It's nothing personal. All we had, all we've got in common is Adam, and if he's gone . . . I think I should just let it all go, you know?'

Angie looked a little mollified.

'What, even if he ends up dead in a ditch?' joked Ben.

'Even then,' said Louisa, trying not to throw up.

She saw them to the door. Upstairs, her father was listening to the *War Requiem* on his Bang and Olufsen, innocently layering an already wretched situation with unbearable pathos.

'Listen, Angie, I have to know. Honestly. You weren't sleeping with him as well, were you? If he's gone, there's nothing to lose by telling me. It's not like you and I are going to see each other again.' She held up her hands and then put them in her pockets to show that she wasn't going to hit her. Angie took a step back in mock self-defence, then grew serious.

'It happened once. Just the once. It was years ago, not long after we'd met. We were both hammered. I think he had to do it to get it out of the way, burst the tension, you know? It would never have gone anywhere. Adam needs complete and utter devotion, passion, adoration, all that truly, madly, deeply stuff. It's not really my style.'

Louisa watched them disappear through the mews gate, Angie's last words turning over and over in her head. She didn't understand. Was there any other way to love?

43

Roseberry Nursing Home didn't look like the photograph on the website. Online, clever angling and soft focus around the edges had connived to portray it as a long, low mansion set in rolling parkland. In fact, it was a row of six post-war, bay-fronted semis that had been run together with little walkways and then painted a dirty red colour. The forecourt had been swept clear of snow to reveal parking spaces so close to the building that cars were parked with their bumpers grazing the front wall. Perhaps that was the reason for the drab net curtains. Louisa had taught him to despise paved front gardens and driveways and he saw the place through her eyes, thinking how they'd have been better off with shingle. And those yuccas in *plastic pots*, what were they thinking? Underneath their topping of snow they were already brittle and yellowing; they needed a thick horticultural fleece if they were to survive another night.

In the lean-to porch, Paul took a moment to kick the snow from his shoes and wipe his soles on the stiff bristles of the mat before pressing the entry buzzer. The nurse who opened the double doors had a tan and red hair that didn't go together, but he couldn't tell which was fake. Her name badge, pinned to a uniform that was so tight that the badge looked skewered through her breast, said that she was called Lenka.

'I came to see Mrs Murray,' he said. Lenka made him sign his name in the visitors' book on the ledge. It wasn't the kind where you left happy comments about what fun you'd had, but a record of who was going in and who was coming out again. Practised now at subterfuge, he wrote *Dan Smith* in disguised writing, the alias hand that had once masqueraded as Daniel's.

'Follow.'

Paul and Lenka, who had a nice arse, an amazing arse in fact, walked a maze of corridors with insipid watercolours on the walls, plastic runners protecting the carpet and railings at waist height. The place stank of cleaning fluid and fish. In the opposite direction, an old man in a medal-decked blazer was shuffling along using two clawed hands to support himself. They appeared to be making their way towards the building's sole source of noise, a vast room crammed with high-backed chairs and a television playing at such volume the words buzzed with distortion.

None of them looked up when Paul came in. One of the inmates – what else were you supposed to call them? – stared right through him, tongue lolling in a toothless mouth. Paul had thought Mrs Ball was old, but these people were in a different league, so aged they were beyond human, and he made a mental note to kill himself before he reached that state. Much as Mrs Ball claimed that all black people looked the same to her, all the elderly women were identical to Paul. Theresa Murray could have been any of them.

'Um, it's a long time since I've seen her,' he said, and was guided over to a dusky rose chair containing the oldest person he had ever seen. She had skin like a dry riverbed. Even so, it was immediately apparent that Theresa Murray was of a different class from Mrs Ball and his own grandmothers. She too wore jewellery, but it was a necklace of chunky amber beads, and the only gold chain she wore held a pair of glasses.

Her hair was short and straight and a huge paisley scarf was folded in half and draped evenly over her shoulders, symmetrical pointed edges resting on each of her elbows. A little red New Testament lay in her lap. She looked smart and alert. Paul felt a flare of panic. There was no way he was going to be able to soft-soap this one, he thought. And then she spoke.

'Alan!' she said, and jerked her body upwards. It was only then that Paul noticed the wheelchair.

'Is not Alan,' said Lenka. 'Is Dan.'

'I think I'd know my own son if I saw him. You've never met him. You people weren't even in this country when he was born, so don't you tell me who he is and isn't.' Lenka wiggled off in a justified huff. 'Alan, darling,' continued Mrs Murray. 'You didn't tell me you were coming! What a lovely surprise. Come here to me.' She patted a brittle-looking knee as though she expected him to sit on her lap. Paul took the seat beside her and she clasped his hand in hers. It was like holding a bunch of twigs in an old leather glove and he had the ridiculous, repulsive, notion that if cut she would bleed dust. He hadn't banked on being mistaken for Alan, although now he thought about it, if the old dear didn't get many visitors and she missed her son it was an obvious mistake for her to make. He understood the need to act quickly, while her delusion lasted.

'You look better than I've seen you in years. Have you managed to stop the drinking?' Paul nodded. 'You have? Darling, that's wonderful. I'm so proud of you. I've been so terribly worried. They thought you were living on the streets, you know, when they couldn't find you.'

'When who couldn't find me?' ventured Paul.

'Oh, Alan, we've been over this a million times. I thought your memory was better? Are you sure you're still taking your medication?'

Paul nodded. 'Um, just a bad day. Tell me what happened again.'

'Nobody knows, dear.' She took on the contented, relaxed tones of a mother reading a familiar bedtime story for her small child. 'You went missing, didn't you, after you were expelled from Wellington. You wouldn't come home to me but we always talked, I spoke to you the day your father died and then when you didn't come to the funeral I was at my wits' end. I knew something was wrong, whatever differences you'd had with your father, I knew you wouldn't have missed that. A mother knows, Alan, a mother knows when her child is in trouble, no matter how old that child may be and how independent he thinks he is. The night you were born, do you remember that? When Daddy had gone home and it was just you and me in the hospital? I said prayer after prayer of thanks while you slept in my arms.' She had a string of spittle, stretching between her teeth when she spoke. Paul recognised the beginnings of irrational distaste and wondered if old age was going to turn into a phobia, like blood. 'I didn't give up. You were on the Missing Persons Register and then one day they said there was a boy in a coma and it was you.' He could barely keep up with her jumbled narrative and he wished he had brought a pen and paper. 'You couldn't remember anything after your sixteenth birthday, when you left home. I had to re-teach you all of it. You kept forgetting that your father was dead. That was the worst of it, the worst of it . . . I had to break the news to you again and again and again . . . it never got easier. Alan, darling, why are you rubbing your eyes? Are you still having the headaches? You know you've got to keep going for check-ups. It's no good giving up the drink if you don't take your pills. There's a doctor here, he can see you now, I'm sure he wouldn't mind. Lenka! Lenka! My son needs to see Dr Venables this instant.'

'I'm all right, M—' He was so into his part that he almost called her Mum.

While Lenka stiltedly explained that Dr Venables was not in the building and that anyway, he was employed to look after the residents, not their family members, Paul concluded that he had gathered as much information as he would get from Mrs Murray.

'Where are you living? You never tell me where you live. Please, Alan. Leave an address for me. How will they know to contact you if anything happens to me? You're all I've got.' She started to dry-heave and it took a few seconds to grasp that she was crying. 'You were such a loving little boy. You were so longed for. We *prayed* for you.'

Lenka returned and stood over them both, arms folded. 'Please to stop,' she said. Paul got up, despising himself for making this poor old woman think he was her son, even if she had started it.

'It's been lovely to see you,' he said. 'But I'd better go now. It's snowing again.'

To his horror, she tried to get out of the wheelchair. 'Alan darling, please come back soon. Please come and see me again. Will you be back tomorrow?'

Tears fell now from the body that had precious little moisture to spare, the water guided through the grooves of her cheeks. She held out her arms and Paul let her hold him for a few seconds, feeling that it was the least he could do. He had expected to recoil from the scent of her but she smelled floral and powdery. The effort of breaking away from her feeble embrace was heartbreakingly small.

'I'll be back soon,' he said, knowing that he could never bear to return.

On the way out he said to Lenka, 'How long have you been working here?' She narrowed her eyes. 'I was just wondering if there was anyone who's known her for years,' he said. 'I've got some questions.' He was met with a shrug.

'Mrs Brown? Maybe she know.'

Mrs Brown turned out to be the manageress, whose office was behind the ledge containing the guest book. She looked up from her desk and did a double take.

'Goodness me, I can see the resemblance,' she said.

'Oh, right,' said Paul, wondering if she was as gaga as her patients.

'Lenka says she thought you were him. I hope you didn't distress her.'

'I didn't mean to. Does she do that with everyone?'

'No,' said the manageress. 'Not at all. But then she doesn't get many visitors, certainly not Alan.'

Paul felt a kind of proxy guilt. 'How long since you've seen him?'

'Years. Nine? Ten? Possibly more. Troubled young man. Well, you wouldn't think he was young, I suppose, but your ideas about youth shift rather when you work here. Anyone under sixty seems young to me.' She couldn't have been far off that herself. 'I only met him once or twice. Drunk both times, of course.' Her voice dropped an octave in a one-sided conspiracy. 'He was losing his looks and he couldn't have been more than thirty. It started after the accident, apparently, although I gather he was a little wayward anyway and that they'd been estranged for some time before that, after he turned his back on the Church. Well, you'd know that better than me, wouldn't you?'

Paul became acutely uncomfortable. Mrs Brown was probably breaching several kinds of patient confidentiality and, more threateningly, he had recognised the hallmarks of the gossip, the slavering for more information, and he knew that his visit would be the subject of staffroom speculation for days to come. It was time to get out before he gave something away. He looked at the white sky. He had used the snow as an excuse but it really was still falling. His bus would never get through the drift if he wasn't careful.

'It's Alan you're really looking for, rather than her, isn't it? Do you mind me asking exactly how you're related to the Murrays?' Did she think he was Adam's *son?* The idea was so distasteful it was almost funny.

'Very distantly,' said Paul, watching her features change as his curt reply made an enemy of her. 'Look, I'd better go. Can I ask you a weird question?'

'Yes, but I won't be obliged to answer it.' She was professional again now, withholding information from him as he had done to her.

'Do you think he's still alive?'

Her face flickered until the urge to gossip trumped propriety.

'I really don't know. We won't find out until she dies, I suppose. You'd be astonished who comes crawling out of the woodwork. Relatives who go to ground for years while they're here suddenly turn up alive and well once they think there's an inheritance up for grabs. Not that there is in this case – the house was sold to pay for her care – so I don't suppose we shall have much cause to search for him. We tried to trace him when she had her last stroke and we didn't think she was going to make it, but there comes a point when you can only expend so much energy. The thing is, some people just don't want to be found; they might as well be dead.'

44

White flakes tumbled through a black sky. The broken spires of the ruin shifted in the flurry. Louisa sat in the canteen with only Radio 4 for company, wearing two coats and lagged again with a horticultural fleece she had found in the boot room and wrapped around herself for warmth. The weatherman was still on about the cold spell, although now, a week into the New Year, it had become the Big Freeze of 2010. They had thought the worst of it was over in December but now they said it was about to enter a second, harsher phase; this new snow veiled lethal week-old ice. Feet were sliding from under bodies; cars were skidding down hills and crashing into walls all over the country. At Kelstice. The Mere was frozen solid, its surface a milky green plate.

It had been dark at four o'clock. Now it was getting on for eight and Paul should have arrived at three. He was always punctual, early even. Periodically she shivered her way to the office and called his mobile; it went straight to voicemail every time. An unanswered mobile was even more frustrating than an unanswered pager. Still wrapped in the fleece, she stared down the ride. Last night's snowfall had hidden patches of frozen brown earth and restored the perfect white mantle. Where *was* he? There was no one around, just a little dun-coloured bird hopping towards her. It left a trail of footprints in the shape of convict-clothing arrows. She went back into the canteen to find a crust for it but it had gone by the time she got back.

In London, she had not had too much time to think about Paul during the day; it had been a relentless stream of activities from the presents to the pantomime and the endless DVDs and tobogganing on the Common. Her niece and nephew were ten and seven; it was the first time they had seen real, lasting snow and their delight was infectious. But at night, between the Cath Kidston duvet cover and the memory foam mattress in Miranda's spare room, she thought of him constantly. Their telephone conversations had been stilted compared with the easy dialogue of their flesh. She found it hard to believe his protestations that he had been mostly staying in with his family – at eighteen, you would have had to cage her to keep her in – and he had missed her call on New Year's Eve, which had been a source of much consternation. She pictured him in a Brighton club, getting off with someone his own age. The jealousy muscle had momentarily flexed, supple and strong despite years of atrophy.

Deliberately they had danced around the fact of her confession. At the time, she had taken it as a sign of Paul's maturity and sensitivity. Now, hours after the tryst, in the swirling shadow of the ruin, she was attacked by a suspicion that turned to knowledge within seconds. It was obvious. He was not coming back.

Her mistake had not been in the telling of it but in its timing. She should have sprung it on him when they had days, weeks, to reflect on her revelation together; she should have been on hand to answer his questions, not unleash him on the world with gaps in his knowledge that she knew from her own experience his imagination would colour in shades of black and red, his initial understanding turning to revulsion. She cowered in her cocoon and cursed her stupidity. Perhaps he had made good on his threat to look up Adam's murder and uncovered some new, terrible truth that she had not imagined, something that had sent him straight to the law. Louisa shrank into the wall as though cornered by police. Would Paul do that? She thought how little she actually knew him, how little she had ever known any of her lovers. She had been a catastrophically bad judge of character in the past and it seemed that she had learned nothing in the intervening years. She had trusted Adam with her heart and Paul with her secret. Neither of them had deserved it. She desperately wanted a drink but the only wine for miles around was in her caravan, so she fell back on an old yoga trick of breathing in through the nose and out through the mouth, trying to visualise the stress leaving her body. It didn't work. Unable to sit still, she followed the swirling cumulus of her own breath and walked out into the night.

At the end of the ride she saw the shape of him, long legs, top-heavy with a rucksack, coming in and out of focus through the blizzard. He put his hand to his eyes as though dazzled by the sun and she waved at him. He broke into a run and her paranoia dispersed as quickly as it had formed. His embrace toppled her, his snowy clothes dampening her dry ones, snow crunching underneath their weight. When he pulled her up there was a single body-shaped impression in the snow, an ice-and-water version of the cop-show corpse outline.

'You wouldn't *believe* the journey I've had,' he said eventually. 'Let's go home.'

She locked up the cabins and together they made their way to the caravan. Snow made a fairy-tale garden of their wasteland. A half moon threw eerie white light back in their faces. They had no need of a torch but it was hard to get their bearings in this new landscape. Instead of Louisa's usual path through the thicket they took Paul's way along the wall. Chattering branches dislodged clumps of snow into her hair, which froze into icicles, and the only noise was the scrunch of snow beneath their feet.

'If this was a book, the monster would know exactly how to find us,' he said.

She glanced back at the prints their boots had made. 'They'll be gone by the morning.'

Inside the caravan, their icy fingers and mouths found the warmest parts of each other. Afterwards, when they had swapped stories about their Christmases and she had silently noted the utter incompatibility of their families, he grew silent the way he sometimes did when he was working his way up to saying something important.

'What would be the best news you could have?' he said. It was an ominous question, despite his confident smile and playful tone. Did he still not understand that news of any kind was anathema to Louisa? 'While I was stuck in Goring I did a bit of detective work.'

'I asked you not to,' she said. She drew the covers tighter.

'Hear me out, it's good.' He was excited now, smug almost. 'I'm just going to come right out and say it. Adam wasn't killed by the car, he didn't die.'

Louisa felt her history warp and reshape itself around her.

'Did you hear me?' His delight was turning to confusion. Her dry lips tried to form words but she felt stripped of her vocabulary.

'But, but, but, but …' she eventually managed, unsure whether she wanted to hear him out or clap her hand over his mouth.

'I found this website that has all the newspapers going back years. And I did a bit of research. When Adam was hit by the car, he had a serious head injury and he went into a coma. He was in it for months, and when he recovered, he was brain-damaged. Not, like, a vegetable or anything, just a bad memory and stuff.'

'But that man, the one who came out of his house … he said Adam was dead. I heard him. He took Adam's pulse and he said, "He's dead."'

'Well, he was wrong,' shrugged Paul, as though this were an insignificant detail. 'He wasn't a doctor, was he? He was just some bloke. Louisa, Adam didn't die in that accident. You didn't kill him. Do you even get what I'm saying? I thought you'd be *happy*.'

'I am,' she lied.

'You don't seem it. Bloody hell, if I thought I was a murderer and then someone said I wasn't it'd be the best news I could have. Don't you get what this means, Louisa? You're free, not just physically but properly . . .' He looked around the caravan as though he was searching for the right word on the spines of her books. '. . . *spiritually* free.' His previous guise of age fell away and he was a child again, wanting instant admiration and petulant when it didn't come. 'I went to a lot of trouble for you. Don't you want to know the details?'

Details were the last thing she wanted; the big picture was painful and confusing enough. 'If he's alive, where is he now?' she managed.

'I didn't say he was still alive, I said you didn't kill him.' The new possibilities bounced off the edges of her mind like pinballs.

'Paul, don't play games.'

'I traced him up to about ten years ago. He was alive then. And then I tried to trace him further but he's just vanished off the face of the earth. He's a registered missing person. That's the next thing we need to find out but I thought we could do that together. I thought you'd be happy,' he repeated sullenly. 'I wish I hadn't bothered now.'

'I don't know what I want, I don't know what I think,' she whispered.

'How can you not . . . ? What's to think about? Let me know when you decide, will you?' said Paul, and rolled over in a sulk. She wanted him out of her home so much that she was tempted to tug her end of the blanket and roll him naked into the snow. In an act of unwitting complicity, he was asleep within minutes. Then she was torn between waking him up and shaking the details out of him and letting him sleep so that she could try to come to terms with what she had heard.

He thought that he had released her from her prison of guilt; how little he had understood her after all. She could still feel Adam's chest against her palms and the force of the temper that had pushed him away from her. In that split second she had wanted him dead as much as any weapon-wielding hitman. And that, she knew, was what counted. That was what Paul didn't *get*. She wished she had thrown his facile, stupid, 'spiritually free' back in his face to drive home that she would always be a killer even if Adam lived to be a hundred and died a peaceful natural death. In all the ways that counted she would always have killed him. The thought was as evil as the deed, wasn't that what the Bible said? Adam would have known.

An idea rinsed around her head; it wasn't a nice idea, she could tell by the way it rushed away whenever she tried to pounce on it. It finally crystallised just as she was about to drop off, and shook her awake. In bringing Adam back to life, Paul had unwittingly killed hope. If Adam survived, she thought, then why didn't he come back for me? In vengeance or love, why didn't he find me?

45

July 1989

Her world dwindled to the footprint of her home. She left her room only to eat and shower, and some days she did neither. She kept the curtains open all night, taking in the view, such as it was, while she could. Elvira had given up on her. Angie and Ben made good on their promise to stay away. News of Adam's death must have reached them by now, but they had not passed it on to her. Perhaps the police, when they found him, had not gone to his current home but straight back to his mother, the next of kin. If they knew, she wondered if they had been to his funeral, and if he had been buried with his father. She was able to hold this projected narrative in her head quite separately from the events leading up to it and wondered how long the respite of numbness would last.

Over time, it became apparent that they were not going to come for her and the reality of what she had done receded. Gradually, her focus switched from how she was going to get through the next hours to how she was going to live out the next fifty years. She felt that her story had ended with Adam's death. Now there were only endpages to fill.

She never made it to the hairdresser's. She let the holes in her right ear close over. The idea of putting make-up on seemed completely alien to her. The clothes she had not given to the charity shop she shredded with scissors, making rags of lace and leather. That was the point at which

Miranda finally told their parents the extent of her concern for her sister. They immediately diagnosed depression; after all, there was no external explanation for this sudden shift in their daughter's looks, energy and character. Had they known Adam, they might have understood the depth of the change; as it was, only she knew about the profound and terrible metamorphosis that had taken place in a part of her the mirror could never reflect. They wanted her to have lunch – at home, no pressure – with a family friend she had always known as Uncle Mervyn, although it was clear that he was being summoned in his capacity as a clinical psychologist and there was nothing avuncular about their proposed get-together. Nick had mentioned that exercise might help to lift her depression and Leah had gone one further and said not to rule out medication, that new treatments were sophisticated and that they would see to it that she had only the best. 'Just a sticking plaster, something to buy you some mental space while you heal,' she said. The thought of taking any kind of drug terrified Louisa. She wasn't even drinking wine with dinner any more. She was aware of a tiny compulsion to tell the truth, minute but constant and always moving, like a mutant cell in her bloodstream. What if these antidepressants magnified it?

'I'm not depressed,' she said.

Still, she found her brave face somewhere in the attic of her spirit and began to wear it whenever she had company. She agreed to take an hour's fresh air every day. The only place she could breathe was in the Roof Gardens; it had been her sanctuary before she had met Adam and her relationship with the place was solid enough to still offer a corner of the comfort it had once given her. She went there most days with the herbology books she no longer had any real interest in, and was aware only of their weight in her lap. One morning, so early that the gardeners were still clearing up from a party the night before, she found herself stopping one of the flamingos from eating a cigarette butt that had fallen down the crack between two stones in the Spanish garden. She handed it to the gardener who was dredging more of the same from the pond.

'To think I trained for three years just to pick yuppies' fagends out of a pond,' he said. Something about his off-the-cuff remark resonated with Louisa. She had never thought of gardening as the kind of thing you trained for; rather, that they were all auto-didact hobbyists who kept learning until some kind of mysterious tipping point was reached and they felt able to charge for their services.

'Where did you train?' she asked. He gave the name of a small private horticultural college in Hertfordshire.

'Best thing I ever did. It felt like someone was showing me a parallel universe.'

That's just what I need, thought Louisa. Later that day, she called Directory Enquiries to find out the number of the college. Because they were a private college, their only stipulations were that she could pay the fees upfront and that she was enthusiastic. Over the phone, she promised that she could deliver on both counts. She was confident of the former, knowing that her parents would support her; and as for the latter, if by enthusiasm they meant was it the only thing she could think of that didn't make her recoil in fear then yes, she supposed she could bring enthusiasm to the course. The forms were faxed to Nick's machine, a cheque was written and posted, and by the middle of the next day she had a confirmed place. As well as meeting the fees, Leah and Nick also paid a year's lease on a little cottage a mile away from the college.

Her remaining clothes barely filled one case: at the bottom of her wardrobe she found the crumpled ball of her blue velvet dress. She held it in her hands for a moment or two before stuffing it in with the shirts and jeans. She packed her essential oils in an old wooden sewing case and arranged for her books to be sent on. She packed her scrapbook, tucking the Roof Gardens photograph of her and Adam into the flyleaf. She took the Glasslake cassettes and the video that she had cobbled together from the live tapes (those she threw into a rubbish bin on the Cromwell Road). She knew she should have thrown everything away – after all, they connected her to a dead man and she could not believe that she would ever watch or listen to them again – but leaving them behind would have felt like killing him all over again.

The first time she performed her ritual was on the anniversary of his death. The summer solstice was rushing up towards her like a runaway train and she was tied to the tracks. On the 20th of June she got as far as the steps of her local police station but never made it to the door. There was a pub directly opposite. It has been a year now, she thought, surely it is safe to drink. After the first glass of wine, she decided it would be safe to see his picture again, and bought a bottle to take home. The next thing she knew she was wearing her old clothes and weeping her apologies to his moving image. Afterwards, she didn't leave the cottage for a week.

She fell into heritage gardening by accident, the first internship she was offered being at a National Trust property in Sussex where they were restoring their Elizabethan maze. She liked the idea of recreating gardens that had fallen into neglect. It chimed with her unmeetable need to undo the damage in her own past. She earned a reputation for bringing long-lost landscapes back to life, for being able to coax rare, endangered, unfashionable plants into leaf from a handful of hard-sourced seeds. She was astonished to find there was always work for her; she never quite lost her Londoner's amazement at the number of private estates in the English countryside. No job ever took her more than three years. Friendships threatened to establish themselves, but she never kept in close touch with people after she had left a project. Like harvests or frosts, she had good years and bad years. In the annual cycle of growth and death she found something approaching peace. In her achievements her family arrived at something approaching pride. She did not return to London until Miranda and Dev moved into their big house in Wimbledon, and it was there she spent most of her holidays. She would tend and till, read and research, plant and sow for as long as she lived, knowing all the while that she would not find ultimate peace until her own body was returned to the earth.

46

Sooty flames made ghosts dance on the walls of the Lodge. He had dragged a brazier up to the centre of the hall to bake potatoes in foil and mull wine; humour and anger had failed to snap her out of her mood so he was desperate enough to try romance. It wasn't going well: the wine was too hot, it scalded their mouths, and the potatoes had been in the brazier since early afternoon but had blackened skins and rock-raw insides. Something in the bonfire caught and crackled, sending a report throughout the hall. It gave an aural illusion that they were surrounded by creeping watchers, dozens of twig-snapping feet.

He wished with his whole heart that he had never told her Adam might still be alive. He could not forget the change that had come over her face; her age caught up with her in seconds and although her face had returned to normal now, twenty-four hours after his revelation, she was different on the inside, somewhere he couldn't access. She was distant from him; everything about her body said, 'Back off.' Tonight, she wore her waxed jacket like a shell, both zips fastened, collar turned up against him as well as the wind. It didn't make sense. You would almost think that she had been happier as a murderer, which no sane person would be. She was acting lovesick over a boy she hadn't seen for twenty years, a boy she'd tried to kill, and it was as though *he* no longer existed.

No matter how hard he tried to understand he could not help but interpret her withdrawal as ingratitude. He told her, more than once, that he had used his credit card and his own money and not asked for any back, and that he had travelled the length of the south coast in freezing conditions – the further into history the journey receded, the more it came to resemble a life-threatening mountaineering expedition in his memory – surely that was what she should be focusing on. To that, she had just said, 'I can't believe that you got to meet his mother. *I* never did.' He had told her what it was like spending time with Theresa Murray, that she was a distressing person to be around, but all Louisa said was, 'Tell me again what she said about Adam.'

She swigged the wine, which wasn't hitting the spot because much of the alcohol had burned off (he hadn't known that you were supposed to heat it gently; she had snarled at him, asking him what the hell he thought 'mull' meant). Then she stared at the dregs, like someone reading tea leaves. He knew she was going to start going on again and sure enough, she said, in that strange, dreamy voice she was using now:

'I can't believe he lied about his name. The thing was with him, there were layers and layers and *layers* of lies and all this time I thought I had finally got to the bottom of them but I didn't even know his name. It's taken me twenty years to process this and now I feel like I'm back to square one.'

He felt a childish urge to upend the brazier and shock her out of the reverie dedicated to another man, but instead he shouted at her, the first time he had done so. 'Do you not think it's a *little* bit fucked up that you're having a stronger reaction to the news that he lied about his name than you did when I told you he might be alive?' A single spark shot out of the brazier and landed on his coat. He hit it harder than was necessary to stop it catching fire, bruising his own arm in real frustration.

'Knowing that I didn't kill him is not the same as knowing he's alive,' said Louisa.

'Why do you still care if he had a stage name? What does it matter whether he's alive or not now? What does *any* of it matter? He isn't here, is he?'

She cast her eyes up to the low pink snowcloud which seemed to be propped up by the jutting peaks of the ruin.

'If you were older, if you had a bit more history with women yourself . . .' He took the words like a blow. 'Oh, Paul, I didn't mean that. Please let's not fall out over this.' She patted the ground next to her. What did she think he was, a puppy? 'I won't deny that it's partly that you've opened up old wounds. But this puts me in a position of . . . there's a world of difference between . . . look.' She slowed her voice as though talking to an idiot. 'Say he *isn't* really brain-damaged and he's looking for me but he just hasn't found me yet. Or say he's told someone else? I know you said his mother was away with the fairies but who's to say who he's been talking to? He might have made contact with the others, he might have gone to find Ciaran, he could be *living* with Ciaran for all I know, he'd probably have loved the chance to nurse Adam back to health . . . Someone else might know and be looking for me now, for blackmail or something. I've got money, I'd be a good target, and I'm hard to find but not impossible. Even if he doesn't remember, it might come back to him; these things do . . . or he might have told the police and they're looking for me . . .'

'For something that happened twenty years ago?'

'I don't know, they could charge me with attempted murder, or leaving the scene of a crime. I don't know, Paul. I don't know how long they wait, I don't know about police and offences and things, I don't know how that kind of thing works—' Louisa's head jerked up and her voice broke off as though the sharp movement had snapped her vocal cords. Paul had heard something too: they both turned to see their visitor at the same time, although he was known only to one of them. He was as solid as a snowman. The bonfire bounced orange flashes from the shaft of the knife which dangled from his belt. Its handle was the colour of clotted blood.

'Lucky for you that I do, then,' said Carl Scatlock.

47

August 2009

He had spotted the school when they had relieved a swathe
of the Essex countryside between Laindon and Colchester of
its street furniture. They had passed through a little hamlet
of weatherboard houses, dotted with the hazy coronas of
reproduction Victorian or Edwardian lamp-posts, elegant
swan-necked designs that looked like wrought iron but must
have been powder-coated steel. 'That's the sign of a rich town,
that is,' said Daniel. 'Any neighbourhood that has them fake
old-fashioned lamps, that means the property prices are sky-
high.' The cars parked in the driveways were big, new and
expensive, which confirmed his theory.

The school was a few hundred yards outside the edge of the
town. It was one of those low stone-walled village schools, only
this one was not tiled in the usual slate; its roof was luminous
turquoise. Daniel had slowed to a crawl as they passed it
and said, 'That'll do nicely.' The little school was vulnerable,
overlooked by nothing except a pylon in the neighbouring field
and, closer by, another curving olde worlde lamp-post whose
bulb had gone. The playground wrapped around the building;
there was a painted snakes and ladders on the asphalt and
bright primary-coloured climbing frames with chipped bark
underneath. A weathervane, a traditional cockerel design but
rendered in some pale grey, modern-looking material, twisted
on the brow of the roof.

'I feel bad, an infant school. It feels like picking on a little kid.'

'Jesus, *how many times*? These places are all insured. They *like* it when you break in: they claim back and bump it up to get more new stuff. Come on. Besides, it's the holidays. They'll have it all patched up by the time the kids are back in. They'll just blame it on some old boy with a grudge.'

He could have said no. Daniel couldn't do it without him. Their abortive attempt to recruit a third man – Hash had relegated himself from potential saviour to Carl's colleague – had only strengthened Daniel's view that it was the two of them against society, Grays Reach, the world, whatever. Besides, Paul was feeling greedy. He had £2,910 in his building society account; there was enough copper in that roof to yield more than the £90 he would need to bring him up to a nice, tidy three grand. He could have said no and saved a life.

That first time, they only looked at the school. After the farce on the railway line Daniel had grown cautious, insisting on a few days between the recce and the job. The night before they returned there, Paul looked around the room they had shared for the last few months and tried to recall some happy times in it that might help to explain the undertow of guilt that dragged and pulled at his mind. He could remember only miserable nights of hearing Daniel's grunts and girls' laughter and sighs curling up the stairs like smoke. He recalled with piercing clarity the night he had betrayed Emily, when he had cried into the hard, flat pillow, and it strengthened his resolve. As though some other authority had taken temporary control of his body, he fetched his holdall from on top of the wardrobe and with automatic precision began to fold his clothes and pack them away. He put his phone charger, both parts of his driving licence and his building society book in the secret inside pocket. When he unzipped it he found the good luck card that Emily had sent him the morning of his driving test.

She hadn't written much, but she had signed her name 'with love' and dotted the card with doodles of kisses, love hearts and L-plates. He stared at it in a kind of trance for a minute or two, then resumed packing for his escape. All that was missing now was the other, more important document. It wasn't on the desk in the room, although he was sure he had left it there. He waited until Daniel took a shower to search downstairs and eventually found it on the kitchen worktop under a sliced white loaf. He read the three stapled pages again; the more often you saw something in print, the truer it became. There it was in Times New Roman font, the confirmation of the place he had scraped on the teacher training course at Brighton University, and the address of his halls of residence. He still found it hard to believe his luck. Brighton was only a few miles from Goring, where his mother and Troy were living. It was the best of both worlds: far enough away from Daniel for accidental meeting to be out of the question, and close to his mother without the liberty-sapping, eggshell-treading reality of living with her. Still, he cursed himself for leaving the letter somewhere so prominent. It might not mean anything to Daniel but Carl – who didn't seem to be around this week, but that didn't mean anything, he came and went without notice – could certainly have read it. He didn't mind them knowing he was going away, but the destination must be kept secret. Telling them without making it sound like an insult was going to be tricky. He was hoping for some eleventh hour inspiration.

Upstairs, clouds of steam from the shower were replaced with clouds of anti-perspirant; he had only a few minutes of solitude left. To throw Daniel off the scent, Paul left a couple of T-shirts he didn't much care for – designer ones that Daniel had bought him – hanging over the back of the chair, and drew some of Daniel's clothes into his half of the room so that it would not look too stark. The letter from Brighton

University went into the secret pocket of his bag. He had packed everything he needed and it was still only half full. It was easy to place it back on top of the wardrobe and crumple it down again as though there was nothing in it. He pictured himself pulling it down, creeping past a sleeping Daniel and walking to the station on his own. It wasn't until then that he fully understood that he had never intended to say goodbye.

48

Carl flicked the blade in and out as casually as someone clicking the lid of a retractable biro. Paul tried to rewind his mind sixty seconds but he could not remember the details of their conversation. How long had Carl been there? What had he heard and what did he know? He could hear the crackle of the fire and the rasp of Louisa's breath.

'Please don't hurt us!' she cried, taking the cabin keys out of her pocket and holding them out to him with trembling hands. 'You can have the computer . . . there's lots of valuable gardening equipment, there are tools you can sell, it's all in the lock-up, just please don't hurt us!'

'Shut her up, Paul,' said Scatlock.

'Do you *know* this person?' Paul saw a flash of that London girl again, ingrained snobbery steeping her voice. Louisa might not be lily-white but her experience of violence was limited. To her, people like Carl were dark-alley encounters, not acquaintances.

'This is Carl Scatlock,' said Paul. 'Daniel's dad.' Louisa's eyes widened. 'How did you find me here?'

'Same way I got your number,' said Carl.

'And how—'

'I'm asking the questions here,' said Carl, still clicking his knife. The blade winked in and out of the handle, flashing like an indicator, constantly making and withdrawing the threat to the flesh. He knows exactly what he's doing, thought Paul. He felt the old dizziness begin to throw him off balance. His problems, so epic and complex before, began to narrow and simplify until the only thing that mattered in the world was not to see blood.

'Daniel's looking at fifteen years because of you, and you're having a fucking picnic with some . . .' Carl turned to Louisa. You could almost see the mental gears shifting as he recovered the memory of what he'd heard when he walked in. 'Where are my manners? Don't let me interrupt your conversation, darling. You were saying?'

Louisa shook her head. Carl walked towards her.

Paul waited for the Louisa he knew to emerge from this tiny, terrified woman and say the right thing, do something that would stop events moving any further forward, but he saw to his dismay that she was looking to him for guidance. He was frozen between flight and intervention. He had felt this twice before, once with his father and once with Ken Hillyard. Carl circled Louisa a couple of times before stopping in front of her, his body a barrier between them. Without retracting the blade of his knife, he put his hands on her shoulders and then, to Paul's further stupefaction, he began to undo her coat. The rustle of waxed cotton and the sounds of the Velcro tabs and then the zip being unfastened seemed unnaturally loud, against the low white noise of the fading bonfire. Carl undressed her with slow, deliberate movements that could, in other circumstances, have been interpreted as tender but now, here, they were almost more terrifying than violence. His heavy hands on her body made Paul feel sick, but he knew that the wrong word or movement from him would rupture Carl's illusion of calm and control and that was not something he was willing to risk while he was so close to Louisa. Carl tugged at her sleeves and removed her coat, tossing it aside; her arms dropped to her sides as though they were stuffed. He rolled up the sleeve of the sweater she wore and the shirt that was under that. He turned it out so the cotton-white skin of her inner arm was exposed and pressed the flat surface of the blade to her wrist. Despite his feeling of paralysis, Paul must have made a move because Louisa looked at him and said 'Don't', in a strangled sort of voice, as though the threat was at her neck and not her wrist. Carl wiped the blade up her arm as though smoothing out plaster, away from her inner wrist and up to the flesh just inside the elbow.

'People always go for the wrist,' said Carl musingly. 'What you want is the brachial artery here, it's much larger. You'll bleed to death in half the time if you slash the brachial.' He pressed down and the dark little river of blood showed purple. 'I'm going to ask you again. What were you saying?'

Paul knew for a fact that the sight of Louisa's blood would kill him. What he said next was as much an act of self-preservation as jumping from a burning building into the unknown dark potential below.

'His name's Alan Murray. He was hurt in an accident in 1989 in Kensington, and we don't know where he is now.'

'I've got a little theory about accidents,' said Carl. 'I don't think there's any such thing. I should know, I've arranged enough in my time. What's the real story?'

'I pushed him in front of a car,' said Louisa in her flat voice. She pinched the bridge of her nose and lowered her eyes.

'You wouldn't want that getting out, would you?' A smile began to crawl across Carl's face. If it had reached his eyes it would have made him look just like Daniel. Did you mention savings? How much?'

'Forty,' she said, although Paul knew it was much more. Carl turned towards Paul without releasing Louisa's arm.

'*You*,' he said, 'will get in touch with the police, make an affidavit on your statement, and my boy will go free and we'll say no more about it. *You* . . .' He pressed the knife flat against

Louisa's skin; she winced as though he had nicked her, and Paul felt the swish of excess saliva that usually precedes vomit. '*You* will get me *all* your savings out, not just the forty grand you're admitting to now, with a full statement, so I can see that you've cleaned the account out, and I won't tell anyone about your part in Alan Murray's accident.'

Paul held his breath while he waited for Louisa to agree.

'Anything,' she whispered.

'You can blame *him* for it,' said Carl, nodding at Paul. 'It's his fault I need the money. Have you got any idea how much a decent brief costs? I'm twenty grand down before the trial even starts.'

'I need to give them three days' notice,' said Louisa. 'I won't be able to get you anything until this Saturday.'

'Then that's when I'll come back,' said Carl, '8 a.m., next Saturday. And when I do, I want you to have changed your statement. Are we clear?' Paul noticed that both he and Louisa were nodding the same way, too fast and for too long.

Apparently as an afterthought, Carl waved the knife and cut off a switch of Louisa's hair, so near to her ear that it was skill, not chance, that stopped him slicing the flesh. He tossed it into the brazier. A few odd strands caught sparks and glowed like filaments, a brief moment of bright shrivelling wire in the dark. The rest of the hair did not seem to burn so much as melt, and the bitter smell of charred human was momentarily on the air.

Neither of them moved until the noise of Carl's engine was an echo in the memory. Louisa was a statue, posing with her hand up to the side of her hair. Paul started throwing half-eaten potatoes and litter into the brazier like someone packing a bag in an emergency. 'We'll take the van and go tonight,' he said.

She shook her head; a little tuft of hair stood out at an angle to her scalp. 'Do you know how long it took me to get that van in there? Do you know how long it's been since it was driven? I don't even know if there's any fuel in it, the tyres are flat.

We'd have to drive it right across the fields, we'd churn up his ground, that's if we could even get it out of the snow, you'll probably have to push it, all in the dark . . .'

'Then that's what we'll do! The van can cope, I can push. I'll do it. I'll walk to the petrol station while you get it ready. We can put air in the tyres in the big petrol station on the Kelstice road. He might come back tomorrow, there's no knowing what he'll do.'

'Paul—'

'We can dump the van tomorrow and get something else to tide us over for the next few days. We've both got savings, haven't we?' Almost without knowing he was doing it he dragged his feet along the ground and started rubbing out Carl's footprints. 'Give me your car keys. I'll go back to Leamington for my bags now. It'll take me ten seconds to pack, I can be there and back in an hour.'

'Paul—'

'No, you're right. The van's too noticeable. We'll just take what you need from here and go in the car. We'll go to Leamington on the way. I'm not leaving you here on your own.'

'*Paul.*' She was almost shouting at him now. 'We can't leave.'

He thought he understood and berated himself for his insensitivity.

'Oh, Louisa, I know, but there'll be other gardens, there must be. I know how much it means to you here but this is your *life* we're talking about. You saw what he was like. He put a knife to your skin. He wouldn't mind that you're a woman. He'll come back and do it for real next time.'

'I'm not just talking about Kelstice. You can't just *disappear*. You're due in court in two months. They know where you're supposed to be. If you run away they'll look for you. You're not just a normal person any more, are you? You're a witness in a murder trial. You go missing, they'll come after you, God knows what they'll unearth about me. You can't go drawing that kind of attention to yourself. If we go tonight, we'll be on the run forever.'

Paul sank down onto the cold earth, heavy with the knowledge that she was absolutely right. Their lives were an impossible maze, each of their problems a twisting, doubling path with Carl Scatlock's grinning face at the dead end. He looked at her through his fingers and saw his own panic reflected. She gave tremulous voice to his own thoughts.

'I just don't believe this,' she said. She was rubbing frantically at the skin on her arm, as though trying to scrape Carl's skin cells off her. His knife had not left an impression on her skin but she was marking herself, fingertips making red comet trails. 'I didn't see this coming. We were so . . . that man, he's . . . everything we've . . . I mean, what's to stop him coming back again and again, Paul?'

He could not answer her. He retrieved her coat from the floor; it was only muddy on the outside, the lining was clean and dry and still retained some of her body heat. He guided her arms back into the sleeves; all the while she was frantic with uncontrolled gesticulations, and he imagined this was how it felt to dress a baby. She broke away and began to pace.

'What's to stop him coming back here, taking all my money, all I've got, and then telling the police anyway?'

'I dunno about *that*, not the police, not him.'

'I think he's capable of anything after the way he just threatened me. You trust him, do you, you take a man like that at his word?'

Once Carl's loyalty would have been one of the few certainties in Paul's life, but not any more. He shook his head.

'What's to stop him taking my money then *killing* us? Jesus, Paul, I can't handle this, I can't believe I'm back here again—'

She broke off and walked away from him, her lips moving rapidly in silent conversation with herself. What had she meant by that, 'back here again'? He had hated her ranting but silence was worse. All of the bad things that had ever happened to him had occurred in some kind of silence, as if evil rushed in to fill the void left by noise.

She stopped pacing as abruptly as she'd started. Her expression had changed again and now she looked almost serene, as though that internal struggle had been stilled. Her features were utterly still and her eyes two points of light. She wasn't smiling, but she had never looked more beautiful.

'What?' he said. 'Have you thought of something?'

She nodded, pressed the heels of her hands to her eyes and took a deep breath.

'What, Louisa? What are we going to do?'

She took her hands away and slowly met his gaze. 'The only thing we can do. We're going to keep our appointment with Carl and, when he comes back, we're going to have to kill him.' She let out a gasp as though she couldn't believe the words had escaped her, and one hand fluttered back up to her mouth.

'You're not serious.'

'I think I am. No, I know I am. Look, I can't see another way out of it. Who knows where it would end? He's not an honourable person like us.' Paul waited for the ironic giggle, but it didn't come. God, she meant it. 'We know when he's coming. We know we'll be the only ones here, look, we've got a shed full of murder weapons and a twenty-acre grave. I'll do the . . . deed,' she said, softly. 'But I'll need your help.'

Fear leaked its way down his spine like a cold trickle of sweat. Escape didn't always mean running away from something. Sometimes, it meant putting your head down and charging at the thing you were trying to outrun.

'OK,' he said. He felt his belly lurch, as though he had lost his footing and was falling. The fire in the brazier let out its death rattle. A single resistant ember sent a line of smoke curling towards the sky, like a soul on its last journey.

49

Something was up with Daniel. He kept taking audible breaths, as though about to speak, then closing his mouth again with a little click. If this behaviour was designed to make Paul nervous, it was working. He was forty-eight hours away from his new life in Brighton. He had tolerated Daniel for five years; why, then, did he feel that tonight was going to be so hard to get through?

Hash hadn't nicked them any old sat nav. They had tried to look it up in the Argos catalogue; it was so expensive that Argos didn't even sell it. It could remember not just their recent destinations but the routes they had taken and the times and dates at which they had driven there. It was simply a matter of asking the device to retrace the previous route. The snaking lane that led them from the A13 to their destination had, thanks to them, only one sign left on it, that white moon with its black sash signalling that the road was governed by the national speed limit. Paul chanced a glance at the little screen on his lap and wished he hadn't; it told him that Daniel was driving at eighty miles an hour. He held on to the dashboard, feeling that he had been stuck for years on a lurching fairground ride he hadn't wanted to board in the first place.

'Should be a good haul tonight,' Daniel said and then, without taking his eyes off the road, 'I suppose you'll be needing money in Brighton.' His voice was devoid of emotion but he pressed hard on the accelerator pedal and took a complicated crossroads without stopping to look or give way. 'Michaela was round the other night, she read your letter. It was fucking embarrassing. I had to pretend I already knew. When were you going to tell me?'

'Tonight,' Paul lied. 'I was going to tell you tonight, just after we did this job. I only found out a week ago. It's all been a bit last minute.' He double-checked the connection of his seatbelt, suddenly convinced that Daniel was about to brake and throw him through the windscreen, but instead he brought the car back down to an appropriate forty miles an hour, smooth as a chauffeur. This self-control was more terrifying than any outbreak of temper.

'I'll drive you down. I might stay for a bit. You've got your own place, haven't you?'

'I'm in halls. Daniel, I'm not sure.'

'It'll be good for us,' said Daniel decisively. 'We could do with a change of scenery. We've outgrown Essex, we need somewhere new.'

'But you hate college, school, everything like that . . .'

'You won't be there twenty-four hours a day, will you? We'll still have our evenings.'

There was nothing he could say. Paul felt a wretched, withering sensation and supposed that it was the death of his dreams. An internal voice told him that that was it, Daniel would follow him around forever, there would be no student parties, no girlfriends, no normal life, just Daniel and petty crime and sharing a room and a friendship that was like a plastic bag over his head for the rest of their lives. Stupid of him really to expect, to dream of, more.

On the outside, he went through the motions of the job, pulling up his hood, slipping on the disposable gloves, guiding Daniel as he parked on the edge of the field next to the school with the copper roof and the aluminium weathervane. Together they surveyed the site for security devices. Daniel might not be able to read but he could recognise the little icon of a CCTV camera when he saw one, and he had even learned to identify the acronym. He established one boxy white camera trained on the main gate and another above the door itself. He too was acting like nothing had happened, as though Paul wasn't leaving him. Paul started to doubt whether they had even had the conversation in the car.

'What they've done is they've covered the legit way in and out but ignored all the back ways. They're so busy thinking about protecting the kids from paedos and that,' – he turned and spat over his shoulder – 'that they overlook the security of the *building*. Not that there's probably any film in them anyway. They're well out of date, them cameras.'

Paul sat on the bonnet while Daniel calculated the blind spots and then, with the snips he carried in his belt, made a hole in the ten-foot-high, diamond-grid fence. From here you could see CDs hanging from the trees as decorations; the children had drawn patterns on them in magic marker. His whispering conscience started to hiss and spit. How the fuck did my life end up here, he thought, tying his hood tight under his chin. At this rate I'll be teaching in schools by day and vandalising them by night.

Daniel, toolbag on his back, scaled a downpipe and went to work. He threw a tarpaulin down and Paul pulled it taut so that it made a chute for the sheets of copper to slide down in relative silence.

He patrolled the rear wall of the school, found the back door and for a second thought that someone else with the same idea had got there before them, that by some incredible coincidence some rival thieves were planning to strip the roof that night. There was a yolk-coloured toolbag containing the tools of their own trade, snips and bolt cutters and saws, but then his eye travelled along the wall to see heavier machinery, a row of unidentifiable tools and a cement mixer, and he noticed that everything was rimed in a coat of light grey dust. He pulled open the bag just in case and saw, on the top, a set of instructions for installing a new surveillance system, carelessly tossed in along with a warranty and what looked like a contract for the job. This was the kind of thing his dad used to do. The line-drawing picture on the front of the brochure looked familiar; when recognition came, it was with a swift, sinking feeling like a pebble thrown in a lake. Paul crept around the side of the building and looked up at the underside of a camera that wasn't out of date, that was cutting-edge. It was the thing they had taken for a defunct lamp-post but now it was obvious that this sleek, modern curve with its black shell like a spaceman's helmet wasn't a streetlamp. It was one of those ultra-modern cameras hidden behind a protective shell, so sensitive that they picked up on the smallest movements and followed them with efficient, electronic eyes. As far as he could determine he was safe down here but Daniel, up on the roof, removing copper panels with the ease of someone peeling foil off a chocolate bar, would be captured in close-up. He turned the page of the instruction booklet, wondering if they had by some remarkable foresight included directions that would allow trespassing amateurs to disable the system and erase the records of their crime. A falling sheet of bright metal missed his head by inches. Paul let out a yelp and Daniel's head appeared over the guttering.

'What are you – are you fucking *reading*?'

Paul automatically hid the booklet in his jacket before looking up. Daniel was hot; he'd pulled his hood off. Paul opened his mouth to tell him about the new cameras and then bit back the warning. All it takes after we get home is one call to the police, he thought, and you won't be following me to Sussex. You won't be able to follow me anywhere. He shivered and wondered if he could really do something like that.

'Keep going,' he said, frightened and excited by the ease of his treachery. 'One more and we've filled up the car, I reckon.'

'I want this first.' Daniel stood on the tip of the roof, as though on the prow of a ship, the tips of his fingers stroking the weathervane. The silvery cockerel swivelled squeakily on its permanent perch, its beak telling them that the wind had just changed from east to north-east.

'That's only aluminium, it's not worth it.'

'I don't want to sell it, I just *want* it,' said Daniel. 'Like a trophy.'

'Whatever,' said Paul.

'It's set in fucking concrete or rock or something,' said Daniel. He used his screwdriver as a chisel, chipping away at the encasing stone. A crack split the air like a sonic boom as it finally gave way. Both boys froze, turning automatically to where the village was behind them, expecting people to come running. But the light that came on was much closer than that.

In the murky playground it had been a dark shadowy block that the boys had assumed was an extension of the school buildings, but now that a light shone from its low square window it was clear that they were looking at some kind of residence. A low fence separated it from the rest of the grounds and a ruthlessly tended garden was visible behind it. A little red front door swung open to reveal the short, stocky figure of a man in late middle age or early old age. Paul's first thought, surreally, was that he looked like a little hobbit coming out of his hole. He was holding a torch. The beam picked its way up the school building, brick by brick, until it located Daniel, weathervane in his hand. The little man walked towards them, his feet accidentally falling into the painted hopscotch pattern. He came to a standstill at the foot of the giant snakes and ladders.

'Put it down, lad,' he said. He had a soft northern accent. 'The police have been called.'

'Piss off out of it, Grandad,' said Daniel. Paul remained hidden at the rear of the building, watching everything through the gap between the wall and a pipe. He came close to shouting out a double warning; to Daniel, to run away now before the police came and to the old man, not to antagonise Daniel.

'Don't call me Grandad,' said the man. 'My name is Ken Hillyard, I'm the caretaker here and you're trespassing. I'm not scared of you, you know.'

'You should be,' said Daniel. Still clutching the weathervane, he swung clumsily down the front of the building and stood at the other end of the painted snake. He was a good head and a half taller than Hillyard, and a lifetime younger, but the caretaker didn't look afraid. If anything, he looked amused.

'Smile, lad,' he said to Daniel, who fell into the trap of following his gaze until it met the all-seeing eye above. His eyes travelled from it to the white box cameras and then to the black and yellow signs.

'Signs are there, lad,' said the caretaker. 'Or can't you read?'

In that line was every teacher who had ever ignored Daniel, every time Carl had dismissed his future, every kid who'd called him thick. He took another step towards the caretaker. Paul saw the arm holding the weathervane twitch and felt his own legs move correspondingly, as if to run in and break up the fight before it happened. But to do that would mean putting his own face on camera. He stayed still and hoped that Daniel's preservation instinct would trump pride and temper.

'What did you say?' His voice was tense and too tight, like a pulled thread about to snap.

'I said, the signs are there, can't you *read*?' said the caretaker.

Paul knew what was going to happen, because he knew Daniel so well. Afterwards, he told himself that he could never have covered the ground in time to stop it, but at the time it felt like he spent minutes deciding whether risking exposure was worth saving the man from violence. He had a furious internal debate. If I get there early enough, I might prevent blood. If I get there too late, there might be blood and I don't know how I will react to that. Either way, my part in this will be recorded and my future is as good as over. Daniel lunged like a fencer, his long legs effortlessly covering the length of the painted snake. His face was as blank as stone but the caretaker's features were distorted by fear and the beginnings of an animal scream that was silenced forever as the arrow marking north pierced his eye with a pop and was buried up to the hilt. The momentum behind Daniel's charge had been such that he took another two staggering steps, the body carried along, before skidding to a halt and letting the body drop.

Ken Hillyard was gone by the time his back made contact with the playground floor, death having come even more quickly to him than it had to Paul's father. No blood issued this time, just an ooze of clear liquid like a tear from the centre of his eye. The other, unbroken eyeball was blind and unblinking.

Paul's heartbeat marked the seconds until he was able to talk.

'Daniel, what the fuck have you done?'

He finally let go of the weathervane and turned to Paul with a look of horrified surprise. It was the kind of expression you'd expect from a witness to a murder, an innocent bystander, someone who hadn't seen it coming.

The decision to run was silent but unanimous. They left behind the copper, and the toolbag remained on the roof where Daniel had left it. They unlocked the car easily but Daniel's hands slipped on the steering wheel and it took him two goes to get the key in the ignition. They drove to the complex crossroads, one they had stripped of its signage, thinking it would be a laugh to leave motorists stranded. Each way looked identical, each exit alternately plausible and implausible. Paul lost his sense of direction, as though someone had blindfolded him and spun him around. The sat nav was taking forever to switch on.

'Which way?'

'I don't know!'

'Use the sat nav!'

'I'm trying!' But although Paul had hit the 'home' icon, the little screen displayed only the navy night-time negative of a map, a single snaking street and a cursive figure telling them how many seconds it had been since the GPS signal was lost. Thirty seconds. Now forty seconds. Now fifty. Paul shook it hard.

'Fuck,' said Daniel, and took a left, at which point Paul knew nothing except that it definitely wasn't left. In the distance they could see the glowing escape route of the A13 but the road they were following seemed to be curving slowly in the other direction and there didn't seem to be any side roads that might lead them the right way. Rather, the road got bumpier and narrower and they were approaching the dead end of a five-bar gate when the sat nav came back to life and said, like nothing had happened, like they had all the time in the world, like they weren't going to hell, *Turn around when possible.*

They became aware of the first flash of blue as Daniel executed the manoeuvre. It grew closer, bathing the late summer landscape in a wintry light. Daniel stopped the car mid-turn so that it rested at a tilt on the uneven camber of the lane. Paul found himself looking up at Daniel, who took Paul's face in his hands and held it. 'Whatever happens, you say nothing. Nothing.'

'But Daniel—'

'Not a grass,' said Daniel. 'Never a grass. What are you going to say?'

'Nothing,' said Paul.

'Run in opposite directions,' said Daniel. 'That way at least one of us goes free.' He pressed the latch that opened both doors. Paul found a gap in the roadside hedgerow and began to tread the uneven ground of an upward-sloping field. The last he saw of Daniel was his back as he vaulted the five-bar gate, his frantic movements slowed to a lazy grace by the pale blue strobe of the police car lights.

50

After making the suggestion, she had slept on it. In the morning it had seemed more, not less, necessary. She acknowledged the horror of it all once, spending the morning alone in the office, staring at the tapestry as though the little lovers in it would come up with a better idea, but looking at their wall-hung world only reminded her how much she stood to lose if Carl Scatlock was not stopped, and soon. From that moment she decided to be professional about it, treating the murder as a project that must be followed through, on time and without setbacks. Thinking like this helped her to speak about it in brisk tones that left no space for interruption, either from Paul or from her own chattering conscience.

It had been his idea to spend the rest of the week in the hotel. She had been touched when he had insisted on paying, calling it a late Christmas present and throwing in a remark about wanting to share a bath with her. The snow was melting frustratingly slowly, each day only exposing a few new pocks of brown earth, and the caravan was, if not inaccessible, then impossible to reach without leaving a crisp trail of footprints telling Carl Scatlock exactly where he could find them. Neither of them trusted him to stay away for the promised four days, and to concede him the power of surprise would have been foolish, possibly to the point of suicide.

They ended up in a Motel Inn at an ideally dull business park between Leamington and Warwick. Its distance from Kelstice and its small population of expense-account transients granted them vital anonymity. Sanctuary was the reason they voiced to each other but Louisa knew that this little holiday was also a kind of last hurrah. What they planned to do would change everything between them. Their relationship had not yet experienced the most basic test, that of being in the public domain; who could tell how they would be together after they had colluded in killing a man? And that was only if it went right. If it went wrong . . . well, that was something neither of them was willing to consider. There was no Plan B.

They hatched Plan A in the bleakly corporate setting of the Motel Inn bar, sitting on a banquette covered with the same pattern as the curtains and bedspread in their room. She took charge; she had to, not just because it had been her idea and because she was older, but because she was afraid that if she relinquished any of the control he would lose his nerve. He said he was as sure as she was that it was unavoidable, but his silences when they were discussing the mechanics of it suggested otherwise. They drank pints of lager and spoke in unhappy whispers under the curious eye of the hotel barmaid, who was also the receptionist who had booked them in and the waitress who took their breakfast order.

They started with the disposal of Scatlock's body and worked backwards. Louisa knew that the only place where the ground was soft enough to dig was the car park. Its raised position meant that it was never eclipsed by the shadow of the Lodge and received all-day sunshine; the snow there was all but gone and the ground was insulated by a semi-permeable membrane, designed to let rain into the water table while simultaneously blocking weeds. The gravel was piled at the side, waiting to be distributed across the site by Nathaniel on his first day back. It would be easy to roll away the sheet and easier still to roll back over his body. Crucially, the diggers were already parked at the top of the hill.

'We need to get him up there somehow,' she said. She spoke about it in brisk tones that left no room for doubt on his part, and went some way to help her get into the part too. 'If we do it anywhere else we'll have to roll his body or drag it up to the car park. It'll take hours and we'll leave a big drag mark in the snow.' Paul winced. 'The only way we can overpower him is if we sneak up on him. I'll come up from behind and hit him with a spade or something. I only need to knock him off his feet the first time.'

She looked to him for feedback but got only a slow nod. While she externalised every thought, he seemed to have a running interior monologue that she could only guess at. It had been one of the things that had drawn her to him in the first place, this stillness, but now she wished that he was more direct. They could no longer afford to attempt to interpret each other's moods. She tried not to let the frustration show in her voice. 'I'm really worried about leaving traces,' she went on. 'We've only got the weekend to make it like it never happened. Everyone will be back on Monday morning. Ideally we need loads of snow or a complete thaw so they can't see where we've been.'

Paul closed his eyes and went silent. For a few, seconds Louisa thought that he was losing his nerve and her guts churned in panic, but when he opened them she saw that he had only been thinking.

'I don't think we need to worry about that,' he eventually replied. 'People only notice what they're looking for. Do you ever see a bit of disrupted earth and think, I bet there's a body under that? They'll just think there was a car parked there or something.'

'I suppose so. And it is only Nathaniel. He hasn't exactly got the most questing mind.'

'Poor old Nathaniel,' said Paul, swilling the foamy remains of his pint around the bottom of the glass and motioning to the barmaid for two more of the same. 'What did he ever do to deserve getting mixed up in all this?'

'Nathaniel isn't mixed up in anything. He'll pour the gravel over the car park and no one will be any the wiser. It's not like we have a *choice*, Paul.'

'I know.'

On the Thursday, they went to Kelstice to rehearse. The car inched querulously over ice both white and black. A couple of times Paul nearly lost control of the vehicle; his ungloved hands were sweating. Louisa too was clammy with nerves as they made their way down the ride but there was no sign that Scatlock had been there in their absence; the only tyre tracks were their own and the ones he had left after his first visit. His three-point turn had made swooping arcs and loops in the slush.

The tool room was a windowless chamber, corrugated steel painted the same dull green inside and out and lit only by a fluorescent bulb that took a few seconds to flicker into life. By its harsh glare they surveyed the implements neatly arrayed before them, rakes and hoes hanging by the necks from wall racks. Louisa caught her and Paul's reflection in the shiny surface of a spade. Side by side, fingers linked, they looked like any normal couple kitting out their garden at a suburban DIY store on a Sunday afternoon. She let the fingers of her free hand trace the handles of the tools she handled daily, expertly, wondering which she would select to change from tool to weapon. Her hands hovered over thick green twine that might double as a garrotte. That rake could blind him. She discounted a huge pickaxe, the size and shape of a liner's anchor: it would be too much for her to handle with precision and everything would depend on the accuracy of her blow. She picked up a small pruning knife.

'Not a blade,' he insisted. 'Anything but a blade.'

Her hand closed over a large blunt shovel, heavy at the spade but with a handle made of light, hollow steel. Its wide, blunt surface would give her a greater margin of error than any other tool. She met Paul's eye. He looked like he was going to be sick, but he nodded. Under his supervision she practised wielding the spade time and time again, like a golfer working on her swing. The difficulty was not in mustering enough force – she was fortified with nervous energy – but in raising the spade high enough to strike the back of Scatlock's head. They went into the trees where there was a limitless supply of wooden targets. After a couple of hours she could land the back of the spade on any given knot at a second's notice. Focusing on the mechanics of the task blinkered her to the horror of it. She was aiming in the first instance to incapacitate him; the second or the third strike would be the one that killed. Somehow she already knew that raising her weapon for the second time would be the difficult part; the challenge would be not the felling of the man but the finishing of him.

They called it a day at four o'clock, when hunger and fatigue and fading light forced them back to the hotel. Paul drove while she tried to massage her neck and shoulders. Her upper body was achy and tender, as though someone had inserted a wooden coathanger into the yoke of her shirt that she could not remove. She took comfort from the knowledge that the death would be at her hands. Paul would be her accomplice and that was all. No matter what he thought, she had crossed that line when she was eighteen. She gave Paul every chance to back out of it. She knew he understood that killing Scatlock was necessary – there was no other way to ensure what she had done to Adam remained a secret, and it was the only way that Paul would ever be free to testify against Daniel – but his reluctance was so obvious that it forced her to hide her own. She had not had time to adjust to or enjoy the liberation that should have followed Paul's disclosure that Adam was still alive, and now her murderer's mantle was heavy on her shoulders again.

'I don't mind doing it on my own,' she said as he followed her through the revolving door of the Motel Inn, although she was calling his bluff; she knew she couldn't go through with it without Paul's strength or sanction. 'You don't have to be a part of this. I won't blame you, I'll understand.'

'Even if you could do it on your own I wouldn't let you,' he said. 'I'm the reason he came here in the first place, and I'm the one he really wants. You're just . . . the icing on the cake.'

The gruesome task on the near horizon took away some of her appetites – food, sleep – and redoubled others – drink, sex. She was surprised, unsettled, to learn that the prospect of death was the strongest aphrodisiac she had ever known. Paul felt it too; he was unusually taciturn everywhere but in bed, the only place the tensions of the week were released. If only it were possible to capture the feeling without taking a life. There was a doomed perfection about those four days in the Leamington Business Park Motel Inn. Nasty wine, cheap bedlinen and a television that didn't work properly took on the qualities of champagne, silk sheets and a virtuoso violinist under the balcony playing their song.

On the Saturday morning they woke up at six and ate a tense, wordless breakfast of boxed cereals and yesterday's croissants; the kitchen did not open till seven. Paul's nervousness had infected her during the night like a virus. Killing Carl Scatlock still seemed necessary but it no longer seemed sexy or easy. The last few days of plotting and practising felt like a game. They weren't Bonnie and Clyde. They were a gardener approaching middle age and a teenage boy barely out of school, taking on an ex-soldier with a vendetta.

They checked out in silence. She couldn't help think that their departure should have contained an element of ceremony; as it was, Paul paid the bill in seconds, using the credit card he had been forced to provide as a condition of the hotel accepting his booking. Their light luggage was thrown into the car. She looked back at the exterior of the building, knowing that within minutes of their leaving she would forget what it looked like. They were the only people in the vast car park. It was still dark, but that peculiar kind of snow-darkness that she had grown used to over the past couple of weeks. The peach-coloured glow of the streetlamps remodelled the landscape. Even shadow and light could no longer be trusted.

She kept the car in second gear, glad that the drive required all her concentration. It took a full five minutes to negotiate the roundabout that linked the business park to the bypass road. The only other vehicle was a supermarket lorry, its cargo snaking crazily behind the cabin, which she hung back to avoid.

'What are you thinking?' asked Paul once they were on the Kelstice road.

He had, in fact, interrupted a terrifying idea that Scatlock might not be alone. She wondered why, when they had gone to such trouble to plot the steps he would take and where he would park his car, they had not factored this in. It was because he had seemed such a solitary man, but he would have cronies, of course he would. She only hoped that her instincts were right, and that a man of such arrogance – and, yes, greed – would go it alone. She knew if she voiced this creeping doubt he would lose his nerve altogether, so she tried to make light of the situation.

'I just can't stop thinking what a waste of fertiliser it's going to be, burying him in the car park. It seems such a shame to compact him down under layers of clay and gravel where nothing's ever going to grow. It would have been the only decent thing he ever did.'

It worked: Paul started to chuckle. 'See what I mean about him being a bastard?' he said. 'He won't even get himself murdered in the spring when the ground's nice and soft and we'd be planting.'

Their respite from anxiety was brief; laughter was snuffed by shock as they rounded the bend near Kelstice Bridge. A line of cars stretched back from the crossing. This was an arresting sight in itself; congestion on the Kelstice road happened occasionally during the rush hour but this early on a Saturday it was unusual even to pass another car. But that was not what made her mouth go dry. It was the sign that sat in the middle of the left lane, white on blue, declaring *Police Roadblock Do Not Cross*.

She managed to put the car into neutral and found that her fingers drummed rapidly on the steering wheel until Paul put a hand over hers to still her and left it there. She could feel his pulse, hot and fast, in the pad of his thumb.

He said weakly, 'He *wouldn't*.'

An officer in a fluorescent yellow jacket, who looked barely out of his teens but who must have been older than Paul, was inexpertly getting the line of cars on the other side of the bridge to back up so that a bus, just shy of the brow of the hill, could turn around. While he was waiting for the cars to accommodate his manoeuvre, the bus driver was shivering, smoking and pacing up and down the queue. Louisa wound down the window.

'What's the problem?' she said.

The driver nodded hello to Paul, who was hunched down in the passenger seat, and lowered his brow fractionally in reply.

'Some poor bastard's gone into the bridge.'

'Oh dear, I hope no one was hurt,' said Louisa automatically.

'I'd say he's got a couple of cuts and grazes, yeah,' the driver sniffed. 'No, he's dead, love. No way you could survive that. The car's all scrunched up. I've got to go all round the houses now. This is a fucking nightmare, excuse my French.'

Louisa tried to compose her features into an expression of sympathy, but he was already gone, delivering his bad tidings to the driver behind them.

They had a brief, fragmented conversation.

'Jesus, I thought . . .'

'Me too.'

'I'm not happy about the police being . . .'

'No, I know.'

'But at least it's not . . .'

'Yeah.'

'Are we still going to . . . ?'

'Of course.'

It was an age before they were allowed to turn their car around. In that time, a low silvery sun had risen and one of the Kelstice landowners, although not the farmer she leased her plot from, had walked into the village and told the police he was happy to let smaller vehicles access the village via a dirt track that cut across one of his fields. Louisa's little car slipped its way along the snow-rutted lane, almost giving up when it had to cross another low stone bridge over the Kelstice brook. It would have been quicker to walk. It would have been quicker to *hop*. The drive took half an hour but they emerged only yards from their point of departure, on the other side of Kelstice Bridge. There was the same Warwickshire Constabulary police car they had seen before, the officer-youth now shouting unintelligibly into a radio pinned to his chest. She proceeded slowly, not just because of the dangerous roads but to see what had happened; her experience with Adam had not cured her rubbernecker's instincts when it came to car smashes. From this angle, the ghastly extent of the damage was visible. The ancient bridge remained intact – not a single stone had been dislodged from its walls – which was a miracle when you saw what had happened to the vehicle. Traffic cones bordered the police-designated accident scene:

its circumference was vast, stretching from the bridge itself up to the village green. Tyre tracks criss-crossed confusingly so it was impossible even to tell in which direction the car had been travelling. Louisa could see a single twisted arc of black metal – a bumper? A wheel guard? A window frame? – lying in the middle of the road. Crystals of shattered windscreen glittered rainbow in the sun. Paul too, despite his professed distaste for the gruesome, was twisting in his seat to get a better look. Something he saw made him draw his breath in sharply.

'Stop the car,' he said.

His tone forbade her from asking him why. She pulled up parallel to a carefully swept pavement. Before she had even put the handbrake on, he was out of the car and running not towards the police tape but up the little mound to the Kelstice Arms. He slipped once, toeing a slice of green in the white, and then, when he reached the top, fell on his backside like a novice skier. When he got to his feet, he peeped through his fingers like a child watching a scary film. He kept them there until she was almost at the top of the hill, and dropped his hands only to catch her own and pull her up to where he stood.

The bus driver had been right; the car was crumpled like paper, its entire front section compressed or sliced off, it was impossible to tell. The snow was washed with engine oil swirled around with something else so that there were streaks of burgundy in the black.

At the bottom of a garden path, a man's plain black lace-up had been thrown from the car, sock still stiff inside it. Louisa winced to consider the kind of impact that could tear the shoes and socks from a man's feet, and watched as a grey cat sauntered over and began to sniff it, at which point Louisa became suddenly, horribly aware that this was because it contained a foot and an ankle. The cat nosed it onto its side, and a single splash of blood made a livid red poppy on the white snow. She fought to keep her breakfast down. Beside her, Paul sucked in his breath and grabbed her arm at the elbow, but when she turned her face to his he was staring not at the severed foot or the stained snow or even at the car but at something else, something with the power to drain the colour from his cheeks and the speech from his lips. He was fixed on two halves of something, black lettering on yellow plastic or vinyl that, on first glance, Louisa identified as one of those Baby on Board signs that Miranda had in the back of her people-carrier. How awful, how horrific.

'Oh, no,' she said. 'Oh, *please* no.'

'I know that number plate,' said Paul, his voice thick. 'I've driven that car.'

She reassessed the scene in the light of his words and this time recognised the broken plastic as the remnants of a car registration plate. Even then, it took her a few seconds to understand the weight of what he was saying.

'Stupid prick always drove like a maniac,' he said in a monotone. He cracked his knuckles. 'Let's get out of here, let's go to the Lodge.' He scrambled back down towards the car without a backward glance, but her eyes were drawn back to the foot once more. 'Louisa, come *on*.'

Not until they had driven the half-mile drive back to Kelstice Lodge, and up the ride, and seen the tools of death laid out at the top of the car park ridge did they break their shocked silence. Paul let out a long, loud noise that was half-cheer, half-sob. She could not bring herself to join him. Her relief was tempered by the sickening knowledge of what they had been about to do.

51

Paul had chosen to run in the right direction (did that mean Daniel's path was the wrong one?). The stubbled field he crossed led him directly to another, larger road that he instantly recognised as the one they should have been driving along to make their escape. He remembered that pair of houses – oddly semi-detached although they had no other neighbours – set a little way back from the road. The right-hand house had a child's bicycle lolling on its side in the front garden. Paul hopped over the low fence and stole the bike, feeling what was left of his innocence desert him. Fairly sure now that he was pointing in the right direction, he began to pedal in the dark. The bicycle's saddle was too low and the wheels were tiny; after a couple of miles he felt his knees begin to ache and was grateful for the little pain. It stopped him thinking about what they had just done. Whenever he heard a vehicle coming he dismounted and hid, at one point throwing himself into a stinking ditch and pulling the bike down on top of him. As the car roared past, he found himself wondering if the bike was postcoded. His dad had always written their postcode on new bikes before they even left the shop so that they would be traceable if stolen – and he wondered if there was any way this one could connect him to what had happened at the school.

The A13 took him by surprise when an unprepossessing road dipped below a whooshing viaduct. Overhead, the lamplit arterial road was almost empty of traffic. Soon he was approaching the local but unfamiliar environs of Benfleet town centre and decided that it was time to dismount. He looked too conspicuous, a man-sized body on a child-sized bicycle, although he didn't feel like a man. He had never felt less like a man. He sent it sailing down the side alley of a mean little house; a family home judging by the *High School Musical* curtains but, from the jumble of white goods dumped in the front garden, not the kind of family that took lost property in to the police.

Walking through the town, he put his hood back up and tried not to look guilty. The station was well signposted and, when he arrived, well furnished with benches. He lay down on the cold metallic surface and hoped he looked like a pisshead who'd missed the last train. Incredibly, he caught himself dozing. He double-knotted his hood under his chin in case it fell off while he was asleep. It deadened some of the sound from the street, making him feel vulnerable, a state which bought him another hour's nervous wakefulness. Every time he came out of the light microsleeps that broke his night he looked around for Daniel on the offchance that his escape had taken a similar route. Even as he craned his neck to take in the whole platform, he knew that Daniel was not free, might never be again. Daniel had said he wouldn't tell them about Paul and he believed him, but that did not mean they would never catch up with him. When all they were doing was stealing copper Paul had been entirely confident that he had dodged the sight lines of the camera. Now that violent death had raised the stakes, the security of that knowledge fell away and he even thought he remembered the soft whirr and click of the camera as it detected the movement of his shadow. Even if Daniel was the only one who had been filmed, they would know the theft was not a one-man job and it would not take much to work out who the second man was. They lived together, after all.

Any Grays Reach resident would tell the police that whenever you saw one of them, the other was never far away. Shit. He knuckled sleep out of his eyes.

The first train to London came at 6 a.m. He boarded it before he had even woken up properly and cowered in the corner of the carriage for the two stops it took to get to Tilbury. To his great relief, the barriers at the station were unmanned. Any kind of confrontation with authority was unthinkable in this state; if he had been nicked for fare evasion he would probably have sung his song of guilt to the ticket inspector.

He could tell by the way the dog greeted him, with a thumping tail and accusing eyes, that no one was in and had not been since the day before. Still he called Daniel's name.

It was only the second or third time he had been alone in the Scatlocks' house. Although he had been living there for months he got the uneasy feeling he had when they were trespassing. Diesel, clearly starving, gave him his usual warm welcome, a headbutt to the groin. Paul got a pouch of wet food out of the cupboard. The gelatinous slab of meat slid out of its packet; the smell turned his stomach. While Diesel slobbered and swallowed, Paul put a wash on, throwing everything he was wearing, excluding his underpants but including his trainers, into the machine. Out of habit, he turned out the pockets and found the CCTV instruction leaflet that Daniel had caught him reading. The blind eye of the device seemed to stare an accusation from the page. It marked Paul out as present at the crime scene as surely as if he'd danced in front of the camera. He turned on the gas hob and got ready to burn the thing. As the flames started to blacken the edges, he saw a scribbled note on the back. He read it in one blink without taking in its meaning and then, as the first orange flame stretched towards the ceiling, he waved the flaming paper around but, instead of extinguishing it, this only encouraged it to burn. He stuck it under the kitchen tap. There was a sizzle as the water doused the fire. Paul spread what was left of the manual before him. It looked like a sheet of old parchment. Bits of it came off in his hands, staining them with soot. All that remained of the note Paul had read was *FAO Nick* at the top of the page and then *New CCTV system to go live 1st September.*

Paul did not need to look at his phone to know that it wasn't 1st September yet. The date was etched in his memory as that of his escape, although now it would be remembered for very different reasons. He was surprised to find that even after the events of the last twelve hours there was room for more sickness and guilt. Daniel might have been the one who killed the caretaker but Paul had encouraged him to stay on the roof, and he had failed to point out the camera.

But the camera had not been turned on. Paul's cowardly scheme to get his own back on Daniel had all come to nothing. No, worse than nothing. Nothing implied that you were back where you started, that you had broken even, that you were no better or worse off than before. A man was dead. This was something. He tried to call Carl but he wasn't picking up his phone. Carl would have known what to do. His mum would not have known what to do but that didn't mean Paul didn't want her. He thought about calling her, but what could he say?

He sprinted up the stairs as though in an attempt to escape himself, and went into the bedroom. His black jeans and a red top were on the back of the chair. When he had placed them there, the previous afternoon, he had still had a future and no one had killed anyone and life had been, in retrospect, gloriously carefree and uncomplicated. He grabbed his bag from the top of his wardrobe and got as far as the bottom of the stairs before realising how hopeless it all was. There was no longer any question of him taking up his place at Brighton. He was inculpated, deeply, undeniably. His prints were on the car, he lived with Daniel; there was no way he would escape from this with his name untarnished. Daniel knew where he was going. If he somehow got away with it, Daniel would follow him. The perfect bubble of his new life had burst like, like . . . like an eyeball, he thought, sickened.

Diesel had finished his breakfast and was pawing at the front door the way he did when he was desperate for his walk. He began to make a pathetic whimpering sound that was more feline than canine. Paul knew that the animal would not leave him alone until he had had some exercise. What harm will taking him for a run along the river wall do? he thought. The river air might help him see things more clearly. Sometimes, standing on the edge of the estuary made everything seem better, the size of the bridge and the cranes and the ships made your own problems seem insignificant.

Even as Paul told himself this he knew there wasn't a structure in the world that could diminish the magnitude of his current problems. The thought came to him that he would rather endure his father's death again than feel the way he did at the moment. He passed the mirror and couldn't look at his own face. He grabbed the lead from its hook on the wall and clicked it onto the dog's collar. He opened the door and walked straight into the man he would very soon come to know as Detective Sergeant Woburn of the Essex Police.

52

The thaw had begun on the morning of Carl Scatlock's death. Now, almost a week on, the air was still cold enough to turn dark shallow puddles to slates that cracked underneath Louisa's boots, but the sky looked different, clearer and less portentous, as though the heavens had shifted from threat to promise.

Louisa felt clean for the first time since Adam. Carl had died without intervention from either of them and in doing so had removed the one threat to their liberty, happiness and futures. It had all been done without Paul having to turn that dark corner; she felt sick to think that she had once intended to drag him into her own particular hell. If anything, the opposite had happened. Paul's innocence – of which she remained convinced despite his constant gnawing guilt – was almost contagious. If blamelessness could be restored to a person then that was what he had done for her.

Things were already changing, suggesting that their luck was beginning to turn. The first thing was that they had been outed, something that had not come as the expected blow but rather as a relief; the logistics of concealment were beginning to bore and exhaust them both. Ingram had seen them together in the wine aisle of Tesco in Leamington, of all places. After some initial acerbic comments ('You're supposed to hug the hoodies, dear, not debauch them') he had been persuaded that to broadcast the relationship would tilt the fragile equilibrium of the Kelstice staff into anarchy, and agreed to remain silent. Doubtless he had told Demetra, but since Louisa had not received an official summons she could only presume that their relationship was to go unpunished.

The second, and more marvellous, thing was that the problem of the meeting with the Heritage Gardens Trust had resolved itself. Joanna Bower had called to express her deep regret that things with the young film-maker had not worked out and that the Kelstice Lodge pitch would no longer be filmed. Joanna had said that they were still keen that the Trustees come to Warwickshire to see at first hand the work they were doing, the plants they had rescued from obscurity, the young people whose work was making it all possible. Louisa had swallowed a cheer, set a date and booked the private room in the Kelstice Arms for their meeting which she could now claim, almost without lying, that the Heritage Gardens Trust had requested themselves. She was almost looking forward to it. Paul was starting to put together a presentation on the computer using something called Powerpoint which, when she had mastered it, would allow her to flash up images of her designs, graphs projecting visitor numbers and even a reproduction of the tapestry itself. She could not wait to see the look on Ingram's face when she unveiled her new technological proficiency, and proficient she must become: Paul could not be there to operate it for her on the day. He would be two hundred miles away, wearing a suit and taking the witness stand at Essex County Court.

Today the Witness Service were taking him on a guided tour of the court, designed to put nervous witnesses at their ease. The police had sent him a copy of his statement to review before his appearance. She had read it, of course. The words were Paul's own but something about the language did not flow, as though it were a document translated from another language. It took two or three reads to understand that the statement had been stripped of the nuances and justifications of emotion; just the bare bones of who, what, where, when, with none of the why. She wondered how the statement she had never had to make would have looked on paper.

The policewoman Christine, the one who was friends with Demetra and had sent Paul to Kelstice in the first place, had also put him in touch with a prosecution lawyer, who had given him examples of how the defence would try to trip him up and shown him how to be on his guard. Afterwards Paul said, 'There's nothing he told me that I hadn't heard Carl say a million times. Ironic, isn't it? Carl taught me how to behave in court and the one time I go there it's to put his son away.' He had given a sad little smile then. 'Still, I suppose he taught Daniel, too, so it's a level playing field.'

She had only in the last couple of weeks come to understand the depth of the boys' relationship and what it had meant to Paul. Apart from his parents and Louisa herself, it was the only deep bond he had ever made in his life. She wished that she could convince him of the confidence she felt in the future. She had not felt this kind of positivity since before she had met Adam – and she wasn't sure she had felt it then. She could not help but interpret Carl's death as a sign that someone up there did not want her to kill. Her sense of reprieve was so strong that it finally granted her absolution for her earlier crime. And as a result, her preoccupation with Adam was fading; it was not a precise or easy thing, like letting go of a balloon, but rather a gradual lifting of a weight she had been carrying for so long it felt like part of her body. She would never be able to think about him without guilt, but to her astonishment she could now do so without longing. Sometimes she even felt a kind of nostalgia for the girl she had been then.

Of course she still wondered where he was, or what had become of him, but without urgency or real fear. Paul had been right; if Adam presented a threat, she would know by now. No matter how long Paul spent online, the trail always stopped in the mid-nineties. The clues pointed to dissolution, vagrancy, death. Further release from the clutches of his ghost had come when Paul had repeated the manager of the nursing home's assertion that Adam had lost his looks. Perhaps she had even passed him in the street somewhere, just another pisshead in a sleeping bag or on a park bench, bearded, bloated, ugly. How could a man like that be a menace to her now?

She wanted to mark this letting-go, not because she was still dependent on the ritual but to formalise the difference between her old life and the new. What she had now – her garden, her boy – were real, and she didn't have hours in her day or room in her heart for ghosts.

And this really would be the final catharsis, for afterwards she would burn the scrapbook that was the only one of its kind, destroy the cassette, unwind it and thread it through the trees, wipe it clean, start again. In her hands it was nothing but a lump of plastic and stretched magnetic ribbon. The only power it had now lay in its potential discovery by Paul. It would be disastrous if he were ever to spot the likeness that had drawn her to him in the first place. He might understand – he could surprise her like that – but it was not worth the risk. She marvelled that Paul had not stumbled across the tape or the scrapbook before. As far as he knew, the bags in her overhead cupboard contained clothes, and the television under its throw he had taken for a side table, balancing his mug on it.

Her watch told her that she had three hours before Paul came back to her; time enough to perform the basic elements of her secret ceremony one last time. She opened up the scrapbook. The glue that stuck the pictures to the pages had shrivelled and dried. Photographs and flyers peeled away from their backing. She spread them on the counterpane before her as she had done on a midsummer evening a lifetime ago. Here was a picture of him onstage, another of the band together, there was the Polaroid taken on the Roof Gardens. The image had almost completely faded, only a soft chiaroscuro remaining, the square returning slowly to its original black void. She held the only professional photograph he had ever posed for, a black-and-white, eyes-to-camera shot the size of a paperback novel. She was astonished to find that his face had lost the power to haunt her. The image remained but not the substance. It was an illusion, like light from a dead star.

The tape slid into the mouth of the machine. This time she didn't reach for the whiskey bottle, nor the vodka. She wanted to be in control, to remember. Neither did she dress up. She wanted to do this as her current self. She slackened into those familiar opening frames, that first surge of music, but the electricity died before he began to sing, leaving her alone in the struggling light. Pulling on boots and jacket, she checked the plug on the outside of the van and found the cable to be securely attached, which could only mean that the bloody thing had disconnected itself back at the mains. The thought of traipsing back through the chattering trees dismayed her, but the need to make her peace and say her goodbye won out. Less urgently, more prosaically, she wanted the kettle to work. She smiled to herself; who would ever have thought that the greatest contentment of her life would have been found drinking tea in bed with a naked teenage boy? Taking care to pull down the trip switch so that there wouldn't be a surge when she plugged back into the main power supply, she began the fifteen-minute hike back to the Lodge. Paul could easily have connected the cable on his way home, but there was no way of alerting him. If I had a mobile, she thought, I could call him and ask him to do it for me. On Monday I will go and buy a mobile phone, I'll charge it and we'll always be able to reach one another.

It was the first time that day that she had been outside the caravan, but Paul had been up early and she noticed that he had left the gate wide open. She made a point of pulling it closed behind her and a mental note to remind him again of the importance of hiding her home. With Scatlock out of the way and Ingram onto them, they had both become lax, and he in particular was absent-minded with the stress of the looming trial, but there was still no reason to invite discovery.

Halfway there, with the ruin in sight – she had grown so used to its shrug of snow that its bare brickwork looked naked – she stopped in her tracks, experienced a brief, excruciating vision of the ensuing mess if Paul were to return to the caravan before she did, if he saw the pictures she had left on the bed or, worse still, if he turned the power back on and the machine started to play and he saw his double singing only for him. But her watch told her that his train was not even due to leave London for another hour, and she walked on.

The cable had loosened itself by less than a millimetre but that had been enough to break the connection. She thumped it back into place with the heel of her hand. There was a little buzz as the current came. Since she was back at the cabins anyway, she opened up the canteen, made herself a cup of tea and drank it on the steps, looking down at the ride. She thought about having a tidy-up of the office before Ingram and the others got back on Monday morning. At one point she saw a figure walk past the gatehouse and her heart gave a little kick of panic. She tipped her drink onto the earth and made to run back to the cabin and hide the evidence before Paul could catch up with her. But the figure, although male, was accompanied by a dog and did not turn into the ride. It took a while for her pulse to return to its resting rate.

I'm getting too old for this, she thought, I'm tired. She had had enough of power cuts and gas canisters and chemical toilets. Paul had awakened a part of her that craved the comforts she had shunned for years. She laughed out loud to find that she wanted to live with him in a house with pictures on the walls and Persian rugs and a kitchen and a bathroom, a sofa from Heal's, arguments about what to watch on television, the lot. She checked her watch again, then made herself another cup of tea. Her goodbye to Adam could wait a while longer.

53

The trial was to be held not at the Old Bailey but at the Crown Court in Chelmsford, which wasn't the intimidating gargoyled structure of Paul's nightmares but rather a bland, redbrick block in the town centre that could have been an office. Only the coat of arms above the door gave it away. He had been cynical when the Witness Service officer – another professional do-gooder, like Demetra – had told him that a tour of the building would prepare him for taking the stand, but he soon had to admit that she had known what she was talking about after all. The courtroom itself was smaller than he had thought and again, its neutral modernity was reassuring. Of course he wasn't looking forward to seeing Daniel but the knowledge that he would be behind glass made him feel somehow safer. The only pity was that Louisa could not be there in the public gallery to support him, but his mother and Troy had pledged their presence and perhaps his courtroom debut was not the best place for them to meet for the first time.

He was almost looking forward to it now: not to the trial, of course, but clearing the last hurdle on the way to the other side. They had told him that he could stay at the court for as long as he liked but one ten-minute recce was all he needed. He would leave Essex now while he still felt strong; stay too long and memories of his home county might pollute his new-found confidence. The train he caught was much earlier than the one originally intended, scattered with shoppers rather than crammed with commuters. In the carriage he had room to chill out, put his feet up on the seat opposite (meekly taking them down when the buffet trolley came round). Returning to Warwickshire felt more like going home than travelling to Essex had. He popped back into his flat to pick up a change of clothes for the morning, bought a cheese and onion pasty and a bottle of Coke from the corner shop and had them at the bus stop. The joke shop was no longer showing its Christmas windows but was back to its default display of fancy dress costumes and feather boas. In a month it would be Valentine's Day and doubtless they would go in for more creative window dressing then. Paul wondered what exquisite tableau they had in mind for that festival; vicars and tarts was about their level.

The bus set him down at the village stop. He checked the time: two hours early. He vacillated between surprising her at the caravan and sneaking a swift pint at the Kelstice Arms. Before he could decide which of these warm welcomes he was most in the mood for, he was winded by a blow to the abdomen, a crouching demon coming out of nowhere that threw him inside the bus shelter. If the wall hadn't broken his trajectory, he would have been thrown to the ground. He struggled to get his breath, aware that there was a solid, moving ball of heat somewhere around his knees and moisture on his hands that felt like blood but couldn't be.

He looked down. Through his fingers he saw the slobbering, happy face of Diesel the dog. Behind the Alsatian, red hair escaping from a big black hood, was a shivering Hash. The dog, who was chained to the lamp-post just outside the shelter, bounced excitedly between the two youths. His panting was the only sound. There was a time when Paul would have been confident of Diesel's protection against anyone apart from a

Scatlock but something about the way he was with Hash said that man and animal had been spending a lot of time in each other's company lately.

Nothing made sense. Paul knew if he thought hard enough he would figure out how Hash had got here and what he was doing. He could tell the truth was there, dancing around in the shadows like a goblin, and on some level he knew that he wouldn't want to believe it when he heard it. Adrenaline is conducive to action, not recollection, and Paul did not have the luxury of contemplation; Hash was bristling with violence. Swiftly he concluded that it was better to take a kicking in the street than here in the murky green recess of the bus shelter. If he survived whatever Hash had in store for him, at least on the pavement there was a chance someone would see his body and rescue him, a passing car or someone from the pub or, if he was left lying in his own blood for long enough, Louisa herself. When the blow came it wasn't the expected punch in the guts but a girlish, two-handed shove and the noise that Hash let out was not a fierce battle-cry but something closer to a sob. This vulnerable state was almost more disarming than violence.

'It wasn't enough for you to get Daniel sent down, you had to kill Carl, too.'

Paul began to inch sideways, towards the freedom of the street.

'Carl? He died in an accident, it was nothing to do with me. What's any of this got to do with *you*?'

'I was living with him.' All the inexplicable things slotted into place, like a series of heavy bolts closing on a door. Paul felt sick, as though he had cut off Carl's head and Hash's had grown back in its place, younger, thicker, even angrier. Diesel, sensing conflict, began to growl; Paul could not tell who the dog was defending and who he was attacking. 'He should have killed you when he come up here.'

'How did you even know about this place?'

'Gavin gave me your fleece to give back to you and it had that receipt thingy in the pocket. It took us straight to you. You'd even signed it.'

Two memories rebounded on Paul, both now loaded with new and terrible meaning. He recalled crumpling up the delivery docket for a tray of saplings and his visit to Gavin's yard, how insistent Gavin had been that Paul's mate was still coming to see him. 'Mate' had only ever meant one person to Paul, and that was Daniel.

'Did you nick my mum's phone as well?'

'Silly bitch left the van door open,' he confirmed.

Bloody Troy and that stupid orange van, marking his mother out as a target. The sickening thought of Hash's fingers all over her handbag, touching that photograph, was quickly eclipsed by another, more urgent worry. Carl might have taken Hash into his confidence. He might have told him Louisa's story and then they would be back to square one. He tried to think of a sly way to phrase it but in the end could only come up with the clumsy, exposing:

'What did he tell you about when he came up that first time?'

'Nothing,' said Hash but that didn't mean anything; he was a born liar and he had as good as said he had nothing left to lose. 'He didn't want to involve me. He was *protective* of me. He treated me like a son, and you went and killed him.'

'I. Didn't. Kill. Him.'

'Bollocks. If it wasn't for you, would he have been up here?'

'You're the one who sent him!'

Hash might have thrown a few punches but Paul was a more experienced receiver of violence than Hash was a giver. The muscle memory of an early youth spent dodging fists aided him; he dropped to his haunches just in time to hear Hash's fist whistle past his ear. The trajectory of the wasted blow threw Hash off balance and he hit the concrete in a perfect pratfall. Coins and keys, wallet and phone and a flick knife all fell out of his pockets on the way down. He scrambled to pick up his scattered possessions. Paul got to the knife first and made sure the blade was tucked in before hiding it in his fist. Crouching, Hash was vulnerable; the dog was tethered too tightly to come to his defence, if indeed Hash was the one he recognised as master. If Paul was any sort of man, he thought, he would knock Hash out now, kill him, extinguish this terrible resurrected threat and drag the body back to Louisa, who would know exactly what to do. But he was a runner, not a fighter, and they both knew it.

He had to get back to the safety of the caravan without Hash watching him go. As he made to run, he trod on a little plastic key, clearly part of the litter from Hash's pockets. He would have kicked it into the gutter, anything to delay or distract Hash, but something about it looked familiar. He stooped to retrieve it; Hash let out an involuntary yelp that was an alarm call to Paul. He studied it, knowing, it was familiar but not sure why. It wasn't a normal door key, it was more like something from Troy's tool kit, or something that operated a machine or bled a radiator or opened the gas box outside his mother's—

Gas box. It was the key that opened the cap that covered the gas canister on the outside of the caravan. Hash had been to the caravan.

'But how did you . . . ?'

His answer was growling beneath the lamp-post. Of course Diesel would have led him straight there. The stupid dog, who had slept in his bedclothes, whose memory and senses were sharper than many humans', would have recognised his scent and chased it across the countryside. Paul balanced the key on his open palm. He felt as though he were holding a grenade with the pin pulled out.

'Hash, what have you done?'

Paul remembered Hash's victory sneer from school.

'Taught you a lesson.'

Reserves of strength and speed that had not come when his father was dying, that had not come when Daniel killed Ken Hillyard, or when Carl turned up, came now. Paul sprang across to grab Hash by the collar of his jacket and shake him so hard that he actually heard his teeth chatter. The dog looked confused, torn between two masters. 'What have you done to the gas? Louisa's in that caravan!' He let him drop.

Hash's eyes darted in the direction of the caravan. 'Who's Louisa?' he said, a very slight quaver to his voice.

'My girlfriend! It's her home.'

Hash chewed his lip in contemplation for a few seconds before smirking, 'You'd better hurry up then, hadn't you?'

Paul ran up the ride. He was newly, acutely aware of the length of his legs; he had not known until now that they could stretch so far, or carry him so quickly. His feet touched the ground only briefly; it felt more like flying than running. He had been wrong to think that each disaster lessened the impact of the next. The clean, perfect terror he felt now was the sum of all his previous fears. She would be there now, waiting for him, a slow leak of gas sending her to sleep or worse. The smallest spark could start a fire and Louisa's caravan was a tinderbox of matches and candles, lamps and oils and books. Depending on how long ago Hash had been there, a light switch might do it, boiling the kettle might do it. He stumbled and fell twice, the second time heavily. Something gave in his ankle but the analgesia of fear allowed him to continue, gaining rather than losing speed. The ruin loomed and vanished in seconds, the cabins whizzed past in a blur like the view from a train window. He was like a dog himself, sniffing the air for signs that something terrible had already happened.

The gate had been double-latched. His fine motor skills had temporarily been sacrificed to the gross; his fingers struggled with the familiar catch as though it were a complicated puzzle, like that ring she wore. There was no time to cajole the latch; he took a step back and, remembering only at the point of contact that he was using his bad ankle, kicked the gate as hard as he could. The rotten, splintering wood gave and the gate fell forwards like a drawbridge, leaving only the swinging iron hinges hanging on to the crumbling brickwork, flinders of wood still in their clutches.

There she was, alive and lovely, her back framed in the narrow doorway of the unlit caravan; she was wearing her coat, and looked as though she had just returned from somewhere. He wanted to wilt with relief, he wanted to collapse on his injured ankle and lie on the ground, but he allowed his eyes to flick briefly to the gas cap and saw that it was ajar. First he had to get her away from that caravan. He called her name and she whipped around. For a second she looked at him as though he were a complete stranger; then, when recognition came, it was freighted not with love but panic.

'Louisa! Don't go in! It's not safe!' he said in a voice that seemed to rise from his toes. She ignored the falsetto siren and disappeared through the opening. 'Get out of the van! LOUISA!'

But she stayed inside. His eyes were used to the dark and he could see her shadow moving inside; still, he barely believed what he saw as she flapped about with swift, agitated movements, bending down and standing up again, as though she were hiding something, as if anything could ever be hidden away in a space that small. All the while he was calling her name. What could she be doing that was so urgent she ignored his screams? He shouted one more warning, feeling his voice go as well as his ankle, but she remained busy inside, leaving him only one option. Wincing with pain, he covered the remaining ground in Olympic strides. By the time his shoulders were in the doorway she was standing in her usual place at the foot of the bed, oil lamp before her, matchbox in one hand, matchstick in the other, poised to strike. He whispered his last 'No' as she brought the sulphur tip to meet the phosphorous.

A ball of blackening orange flame guzzled metal and flesh, paper and oil. The boom of the explosion and the noise from the fire were heard for miles around, but the ash fell in silent flakes, like snow.

EPILOGUE

July 2012

Elaine drove along the uneven lane smoothly and without hesitation. The Big Freeze had been two years ago but its legacy of potholes remained on these country B-roads. On days like today, conceived, planned and executed without his consultation, he felt she was being capable *at* him, that her competence was designed to highlight his own shortcomings. He kept his eyes on the road not because he was navigating – Elaine was doing that, from memory – but because if he took his eyes off the horizon for one minute motion sickness would strike. He was sick of being sick in front of his children.

'Here we are,' she said.

The tumbledown gatehouse had been restored but not with brick; it had been domed in glass and wood, a giant, ultramodern cloche protecting the ancient ruin. It had had its old role restored; a woman smiled in the open window and took their money in exchange for stickers that gave them the freedom of the site.

'Twenty quid to get in?' he said as the car scaled a shallow hill and entered a perfect gravelled oblong of parkland. 'And me on benefits. It should be free to people like us.'

'Well, the kids were free, so that's something. And I suppose they've got to make money somehow,' said Elaine, her reasonableness as grating as her competence. The boys had the back doors open before she had finished parking and were out, stretching their arms above their heads and churning the gravel with their heels. 'Please don't kick off today,' she said in a low voice. 'I just thought we could all do something *nice* for once. And history's the only thing Jonah's shown any interest in all year.'

'Sorry,' he forced himself to say. 'I'm not feeling too good today.' It was one of those days where he felt he had one headache on top of another, rival sources of pain in different parts of his cranium, competing to see which would be first to split his skull.

'I know, love, but try, for the kids. For me?' She pressed the heels of her hands into her eye sockets and he saw how tired she was; not his kind of tiredness, the wired, edgy aftermath of a sleepless night, but the exhaustion of years of marshalling a husband and two sons.

'Of course I'll try. It'll be fine.' He reached into the glove compartment and popped two pills out of a blister pack. He swallowed them dry with the practised peristalsis of the chronically medicated.

It was the first day of the school summer holidays and the place was thronged with families with the same idea. Jonah skipped along the ride with its spindly trees and proudly showed his sticker to the steward at the main entrance. When he was given a worksheet and some coloured pencils he turned around and faced his parents with an expression of unreserved glee that was bittersweet to observe. It would not be long before this engaging little boy became a sullen teenager like his brother. Jonah was eight now. Elijah was thirteen and three years into an awesome sulk. He was behind them now, sauntering deliberately and playing music out loud on his phone.

'Eli, *not here*,' hissed Elaine, scarlet with embarrassment. 'I *told* you.'

He watched his eldest son with the usual mix of wonder and jealousy and was bewildered again by the people who claimed to enjoy living vicariously through their children. Watching Elijah grow up, grow strong, grow beautiful, aroused no pride, only bitter, toxic envy. And it would get worse. In five years' time Jonah would be a teenager too and there would be two of them under his roof, getting off with girls, staying out late, taking drugs, all the good stuff that he had been told he had done to excess in his own youth.

Did Elijah understand that there was a direct correlation between his behaviour and the pain in his father's head? The tight iron band around the temples was winning out over the dragging ache at the point where his head met his neck. He reached into his pocket to check that his emergency painkillers were there. Just touching them made him feel better. Reluctantly the boy plugged himself back in.

'This is spasticated,' he said. 'I'll be over in the corner,' but the parental hand that grabbed him roughly by the shoulder had other ideas.

'We're doing this as a *family*,' snarled his father, loudly enough that a catalogue-perfect blond family, the real thing, turned to stare.

'Whatever,' said Elijah, but he was clearly shaken. Elaine gave him a look that was part mortification, part reproach.

The garden itself was only two years old and its immaturity was obvious, a barrier to the sense of history the place was clearly designed to evoke. A great deal of planning must have gone into it but many of the intricately planted bushes and shrubs were still gappy and short. It felt more like a suburban garden centre than the brochure-promised journey into the past. It was richer in scent than sight. The smells came in bubbles; when you turned a corner you sniffed a new one, as dramatic and discrete as though you were entering a new room with different coloured wallpaper. Some of the smells were strange to him, many familiar, like the box and the stock they grew in their back garden, and one was unwelcome: the bobbing purple antennae of the lavender released that cloying perfume that had always made him uneasy, for reasons that remained comfortably just out of his grasp.

Jonah had obtained a wooden sword from somewhere and, worksheet forgotten, was charging along the paths of sand that glittered like gold between the regimented beds. He chased Elijah, who was trying to pretend it wasn't funny. Elaine took his hand: they followed their sons up the staircase and into the shell of Kelstice Lodge. The brickwork reared up on all sides, dark and damp and soothing. He pressed his temples against the cool stone; instantly the pain subsided and he loosened his grip on the blister pack in his pocket. Together they climbed to the viewing gallery, another sensitive wood-and-glass creation that sat happily with the crumbling brickwork and afforded snatched scenes from glassless windows. From above, the garden made perfect sense. Red, yellow and white flower heads bobbed, softening the sharp angles of its geometry. The artificial had been made to seem organic.

Jonah the warrior led them back down to the centrepiece of the garden, a fountain of marble and granite. The design was the kind that must have been classical even then: stone men and women shrugging off marmoreal togas and holding great stone balls above their heads. The innovation was all in the water, which arced and criss-crossed in the dead centre. The effect was oddly futuristic.

'Think of the planning that must have gone into that to get it perfect,' said Elaine. 'That's real precision engineering. You'd have to get the water pressure and the positioning of those fountains right to the nearest millimetre.' To test her theory, Elijah put his hand in front of one of the jets and the whole pattern fell apart. Jonah chopped the water into droplets. Elaine crouched in the spray to read a plaque that was set into the base of the fountain. Unlike the coloured signs telling the history of Kelstice, this was not part of the narrative but reserved for those in the know, or for the kind of person who stopped to notice all the details.

'Oh, that's so sad,' said Elaine. 'Look, they died.'

He dropped to his knees next to his wife with no small effort; automatically she put out a hand to steady him. The inscription was gold letters on black stone.

> THIS FOUNTAIN IS DEDICATED TO THE MEMORY
> OF LOUISA TREVELYAN AND PAUL SEAFORTH,
> WHO HELPED TO CREATE THIS GARDEN
> AND WHO DIED IN A TRAGIC ACCIDENT
> ON THIS SITE ON 15TH JANUARY 2010

Louisa Trevelyan, Louisa Trevelyan … It was like a very beautiful, very short poem, or a prayer. The worst headache of his life threw him to the floor. Spitting sand and tasting blood, he curled up in a ball and sealed his eyes against the image of her face and her little silver-ringed hands, reaching out to push against his chest. A dozen forgotten songs played in his head at once in a blaring cacophony.

'Al, what's wrong?' said Elaine. She crouched over him, blocking the sun. 'Alan?'

He opened his mouth to scream.

AUTHOR'S NOTE

The Warwickshire village of Kelstice is my own invention, although the garden restoration project was partly inspired by a similar one at Kenilworth Castle, just a few miles up the notional Kelstice Road. I have played similarly fast and loose with the geography of my home county, Essex, superimposing the Grays Reach Estate on a blameless commuter development on the river's edge.

The Roof Gardens are real, and Kensington Market was for decades a thriving hub of alternative youth culture. Despite vigorous campaigning from the people who loved the place, it was pulled down in 1997. The site now hosts a branch of PC World.

ACKNOWLEDGEMENTS

Writing can be a lonely profession but the support and encouragement of the following people made this book feel like a group effort. Huge thanks and love to Team Sick Rose: Sarah Ballard, Suzie Dooré, Jessica Craig, Eleni Lawrence, Lara Hughes Young, Michael Kelly, Lynne Kelly, George Lewis, Michael Moylan, Helen Treacy, Francine Toon and Jennifer Whitehead Chadwick.

The Sick Rose

A READING GUIDE

Further Reading

Novels that share themes with *The Sick Rose*:

> *Boy A* by Jonathan Trigell
> *The Hours of the Night* by Sue Gee
> *A Judgement In Stone* by Ruth Rendell
> *Notes on a Scandal* by Zoë Heller
> *Sheer Blue Bliss* by Lesley Glaister
> *The Thirteenth Tale* by Diane Setterfield

Books that helped inspire the author:

> *The Lost Gardens of Heligan* by Tim Smit
> *The Morville Hours* by Katherine Swift
> *Elizabeth in the Garden* by Trea Martyn
> *The Encyclopaedia of the '80s – A Decade of I-Deas*
>   by *i-D Magazine*

- What do the above novels have in common with *The Sick Rose*? Can you think of any other books that could be added to the list?

- *The Sick Rose* bears many hallmarks of Gothic fiction; darkness, the supernatural, superstition, doppelgängers and dual narrative. Can you think of any other contemporary novels that play with these conventions? How does *The Sick Rose* compare?

- Most Gothic novels are dominated by a house or other building that is central to events, and some scholars have theorised that this represents the maternal body and the universal desire to return to it. Does Kelstice Lodge fit this theory?

- Why do you think gardening is so important to Louisa?

- And why is reading so important to Paul?

- Was Louisa really in love with Adam, or was it merely an infatuation? To what extent has her obsession become part of her identity?

- Why do you think Daniel chooses Paul to be his confidante and accomplice, rather than, for example, Hash? And what is revealed about Daniel when he secretly pretends to be Paul?

- *'You kept my secret. I know yours now. That makes us even.'*
  In what ways do Louisa, Adam, Paul and Daniel all lead secret lives? How does this affect the decisions they make?

- Consider the collective guilt of Louisa and Paul's planned murder, and whether culpability can ever genuinely be shared. She ostensibly goads him, but is it a question of good versus evil or strength versus weakness? Would they have been physically and emotionally capable of following through with the murder, and if they had would it have been more of an issue in their relationship than the age gap or class divide? Would it have brought them closer together, or driven them apart?

- When Louisa finds that Adam is alive, the knowledge barely lessens her guilt – she says that the thought is as evil as the deed. Do you agree with this? How guilty is Louisa?

- The idea of arrested development posits that traumatic events 'freeze' a person at the age when it happened – ten in Paul's case, eighteen in Louisa's. Do you think this is true? What of the other pivotal characters like Daniel and Adam – were they 'frozen' by the time they came to play a part in the story, and if so, how does this affect their personalities?

- Did the double death near the end feel inevitable to you? If so, what is the last point at which they could have rewritten this fate?

Scan the QR code with your phone to watch
Erin Kelly talk more about THE SICK ROSE:

Find out more about Erin Kelly online:

www.erinkelly.co.uk

www.twitter.com/mserinkelly

'Like' Erin Kelly's Facebook page by
scanning this code with your phone:

'Dark, poetic, gripping, totally brilliant.' *The Times*

'A terrific suspense debut . . .
This one gets the writer's ultimate bit of praise:
I wish I had written it.' Stephen King

OUT NOW IN PAPERBACK